THE SLEEPING DICTIONARY

THE SLEEPING DICTIONARY

Sujata Massey

G

GALLERY BOOKS

New York   London   Toronto   Sydney   New Delhi

G

Gallery Books
A Division of Simon & Schuster, Inc.
1230 Avenue of the Americas
New York, NY 10020

First Gallery Books trade paperback edition August 2013

GALLERY BOOKS and colophon are registered trademarks
of Simon & Schuster, Inc.

For information about special discounts for bulk purchases,
please contact Simon & Schuster Special Sales at 1-866-506-1949
or business@simonandschuster.com.

The Simon & Schuster Speakers Bureau can bring authors to your live event. For more information or to book an event contact the Simon & Schuster Speakers Bureau at 1-866-248-3049 or visit our website at www.simonspeakers.com.

Designed by Davina Mock-Maniscalco

Manufactured in the United States of America

10   9   8   7   6   5   4   3   2   1

Library of Congress Cataloging-in-Publication Data

Massey, Sujata.
  The sleeping dictionary / Sujata Massey.—First Gallery Books trade paperback edition.
    pages cm
  1. Young women—Fiction. 2. Passive resistance—India—Fiction. 3. India—Politics and government—1919–1947—Fiction. 4. India—Social life and customs—20th century—Fiction. I. Title.
  PS3563.A79965S54 2013
  813'.54—dc23   2012042498

ISBN 978-1-4767-0316-9
ISBN 978-1-4767-0325-1 (ebook)

This book is for my father
Subir Kumar Banerjee

CAST OF CHARACTERS
(IN ORDER OF APPEARANCE)

Pom, Sarah, Pamela, Kamala: a peasant girl called by many names

Rhumi and Jhumi: Pom's young twin sisters

Dadu and Thakurma: Pom's paternal grandfather and grandmother

Baba and Ma: Pom's father and mother

Bhai: Pom's newborn baby brother

Jamidar Pratap Mukherjee: major landholder in Southeast Bengal. The jamidarni is his wife. His daughter is named Bidushi.

Dr. Andrews: Scottish physician at the Keshiari Mission Hospital

Nurse Das: nurse at the Keshiari Mission Hospital

Nurse Gopal: nurse at the Keshiari Mission Hospital

Rowena Jamison: British headmistress at Lockwood School

Abbas: Muslim driver for Lockwood School. His wife is Hafeeza.

Miss Rachael: Indian-Christian head of housekeeping for Lockwood School

Jyoti-ma: a sweeper at Lockwood School

Claire Richmond: British literature teacher at Lockwood School

Pankaj Bandopadhyay: Calcutta lawyer and Bidushi's fiancé

Nurse-matron: nurse at Lockwood School

Rose Barker, also known as Mummy: Anglo-Indian proprietress of Rose Villa, Kharagpur

Mummy's Roses: Bonnie, Lakshmi (also known as Lucky), Natty, Doris, Shila, Sakina

Chief Bobby Howard: senior police official in Kharagpur

Dr. DeCruz: physician

Ralph Abernathy, also known as the Taster: acting chief of Hijli Detention Camp

Bernie Mulkins: Australian photographer

Jayshree and Tilak: brothel owners

Lina: oldest nonworking child at the brothel

Kabita, also known as Hazel and Zeenat: an Anglo-Indian foundling

Simon Lewes: Indian Civil Service officer, political sector

Mr. Lewes's staff: Shombhu, chief bearer; Manik, cook; Choton, cook's assistant; Jatin, assistant bearer; Promod, gardener; Farouk, chauffeur, later replaced by Sarjit and then Ahmed

Wilbur Weatherington: Mr. Lewes's ICS colleague

Supriya Sen: Bethune College student; her younger sister is Sonali and younger brother is Nishan. Her parents, Mr. Sen and Mrs. Sen, also known as Mashima, own Sen Bookbindery and Publishing on College Street.

Supriyas's friends: Ruksana Ali, a Muslim student from Calcutta, and Lata Menon, a Hindu student from Travancore and leader of the Chhatri Sangha student activist group

Arvind Israni: friend of Pankaj and a political activist

Bijoy Ganguly: friend of Pankaj and a political activist

Reverend John McRae: Scottish Presbyterian minister

Historical Figures Who Appear in *The Sleeping Dictionary*

Sarat Bose: Bengal Congress Party leader and elder brother to Subhas, from a prominent Bengali Hindu family of lawyers and activists

Subhas Chandra Bose, also known as Netaji: a former mayor of Calcutta, two-time Congress Party president, founder of Forward Bloc party, and commander in chief of Azad Hind Fauj government and Indian National Army

British governors of Bengal: Sir John Arthur Herbert, a conservative who served from 1939 until his death in 1943; Richard Gardiner Casey, an Australian appointed for 1944–46; replaced by Sir Frederick Burrows, the final British governor of Bengal, 1946–47, who did not favor partition.

British viceroys of India: Lord Victor Hope Linlithgow (the 2nd Marquess of Linlithgow) 1936–1943, a hard-liner against Indian independence; served the longest tenure of any viceroy in the Raj. Succeeded by Lord Wavell (Earl Archibald Wavell) 1943–47, who favored independence but was opposed by British prime ministers Winston Churchill and Clement Attlee. The last viceroy was Lord Louis Mountbatten, appointed in 1947 to oversee the transition to independence. Lord Mountbatten served as the first and only governor-general of the Independent Union of India (1947–48).

Mohandas Gandhi: Hindu lawyer turned activist, who is better known abroad as Mahatma Gandhi and by Indian followers as Gandhiji. He was the founder of India's best-known resistance movement based on nonviolent protest. Married to Kasturba.

Sir Khawaja Nazimuddin: Muslim politician appointed as education, home, and chief minister of Bengal during British rule. He was also a former Muslim League head for East India and eventually because a prime minister of Pakistan.

Jawaharlal Nehru: Hindu lawyer and politician also known as Panditji; left-wing Congress Party leader mentored by Mahatma Gandhi, eventually elected first prime minister of the Republic of India.

Husseyn Suhrawardy: Muslim lawyer and politician who served as minister of labor and minister of civil supplies under Nazimuddin. During 1946, he was head of Bengal's Muslim League party. He has been accused by some of inciting rioting on Direct Action Day, while others credit him with persuading the British government to bring army troops back to the city to put down the violence. Suhrawardy later became a president of Pakistan.

Rabindranath Tagore: world-famous Bengali poet, novelist, playwright, artist, and musician, 1861–1941. Tagore, known by his admirers as Gurudeb, was the first Asian to win a Nobel Prize. A longtime independence activist, he repudiated his British knighthood in 1919 as a statement of his desire for Indian freedom.

HINDI/BENGALI/ENGLISH GLOSSARY

I have used regional Indian and British spellings whenever possible, especially of the time and place.

aadab—a polite greeting made to and by Muslims

aey—an exclamation, like "hey"

almirah—a freestanding cabinet that locks

alpana—colored rice flour designs used to brighten a doorstep to welcome guests

Ananda Bazar Patrika—Bengali-language newspaper owned by same Indian publishing company as ***Amrita Bazar Patrika,*** an English-language paper

Anglo-Indian—a term that refers to persons with mixed Indian and British ancestry, and also to the British living long-term in India

anna—a small change coin; at the time of the story, four paise made up one anna, and sixteen annas made one rupee.

ayah—a female household servant to children or adults

baba—term to address one's father

babu—a gentleman or professional

Baidya—Bengali Hindu caste of doctors prescribing Indian medicine, the second highest caste in the province

baksheesh—a tip or bribe

bearer—a head male servant; similar to a butler

bed tea—the first cup of tea of the day, usually served in the bedroom

Bengali—also known as Bangla, the language widely spoken by people of the northeastern state the British named Bengal. Also, a person from this region is called a Bengali.

beti—Hindi word for daughter

bhadralok—Bengal's upper and educated class, composed of Brahmin, Baidya, and Kayastha castes; people born from the top of Brahma's body

bhai—brother or male friend

bhisti—a water-carrying servant

boudi—term for eldest brother's wife

Brahma—the creator in Hindu theology

Brahmin—the top priestly caste in Hinduism, believed to have sprung from Brahma's head

bungalow—an expansive house favored by British residents, often two-story

burka—a long one-piece black cover-up worn by some Muslim women

burra-saheb—big boss; female version is burra-memsaheb. (In parts of India outside of Bengal, *saheb* is spelled *sahib*.)

bustee—slum neighborhood

cabin—small, casual tea- or beer-drinking place

Calcutta—West Bengal's capital city, which, until the building of New Delhi in 1911, was known as the crown city of the British Empire and the administrative capital of British India. Now it is known by the Bengali name Kolkata.

caste—a social level that a Hindu is born into; Brahmins at the top and Untouchables or Harjians at the bottom

chacha—a term for an uncle or respected close elder, used by younger people toward Muslim elders; a chacha's wife is a chachi.

chai—tea. A chai-wallah is a tea-vendor.

channa dal—dried chickpeas

chapatti—unleavened round bread

chappals—sandals

Chhattri Sangha—a women's students association founded in Calcutta

cholar dal—Bengali split chickpea dal flavored with coconut and sugar

chowkidar—a watchman; similar to a darwan but more likely to be employed by an office or business

coolie—a boy or man who carries things; still commonly used at train stations

dacoit—bandit usually operating in the countryside

dada—warm form of address meaning older brother. Also, a first name plus the -da suffix means the same thing.

dadu—paternal grandfather

dai—a midwife

dal—lentils cooked into a thick soup

Darjeeling—hill town in Bengal's North, near foothills of the Himalayas; also a type of tea

darwan—a watchman; similar to chowkidar but usually employed by families to guard their homes

darzi—tailor

dharma—moral law combined with spiritual discipline specific to one's life

didi—big sister; used literally or for close female friend

Digha—a seaside town in South Bengal, near Orissa

dhobi—a washerman

dhoti—a length of cloth that primarily North Indian men wrap and drape to cover their hips and legs

Dom—a low-ranking caste whose exclusive duties are the handling and disposal of corpses

dhonekhali—regional Bengali cotton textile, especially known for stripes and checks

Durga—the much-loved warrior goddess who is worshipped in Bengal in a weeklong puja followed by Diwali (Kali-puja in Bengal)

ghat—area of river close to shore that is used for bathing, washing clothes, and drawing drinking water

ghee—clarified butter used in cooking

goonda—like a dacoit but more likely to be organized criminals operating in cities

hartal—a work stoppage or strike

Hindi—most widely understood language in North India, in the past referred to as Hindustani. Its roots are a combination of the Sanskrit and Urdu languages

ICS—Indian Civil Service; an elite corps of administrators usually born and trained in Britain

imam—religious leader in Islam

INA—Indian National Army; an Indian-led force built from Japanese prisoners of war during World War II who fought alongside the Japanese in the hopes of gaining India's freedom from Britain.

Indian Army—the military force serving under the British rulers of India that, by World War II, included Indian as well as British commanding officers.

Ingrej—an English person or people

Jagannath—a reincarnated form of Shiva, god of destruction. The most famous Jagannath temple in India is in the state of Orissa.

jamdani—a type of Bengal handloomed sari known for gossamer weave and fine embroidery. There are many kinds of jamdani saris including a dhakai, from the Dhaka area of East Bengal, extremely fine and chosen for parties and special occasions.

jamidar—landowner. His wife is a jamidarni. In other parts of India, he would be called a zamindar.

jao—command to go

jelebi—fried lentil flour sweet

Kali—fierce goddess who is very popular in Bengal

Kayastha—the record-keeping caste of Hindus, usually judged third highest in Bengal

khadi—homespun cotton cloth made famous from Mahatma Gandhi's home-spinning campaign

Kharagpur—a railway-dominated town in south-central West Bengal (called Khargpur by Europeans)

Krishna—Hindu god of love, also the charioteer of Arjun in Mahabharata

kedgeree—a mixture of rice, dal, and spices often served at Anglo-Indian breakfasts

kurta—a pajama tunic with drawstring waist trousers; worn in the past primarily by Muslim men

Lakshmi—Hindu goddess of wealth and abundance

lathi—stick weapon

luchi—puffed fried wheat bread

ma—a term to address one's mother or a very young girl

mali—a gardener

mashima—aunt, especially a senior aunt, also children's nurse; means mother's sister or very senior female servant (can be shortened to mashi)

masho—a mashima's husband, a warm form of address for older men

maund—an equivalent of 82.6 pounds, often used to describe weight of a large sack of rice

memsaheb—a term of address for a gentlewoman. (In parts of India outside of Bengal, *saheb* is spelled *sahib*.)

mishti doi—baked yogurt pudding

Murshidabad—a town in Bengal known for producing natural tussar silk saris with broad red borders favored by middle-aged, married women

namaskar—the Bengali version of the namaste greeting; said aloud and signified by folded hands

Napit—the barbering and nail-clipping caste

nawab—royal ruler, also called a maharajah in other areas

neem—tree with fragrant soft twigs used for cleaning teeth

paan—betel leaves that are wrapped around a filling and chewed after meals to freshen breath and serve as a psychoactive stimulant

paisa—one-penny coin. At the time of the story, four paise to one anna, sixty-four paise to a rupee.

pakora—spicy, savory fried snack

pallu—end section of sari that hangs over the shoulder or covers hair

pandit—Hindu priest; also a respectful prefix used for great leaders, such as Pandit Nehru

papadum—chickpea flour cracker bread

Parsi—a follower of Zoroastrian faith, refugees from Islamic Iran

phuchka—a street-food snack, miniature puffed breads stuffed with spiced vegetables

phuluri—Bengali vegetable fritters. Elsewhere they are called pakoras

pillau—a Bengali rice dish with Persian roots

puja—the act of worship, or religious holiday

punkah—ceiling fan

purdah—the custom of keeping women indoors away from others' gaze, practiced by Muslims and some Hindus

quisling—a World War II–era word for traitor; inspired by the surname of the Norwegian official who assisted the Nazis in Norway

rickshaw—a two-wheeled cart that is pulled by a human running or riding a bicycle

rupee—the Indian unit of currency. During the time period of the book, forty rupees equaled one US dollar.

saheb—a term of address for a gentleman, high-ranking Indian or English

salwar kameez—a long tunic with drawstring waist trousers worn primarily by Muslim women at the time of this story. Later on, this dress was adopted by Indian women of other religions.

sari—a wrapped eighteen-yard length of cloth that is a traditional Indian woman's dress

shingara—a Bengali vegetable- or meat-stuffed pastry similar to a samosa

Shiva—the god of destruction, husband to Durga

shondesh—a Bengali milk-based sweet

Sikh—a follower of Sikhism, India's third major religion

sleeping dictionary—the metaphor used by the Dutch and British colonialists to describe girlfriends who also taught them languages and customs

Sudra—a person belonging to one of the lower castes believed to have sprung from Lord Brahma's legs

sweeper—a person from the caste of floor washers, toilet cleaners, and night-soil removers

tiffin—packed lunch eaten away from home, served from a tiffin box, a circular set of stacked tins with a carrying handle

tika—pigmented substance applied to forehead as symbol of Hindu blessing, usually red vermillion powder

Thakurma—paternal grandmother

tonga—a horse-drawn two-wheeled carriage with a shaded seat for passengers behind the driver's platform

topee or sola sopee—hard-brimmed pith helmet

Urdu—language spoken by Muslims in South Asia with ties to the Persian language

Vedas—the four religious texts of Hinduism

Vishnu—Hindu god of protection

wallah—a person who sells something, like a newspaper-wallah, corn-wallah, etc.

wog—disparaging term used by colonials to refer to Asians, especially those suspected of intellectual or social ambitions

zari—gold thread embroidery for a textile

FRAGMENT OF A LETTER FOUND BY THE ARJUN CLEANING AGENCY IN 1947 AT 22 MIDDLETON STREET

Middleton Street, Calcutta

. . . concerning a long-running rumor that I know to be fact: your hiring of a native female as your assistant. Several colleagues have already called into question her background. The young lady may speak four languages; that is not unusual in this land of polyglots. As Mr. Pal has explained, it is highly unlikely that any upper-caste Indian would permit his daughter to work. Another on staff has ascertained that the boarding school from which your assistant claims to have matriculated does not have any record of past enrollment.

The women of Calcutta are alluring. It is easy for a man to lose his head. I recommend that you terminate this employee if, in fact, she has been hired for pay. And . . .

BOOK ONE
JOHLPUR
Spring and Summer 1930

Thunderous clouds loom in the sky
It's the middle of monsoon,
I wait anxiously on the riverbank
As rain has come too soon.

Rabindranath Tagore, "Golden Boat," ("Sonar Tori"), 1894

CHAPTER
1

The Flower says I was born from the dust.
Kindly, kindly
Let me forget it
Let me forget it
Let me forget.

—Rabindranath Tagore, "The Flower Says," *Chandalika*, 1938

JOHLPUR, WEST BENGAL, 1930

You ask for my name, the real one, and I cannot tell.

It is not for lack of effort. In a proper circumstance, the narrator must give her name. In fact, one of the first English phrases I learned was "What is your good name?"

Over the years people have called me many things. Not all of them are repeatable. But in the early days, I was always called Didi or Pom, the last being a village nickname you will not find in any book. To me, Pom sounds hard: a hand on a drum, or rain pounding on a tin roof. Both are sounds that I remember from the Bengali village where I was born: Johlpur, the Town of Water.

Pom, Didi, Pom! Those who shouted for me the most were my younger sisters, Rumi and Jhumi, twins who looked as similar as grains of rice. But what a difference between them! Rumi was the easy one: quiet and helpful. Jhumi cried more and always demanded to be carried, even when she and Rumi were big strapping girls of six. Double curses was what my grandmother Thakurma called them. But when our father, who we called Baba, was alone with us, he would sometimes say that a daughter's birth lengthened a father's life and that for having three strong girls he might live to one hundred.

I tell you this only so that you will understand how rich I once was.

But nobody in my family understood that those days were perfect ones. Most mornings when my mother made her prayers, she whispered her hopes for a son. If Goddess Lakshmi would bring one, my mother was willing to give her a goat. Or five rupees. Anything, for the boy everyone wanted. Then, in the spring of 1930, the flatness under Ma's sari rounded. Thakurma and Dadu—my grandparents—were suddenly happy with everything she did, and my father sang songs every evening.

As summer came, my mother's belly expanded to the size of a good pumpkin. I marked my tenth birthday, and we ate sweet payesh pudding to celebrate. It was the same time that the daughter of Jamidar Pratap Mukherjee, the landed aristocrat who owned all the rice fields, was studying with a foreign governess. The jamidar's daughter had long been my object of fascination because of her lacy pastel frocks and the white-skinned doll she carried. I did not know the little girl's name then, for we could not ask such a thing of our superiors. In my mind I called her the Princess; and that was not out of envy but amazement that another little girl could be so different.

My acquaintance with the jamidar's household formed at the time I was about seven, old enough to walk distances carrying a bundle of homemade brooms that Ma and I sold throughout the villages. When we reached the jamidar's estate, the ritual was always the same. A servant would call for the jamidarni to see us; she would come out with her daughter hiding behind the folds of her shining silk sari. Then our two mothers would examine the brooms: hers looking down, and mine squatting on the stone veranda, turning over each of our brooms to find her the best. The jamidarni would suggest that her sweeper didn't really need a new broom, then my mother would counter, *Jamidarni-memsaheb, the rains are coming and with them, mud!* Or, if it were a few months earlier: *This is a frightfully dry season, please look at the dust on your veranda; it's a shame that your sweeper missed it. Not the woman's fault, just the broom's.*

On our last call to the estate, my mother was heavily pregnant and could not make her usual bright banter. Perhaps because of my mother's condition, the jamidarni gave me a gaze that seemed especially soft. This gave me the bravery to ask where the Princess was hiding herself. The jamidarni replied with a word I hadn't heard before: *school.* Two Ingrej women came to the house to teach the Princess reading and writing and numbers—all in English! The Ingrej had turned a parlor into a proper schoolroom with a desk and chair and a blackboard on which they wrote with a short white stick.

"Would you like to see her?" the jamidarni asked in her gentle voice.

As I was nodding my head, Ma said no. Disappointment flooded me, but she ignored the look I gave her.

The jamidarni asked my mother why I wasn't in school. She'd heard some village children were learning to read and write under the banyan tree behind Mitra-babu's shop.

Then I understood what she meant by the word *school,* because I'd seen boys sitting in Mitra-babu's yard, scratching with reeds on palmyra leaves. For a girl like me, there would never be time to sit under a tree; that was why Ma hadn't wanted me to see the jamidarni's daughter in her special room.

I said to myself that it didn't matter; I didn't want to be the only girl studying with those boys, and I was already doing something more important than they: I was with Ma, earning money for the family.

And I didn't need a numbers class to know how to count coins; by the age of ten, I was proud that I couldn't be cheated. All this I wished I could say to the jamidarni, but it wasn't my place.

Ma was murmuring something about needing my help now that a baby was coming. She placed her hand on her belly, emphasizing this, and the jamidarni pledged that she would make a special prayer for a boy. Ma smiled at this, looking as grateful as if the jamidarni had bought ten brooms. And that day, the jamidarni bought her broom without bargaining.

We did not have such luck at other places on our route. By midafternoon, my mother and I slowly trailed home, the heat wrapping itself around us like a scratchy woolen shawl. We were still a month from the arrival of the monsoon, and the last weeks were always the worst. By the time we were home from broom selling, I was as wet as if I'd played the Two Turtles game in the pond with Rumi and Jhumi. I knew that for my mother to carry her waiting baby during that last hot month was not only uncomfortable but also physically risky. Some women in the village had even muttered to one another that it would be a blessing if Ma lost the stone she carried, because three girls first was only likely to bring a fourth.

Everyone knew that we'd had trouble. Dadu was forced to sell the one rice paddy he owned to meet the debts of our family, and now his son, my Baba, farmed for others, receiving as payment a portion of rice. Still, we were not poor like the ragged ones living in the alleys of the village. These were the ones my mother called lost souls, and if they came for food, she still always gave something. We had potatoes and eggplants and tomatoes and greens from our own vegetable garden. Fruits beckoned from old abandoned orchards and from neighbors who did not mind sharing. To buy foodstuffs we could not grow, my mother raised a small amount from selling the brooms in summer and catching fish during rainy season. I would do all this work with her until it was time for my marriage, and then Rumi and Jhumi would do the same.

"Your face is our jewel," Ma would say sometimes, and I would laugh and crinkle my nose in embarrassment, because I felt awkward compared to the rosebud prettiness of the twins. But I knew that of all the girls in the family, I looked the most like Ma. It might help me get a husband, especially since there was no dowry we could give. At ten, I didn't think much about marriage, even though my mother had married at eight, moving into my grandparents' hut to live with them and Baba when she was thirteen. I was born two years after that. Sadly, Ma's parents died from typhoid before my annaprasan, the six-month first-rice-eating celebration of a child's life. So I had nobody around except my two sisters, my parents, and one set of grandparents. In our village, this was a very small family.

Two nights after our final broom-selling journey, I awoke to realize that Thakurma was hovering near Ma. Baba was lighting the oil lamp. Thakurma whispered to me that my mother was going to have the baby soon, and that I should take my sisters to sleep outside and then fetch Chitra-massi, the dai who lived in Johlpur village. Thakurma reminded me to call Chitra-massi's name four times at the door: to call her once or twice might lead her to worry that I was a nighttime ghost. I thought this was nonsense, but her door did not open until the fourth time I called. Together, Chitra-massi and I raced back to the hut, carrying her special bucket and cloths. Then Thakurma took her inside and ordered me to rest with the twins.

It was a hot night, so it should have felt easier to sleep outside. But how could any of us sleep as the minutes turned to hours and our mother's groans evolved into a tiger's roar? Village women flowed toward our hut like ants on the trail of a dropped piece of sweet shondesh. I knew they felt especially concerned because Ma could not go to her childhood home to give birth, since her parents had passed.

Ma's cries grew wilder, but still the baby would not budge. Eventually Chitra-massi told my father to fetch Dr. Dasgupta from the next village. My father rode off with a neighbor in his cart; it was some hours later that they returned with the doctor. The sky was light and my mother was hardly crying at all, which made me fear for her all the more.

I watched the doctor's black case bang against his legs as he hurried inside. What did the case hold? I did not trust doctors and their tools. If he had a knife, he could kill my mother or the baby by accident. Silently, I begged the goddess Lakshmi to watch over my mother and the baby. I was beyond wishing for a little brother; I just wanted whoever was inside to come out alive.

Morning traffic to the river was under way when new sounds broke from the hut: happy cheering and laughter. Thakurma emerged covered in sweat but with a smile as wide as the lightening sky. She told us that a little brother had been born, with big ears for listening to his sisters and lots of black curly hair. He had been locked inside of Ma, and Dr. Dasgupta had used something called forceps to free his head. She said she'd almost fainted from the sight of it, but it had worked. Ma was quite tired but wanted to see us.

My sisters and I could not get inside the hut quickly enough. The air was full of heavy smells: incense, the afterbirth, and sweat. After kissing Ma's damp cheek, I turned to look at the new one in the family.

"Bhai," I breathed softly. Thakurma gently lifted part of the red swaddling cloth to show his miniature boy's face with closed-shut eyes. His skin was fair, but the sun would darken him to the same golden-brown color as me.

"Double curses wiped out by a gift from Krishna himself. We will give ten rupees to the temple!" Thakurma hugged me against her thin frame.

It didn't matter whether Krishna or Lakshmi or any other deity was responsible, I thought while studying my brother's wet curls plastered from the sandalwood-scented bath he'd just taken. He was so beautiful that calling him Bhai—*brother*—seemed too ordinary. All the other children in Johlpur called their brothers Bhai. And they had not prayed as hard for a miracle.

As I retreated back to the sleeping mats and settled between Rumi and Jhumi, I drowsed off, pondering what kind of name my grandfather would choose for my little bhai. Then another worry came: how would we ever come up with the goat Ma had promised Lakshmi and the rupees owed to both her and Krishna?

You may think such karmic debts are old-fashioned Hindu superstitions worth as much as an Englishman's crossed fingers or thrown salt. But I have sometimes wondered whether paying those heavenly debts right away might have kept them from becoming my burden. Then I would never have left the beautiful shores of Johlpur, and I would be able to tell you my name.

CHAPTER

2

The sea, one massed foam,
clamors with its million up-thrust arms,
"Give! Give! Give!"
Wrathful at the delay, foaming and hissing
The aura Death grows white with mighty anger.

—Rabindranath Tagore, "Sea Waves," ("Shindhutaranga"), 1887

After Bhai had turned six days old and had his nails clipped by the Napit woman, people stopped talking about him and thought only of the monsoon. Mitra-babu, the shop owner, said that the rains had fallen on Travancore, the province at India's southernmost tip, and were traveling upcountry. A second monsoon wind was sweeping the Indian Ocean to break at Bengal. This was the real storm, and from the shore, one could see it coming like the most magical blackness in the world.

The day those rains came, a slow parade of tongas, cycles, rickshaws, and cars snaked along the coastal road. This spectacle of sightseers was almost as exciting as the pending monsoon. The year before, a white man sitting in the back of a big Rover had come past. The village children said he was called the Collector. When I asked Baba whether this was English for devil, as my friends had said, he laughed with a harsh sound. Baba said the Collector was the jamidar's good friend. He worked for the government and gave the district's harvested rice to the people in England and other countries the Ingrej owned. *Does the Collector pay you, or the jamidar?* I had asked. *Neither,* answered my father in a short, hard voice. *There is no pay. Just whatever bit of rice they let us keep.*

I did not see the Collector's car today, but that did not concern me. I was more interested in the holiday makers: the well-dressed ladies who shrieked and clutched their saris that the winds tried to take from them, and the valiant husbands who struggled in vain to keep umbrellas from taking flight. I loved to see the rich people in fine clothing; to me, they were as amusing as monkeys playing games in trees.

Stillness precedes the rains: a kind of energy that holds you and everything else motionless. It was holding us then. My sisters and I went inside as the sun had slipped away behind the clouds. The hut became so dark that I had to squint to properly see the dal I was picking through. Silently, Rumi fanned the sleeping Ma and Bhai, who had a black spot drawn on his face to ward off the evil eye. Nearby, Jhumi was snuggled against Thakurma's thick, comfortable belly.

Into this peaceful silence, a neighbor boy outside called: "Look! It comes!"

Rumi left off fanning and ran outside, while Thakurma slowly arose and took Jhumi with her to check the weather. I stayed at my job so Thakurma wouldn't have reason to scold me. When they all returned, both sisters jumping and tugging at Thakurma's sari, my grandmother said, "Rain is here."

"Let's go!" Jhumi hugged Thakurma. "You promised we could!"

The twins were desperate to see the monsoon arrive because

they'd missed going the previous year. It was because they had misbehaved, snatching a rose apple that Thakurma had carefully placed at
her altar to Lord Krishna. My sisters had wept while I was allowed to
join the rest of the village in celebrating the rain last year. They had
been five. Now they were six, but still too wild, everyone said.

"No, wait," Thakurma said to the twins. "When Baba's back, then
you go."

"Yes," Ma said, sleepily awakening. "Baba will surely be finishing
his job and coming home soon."

"What if he's late?" Jhumi asked. "What if he is so late that we
miss the cloud?"

It was only midafternoon; Baba usually worked until the sun
faded. He'd been very busy lately, working every day to irrigate the
jamidar's dry fields.

"You cannot go alone!" Thakurma scolded. "Your mother is staying
here with Bhai, and Dadu and I are too old for the comings and go-
ings. Yesterday somebody else shouted the rain was about to fall. And
it did not!"

"I could ask what Baba thinks," I suggested, seeing in Jhumi's
eyes a glare that could easily earn her a cuff from Thakurma. "Perhaps
the overseer will let them all off before the road floods. And if Baba
can't come"—here, I turned to nod respectfully to Thakurma—"I can
explain to Rumi and Jhumi and we will all wait together."

Thakurma gave me a shooing gesture. "Yes, you go, but quickly.
Before it becomes darker."

"Wait, Pom!" Ma said suddenly. "Remember, don't take the jungle
path."

My pleasure at being allowed out to find my father was dulled by
my mother's command to take the longer route. She had loaded me
with many frightening tales about the jungle hideaways of the revolutionaries who robbed innocent country people in their efforts to
raise funds for antigovernment activities. When my mother wanted
me to understand something, she told a dramatic story. Thakurma did

as well. Perhaps it was because they knew I paid more attention to stories than anything.

There would be no dacoits hiding in the jungle today, I was sure. When I was out of my family's eyesight, I slipped off the main road and through a cassia grove into the jungle, where a shortcut led to the rice fields. It was not like me to break the rules, but I had a feeling the rain was very near, and I wanted to be with my father when it struck.

The narrow path through the jungle was easy to miss, but I recognized landmarks like the supari tree on which always hung a jug of rainwater for wandering holy men. I supposed that dacoits might drink from it, too; I was careful not to go near it. As I passed a small grove of papayas, I picked up a couple of freshly fallen ones and tied them in my sari's pallu to share later with my family.

The sun was almost gone when I reached the edge of the fields where a few men raked the dull, dry earth. That group didn't know of my father, so I walked on. I already had a few cuts on my feet that smarted as I continued on the pebbled path. The fields themselves would have been softer, but I didn't dare trample on the precious seedlings.

The sky was darker now and slightly green. I felt an absolute quiet in the air—not a single leaf moved. Then a cool wind rushed over everything, rippling the trees, grasses, and my hair. In minutes, I imagined, the storm cloud would arrive.

As the raindrops began falling slow and thick, I hurried on, wishing I'd found my father. The next field had workers, some of whom were already dancing in the rain, but far more were still bent over, hoeing channels for the heavenly rain. This was my father's group, but the men said he'd gone home on the longer route with several others an hour ago on the company cart.

So my father was in another place; I'd missed him. I felt my heart pound with the frustration of it. If I'd taken the main road as Ma had ordered, my father would have seen me and probably swung me up to ride along on the cart. We would have returned together. Now everyone would be waiting for me and becoming angry.

"Another cart comes through in a while." One of the workers stretched his lips into a grin that made me feel sick. "You can ride on it with us."

It would have been fine to ride home alongside Baba. But if Ma or Thakurma heard from anyone that I'd ridden on a cart with strange men, some of whom were Muslim, I would surely be beaten. I didn't hesitate in my quick reply. "No, Uncle. It is not far. I will walk."

The trip home was downhill, so it did seem faster. My feet moved so quickly I hardly felt the thorns. I opened my mouth wide, tasting the cool, fresh rain. I was not on the beach; but I was still enjoying the rain. Then I passed the papaya orchard, and from a slight rise, I was able to glimpse the thatched roofs of Johlpur and the great sea beyond. Several cars had parked on the beach, and many tiny figures ran along the sandy beachfront, arms outstretched to the massive dark cloud. As I lingered, I thought I heard some people shouting.

A great wave was rolling in: a wave so tall, so long and thick that it resembled a wall. The highest walls I knew were the stucco ones that surrounded the jamidar's estate; this wall of water was much higher, and it bore down on the beach as I had never seen.

Everyone on the sand was running, but the wave was closing in fast. Then it rushed right over them, sweeping away the land beneath. Where was the shore? I stared hard, but all I could see now was endless water with small black specks floating.

The rain continued to fall in great cold sheets that stung. Without having seen the people reappear, I turned away and continued into the jungle. In the darkening evening, everything seemed foreign. The ground's stones and nettles were covered with water high enough to touch my ankles, and I could not see through the trees to where I was going.

I did not let myself worry, for the path home was quick. Everyone would be waiting at the hut. I would tell them about the strange sight at the beach while Ma cleaned my cuts with mustard oil. But as I descended into the jungle's end, everything seemed to dissolve into a giant puddle. My walking slowed, and the puddle rose to my knees. There were floods in Johlpur every year, for at least some of the rainy season—but always in the low areas and along the village road. I couldn't remember anyone talking about floods entering the jungle.

Just a bit farther was a tall, sturdy date palm, with enough branches to get a foothold. I pushed my way through the water that had risen to my waist and pulled myself up the tree. I was attempting something I had heard my grandfather talk about doing once when he was a young man, to survive a very bad storm. I climbed as high as felt sturdy and unfurled half of my sari to tie myself into the embrace of the tree. I felt warm for a moment, remembering the way Ma tied Bhai against her body. My little brother would be frightened by this change of weather; thinking about Bhai's fears took away my own. I remembered the papayas I'd tied in my sari and ate the first one.

I had no idea about the passing of time, for it had become dark and the rain never stopped. Despite this, I slept fitfully. When I awoke for good, the sky was a soft purple color, and the crows were crying. I couldn't make out a break between sky and water, just an endless purple-blue. Eventually, the rain slowed to a drizzle, and the sun appeared.

I struggled to identify the clearing where our settlement of huts should have been, but it wasn't there. All that stretched ahead was brackish water that grew steadily clearer and bluer as it met with the sea. My memory returned to the wave I'd seen, so strange and high that it might have sprung from one of Thakurma's religious stories. The water moved slowly, carrying things past the tree where I had climbed up. Trees, branches, and roofs. Goats and donkeys and water buffalos. Even the jamidar's silver Vauxhall, which lay sideways as it floated past.

Dead people were also part of the tide. At first I did not want to look at them, but then I knew I had to, for with every one I didn't recognize, it meant that my family might be safe. By then I was crying, silent heaving sobs, because if the sound were audible, it would mean my mourning was real. I knew the wave had taken away the people on the beach. I knew, too, the water must have swept over the place where our hut was. But maybe not; I held fast to my belief that if I were patient, Baba would find me.

The rains came and went all day, bending the branch that had become my savior. Then the night came. I fell into a strange sort of waking dream, where every sound I heard was Baba's firm, reassuring footstep; although I understood, in my heart, there could be no sound of walking when all the earth was covered with water.

The next morning followed the same pattern as the one before: a purple sky growing paler, then sunlight, with monkeys and crows chattering. I ate the second papaya and watched more bodies float in the water. The outside of my sari had dried into a stiff, dirty shell, but drops of water remained inside some folds. I unwound the cloth and sucked it, trying to ignore the tastes of earth and salt. Then the torture began: tree ants climbed my legs and arms and bit me in places that I couldn't reach. I tried talking to them, explaining that I did not want to be in their home and begging them to leave me in peace. How tired my arms and legs were, but if I lost hold, I would drop to the water. I was a good swimmer, but there was no land to reach; I would be lost.

Hours later, I thought a miracle had arrived: a fishing dinghy loaded with living people. I called down to them as they approached, but the men paddled on without a glance. I hadn't wept since the night before, but now I did. Twice more boats passed slowly, all of them overloaded with people and animals. I called to them each time with the small, rough voice I had left. *Look! I'm here! Save me, please.* How thirsty I was. I feared I might wither up where I was, like a dry leaf on a tree.

Then, late in the day, I spied a small fishing boat occupied by what looked like a single family: two grandparents, a man and a woman of middle age, and two young boys. The boys were pointing at some animal swimming in the water and laughing as if it were an ordinary day.

I shouted louder than I had before, and the brothers stopped laughing and looked. I could tell the children had not yet seen me. Quickly I pulled off my sari and, holding one end, flung it out like a flag. Now the children pointed at the dirty, cream-colored cloth, and to my joy, the father changed course and rowed toward me.

As the boat approached, I wrapped my sari and descended the tree that had saved me: a difficult operation because my limbs had not moved for so long. But I finally reached the water and swam the short distance to the boat. The boys' father held out an oar that I caught.

"Thank you," I whispered. "Thank you very much."

"Good that you can swim," said the father, and he gave me a small smile that made me feel safe.

"Girl, where is your family?" asked the wizened old man who was likely the family grandfather.

"I don't know!" I said, as I clambered aboard. "We lived in Johlpur, but it is gone."

"We're from Komba. Our place is gone, too," the younger boy said, sounding almost excited.

"A terribly big wave swallowed the beach," I said as the boat moved along, passing thick mangrove forests on one side and open sea on the other. It was a landscape I knew well, but seemed alien with so many of the mangroves uprooted and leaning crazily.

"Not a wave. It was Goddess Kali's doing," the grandfather said in a stern way.

"We can't give you food or drink, as there is not even enough for ourselves," the thin grandmother told me. "But it is a sin not to help. We will take you to shore. From there you can find your people."

"But her family is gone," the father said.

"On land someone will help her." The boys' mother spoke quietly. The water had stained her white sari gray, but I could still see the thin red border. She was well-off to have a sari woven in a mill.

"Who will help?" I asked, for I was starting to understand that my old life might be over. A new wetness trickled down my cheek, and my thirsty tongue crept out to catch the salty tear.

"Boudi just told you: someone will. We have provided a ride to you; that is our duty." The grandfather's voice was as rough as the crows that had wakened me that first hellish morning, and I imagined that he might become tired of me and let me go overboard like the horrible debris around us.

I began an apology. "Forgive me, please. I am so grateful that you saved me—"

"Quiet!" the old man snapped.

I said naught until the next morning, when we touched land.

CHAPTER
3

How many of us have sighed for a drink of clean *water,
not boiled, from a* clean *well, removed from drains,
from a* clean *bucket in which hands have not been washed
surreptitiously, from a* clean *cup which has been already
wiped on a* clean *towel (not previously used for toilet purposes),
and cleaned previously in* clean *water, in which lurk no germs
of disease!*

—Margaret Beahm Denning, *Mosaics from India,* 1902

My eyes were dry and tired, but I kept them open as the father and grandfather climbed down into the shallows to bring the boat to land. The waters were filled with discarded logs, boards, and tires. A family of five paddled in on a simple wooden board; on closer inspection, I saw on that board a child my size lying motionless and covered with flies. Dead; but they had not let the child go.

During my journey, I had seen so many floating deathbeds and I had hoped for all of them that they would come to land and have cremation. Hindus who weren't cremated would have their souls trapped between worlds, a fate that Thakurma told me was worse than anything. Now I had to bear the thought of my own family wandering eternally, because I had been unable to send them on to better lives.

On the walk that ran near the sea, I could see all manner of folk: wild-haired beggars, laborers, constables in crisp uniforms and hard topees, and gaunt holy men clothed in saffron robes. Later, I would know India's greatest city like the back of my hand; but at that moment in my young life, the sight of this seaside town called Digha was as impressive as Calcutta and Delhi and Bombay put together and topped with silver leaf. For what I saw on the path along the water's edge was food! Cauldrons of boiling chai, snack stands selling crispy delights, and piles of fruit and vegetables abounded. Everywhere was nourishment, the luxury I had been without.

First onto shore was the grandfather, who took the hand offered to him by a young man standing on the dock. Then the father went up, and the mother helped the grandmother be lifted to safety. The boys were lifted off, then the mother, and then I pulled myself up to the dock.

"I've been told there are several wells very close," the father said to all of us. "I'll bring water."

"But what is there to carry the water in?" the grandmother grumbled.

"We have one jug," the mother said, showing the container she had carried off the boat with her. "Let's all walk together and drink what little bit is left. Then we will have good fresh water from the well."

"She cannot drink from our jug," the grandfather said, jabbing his chin toward me. "We have not come so far only to ruin ourselves."

"Yes," said the father. "We have done what we can for the girl. It is time to let her make her own way."

I was confused, because they had taken me in the boat without question; but everything was different now. How had they guessed that I was low caste? At the same time I pondered this, I was also thinking about how to get a cup. The chai-wallah's customers tossed their used clay cups to the ground; it was possible I might be able to take one that hadn't broken.

The line at the well was long, full of the town's regular residents and, of course, all the refugees. Nearby, in front of a tall stucco building the likes of which I'd never seen, there was a veranda shaded by an awning, and sitting at a great wooden table, surveying the scene, were two Ingrej men in suits, talking to each other in their sharp-sounding, funny language.

I'd never seen an Englishman except for the Collector, and that was not close. Now, I could see the veins in one man's head and the extreme fairness of his skin. A child in Johlpur had been born with skin as white as rice, hair of red, and eyes a curious shade of green. Thakurma said that a demon had taken up inside him, and I wondered now if these white-skinned men were also demons.

As I fearfully looked away, my attention turned to a tea drinker who was finishing his cup of tea. Excitedly I darted forth and caught it in midair. Some people laughed, but the boys' father shouted so loudly that my fingers slipped, and the cup smashed to the ground.

"Don't steal!" the father chided.

"Forgive me," I whispered in my dry-throated, painful new voice, aware of the brothers greedily drinking down the water from the jug the mother had filled since she'd finished in the well line.

"The child can have this!" A deep, warm voice spoke from somewhere behind me. I turned to discover a man in a clean, finely woven kurta and dhoti. His light skin was closely shaven and bore a trace of saffron in the center of his forehead, the sign that he was a Hindu who had recently been blessed. From his unrumpled appearance, I knew he could not have come on a boat but must have lived in the town.

"Babu, she is not our daughter. We know nothing about her caste. She will contaminate your well." The grandfather seemed to puff up as he spoke.

"I have drawn the water myself, so there is no danger." The man made a sign of blessing toward the father. "Surely you will be rewarded for taking care of an orphan."

Was he a priest? I wondered. The conversation between the gentleman and the boys' father ran along as merrily as the sound of good sweet water sloshing into urns and jugs and pails, water so close to me yet unattainable. Something in my head seemed to explode, and then my hands were cold, for the gentleman had put a cup full of water into my hands.

"Drink," he said, and I remembered what Ma had once explained, that even though Brahmins only ate food or drink prepared by their own kind, they could give others nourishment, as this man had decided to do for me.

There are few sensations I remember more strongly than the feeling of drinking water after almost three days without it. It was pleasure mixed with agony, because my throat had become sore with dryness. The water rushed through my arid throat to my belly. Such delicious, lovely water; but the Brahmin was cautioning me to drink slowly, for taking water too fast would make me sick.

"There will be more water where we are going. Food, too. Keep hold of your cup." Then the stranger told the father that he would like to bring me to a temple in the next province, Orissa. Normally, very few girls were selected to become temple servants; because of the floods, the priests were generously opening doors.

Johlpur was so small we had only roadside shrines for the various gods. I had heard about temples but had never been to one and certainly hadn't known children could live inside. But the saheb was saying that girls were given food and clothing and grew up to dance and give prayers to Jagannath, a reincarnation of Lord Shiva. The saheb had been commanded by the priests to bring orphan girls coming into Digha to their temple.

As he spoke, I saw the mother's dry lips relax from their tight line. She bent to look into my face and said, "Surely it was Lord Shiva's doing that we came to this well just when the good saheb was arriving. You must thank him for his kindness. Go on, touch his feet."

I did so, and then the saheb gave some coins to the father, who at first protested but finally accepted the money, raising it to his forehead in gratitude. All around us people stared and pointed their fingers, asking why they could not also receive money from the saheb.

It was a struggle for me to be bold enough to speak, but I was truly desperate. I said, "But, Saheb, if I stay in a temple, my parents will never find me!"

"If they are alive, they will surely come to the temple to pray! Many people travel to worship at Jagannath Temple. You will see." Then the saheb wrapped his strong hand around my wrist and led me away from the father, mother, and the rest of them.

This had happened so quickly that I was frightened, but my rapid heartbeat slowed when he brought me to a food stall. Hungry people were lined up three-deep, but he shouldered his way to the front and had the vendor fill a banana leaf with rice and dal and greens. I followed his directions to take time eating. As food filled my belly, I felt sleepy with contentment. I put away my uneasiness about the man's shifting gaze, because in truth he had been the kindest stranger I'd ever met. I could imagine Thakurma telling me to show thanks properly.

The saheb still had more for me: sweet jelebis that he bought on the next street. Now he did not need to hold my wrist. I followed him into a quiet area near some trees where he'd left his cart. There was a seat in front for the driver and, behind that, a shaded compartment where I guessed that the saheb and I would sit. As he discussed something with the driver, I roamed a few steps backward, for I was seeking a place to relieve myself. As I passed the back of the cart, I noticed the cloth cover moving as if something were alive beneath it. I heard a strange, strangled sort of noise, and peering into the gap between the cart's side and the cloth, I saw an eye. I moved the cloth very slightly and saw the face of a girl about my age and near her, another girl's face smeared with vomit. A rough rope tied the two girls together; and as I lifted the cloth farther, I saw more girls and a few boys all lying together, connected by ropes and with cloths tied over their mouths.

Time seemed to pass slowly, but in hindsight, I know that I made up my mind about what to do in just a few seconds. I walked away from the cart, pretending I'd not noticed anything, and when the saheb looked at me with his false friendly face, I begged him to allow me to relieve myself behind the tall trees bordering the road.

He agreed easily, but I felt his eyes following me until I had reached a thickly forested section. I moved into the dense grove, stepping as soundlessly as I could until I found a very large tree with a good covering of leaves. I climbed up, for by now I knew the trees were friends. This one would hide me, I was sure.

After some minutes, the saheb ran with his driver through the trees, shouting threats of what they would do if I didn't come forth. Up in the tree, I was shaking so hard I feared rustling the leaves. The saheb was not good; he was an evil being. If I had not seen the tied-up children, I would be with them.

The saheb could spot me if he lifted his head. I tried to still my shaking, and my mind sent pleas to the birds to stop their chattering. But he did not look high; he passed under the tree and spent a long time angrily pulling apart branches. Eventually, the driver told him time was short, so he left. Through a gap in the tree's leaves, I saw the saheb push the covering tightly around the living cargo and then mount the tonga bench. When the driver whipped the horses to go forward, I finally released my breath.

It has been many years since I saw those children in the cart. Now I wish I'd done something, perhaps run to find a constable and tell him about the saheb. But in those days, I'd been a low-caste young girl without a voice. Nobody would have believed me.

I crept through the alleys, keeping my eyes open for constables or anyone else who could apprehend me. I turned a corner and saw a family of miserable waifs huddled in a doorway. As terrifying as the saheb's temple plan was, I could not picture living without a home among the lost souls. I wandered into another alley, vacant except for a large pack of mangy dogs surrounding a stamping, wild-eyed water buffalo that had been left tied to a hook. What a pretty beast she was, with big soft eyes that were set with fear. The dogs would kill her; this she seemed to know.

I felt her fear as if it were my own, but I knew the dogs were not as terrible a foe as the saheb. Even though dogs had sharp teeth, they couldn't speak lies, and they had no hands to catch children or pay money to people to help him. Then I had an idea so daring that it frightened me. Instead of walking on, I could beat away the dogs and take the water buffalo for my own.

To take someone else's water buffalo was stealing. There was no doubt about this, and stealing was a sin. However, to take the poor beast from the dogs was also protecting it. I had not done anything for the children in the cart. But if I saved this buffalo, she would be joyful, and she could carry me away and feed me her good milk.

I passed a bush, breaking off a long branch that I waved in front of me while I shouted in a deep boy's voice, as if the water buffalo belonged to me. The dogs formed an ominous circle around me and barked all the while I unhitched the water buffalo. The biggest one snapped at my leg. I hit him roundly with the branch and made such a terrifying roar that he fell back. He kept up an angry bark until the water buffalo and I had rounded the corner and I found a barrel to step up on to mount her.

She waited patiently and gave a slight sigh when I was on top. She seemed happy I'd taken her. That moment, I decided we were to be friends, and she needed a name. I decided to call her Mala, a name that meant garland, for I intended to weave a garland of flowers for her neck when we were in the countryside.

The road out of Digha was simple to follow. My spirits rose at the occasional glimpses of a blue river, which meant drinking water and fish to catch. Then rain returned, so it was a great deal harder to proceed. It was evening when we finally reached the river's edge. Mala dropped her head and drank. Hiding from the saheb, I had lost my cup, so I used half of a broken coconut shell from a nearby grove to scoop up and drink the cold water that tasted of grit.

The moon rose as I brought Mala to graze on weeds and looked around for something for myself. Close to the water's edge, I came upon some snails. Just as I'd done at home, I smashed the shells and pulled them out. There was no cooking fire, so I ate them as they were.

So this was how one day passed, and another. Each morning I milked Mala, squirting her milk into one coconut shell half, drinking it, and then filling it up again with more of her milk. I got the idea that if only I had a pail, I could make a living as a milkmaid; so I kept my eye out for anyone who might have one to give me, in exchange for free milk for some time. All these ideas I spoke aloud to Mala, just as I told her about my family: how I loved them and the terrible guilt I felt for going away and leaving them to the flood. As I spoke, I sensed that Mala was treading more slowly, as if she needed a good rest or food and water.

We plodded along, passing by fields of maize and mustard greens. I saw a peddler and called out to him, asking him if he had a milk pail. But he said all his containers were sold because of the cyclone that had struck the coast. And he said I should go home, that it was not safe for a girl to be riding about on an animal that looked as if it might collapse any minute.

I kicked Mala's sides a bit harder to see if she might move faster for me. There were sharp pains in my stomach, no doubt from hunger, and my head was throbbing. At the river again for supper, I watered Mala and gave her ferns, which I ate, too, along with the few snails I found. I remembered the garland I'd promised to make her, but I was too tired.

Mala chewed up the ferns happily, so I thought she would do well when we set off again. But in my position atop her jouncing back, my stomach was becoming unsettled, and I was struck by unusual thirst. I dismounted and scooped some river water into a shell for drinking, but that only made me feel worse.

On the damp earth, I crouched weakly while everything inside me rushed out. And then, as I struggled to stand, I felt a second rush of sickness, and I knew I'd shamed myself. With supreme effort, I raised my head and saw Mala slowly ambling alone toward the river.

Don't leave me, I begged her silently. If she did, there would be only vultures to take my body away. I lay where I was, because my legs weren't working anymore. After a while, though, I felt Mala nuzzling my back. Using every last bit of strength, I tugged until she lowered herself to the ground; and then I clung to her until she arose. I could guess from her flaring nostrils that she smelled my sickly odor. But she was a good friend and carried me until I slept with terrible dreams.

I was in the boat with the family again, but this time the grandfather pushed me over the side into the contaminated sea. I came up gasping for air and swam all the way to a cool green pool. There I saw Thakurma's familiar rough khadi sari trailing in the water, but when I reached out, I was wound in it so tightly I knew I would drown. Against my grandmother's pleas for me to remain, I struggled upward until hands reached down to grab me. And then I was no longer in water but lying on something hard that felt like the back of a cart. I had no strength to run away. All I could do was roll back and forth in agony, knowing that my brief fantasy of a free life was lost.

BOOK TWO
MIDNAPORE
Summer 1930–Summer 1935

There was a bird in a cage of gold,
another free in the woods.
One knoweth not what whim of God
Brought the two together of a day.
'O, my friend in the cage,' said the bird in the woods,
'Let's fly away to the woods.'
'Let us live quietly in the cage,'
rejoined the bird in the cage.

Rabindranath Tagore, "Two Birds," ("Dui Pakhi"), 1894

CHAPTER
4

MEMSAHIB, S. This singular example of a hybrid term is the usual respectful designation of a European married lady in the Bengal Presidency; the first portion representing ma'am. Madam Sahib is used at Bombay; Doresani (see DORAY) in Madras. (See also BURRA BEEBEE.)

—Sir Henry Yule and Arthur Coke Burnell, *Hobson-Jobson: A Glossary of Colloquial Anglo-Indian Words and Phrases*, 1886

I floated between two worlds: the alluring, cool pond where my family swam and the hard, hot cart. Leaning over the cart was a colorless woman with a huge hat and all around me were children who had been turned into boxes. Then I was in the water again and saw my sisters and brother swimming by, their hair spreading around them like the petals of lotus flowers. Thakurma and Dadu floated past on their backs, their homespun clothing drifting downward. Ma was closest, treading water beside me, beseeching me to open my mouth and drink, and when I did, the water tasted cold and sweet, as if it came from our clay jug at home. But my father was swimming away and calling the others to join him. I begged him to come back for me, but my father turned once to look with loving eyes, and then he swam on.

Bright light pierced the water, and I awoke. I lay on a cot covered with white cloth. A European stood over me; his head was bare and sun mottled, with a small amount of reddish fur around the sides. The man shook at a short glass stick, held it close to his gold-rimmed spectacles, and then put it underneath my arm. My arm was not free but had a long soft tube going into it; the whole thing was attached to a bag of liquid that hung on a metal stand. The man had caught me and was giving me poison!

Then two Indian women came to the Ingrej demon's side. They wore peaked caps and pale blue cotton dresses with long sleeves and high necks. I was so caught up in staring at them that the glass stick fell out. Both ladies exclaimed. The stout, sterner one tucked the stick back in place, telling me firmly not to let it move again. Then the thin one said that I'd been found near the river ten miles away, sick with cholera. I was brought to them by a man who'd found me hanging upside down on a wandering bull.

"My water buffalo! Where is she?" I felt worse at the thought of this loss.

"The man who rescued you, Abbas-chacha, tied her to the side of his tonga and brought her back to the school where he works." The thin lady stroked my forehead. "They will care for the animal there until you can return with it to your family. They must be worried."

"No, they aren't worried. They are dead." Overhead, a giant fan whirled, moving air that smelled like medicine. If only the fan could move away all that had happened, send me back on a gentle wind to my family.

The white man joined the conversation, speaking in his own language to the nurses and then to me in slow, peculiar-sounding Bengali. I learned that his name was Dr. Andrews and the stout lady was called Nurse Das and the more sympathetic one was Nurse

Gopal. Dr. Andrews listened to what the nurses told him about me and then said he thought my family members were victims of a tidal wave that had swept southern Bengal.

Over the next few days, I took only water and cooked egg whites until Dr. Andrews deemed me strong enough for boiled milk, rice, and dal, which tasted like a feast, just as the clean cot I lay on felt like a goddess's cradle. I slept for a long time each night, and when I awoke, I talked with the other patients who were interested in conversation. I was intent on not thinking about what had happened to me and what I'd lost.

After five days, I was walking and had become, as Nurse Das said, a healthy girl needing occupation. Dr. Andrews must have noticed, too, for I was told he wished to speak with me in his office. As I waited, standing just inside the door, my attention went to his desk, which held a very thick book with many pages. I had seen him looking at it before, and now that I was alone, my fingers itched to open its leather cover and turn the pages.

"Hello, Child," he said from behind me. This was what he called me and every other young person, because there were so many of us in the hospital.

"Hello, Doctor-saheb." I ducked my head in respect, hoping that I'd not been called in because I'd done something wrong.

"You are looking at Dr. Osler's book," he said, nodding toward the large book at the table. "It's the doctors' bible."

I had heard that word before but wasn't quite sure what it was. "Is it your holy book?"

"Almost." A half smile stretched his faded face. "The book describes illnesses and their treatments, for instance, the cholera Asiatica that you caught. If I did not have this book to turn to, I would not know all the different ways to help."

The doctor was now speaking a mix of Bengali and English that was hard for me to entirely understand, but I listened carefully, nodding all the while.

"The nurses say you cannot read or write."

"That is true, but I want to learn." Perhaps because I spoke so much to everyone and had learned a few English words, he might have expected more from me. This made me ashamed.

"I wish that for you, too, but what can be done? The collector from your locality says your village was destroyed. Your family has not reappeared anywhere. I cannot send you back." As he spoke, he looked at the small board the nurses often carried. "It was suggested by Nurse Das that you be placed in a family seeking a bride. I don't like child marriage. However, you have no skills to earn a living."

How ignorant this doctor was: not knowing that children younger than me pulled weeds and herded cows. "If I have a tin pail, I can sell my water buffalo's milk. Then nobody needs to care for me."

"The water buffalo is currently stabled at the Lockwood School. But even if you had her, the countryside is not a safe place for a child to stay alone."

"May I work here?" The tremble in my voice was real, for I was afraid of leaving the place that had brought me back to life. Despite its strong smells and the anguished cries of patients, it felt like a second home.

"We require education for our nurses and even their assistants." He paused. "Perhaps that school would take you as a servant."

There it was: that word, *school*. I'd heard it a lifetime ago from the jamidarni's pink lips, a promise of something I never thought I could have. I looked at the book on the doctor's desk. If I was in a school, I could learn to read books. To be like Nurse Gopal, who always had a novel in her pocket, or the Princess.

"Would you go?" the doctor asked.

"Mala is still there? Alive?" I knew Ingrej ate cows, which meant there was a chance they ate water buffalos, too. I could not bear to arrive and find her gone.

He looked at me sternly. "Of course she is, but you must not use her to run away. If you do, Miss Jamison will be so angry she may never again help our patients. She is the headmistress and regularly brings us supplies. We are very grateful."

"Yes, Doctor-saheb," I said, though I was suddenly uneasy. A white devil woman had loomed over my feverish dreams. Would Miss Jamison look like her?

❧   ❧   ❧

I'D ARRIVED AT the Keshiari Mission Hospital in a bedraggled scrap of a khadi sari, but I left in an English frock. The garment came from one of the boxes of donated clothes that had been packed closely around me in the tonga. The frock Nurse Gopal chose reached almost to my ankles, which she said was good because I would grow into it. It was a faded blue color like the midday sky, and some of the buttons for closing up the back were gone. I knew not to complain, but I did not like the idea of anyone seeing my skin.

Knickers were also provided by the Lockwood School charity. I was quite puzzled until Nurse Gopal explained the thigh-covering pants were to be worn under the frock and not shown to anybody. I was to wash them each night. As she helped me into my garments, she grumbled about the missing buttons. She vanished for a minute, then came back with a needle and two buttons. They were not the same color as the ones on the frock, but they were the right size for closing the gap that had left part of my back bare.

"I won't ever be able to put on this dress without you," I mumbled as she began working on the back of my dress. "I wish I could stay."

Nurse Gopal turned me around so I could see her gentle expression. She said, "Pom, you are very lucky! For Doctor-saheb to convince the school to take you as a servant was a great thing for him to do. And Miss Jamison's school is the finest in the area."

"But her face . . ." When Miss Jamison had arrived an hour earlier, I recognized the wide solar topee with a mosquito-netting veil. When she removed it, I saw a long pale face wrinkled like old fruit. She was the being from my nightmare. After she looked me over with strange green eyes, she said something to the doctor that I didn't understand, but it sounded unfriendly.

"She looks that way because she is a serious woman. She rules over many teachers, and she teaches religion, too." Nurse Gopal finished securing one button and started on the next.

"Oh! Is she a priest?" I had wondered about the plain beige dress that went down to the bottoms of her thick calves.

"No. The Ingrej will call her headmistress, but you will call her Burra-memsaheb." Nurse Gopal's words came fast, and her hold on my dress tightened. "She is the leader of the school. If you are obedient and work hard, they may keep you for quite some time. It is a blessing."

"Please don't leave me!" I said, sensing from the nurse's fast stitching that I would soon be properly dressed and gone.

She snapped off the thread, knotted it, and turned me around. "I must. I am needed on the ward."

As Nurse Gopal hurried off, I saw that two buttons were gone from her apron's waistband: the buttons she had given up for me. I knew I should call out thanks, but I was afraid that if I opened my mouth, I would weep. So I stayed silent instead.

❧   ❧   ❧

I NEVER HAD sat next to a man other than my father, so I was anxious when the driver called Abbas indicated I should join him on the front driver's bench of the tonga. The burra-memsaheb, Miss Jamison, was already comfortably settled behind us on her own seat that had a cushion. Overhead, a cloth awning shielded her from sun and rain.

"Indians stay together, Ingrej in the back. It is the way, Beti," Abbas said in Bengali. I climbed up, trying not to look at Nurse Gopal standing outside watching after me, lest I cry. I found that Abbas had placed three brass tiffin boxes between us, making a small sort of barrier. He told me it was my job to keep these boxes safe. I was glad to have something to do and kept my hands on them.

Abbas was about my baba's age, but a little bit plump. He wore a long cotton kurta that strained against his belly, pajama trousers of the same color, and a small crocheted cap. I knew that this clothing meant he was Muslim, another reason I should not have been sitting beside him. But the nurses had told me that he saved my life, and he had already called me daughter.

"Abbas-chacha, I must thank you for what you did." Consciously, I used the Muslim honorific for *uncle*, because what he had done made him much more to me than a stranger.

"I was only following Allah's command." Abbas had a warm voice, and the skin around his eyes crinkled as he smiled at me. "Every life has value; it was my duty to stop. Normally, we would not have been driving that way. We changed our route because of puja celebrations happening in some villages that day. The memsaheb does not like to see such things."

"I thank your Allah then." I paused, wanting to say more. "But also you for listening to him."

Abbas raised his eyebrows and said softly, "Once you learn English, the burra-memsaheb is the one who needs proper thanking. It was only with her agreement that I could carry you to hospital."

I glanced behind and saw that the strange Englishwoman was reading a book. She could have left me to die but had not. I turned back to Abbas and whispered, "I will always be afraid to speak to her!"

"They will like you at Lockwood School then," Abbas-chacha said in a joking way. "Quiet is the rule. Don't ask about your pay; for young ones like you, Miss Rachael keeps it safe. It is only a few rupees each month, anyway."

Not ever having held a coin as valuable as one rupee, this news did not disturb me. But something else did. "Do you stay at the school?"

"No, I live in town with my wife."

"And how many children?" He struck me as being a very funny, kind father. Different from my own, but probably just as good.

He shook his head. "My wife is a good woman, but we were cursed—we have no offspring. We live alone!"

"Oh," I said, unable to imagine this. "Nurse Gopal said many of the girls sleep at the school. Have they lost their homes, too?"

"Not at all. They are Europeans," he said, and at my blank expression, he laughed. "Ingrej and children from other countries are called Europeans. They often fall sick in Bengal; this school was built one hundred years earlier because it is on high ground believed to have better air." He was describing the countries in a place called Europe that the foreigners came from when Miss Jamison's low, grumbling voice came from behind.

"Yes, yes, Burra-memsaheb!" Abbas switched to English and his pitch became higher, and he began bobbing his head as the headmistress continued in her address. He answered her in that high, falsely happy voice after a bit; I could not understand any of it except for the name I'd told him, Pom. The burra-memsaheb spoke again, and then Abbas told her "Yes, yes!" and returned his gaze forward.

The horses picked up speed with a flick of his reins. Under his breath he said to me, "She says your name is too strange. From now on you shall be Sarah. She wants me to tell you it is a good woman's name from the Christian holy book."

"Say-ruh." I pronounced the strange, sharp-sounding name the way Abbas had done and repeated it to myself silently for the next several miles. I should have minded losing my name, but the thought of getting a fresh name to go with my new clothing seemed fitting.

We made a stop in some hours' time for lunch, and it turned out each one of us had our very own tiffin box. After that, there was more driving. There were fewer rice paddies here than in Johlpur, and many more fields of grain. At last, the land changed a little, with some villages and a big road leading to a town called Midnapore. But we turned off in a different direction, up a long, slowly rising hill.

"A sign for the school." Abbas pointed to some English letters printed on a white board. Below it were two crossed strips of wood painted gold that he said was the symbol of their religion. I looked at the cross, trying to quell the rapid beating of my heart. We were here, and the wide, tall building ahead was like nothing I'd ever seen before: built not of mud or wood but something entirely foreign.

"The school is built of bricks." Abbas-chacha seemed to sense my unspoken question. "They are strong enough to resist wind and rain and everything else. The Ingrej sometimes call a person a brick; he is one with a determined, hardworking manner who does not complain."

I nodded, understanding why he was telling me this. It was how I should behave.

Two bearers in green costumes stood in front of the school's grand sculpted brass doors. Then two Ingrej girls stepped out the front door toward us. They are here to meet me, I thought with some excitement, but their eyes slid past as if Abbas and I weren't present.

"Oh, Miss Jamison," the tallest girl called out, waving a book in her hand. Then she spewed many more English words I couldn't understand. I stared at her face and that of her companion: not colorless like Miss Jamison's but a bright pink. Both girls wore neckties like Englishmen with white blouses and dark green skirts almost as long as Miss Jamison's. Their legs were shielded by thick gray stockings, and their feet were covered in heavy black shoes that tied with laces. I curled my toes, feeling self-conscious about my rough bare feet.

The bearers came forward to help Miss Jamison off the tonga, and then she went inside with the girls. I stayed on the cart bench as Abbas drove us around the school building and past a large garden bordered by square hedges. Inside the hedges were round clipped bushes of flowers; a thin old man moved between the plants, pouring water over them. Beyond the flower garden lay a field of short grass; horses were skipping around it with girls dressed in men's trousers and jackets riding on top.

Abbas drove the tonga straight into an open building where there were other horses, carts, and carriages. A group of men who had been lounging inside the darkness came forward to detach the horses from the cart's harness. As two workers led the horses off for a drink, Abbas introduced me to everyone as the new house girl, Sarah.

"Hindu or Muslim?" one of the stable hands asked, looking me up and down.

"Christian," Abbas said quickly. "Come, Little Sarah, I will show you the animal you have been missing."

"Am I really to be Christian?" I whispered to Abbas as he walked me deeper into the stable, away from the crowd of stable hands.

"Miss Jamison wants you to convert. Not having parents to speak up, you have no choice."

My body stiffened at this. Changing a name was one thing, but changing religion was quite different. It didn't seem safe. Where would I go after death if there were no chance for reincarnation?

"Christians are favored here, Beti." Abbas was whispering in the same reassuring way he had during the tonga journey, but his eyes weren't smiling. "Miss Rachael, the housekeeper, is Christian. She will treat you better if she thinks you are like her."

"But I cannot be Christian. I don't know their gods' names except for Mary and Jesus, and I know nothing of the prayers!" And what of my beloved Goddess Lakshmi or Thakurma's favorite, Lord Krishna? Goddess Durga, Lord Shiva . . . I resolved never to forget these holy friends, no matter what the Burra-memsaheb or Miss Rachael wanted. I would not speak their names aloud, but I would keep them in my heart.

"You will learn those prayers." Abbas beckoned me forward. "Come see your old friend."

I recognized Mala's sweet brown face peering out from the midst of other buffalos and cows and hurried forward to greet her. Where pointy ribs had stuck out before, there was a smooth layer of fat. As I reached my arms toward her, the new, healthy Mala stamped, forcing me to step back. She bent her head and continued eating, not giving me a second glance.

I was taken aback, for Mala seemed to have forgotten how I'd rescued her from the dogs and fed and watered and milked her during our long journey together. I had become as invisible to her as I'd been to the English girls. And this lonely bit of knowledge gathered so quickly upon my arrival turned out to be an accurate prediction of how the next three years at Lockwood School would pass.

CHAPTER
5

VOUCHSAFE: *1. To confer or bestow (some thing, favour, or benefit) on a person. 2. To give, grant, or bestow in a gracious or condescending manner.*

—*Oxford English Dictionary*, Vol. 12, 1933

In no time at all, I lost track of the traditional Bengali seasons. A year was divided into three academic terms, and that was how I thought of things: whether the girls were almost to Christmas holiday or summer leave or October's puja days. But while Lockwood students were promoted to a higher standard each year, things did not change for me, even though it was 1933, and I was thirteen years old.

I spent the early mornings bringing bed tea to sleepy teachers housed in their private rooms off a long red oxide corridor. It rattled my nerves, even after all this time, to be the first each morning to enter these bedchambers with their exotic furniture—tables designed just for one person to sit and write; wooden cases filled with books and papers; and a tall, netting-draped bed that belonged to a memsaheb who expected morning service of tea and biscuits her own particular way, without fail each morning. After delivering the teachers their bed tea, it was time to set up the dining hall. I did this for each meal and afterward washed the room clean. Times in between were spent dusting, polishing, and cleaning other parts of the school, depending on Miss Rachael's wishes.

Abbas had warned me that Burra-memsaheb Jamison was the most important person at Lockwood, but I did not see her nearly as much as Miss Rachael: a tall, strong Christian woman with skin like copper who wore a sari in the same green as the school uniform, which was mill-woven with a fine border of white. The directress of housekeeping seemed older than my ma but younger than Thakurma. The other servants said she was married to a man who worked as a driver in Calcutta, but had never had any children. Because of this, and my Christian conversion, Abbas thought she might take a liking to me.

He was wrong. From the moment she'd received me, there was never a smile or laugh, only criticism. Miss Rachael sang at Sunday services in a tuneless shout that reminded me of the way she called after me in the school hallways. *Sarah, get here now. Fans are dirty. You missed a dead cricket near English classroom. Pick up your feet, close your mouth!*

Miss Rachael was the one who decided I shouldn't sleep with the other servant families in their huts but on a mat in a tiny lean-to occupied by Jyoti-ma, the old widow in charge of collecting and washing all the students' and teachers' used sanitary cloths. Jyoti-ma snored, groaned, and coughed in her sleep, but I didn't mind; it made me feel safe on dark nights.

Jyoti-ma was able to kill mice without even needing a candle to see them. She was also the one who helped me on the morning I awoke to find blood on my thighs. I was twelve, but with no understanding at all of what was happening. Jyoti-ma taught me how to tie long cloths around my middle and gave me an old bucket that I could use for soaking them. Of course I washed the cloths myself, as I did my dress, with water gathered from the courtyard pump.

I had shot up like bamboo just before my first bleeding, and after that, my breasts kept growing. My blue dress that once grazed my calves had become indecently short in length and tight across the chest. When the male staff began teasing me about it, Miss Rachael replaced the blue dress with a gray one from the charity collection. I was glad, because I wanted to look respectable for the one job at Lockwood I thoroughly enjoyed: moving the punkah in Miss Claire Richmond's classroom.

I had become a fan puller whenever the electrical generator at Lockwood broke down. The first time the electric fans stopped and lights went dark, Miss Rachael shouted for me to go into Miss Richmond's classroom. Her room was part of the oldest section of the building, with wooden fan blades attached all the way across the ceiling. These blades shifted back and forth, moved by the power of a servant sitting in the back with a cord tied to her foot. I enjoyed being in the back of the room, lazily moving my foot back and forth and observing pretty Miss Richmond, who gave her students real smiles and spoke in an accent as rich as her orange-gold hair.

The first six months I was utterly confused about the meaning of her speech. But as time went on, her vocabulary flowed into my brain without need for translation, and with my finger touching my dress, I traced the same words she wrote on the blackboard. And then I was reading: first the books for the littlest ones and then the *Just So Stories* of Rudyard Kipling, followed by *Treasure Island* and *A Little Princess*. Miss Richmond maintained a side shelf for borrowing what she termed *pleasure reading*; almost every evening I sneaked one of these to the lean-to and brought it back in the morning before classes had begun. When I came across an unknown word, I memorized its spelling and investigated later in Miss Richmond's *Oxford English Dictionary*. As I continued to study, I felt secretly rich: for each word I learned was something that could never be taken away.

I wanted to speak English, too. The Irish and English and Australians and Anglo-Indians all spoke slightly different-sounding variations of it; with so much confusion, I chose to pattern my English after Miss Richmond, the only English person I admired. In the back of her room, I whispered along with her; when I visited Abbas, who was cleaning and polishing the tongas in the evening, I repeated those phrases more loudly. He encouraged me with praise and small gifts, such as pencils and paper. However, he warned me to practice where the other servants would not see or overhear, for they could become jealous. As a result, after three long years at Lockwood, I could speak and read English. Yet very few knew.

I had grown accustomed to an almost-invisible existence until the day that changed everything. It was at the end of morning lessons in late spring of 1934, and although the electric generator had begun working again, I'd lingered in my fan-pulling corner to hear a few more sentences from *A Room of One's Own*, by Virginia Woolf. Then Miss Richmond raised a discussion about whether young women living in a crowded school might like occasional solitude. If I had been one of her students, I would have raised my hand to say that any person could build a room of her own in her mind, just as I had an imaginary cupboard where I kept Thakurma's and Ma's stories to comfort me. And then, like a voice from that cupboard of childhood dreams, I heard a girl's voice say: "Aey, Broom Girl. Aey!"

The voice was not inside my head but somewhere nearby. I jerked my head up, thinking I must have been daydreaming. But then I saw the new Indian student who'd arrived the previous week: a pretty, plump girl with untidy black braids. I was confused again, for how could anyone know that I'd once sold brooms?

"You don't remember me," she said in Bengali, and the disappointment in her voice gave me the courage to look again. In a flash, I recognized the long-lashed eyes that had watched me years ago from a veranda in the countryside near Johlpur. It seemed unbelievable, but this new student might be the jamidar's little princess daughter.

"When I was younger, I sold brooms. Did you know my mother and me?" My tongue curled at the unfamiliar feeling of our shared old dialect.

"Yes, certainly. You came to my house when we were very little girls." She spoke in a manner that fit her high caste—but without impatience or anger.

"I called you Princess. I remember your frocks," I blurted.

"Yes, I liked them much better than what I'm wearing now." She flicked her stiff green school skirt. "My name is Bidushi. Bidushi Mukherjee. What is yours?"

It was unusual for someone high up to declare her name to a servant. But she was looking at me in a kind way, so I mumbled my new first name, Sarah. How I hated it; but I understood that it was just one of many changes I'd had to make to live under the protection of Lockwood School.

"Sarah! Must everyone call you that now? It sounds strange, doesn't it?"

"I've become a Christian." I dropped my head, expecting that the conversation was done, but it seemed that Bidushi expected more. Clearing my throat, I asked, "And how is your esteemed family?"

Bidushi pressed her rosebud lips together for a moment. Then in a somber voice, she said, "Four years ago, a tidal wave killed my parents."

"I know that wave!" I said. "I saw it. That same wave took my whole village and family. I escaped only because I was on higher ground in the jungle."

"I suppose that we were both lucky," Bidushi said, but her voice was heavy. "They didn't take me to the beach because I needed to finish my lessons. The next day, the Collector came to explain to my ayah and me that all of them had drowned."

"Have you been alone since then?" I ached for her.

"My father's brother and his wife came to take over the estate. My aunt began keeping me inside, because well-bred girls should not be seen outside the family. I have been trapped inside the walls of our estate until last week!" From the tone of her voice, she sounded glad to be away.

Feeling shy but wanting to reassure her, I said, "Welcome to Lockwood School. I hope it will be a good home for you."

"Yes, because you are here." Bidushi's eyes shone. "We are the same, two Johlpur orphans alone in a strange place."

But we were not the same. I was a servant, and she was a student; and she still had her relatives' protection and money, while I had a stipend that I'd never seen because Miss Rachael was keeping it for me. But I could not say all of that. Instead, I asked why she was studying in such a faraway school.

"My uncle and aunt didn't really want to send me. But a plan was made many years ago for me to marry my mother's cousin's son from Calcutta. Recently, his parents inquired about my education. You see, Pankaj—that is my betrothed's name—is in England studying law at the University of Cambridge."

"I have heard of Cambridge!" I knew that Miss Richmond was a graduate of Newnham College, Cambridge, and that many Englishmen who'd been at Cambridge or Oxford ruled within the government of India.

"Yes!" Bidushi straightened her shoulders and beamed. "Pankaj-dada told his parents he would never marry a girl who was uneducated. So my aunt and uncle quickly had to send me somewhere. My old governess said that I would be happy here, but I don't like all these English girls pointing at me and not wanting to have their bed near mine. And I've forgotten all my English. When my aunt moved into the house, she stopped allowing my governess to come."

"Miss Richmond is a great teacher, and not every girl here is unkind," I said, trying to raise her spirits. "There are some friendly girls, especially the ones who like games. You must learn badminton! You don't need to speak much to play."

As I finished speaking, I had an odd feeling of being watched.

Two English girls passed closely, their oxford shoes clipping the floor like horse hooves. The first girl, who was called Anne, narrowed her eyes as she looked at us.

"There you have it," Anne said in a brash, loud voice. "Wog-to-wog gossip! What is that, Hindustani or Bengali?"

"Wogoli," said her friend Beatrice. "Or should we say, Wiggly?" The two dissolved into snickering laughter.

Inside of me, rage flared. I was accustomed to mocking words, but Bidushi was a princess who shouldn't have to hear it. But I couldn't speak back to an English student; it could mean being thrown out of Miss Richmond's room for good. So I stuffed my upset into my imaginary cabinet, hoping that Bidushi hadn't understood their teasing.

Too upset to say good-bye to Bidushi, I bobbed down into a short curtsy and crept toward the door.

"Just a moment!" Miss Richmond said in her pay-attention voice.

My stomach was filled with a fluttering, as if one of the beautiful yellow butterflies from the garden were trapped within. If Miss Richmond told Miss Rachael I'd been speaking Bengali with a student, she might beat me. And Bidushi might get a black mark, which could mean she wouldn't get pudding on Sunday or something even worse. But Miss Richmond's first words weren't addressed to me.

"Bea and Anne, that's enough, and you'll have a reprimand if you do it again. Go!" After the two had left, Miss Richmond looked at Bidushi and said in soft, slow English, "I should remind you that Hindustani is not supposed to be spoken. You are here to learn our language. Were you told that upon arrival?"

Bidushi remained silent, clearly not understanding or having no words to respond. And so, in her defense, I found my own voice: the English one I had practiced and practiced, but not yet used with an English person.

"Memsaheb, I apologize. We spoke Bengali only because she knows so little English. Her English governess was sent away four years ago, after her mother died, so she has forgotten the language. I vouchsafe that Bidushi will try very hard to learn English here. Please permit her."

"Yes, but—*vouchsafe?*" Miss Richmond looked at me with an odd expression. "Who are you?"

"I'm called Sarah, Memsaheb. I came to your room today to pull the fan." Inside, the butterfly was going mad trying to escape.

"Of course you were here; I rang for you. You are here quite often, doing that. It must be boring."

"Oh, no, Memsaheb! To be in your class is a joy." My words might have sounded like flattery, but they were true.

"Where did you work before you came here?"

"I lived in a small village near the coast with my family, who are now deceased, God rest their souls—"

Miss Richmond interrupted. "And were you schooled there in English?"

I shook my head.

"Then how did you learn the expression *vouchsafe?*"

I was afraid to admit that I hunted many of her long and lovely words in the *Oxford English Dictionary*. It was probably against school rules for someone like me to pollute the dictionary with my touch. So I said, "In here, Memsaheb. You are a great teacher."

Miss Richmond was quiet for a moment, then said, "Sarah, speak some more."

"I'm very sorry, but I don't know what to say." My face was hot with shame, for I knew this conversation had gone on too long. I had not intended to call attention to myself, only to rescue Bidushi.

"If you've been learning from me in this classroom, will you please recite something?"

So I recited the part of *A Room of One's Own* she had just read aloud to the class. Perhaps I had gotten a few words wrong, but at the end, Miss Richmond asked me some questions to see how much of it I'd understood. I explained the various themes and about my idea of keeping a cabinet in one's mind. She nodded and said, "You understand everything, and your intonation is remarkable. And you must read plenty of books, obviously, to have followed all that figurative language."

"I do read," I said cautiously, praying this would not lead to an inquisition about which books I had touched. "But my handwriting is not up to the mark."

"Handwriting can be improved—but, Sarah, you have a gift for language. You have given me an idea for Bidushi." Bidushi had been looking blank, but her eyes widened at the sound of her name. Miss Richmond continued: "You shall become her special helpmate. An extra desk will be brought to this class and placed next to her. When Bidushi does not understand a word, she shall touch your desktop, and you may translate in Bengali—but in a whisper, so as not to distract the others. Please explain this."

I translated quickly for Bidushi, and her lips slowly curved into a smile. In heavily accented English, she said, "Thank you, madam!"

"Oh, don't thank me; it will be Sarah who deserves that." Miss Richmond's voice was brisk. "Now, Bidushi, shall we go into the dining hall? There are only friendly girls sitting at my table."

%   %   %

SUDDENLY, MY LIFE had become quite bright, with a girl just my age who shared my past. In *A Little Princess*, a novel that Miss Richmond always had the nine-year-old class read, the rich student called Sara, and the scullery maid Becky, were kind to each other. It was almost the same, except for the reversal in our names. And I was aware that, although I now tutored Bidushi, I still had to honor my other responsibilities. If the electricity failed, I rushed from my desk to the back of the classroom to work the punkah, causing giggles among the girls. But such nonsense paled in comparison to Miss Rachael's anger at losing my hands for several hours each day. In retaliation, she set me to doing more in my reduced hours. But I hardly minded, because

I adored helping Bidushi. Learning English was like catching fish without touching water, as Thakurma used to say about good things that came too easily. I wanted it to be that way for Bidushi, also; but it was not.

"I cannot learn this language," Bidushi whispered in our forbidden Bengali during the late-afternoon study period. "It is an embarrassment with my name."

Bidushi's name meant knowledge; I thought how lovely it would be to have such a lofty name instead of Sarah, an old wife in the Ingrej Bible. But I could see that Bidushi felt too sorry for herself. I had grown comfortable enough to know that if I teased her, it might improve her outlook.

"Oh, there's no need to work at it," I said lightly. "If you don't care to please your husband and his English-speaking friends, he can return you to Johlpur, where you can speak Bengali with your dear aunt."

Bidushi made a face but did work harder. Together we recovered the long-lost vocabulary, and she learned enough new words to recount life when her parents were alive. What a beautiful world it had been! As a young child, Bidushi tottered around a lace-covered table until European lady guests reached down to take her up on their laps. She moved on to thirty-course dinner parties at which royalty and government officials mingled. All the while the jamidarni was schooling her in menus, jewelry selection, and sari draping: details of the Indian aristocratic life that I savored.

Once she became more confident, I made Bidushi write her English sentences next to Bengali translations; I used this to help me learn the writing of Bengali, for up to this point I spoke my mother tongue but could not read or write. In this way, Bidushi taught me as much as I taught her, without her noticing. I feared that if she knew I was so uneducated, she might treat me like less of a friend.

Bidushi smiled and joked more as her English came along, although she retained a strong Bengali accent that the other girls mocked if the teachers weren't listening. I'd hoped Bidushi would find solace with the two other Indian girls at Lockwood, but they walked past her as if she didn't exist.

"It's because I talk with you, Didi, but I don't care," she said one evening in the garden, where we had gone for fresh air after studying inside. "I've never had a true friend like you, and those two aren't worth two paise. The others, even less." And then she told me something that I had not understood. Indian Civil Service and army officers did not send their daughters to our school, which wasn't top-drawer. Lockwood was stocked with the daughters of ordinary merchants and missionaries and railway men, and a few wealthy Indians from nearby. Out of this mishmash, the girls built their very own caste system.

Indians were, of course, at the ground floor. The Anglo-Indians, Armenians, and French socialized well together; but it was the girls from Britain and her colonies who were on top, though they occasionally warred with one another. The British called the Australians Aussies, and they in turn called the English ones Poms, which meant Prisoners of Mother England. When I learned this, I was quite relieved nobody knew my old village name.

Bidushi did not call me Sarah, only the loving term *didi*, meaning big sister. It was ironic, because she was slightly older. But in many ways, she seemed younger; and as months passed, a feeling grew inside me that I was intelligent and had value. It was as if Bidushi's affection and Miss Richmond's expectations were making me into someone new.

IN SHORT ORDER the weather turned from pleasant to sweltering. The girls played tennis in sleeveless white blouses and skirts that barely brushed their knees. Even Bidushi wore a tennis costume, and I silently cheered as she grew in skill enough to triumph over an English girl. I was happy for Bidushi, and the next time that we were taking our evening constitutional, I confessed that I wished we could always be together at Lockwood.

Bidushi bent to snip off the blossom of one of the rosebushes and held it to her nose, inhaling deeply. "First, you'd have to change this place by sending away all the pale people with their unkind thoughts. And the hot air in this locality makes me feel ill from late morning into the night. I long to hear the sea again and feel the cool breezes."

"But Pankaj's family doesn't live near Johlpur—aren't they in Calcutta?" I asked, watching Bidushi idly twirl the rose in her hand. If the gardener had seen, he would be angry; clearly, Bidushi wasn't afraid of anyone.

"Yes. The City of Palaces, as they call it! It's going to be a terrible hustle-bustle there, with all the trams and cars, but the Bandopadhyays live in a very beautiful calm section. They call that place Ballygunge."

"What a lovely house name," I said, spelling it out in my mind.

"No, it is not like the countryside!" Bidushi said, casually dropping the rose to the gravel path. "Their bungalow has a number on the street—27 Lower Circular Road—and it is built with four levels, just like a tiffin container. Every bedchamber has its own bathroom with running hot and cold water. There is a large room just for parties, and in it a grand piano like the one in Miss Jamison's parlor."

"The street a circle? And the house like a tiffin box. It is too much!" I spoke knowing that I would never see such a place, except in my mind. And for a moment I felt jealous.

"But it's really like that. I was there many years ago, visiting Calcutta, and Pankaj was describing it again in the letter he sent from England."

"What? He sent you a *love letter*?" I whispered the forbidden, racy words in English.

"Go away!" She punched me lightly. "Nothing is bad about the letters he sends. But I cannot decide whether to write back. My aunt and uncle would be too angry."

"They are too far away to know what you're doing." I was thinking how much I would like to see one of those letters for myself. This year, I had begun to feel that certain parts of my body were awake and restless; the idea of Bidushi receiving inappropriate correspondence inflamed me.

"I don't know what to write to him. He is ten years older and so intelligent." She looked at me anxiously. "Will you help me?"

Warmth spread through me at her words; for this was exactly what I wanted.

During the next day's study hall, we finished Bidushi's homework, and then she laid a delicate paper across her notebook for me to read. I inhaled the letter from Pankaj the way she had the rose; but to my surprise it was more friendly than lover-like, full of talk about his classes and the English weather and his longing to return to Bengal. I began work that day on a reply in Bengali and made several drafts, the last of which we both approved several days later. In five hundred words, I had created a humorous depiction of Bidushi's school life, making observations about the English girls' odd behaviors. I included questions about Pankaj's daily life and Bidushi's anticipation of seeing him, throwing in a few English phrases to show how worldly she had become.

Bidushi copied my words into her own neat handwriting and posted the letter with the regular school-mail collection. Letters going overseas were very common, no cause for notice. However, letters to men outside of the family were forbidden, so we always put *Miss* on the envelope addressed to Pankaj. Miss Jamison, who checked over the incoming and outgoing student mail, couldn't pronounce Indian names. We realized with great delight that she would probably never guess that Pankaj was a male name, especially since he'd got in the spirit and wrote his name on the back of the envelope as Miss Pankaj Bandopadhyay, Esq.

The letters flowed back and forth, at least one per fortnight. By 1935, the correspondence between Pankaj and me posing as Bidushi became almost flirtatious. I was happy for Bidushi and proud of myself for engineering such a strong romance. I'd also gotten much better with my Bengali writing, although Bidushi was the one who always wrote, in her handwriting, the final version of the letter to be mailed.

"If you give a beggar a pitcher, he will never stop drinking," Miss Rachael said one afternoon when I'd come back from the study hall. "Your association with the Mukherjee girl is not good. And what would her Brahmin family think if they knew who was sitting so closely to her every day?"

If the directress of housekeeping understood the extent of what was going on, she would have been even angrier.

CHAPTER

6

February 14, 1935

12 Milton Road
Cambridge, England

My dear Bidushi,

May I call you dear? I have found myself struggling not to use endearments when I think of you. That is why I have enclosed this pendant. Your family will give you jewelry to take to our marriage, and perhaps not all of it will be to my liking. Therefore, this is my gift to you.

Your most recent letter was my favorite to date. How your descriptions of the school setting and your teachers amuse a very bored and homesick student! You may not remember, but when we were small, I played school with you once when your family visited us. Of course, I claimed the right of teacher and used our darwan's lathi to great effect as a pointer. Your mother took fright and brought you back to the other little girls who were making alpana designs on the veranda. But you were brave, and I believe you enjoyed playing my student, and I am pleased that you were willing to leave the comforts of your home for the rigors of school.

I'd like to say that I am as happy in England as I was upon arrival three years ago, but that is not the case. The

*laws I memorize form a droning sound in my mind, rather
like the Vedas Brahmin boys are forced to learn. And to what
end? Indian lawyers are a penny for a pound in Calcutta,
and the thought of serving at the pleasure of a white-wigged
English judge does not appeal. If only I could combine law
with nationalism. To take risks in the name of India's freedom
would be my privilege. I have doubts about the likelihood of
what Gandhiji says about the British granting us self-rule. For
England has built its wealth on our backs, and if that wealth
vanishes, how can they survive in this new century? What is
your opinion of Gandhiji's hope?*

*As ever, I am your devoted,
Pankaj*

The day the envelope came, Bidushi took it to open with me
on the evening walk. She jumped up and down in excitement at the
gift, a ruby pendant that hung from a long, delicate gold chain. Lockwood girls could wear only religious medals or school rings; and even
though Bidushi kept her collar closed to the neck, there was still a
chance of discovery. Still, she demanded that I secure the clasp behind her neck.

"What is wrong, Didi?" Bidushi asked, as if sensing something
was amiss.

"Nothing's wrong. Ruby looks very well on you." I was thinking
that the gift had been given because of the sweet words I had written;
but it wasn't jealousy I felt as much as foreboding, an undefinable
anxiety that had settled in the bottom of my stomach like one of the
bricks in the school wall.

"Why are you frowning, then?"

If she were truly my sister, I would have put a black mark on
her face to prevent the evil eye. That was how strongly I felt that she
needed to be protected from whatever misfortune lay ahead. But I

could not paint her with Hindu preventives in this place. So I said, "I only hope you won't be caught."

"If I am, I'll say wearing this is part of my religion." Lovingly, she caressed the pendant. "And Pankaj is wrong in thinking my aunt will give any jewelry for my dowry."

"Don't mind her not gifting you!" Privately, I thought Bidushi sometimes complained too much. "Your mother's jewelry must be exquisite. Enjoy that when it comes to you."

"Oh, Auntie took it all as her own!" Bidushi's laugh was brittle as a papadum wafer. "Anyway, I am pleased with this, but look at what he wrote, asking my opinion of Gandhiji. How shall I reply to him?"

"Tell him what you think."

"I don't know what to think! You have always given the ideas and sentences for me to write."

"Bidushi, try it for once." As I spoke, I resolved not to write the entire reply letter. We could consult an expert together, and Bidushi would pen her own thoughts after learning something.

The opportunity to ask Abbas-chacha arrived by chance. Miss Richmond became interested in the great poet Rabindranath Tagore's writings, and she requested that I go into town to buy his latest Bengali publication and later translate it. I was delighted at my first trip to the town, to see a real bookstore and who knew what else. And the best part was that if I found the right book to bring back, Miss Richmond would teach me how to use her handsome typewriter for the translations.

Miss Rachael didn't like the plan, and when I asked her for a fraction of the stipend she'd been keeping for me since I'd started working, she refused. I was disappointed not to have a little spending money for myself, but I was glad at least to be going.

The following Saturday afternoon, Abbas-chacha brought the tonga up to the school's portico for our journey. Bidushi climbed straight up to the backseat without waiting for assistance. There, she bounced happily and urged me to join her. After an initial startled look, Abbas nodded his assent.

"Uncle, what do you think about the British giving us self-rule?" I started the interview once we were off school grounds.

"Hush!" Abbas scolded from the front bench. "Do not disturb the young mem. She comes from a jamidar family—they like the British."

"But I want to know about it," Bidushi said. "Gandhiji is certainly trying for India to get dominion status. He was invited to England to talk about it at a roundtable, wasn't he?"

"There were no congressmen or Indian nationalists there to support him, just Indian royals who like what the British do for them," Abbas said. "He was speaking into the wind; nobody agreed."

"But how can change ever come, then?" I asked.

"Change won't be made in the halls of English Parliament by Englishmen and Indian nawabs—but here, by us. Remember Gandhiji's march down to the sea to rake salt?" Abbas turned around to look soberly at the two of us. "That was something important."

"I thought salt only came from shops?" Bidushi sounded puzzled.

"No Indians are allowed to collect or sell salt," Abbas called back to us loudly over the sound of the moving horse hooves. "The British have a monopoly on it. Gandhi was put in prison for picking up a piece of natural salt, and many of the people who went with him were beaten to death by the police. You girls weren't here at the time, but our cook, Lalit, stopped cooking with salt out of sympathy. The food he makes for the teachers and students is so mild anyway that nobody complained right away. But then Burra-mem realized, and Lalit had to put it back in."

Bidushi sighed. "Burra-mem stops everything, doesn't she? And Gandhiji's salt walk didn't work, if we're still not free."

Abbas turned around to look at us soberly. "Because it became public, the British were embarrassed. Read the newspapers. Now they talk about wanting to treat us honorably."

"But it's like school, isn't it? If a teacher gets embarrassed, she only make things harder on the student."

"If that is what you feel, it's how you must write." I was pleased by Bidushi's independent thinking. "Pankaj will be interested."

Abbas turned back and stayed out of conversation the rest of the trip; I did not know if it was because he had decided to stop talking about politics or that he had heard me speaking the name of a man. Years ago, Abbas had taught me that the rule of Lockwood School was for servants to be quiet; in my relationship with Bidushi, I certainly had broken that.

Abbas brought his horses to rest in the shade of some trees and pointed to the direction of the main bazar. It was easy to find the poetry book at a bookstall; there were several annas left over, which I tucked into the pocket of my work dress to bring back to Miss Richmond. Bidushi was elated to be walking through a real bazar and bought us both snacks of crunchy phuchka from a street hawker. As we approached a sari shop, she licked the last of the tamarind-water dressing from her fingers and said, "I think you need something new to wear."

I laughed lightly to cover up the sadness I felt. "When Miss Rachael thinks the same, she will take out something for me from the charity donations."

"But you are so tall now that your dress is indecent. You should be wearing a proper sari."

"What about you?" I gestured toward her boxy Lockwood uniform that hung to midcalf.

"I *must* wear this because I am a Lockwood girl. But you have freedom. Come, Didi. I shall buy you a sari and blouse set. I should have given something like this to you last Durga Puja anyway."

Bidushi had learned bargaining skills at her mother's knee; something I watched with fascination in the sari shop. She bought two saris and extra material that the shop's tailor would make into blouses and petticoats. Although they were ordinary hand-loomed cottons, one sari was a pretty light green color, with yellow threads shot through it, and the other as pink as bougainvillea, a color that Bidushi thought suited my skin.

"I cannot work in such fine saris," I said, looking in fear at the yards of fabric fanned out before us. The khadi saris Thakurma had woven for my mother and me had been much shorter in length and always a dull beige-brown color.

"Fine saris are always silk. These are not," Bidushi said. "Let me show you another way to wrap. You must make the pleats fall just this way."

"How do you know so much?" I asked her, as she worked around my body, shooing the shop assistants out of the way. The thickly tucked fabric felt uncomfortable at my waist, and I felt as though the pallu hanging over my shoulder could slip at any moment.

"My mother always had me fix her sari pleats. She would be happy to see you looking like this. Now you look like a smart young teacher at an Indian school."

A teacher! I was almost fifteen, but I supposed with my height and figure I might have looked a bit older. What a pleasure teaching would be; but to do that required not just finishing school through the twelfth standard but also an advanced degree. Two things I'd never have.

Outside the shop, the bright sun was blinding. As we walked back toward where Abbas was waiting, a group of people moved in front of us. A mean-looking man walked straight up, demanding that we give him the shopping bag filled with cloth that we had purchased. My stomach cramped with fear, but I knew I'd have to defend us both.

"Go away, dacoit!" I shouted, hoping others on the street would notice and come to our aid. But nobody did and the man with red eyes and an angry scowl still was reaching for the bag. In a trembling voice I said, "Shame, shame, to bother girls! Where is your honor?"

"Nobody should shop at Atul Ganguly's shop until he stops carrying foreign cloth," the man retorted. "Indians pay taxes on the silks and chiffons and so on from England and Japan. Your memsaheb is selfish to think of herself and not the country."

"This cloth is not foreign," Bidushi protested before I could defend her. "It is simple cotton woven by people living in Dhonekhali."

"Is that so? Let me look." A woman with the group came forward now and grabbed the bag from my hands. I watched helplessly as she shook each one of my folded saris. The fear I'd felt was turning to horror at the thought of my wonderful gift from Bidushi being stolen away.

"Please don't!" I cried.

"It is not khadi, that is for certain," the woman said, looking critically at the cotton's weave.

"That's true, but it is still cotton grown and spun in Bengal." Bidushi snatched back the saris. "It is for my friend, since she would rather not wear any more English clothing."

The woman and man looked at me in the ragged old dress; in their eyes, I had been just the servant, not worthy of notice. Bidushi's arm was around me firmly like a sister's. How much I loved her at this moment, for her bravery against these grown strangers. And then Abbas ran up, shouting at the people to let the little girls go and save their action for real villains. In moments, he had hustled us and the package of saris back onto the tonga.

"Who were those dacoits? And why can they move freely about town?" Bidushi demanded as Abbas hit the horse with his crop.

"They are not criminals; they are members of the Congress Party." Abbas explained that the political party boycotted cloth made outside of India, and we had walked straight into one of their protests. He added sternly, "You were not supposed to go about everywhere, just to the bookshop."

"Yes, Chacha. I'm sorry," I apologized. Abbas was my friend: I didn't think he would tell on us, but I hated his thinking I had disobeyed.

"I understand not buying English salt, but clothing is necessary, and how can we tell where it is from? It is only lucky the tailor mentioned the name of the village." Bidushi seemed very cross now that the danger was past.

I also was angry about the way the strangers had reached in and soiled my fresh new saris with their touch. I would wash them, but I didn't know if I could erase the taint the activists had made on my first free afternoon in town.

❧   ❧   ❧

Dear Pankaj-da,

May I call you by the name of older brother? It might seem funny or impertinent, but I don't know that I can ever adjust to the English custom of using first names. This is how the English girls refer to each other, and my goodness, what names they have: Amelia and Anne and Emily and Mary. Always so similar and plain! I wonder if their names have deep meanings like ours do. Living with my name, which means knowledge, has been quite a cross to bear, but fortunately my marks are improving. Writing to you in Bengali is a true pleasure, as it is not supposed to be spoken aloud.

You asked what I thought about Gandhiji's promises of our freedom earned eventually. I sometimes think mistake upon mistake has been made in our freedom struggle, even by one as great as he. I am intrigued by the other nationalist who speaks boldly of confrontation rather than waiting for the British to pronounce their terms. I am referring to Mr. Subhas Chandra Bose, also known as Netaji. I wonder if you ever saw him when you were living in Calcutta, which is also his home, although he has spent many years in prison. I heard that he was released to recuperate in Austria last year and since then has been slowly traveling through Europe, telling many kings and prime ministers of India's right to freedom. The newspapers do not give exact details on his words, but if you have heard anything about Mr. Bose's statements, I would be most pleased to learn.

I remain your true and admiring friend,
Bidushi

Despite my desire that Bidushi write her own letters, this one was again written by me. She had pleaded that I help her, just one more time. I had thought of telling about what the Congress protesters had done in Midnapore, but I could not figure out a way to describe the incident without mentioning my role in the outing, which would only confuse things.

Two days later, the tailor's boy bicycled to school with the package of stitched blouses and petticoats. Bidushi was eager to see me wearing them, but there was no time for changing dress in the middle of the day. So I took the package with gratitude, and the next day slipped into the new blouse and petticoat. Then I wrapped the sari the way Bidushi had taught. Jyoti-ma gave me some pins to help keep the sari in place and said that I looked very nice.

"What nonsense is this?" Miss Rachael shouted when I arrived at the kitchen to get bed tea for the teachers. "Where is your dress? And how did you get that sari?"

"This was given to me," I said, straightening my back. "Because I am a woman, I must wear longer lengths for modesty."

"You are impudent!" Rachael shook a finger at me. "Only I can decide what you wear. Answer my question: From where did you steal the sari?"

"It's a gift from a young memsaheb." I felt smug, because I knew she could not cross a student.

"I can guess which one: Mukherjee-memsaheb, who seems to have forgotten everything about caste. Give that sari to me for safekeeping and wear your old dress."

"The dress is gone."

"What do you mean?" She had moved so close that there was nowhere to step back.

"The dress was fraying badly. I gave it to Jyoti-ma, and it has already been cut for rags that she needed." I kept my voice steady, despite the quaking inside.

"Without permission? You have defiled school property." Her

breath, a poisonous mixture of mustard and garlic, made me wince. "I will tell Miss Richmond what you did on your trip to town."

I relived the scolding in my mind as I slogged through delivering tea and all my other morning jobs. Miss Rachael's words had worked their poison; now I felt shy and awkward. In class, I could hear whisperings from the girls about Sarah Going to a Party and Green Parrot Girl and so on. I had turned from Cinderella the scullery maid to a young lady in a ball gown, with too many wicked stepsisters nearby.

"It's not too fancy," Bidushi whispered from her desk next to mine. "Don't feel badly. They are only jealous that you can wear a pretty color when they are buttoned into their ugly uniforms."

After class, Miss Richmond called for me to wait. When the girls were all gone from the room, she asked in a serious-sounding voice if I'd used her money to buy the new clothing.

At these words, I was so shocked that for a moment I forgot my English. In a faltering voice, I said, "No, Miss Richmond. It was a gift from Miss Bidushi. I gave the leftover annas to you Saturday evening."

"All of them?" she asked quietly. "Miss Rachael said she thought you two girls spent a suspicious amount of money."

It must have been Miss Rachael who'd persuaded Miss Richmond into thinking me dishonest. Sweat broke out under the fine new cotton as I scrambled to think of how to save myself. Then I remembered. I went to Bidushi's desk, where I'd last placed the book, and put it in her hands.

"Memsaheb, inside the front pages is a small paper the merchant gave me, which has the price of the book listed, so you can be certain of the change. As for the saris, they cost a bit over five rupees, and Miss Mukherjee paid with her own pocket money. It is possible she still has such a paper from the tailor shop—what is it called, the recept?"

"Receipt." She pronounced it clearly, and I remembered it from my mind's dictionary, spelled almost like deceit. Which was what she thought of me.

"Yes, here it is," Miss Richmond said after she'd opened the book. "All clear. I'm sorry for the misunderstanding, Sarah." Her white face had pinkened, as if she felt badly. "However, Miss Rachael is quite hot over the situation and would prefer you not to continue helping Bidushi in my classroom. I told her that it will only be for a few more months' time, but still—"

"Why only a few months?" I was utterly puzzled, for Bidushi was a year and a half from taking the Senior Cambridge examinations.

"I'm disappointed about Bidushi's leaving, too, but I understand a traditional wedding is being planned for the autumn." Miss Richmond paused, then added, "You are so close. I thought she'd told you."

I was so upset that I could not respond other than to bob my head and hurry away, lest she see the tears that were starting. The rest of the day I thought, How could she? How could Bidushi not have mentioned that this would be her last term at Lockwood? If she left, I would never again run through the trees with my companion, or sit at a desk beside her like a real student. I would be out of Miss Richmond's bright universe and back in the small, mean world ruled by Miss Rachael.

🌼   🌼   🌼

"WHY SUCH A heavy face?" Bidushi asked when we met in the un-cultivated forest just past Lockwood's manicured gardens, the only place private enough to speak Bengali without being caught. We had to watch for snakes, and the insects were fierce, but this seemed a small price to pay for being away from the rest of Lockwood's population.

"I know the saris were a good-bye present," I said, watching my friend's eyes widen in surprise. "Don't think that they can make up for your leaving."

Bidushi spoke fast, her words tripping over each other. "I didn't do it for that reason. I gave them to you because I love you. But it is true that I have to go."

"Why didn't you tell me?" I cried. "The teachers know, but not me!"

"It pains me to leave you!" Bidushi put her soft, fair arms around me. "You know that I could not have borne this school without your help. It would have killed me."

"But you *shouldn't* leave," I said, trying a new tactic. "Pankaj wants you to take the Senior Cambridge examinations. He will not marry an uneducated wife."

"It was Pankaj who wanted me sooner," Bidushi said quietly. "I did not show you the letter that came before the last one because I knew it would make you sad. He said that he had passed the London bar examination and thought the best way to celebrate was by beginning our life together."

He was in love because of the letters I'd written to him. My very best efforts had hastened the future for Bidushi—the future that I had longed not to come. I was suddenly filled with despair, knowing that I'd braided an escape rope for my princess but not for myself.

"Didi, I can't bear to leave you!" Bidushi said. There were tears in her eyes, too: real tears of love and sadness. Suddenly, I felt guilty, because I did not want her to suffer.

"Don't cry," I said, laying my own damp cheek against hers, which smelled of the sweet dormitory soap. I would make the most of every last minute; that was all I could do.

"I cannot have a happy wedding knowing that my dear friend is in misery," Bidushi wept on.

"Won't you take me?" I whispered, remembering the happy ending of A Little Princess, where poor Becky is invited to become Sara's personal attendant. "You said there were many servants in Pankaj's house. They will want you to have your own ayah. Why not me?"

Bidushi drew in her breath. "But you are so intelligent! I could not possibly order you to brush my hair or dress me as I would a common ayah."

"After you leave here, all I will do is scrub floors," I protested. "If

I'm lucky, I will get a few hours pulling the fans in the classrooms, like I used to do."

"If you came to Calcutta with me, you would never scrub floors. Pankaj's family has sweepers for that. But . . ." Bidushi hesitated. "If you were my ayah, we could do some other nice things. A lady's ayah sometimes accompanies her outside for shopping and so on."

"Nothing on this earth could make me happier." A small bright hope flamed within me; it was as if Bidushi held one of the small clay lamps that Hindus light at Diwali in order to push away darkness and bad luck. "There is so much in the City of Palaces we could see together! Victoria's Memorial, Chowringhee, the Kali Temple! Please tell them I don't want money. Just a place."

"I want you to come, but I don't know whether Pankaj's parents will allow me to choose my own ayah." Bidushi fell quiet after that and sat very still; so still that I had to reach out and slap a mosquito settling on her leg. "I shall ask Pankaj myself, but I will wait until after the first engagement ceremony. Otherwise his family might think me improper."

"Nobody would ever think you are improper," I said, feeling a rush of gratitude at her promise. "And we will not behave like sisters before anyone's eyes, I swear to you."

If anyone could get what she wanted, it was my sweet Bidushi. I told this to myself as we slowly walked back between the red and orange rows of geraniums and marigolds, back toward school and our uncertain futures.

CHAPTER
7

The common people in Bengal, however, though they speak a very circumscribed language, do not so frequently violate the rules of Grammar as might be imagined. They are, it is acknowledged, ignorant of many refined modes of expression; and, as may be expected, rustic in their conversation: but they appear to surpass many other nations in correctness.

—William Carey, *A Dictionary of the Bengalee Language,* 1825

As spring turned to summer, Lockwood's brick buildings turned into ovens. There was no relief for us servants, who had neither fans nor awnings to cool the rooms and halls where we worked. But the students and teachers suffered, too. Sports practice was shifted to the morning, and the girls were allowed to wear short socks instead of stockings and made to drink water every hour. To cool jugs of water and food, blocks of ice came from Kharagpur in large boxes packed all around with hay. How I longed to touch the ice, but if Miss Rachael caught me, there would be hell to pay.

Pankaj would arrive in this humid Hades. He posted a letter to Bidushi just before boarding the steamer *Percival* saying he hoped to arrive by mid-June 1935. If Bidushi's aunt and uncle permitted, he would call on her at school before the formal engagement ceremony.

"They won't allow it," Bidushi said, pacing back and forth in the study hall. "They would never allow us to see each other before the wedding. But I suppose it is for the best."

"Why do you say that?" I didn't understand the drop in her voice and her suddenly obedient words. I wanted him to come because I wanted to know the man who was my close correspondent. Did he have a mustache? Was he tall or short? Was his real voice as charming as his written one?

"If Pankaj visited, it would disturb my mind so much that I could not return to studying." Bidushi sank into her chair and grimaced at the pile of books on her desk. "I cannot fail my last exams. My school record will be used for the application for the Calcutta school where they want me to finish. And I might not be admitted."

"Of course you will! You've learned so much!" Yet I knew that academics were not Bidushi's strength. Perhaps it was because of her long time at home without any teachers or because she had no joy sitting with her Lockwood classmates. She was afraid Pankaj would not think her intelligent. And while I knew she was clever, her cleverness was about wearing clothes and jewelry and setting a table: not sums or literary quotations or politics.

Sometimes I thought, If only Lakshmi could work her magic to make the two of us one. This ideal young lady would be as fair and sophisticated and confident as Bidushi, yet also have my voice for English and my head for numbers. Melded together we would have four slim arms like a goddess, all the better for embracing the man we both loved! But it was sacrilegious to dream such things. There was no way to share Pankaj with Bidushi. If I could ride to Calcutta on her coattails, it would be the luckiest thing that ever could happen.

With renewed vigor, I helped Bidushi review her academic subjects; I thought that if she could read with enjoyment, she'd have something to share with Pankaj. She would please him so much that he would gladly allow her anything, especially her request for me to become her ayah.

For the next week, we spent all our study-hall time on books instead of letters. During our evenings in the garden, I spent the time quizzing Bidushi instead of falling into our usual chummy gossip. The readings were baffling for my friend, because Miss Richmond had assigned books by George Eliot and Charles Dickens that had English peasants speaking their language incorrectly. I had been at Lockwood long enough to know the difference, but Bidushi did not.

Sometimes, it seemed like Miss Richmond was trying very hard to show the lives of poor people to her well-off students. The teacher was also quite interested in Indian writing translated into English. She had declared the Tagore translations I'd done "naturally poetic" and had asked me to work through the whole poetry anthology in advance of the next school year. At night, I would study these Bengali poems by the light of a jar filled with fireflies. Sometimes my eyes were so tired that I wanted to close them, but I reminded myself that everything I finished could be typed up the next day on Miss Richmond's Smith-Corona, the promised treat she had begun allowing me. The typewriter was kept in her bedroom, which was rich with rows of books. Miss Richmond saw my interest and explained the organizational system, and soon I was shelving and dusting her books.

Now that I was fifteen, Virginia Woolf, E. M. Forster, and the American John Steinbeck were some of the authors I read, at Miss Richmond's suggestion. I was grateful for these recommendations and the other things the teacher gave me: old newspapers and magazines and stubs of pencils and paper scraps. She taught books that the other teachers in school thought were unsuitable, which made me even more interested in reading them, as well as the beautiful poems by Tagore.

"Why are you still lingering? People are waiting!" Miss Rachael barked when she came upon me in the scullery using a handed-down notebook to finish a few more lines of a poetry translation.

"Miss Richmond wants this." My voice was short, because she had interrupted me when I was on the verge of finding the right word to finish a couplet.

"Miss Richmond wants! Mukherjee-memsaheb needs!" Miss Rachael wagged her head back and forth. "Their wanting you is like pouring ghee on a fire."

"There is no fire." Tired of her proverbs, I closed the notebook and got to my feet.

"The fire is you, already too hot and proud. But after that Mukherjee-mem is gone, I shall give you duties building fires and collecting ash. It is what you deserve!"

I regarded Miss Rachael's flushed round face, thinking how different she was from my mother. I didn't allow myself to think often of Ma, but now I remembered her praising me as I mastered my duties in the house. She always expected me to work hard and would have criticized me when it was due, but not given me work out of malice.

"There is no reason for you to do anything with books or papers again. Here, give me what nonsense you were writing!"

"No!" I reached out in vain as Miss Rachael's rough hands opened the precious book where I had written pages of Bengali and English side by side.

She tore out a page and held it up to me. "Good kindling for the kitchen fire, isn't it?"

Panic and anger surged in me. As I struggled to keep my grasp on my writing, she hit my arms and then face. Still, I kept my hands on the notebook. I could not imagine coming up with the same words and phrases again to reflect the calm beauty of Tagore's poetry.

Behind me I heard the clearing of a throat. I turned and saw Miss Jamison, who had come in without being heard.

"Stop it!" said Miss Jamison, who must have come from her sleeping quarters as she still wore her high-necked dressing gown. "If you spend time beating the girl, she cannot bring my tea or anyone else's. I've been waiting ten minutes!"

"Burra-mem!" Miss Rachael brought her reddened hands to her face, and her breathing slowed. "It is because of that lateness that I'm punishing her! Sarah is a very bad girl."

Miss Jamison shook her head at me and then, stern-faced, looked back at Miss Rachael. "Tardiness is a situation for reprimand, not a beating. This is a Christian school."

I breathed deeply and hugged myself. I was relieved that Miss Jamison had intervened, but I didn't dare tell her what had really happened with the notebook. I wasn't stupid enough to violate the servants' code of silence.

"Sarah, there's something else."

I bobbed my head, wondering what punishment Miss Jamison was going to mete out.

"The student whom you tutor in English took ill last night. Matron came to me and said she was asking for you."

"Miss Bidushi?" The aches in my body from Miss Rachael's beating subsided as a strange new fear filled me.

"Yes. Come along to the infirmary, and Nurse-matron will speak with you."

As we left, Miss Rachael made a parting shot at me in Bengali. "The best medicine is beating!"

※   ※   ※

LOCKWOOD'S NURSE-MATRON WAS someone I didn't know much about, except that she was a large Irishwoman with very pink skin that was always sweating, regardless of the season. Today, a thin cloth mask covered the lower half of her face. This was wet, too.

"What is Miss Bidushi's illness?" I asked.

"I don't really know; it could be anything," she said in her rolling accent. "The fever hasn't broken. She's got the chills something awful, but I can't wrap her lest I raise her fever."

I looked past the blue-and-white-striped mountain of Nurse-matron and toward the infirmary's rows of beds, all empty save for one occupied by Bidushi. Nurse-matron's mention of chills reminded me of my own episode with cholera. It seemed unlikely for Bidushi to have caught that disease, because all the students and teachers drank boiled water.

I approached Bidushi's cot. A mosquito coil burned nearby, its noxious perfume flung across the room by the whirling overhead fan. I put my hand on my friend's cheek; it burned like fire. Underneath her closed lids her eyes were moving, dreaming about something that made her whimper.

"I'm here," I said in English, getting as close as I could given the mosquito nets guarding all sides of her cot. "What's wrong, dearest? Where does it hurt?"

She didn't answer, although her eyes flicked open for a moment. Something was wrong with them. I realized then that this could not be an ordinary fever. My friend was deathly ill, and I could lose her.

"Speak to her in Bengali," Miss Jamison commanded from behind me. "Perhaps then she'll hear you."

"Yes, madam." Struggling to sound calm, I said, "Bidushi, I am worried about you. Please tell me what you are feeling."

I regretted my words for they were lost in a paroxysm; Bidushi shook and tossed her head from side to side so much that the front of her nightgown opened, revealing the ruby pendant plastered to her damp skin. Her eyes opened, and I could see only the whites that were not white at all, but a pale yellow.

"God Almighty, is she epileptic?" Nurse-matron cried, pulling up the mosquito net as Bidushi's body continued its sharp, fast vibrations. "Fetch a towel, girl!"

I ran for the clean laundry cabinet and brought a cloth that Nurse-matron twisted and slipped inside Bidushi's mouth. The violent shaking continued for another minute and then slowed until she was finally still. But not dead, I realized with gratitude, as I slipped my own hand over Bidushi's hot, wet one.

"Did you think her eyes looked yellow?" I asked Nurse-matron.

"The girl may have the yellow fever and the jaundice. That's more than I can treat; we must have a doctor come." Nurse-matron gave Miss Jamison a look that said *Do something*.

"Unfortunately, her guardians already made clear she cannot be examined by a male doctor." Miss Jamison's voice was grave. "Dr. Andrews from the Keshiari Mission cannot be called. There are Indian doctors in Midnapore, but I imagine they won't allow them either because they are men."

"I would send for any doctor and not tell them about it. Surely they'd rather have a live girl than a dead one!" Nurse-matron's eyes flashed as she straightened the sheet over Bidushi. I admired the Irishwoman for talking so strongly to the headmistress.

"But there is also her fiancé's family to speak with," I said, remembering what Bidushi had told me about the Bandopadhyays' modern ways. "She is to be married in a few months, and they are a very educated and modern family. I'm sure that her health is very important to them."

"Yes, I know about the forthcoming marriage." Miss Jamison sounded thoughtful. "I suppose they might talk sense about the doctor to the Mukherjees. But I know nothing of their whereabouts."

"Her father-in-law-to-be, Mr. Bandopadhyay, is a lawyer at Number 27 Lower Circular Road in Calcutta's Ballygunge section." I said it swiftly, because I had memorized the address of where I dreamed of moving.

Miss Jamison nodded. "If there is a telephone on the premises, I will be able to call. Otherwise, I shall send a telegram."

"May I please help with the feedings? And I should like to watch over the young memsaheb as much as I can." I spoke pleadingly, for I could not bear to leave Bidushi when she was so weak and miserable.

"It would be a bit of a help," Nurse-matron said, patting me on the shoulders. "Our Sarah, she's a good one."

"Very well then," Miss Jamison answered with a thin smile. "Sarah shall temporarily halt her housekeeping duties. Use her as you wish during the day and have her sleep in the room at night."

❧   ❧   ❧

I WAS ALLOWED to bring my sleeping mat from the lean-to and placed it on the cool floor near Bidushi's bed. She slept quietly that evening, and the next morning her fever was gone. She was able to take water, weak tea, and dal soup, but nothing more.

"I'm sorry," my friend murmured as I wiped her hands and face clean with a damp cloth.

"Sorry? I am so very happy to hear you speaking!"

"Sorry for being weak like this," she whispered. "We must prepare for the examinations. How many days have I lost?"

"Just two," I said, stroking back her hair. "And they are nothing to worry about."

Bidushi ate some more soup and was well enough to have a bath. The next day, however, the fever returned, and her body shook for hours. Although she did not hear or feel my presence, I washed her and put water to her dry lips. How ironic that she had lost her parents in a flood but now was struggling because of a lack of water inside her. I had to get the water down, I thought as I tilted the cup into her mouth. She was like a fading flower, and flowers needed water to live.

The third day, Miss Jamison told Matron that the Bandopadhyays had found and spoken with a female physician, Dr. Sengupta, who could arrive tomorrow. I worried about that long delay, although Bidushi's fever had again broken, enabling her to converse weakly and take more food and drink. Fever on, fever off; that was not the way cholera ran. Nurse-matron thought that her illness was starting to resemble malaria.

❦   ❦   ❦

THAT NIGHT, AFTER I'd lit the mosquito coils and begun to tuck the mosquito net around Bidushi's bed, she whispered, "Sleep with me tonight."

"I will, dearest. My mat is here, and I will lie close by." She didn't know that I roused myself several times each night to put my face close to the net, to hear that she was still breathing. But what I heard—the fast, ragged sounds—did not reassure me much.

"No, inside the bed. Only you can stop Ravana from taking me tonight."

She was speaking of the demon king who kidnapped King Rama's wife, Sita. The holy story of the Ramayana, so loved by children, must have begun to infuse her dreams. I said, "That cannot happen."

"I have not slept with another person since my mother, when I was small," she said.

"Soon you will lie with Pankaj on a bed strewn with rose petals," I said, willing it to be true. If Bidushi survived to leave Lockwood without me, I would not be the slightest bit envious or resentful. Just glad she was alive.

"Do not leave me, Didi," she breathed. "Come inside my bed."

I wasn't frightened of catching her illness, but I did not know what Nurse-matron would think. The school's Indian servants would be shocked, because for a Sudra to lie with a Brahmin girl would ruin her chances for a good afterlife. I thought about this seriously.

My friend moaned, and that decided it. I lifted the mosquito net enough to creep in beside her. How strange the bed was with its soft mattress covered with smooth white cotton. Under the sheet, we laced hands, and something jolted my heart. This girl, in the space of a few years, had replaced the sisters I'd lost, as well as my brother, parents, and grandparents. I clung to her because of my own longing, not just hers.

"You must take care of Pankaj," Bidushi whispered to me. "Will you promise?"

"He will soon be here," I soothed. "He is aboard the ship and will be in India soon."

"Write a good-bye letter for me," Bidushi whispered.

This was the wrong way for her to think. Without hope, she would not have the strength to live. "There is no need for a letter. The doctor is coming tomorrow. You will feel better once you have the proper medicine."

"No. I am already gone! I feel it."

"Don't talk nonsense." I pulled her so close that her heart beat against mine. "Everything will be right as rain."

"No," Bidushi repeated sadly. "The rainy season will come, but I will not feel a single drop."

And that night, I was awakened not by any cries from her, but by her fast breathing and burning-hot body. I left the cot to soak cloths in cold water and press them all over her, but to no avail. I was so frightened by Bidushi's condition that I went to call for Nurse-matron, who slept in her own small room just outside the infirmary. She rang for the bhisti, who came rubbing sleep out of his eyes to carry buckets of cool water into the infirmary bathtub. Then I carried my friend, who in just a few days had shrunk to such a low weight, into the water.

Bidushi was back at 105 degrees Fahrenheit when Dr. Sengupta arrived in the tonga driven by Abbas the next morning. From the corner of the infirmary, I watched the small woman with large spectacles examine Bidushi and take a needle to her arm to collect blood. This blood went into a glass tube set into a flask filled with chilled water. She told me to give it to Abbas to bring right away to the Midnapore clinic. I admired the doctor's calm, directive manner, and marveled that an Indian woman had this job that I thought only

Englishmen could do. How clever she must be; surely she would save Bidushi.

The next morning, the clinic's doctor confirmed that Bidushi had malaria. A driver came with medicine and a metal stand that held bags of liquid that dripped through a tube into Bidushi's arm. Dr. Sengupta started giving Bidushi the medication mepacrine and asked that Bidushi's aunt and uncle be summoned.

Around teatime the next day, the chowkidars who guarded the school's gate sent word up to the building that the jamidar-uncle and jamidar-auntie had arrived. Miss Jamison sent me out of the sickroom to give the Mukherjees privacy with their niece. My head rebelled against this, knowing how Bidushi felt about them, but I knew it was their right.

Miss Rachael put me on duty washing the baseboards along the hallways. I made sure to work slowly in the hallway outside the infirmary, so I could spy on the visitors. Bidushi had told me enough about her aunt that I easily recognized her puffy face with eyes as small and hard as black dal. She was wearing a good bit of jewelry—Bidushi's mother's, I guessed. The lady's husband, Barun Mukherjee, was almost as tall as his elder brother, but was lacking the old jamidar's kind features.

Two of the school's guest rooms were occupied now: one by Dr. Sengupta, and the other by the jamidar-uncle and his wife. Their arrival caused notice by the English and Anglo-Indian girls who joked about the jamidarni-auntie's heavy jewelry being paste. Lalit, the Brahmin cook who normally just prepared simple meals for the school's few Hindu students and large Hindu staff, suddenly had to cook fancy vegetarian meals for the Mukherjees. He grumbled about it mightily, so I offered to help with kitchen cleaning, because, of course, I could not touch their food.

The next day as I was scrubbing out a pot with ash, Miss Rachael came into the kitchen. She stood watching me for a while before saying, "You're looking thin."

"It doesn't matter." It was true that I'd barely eaten over the last few days; yet she could not be asking because she was concerned about me. It was leading to something else.

"Why are you in this kitchen?"

"Lalit-dada is cooking many more dishes now and asked me to help with cleaning," I answered, keeping my eyes on the pot, because I didn't want her to accuse me of disrespect; I just wanted her to go away.

"Well, there's a great deal more I have for you to do, but let me tell you some news: Your friend is dying. The bhisti heard the doctor tell her parents."

"They are not her parents," I said as my mind whirled. Bidushi had medicine; she could not be dying. Miss Rachael had lied to me and other people before. This could be another of her cruel fabrications; I would not believe it.

❦   ❦   ❦

THAT NIGHT I went to the infirmary door and was told by Nurse-matron to sleep in the lean-to. This troubled me, for I worried whether it might be true that Bidushi was doing worse. Matron would not say, and I couldn't bear not knowing. So the next morning, even before the crows cawed, I went silently to the outdoor tank to bathe. Just as I was tying on my clean pink sari, a car horn sounded.

The only reason for the noise was a visitor outside the school gate, which was locked every evening. I hurried to the stables and called to the boys who slept there about the horn and then hastened down the driveway myself. A taxi had come with a turbaned Sikh driver at the wheel. In the seat next to him was a clean-shaven young man wearing glasses, and in the back was an older well-dressed couple still half asleep. I waited at the gate until the stable boy came running with a key to unlock the padlock.

I followed the car as it drew up to the portico. Without waiting for a chowkidar's aid, the young man unfolded himself from the car. He was tall and wore a Western gentleman's suit. His dark hair waved back from a high, intelligent forehead. He had round gold-rimmed spectacles that made him look wise beyond his age. I stared openly, realizing he was as fine and beautiful as the words he'd written to me. I loved him; so would Bidushi.

"Will you please tell the authorities that the Bandopadhyays are here to consult with Dr. Sengupta?" Pankaj Bandopadhyay's voice was courteous and carried what I guessed must be a sophisticated city accent. How breathtaking he was: even more than I imagined.

"Yes, of course. I'd almost forgotten you were coming!"

He paused, as if my words had startled him. Then, looking at me strangely, he said, "I reached Calcutta yesterday. My parents and I have come to see my fiancée, Bidushi Mukherjee. She is a student here who is seriously ill."

"Yes, I know. I will tell them. Please wait." I ran back to the school building, elated that Pankaj had come, like a prince to awaken and save the sleeping princess. I awoke the bearer who was sleeping in the hallway and asked him to summon the bhisti to bring hot water to the infirmary, while the kitchen staff needed to make tea for the visitors and doctor. I next rapped on the doctor's door and called to her that bed tea was forthcoming and that the Bandopadhyays had arrived.

But when I reached the door to the infirmary, it was still locked. Desperate to awaken and bathe Bidushi, I went out a side door into the garden and came around to one of the infirmary's open windows and pulled myself up through it into the room.

To my relief, Bidushi's stomach was rising and falling with her breath. Her stomach was hard and round, protruding more than be-fore. When I approached her and touched her hand, her eyes flick-ered.

"Pankaj is here," I said. "We must prepare for him!"

Slowly, she turned her head toward me.

"He came straight here with his family. I will wash you because they will come to your bedside later on." I was filled with urgency that she appear as fresh as she could. Her beauty was gone; maybe with washing I could bring it back.

"Too cold," whimpered Bidushi, although the temperature of her hand was pure heat.

"Heavens, what are you doing in here?" Nurse-matron had unlocked the main infirmary door and come inside. The bhisti was behind her, carrying his heavy drum of water.

"Her fiancé just arrived. I came to clean her and change her sheets."

"Yes, I've heard about the visitors. They're in the parlor having tea. All right then, you may help with her bath, but let me take her temperature first." She put her hand to Bidushi's forehead. "God only knows why this medicine is taking so long to have any effect."

At least now Bidushi knew Pankaj was there. Because of this, I thought she could rally. After all, love was the most powerful medicine. Not just what Pankaj felt for Bidushi; but what I felt for both of them, too.

Why is it that the best moments pass fleetingly—and bad minutes feel like days? I paced the hallway, ready to run for supplies if Matron or Dr. Sengupta put their head out the door. I was not allowed at the bedside but knew her aunt and uncle were there. Every so often they would exit to drink tea in Miss Jamison's study, while the Bandopadhyays took their turn. All this switching had come about because Dr. Sengupta thought too much company would tire Bidushi.

"That sick girl will ruin chances for a wedding." I overheard the jamidarni-auntie fretting to her husband. "If she has another fit, they'll believe that a devil's inside her. I always suspected, but here is proof."

"We don't know what they think." The jamidar-uncle sounded more tired than anything. "They are a good family with a long link to ours. Over the generations, there have been many Bandopadhyay-Mukherjee marriages. Remember that."

"She never should have come to this place," his wife hissed. "If she'd been kept in purdah at home none of this would have occurred."

It was because of Pankaj's request that Bidushi had come to school; I wondered if he was thinking about that, too. Later that morning, I glimpsed Pankaj seated in the chair closest to Bidushi's pillow. There were no indications any conversation was taking place between them, and I felt dejected about how sickly Bidushi looked. I hoped that would not deter Pankaj. If he kissed her brow, perhaps she would come back to life like Sleeping Beauty in *The Arthur Rackham Fairy Book*. Bidushi had said that if she died, I would have to watch over Pankaj; but how could that be, with me a lowly servant he clearly hadn't recognized as his companion of letters? The request was impossible. The only way I could care for him—and for her as well—would be for her to survive this terrible turn of events and get away to Calcutta.

I worked in the kitchen that afternoon, chopping fish for a curry that would be served to all the Indian visitors. A special table had been created for them near the headmistress's. According to Lalit, the new Indian table had triggered unrest among the English girls. Upon seeing the Bengali dishes spread elegantly on the table, some students were demanding the same instead of boiled meat and potatoes.

It was a struggle to concentrate on Lalit's conversation. I could only think of Bidushi slipping away and my future burning up alongside her on the cremation pyre.

In the late afternoon, I begged to bring the tray of tea and sweetmeats for the visitors to Miss Jamison's parlor, in order to overhear any possible news. Lalit was uneasy, for what I'd volunteered to do was typically a male bearer's job, but he finally agreed to let me bring in the freshly ironed tablecloths and napkins to set the table at which everyone concerned with Bidushi would take their tea.

I walked with my arms full of fresh-starched cloths to the empty study, wishing for a way to make the job last longer. I had an idea. I'd slip into the garden and see if the mali would allow me to cut some roses. Then I would arrange a vase for each table. The fragrance would revive the visitors after the harsh smells of the sickroom.

As I walked through the school's flower garden looking for the freshest open roses, I noticed that Bidushi's fiancé was walking, too. As Pankaj drew near, I saw his head was bowed and tears were streaming from beneath his spectacles. He half-fell onto one of the marble benches and then buried his face in hands.

I had grown up believing that tears were a sign of womanly weakness. Yet here was the man Bidushi and I had both dreamed about in uncontrolled despair. How moved I was by the sight of him; his tears made me love him for everything he was and for how deeply he adored my only friend. Now I regretted not having written the final letter Bidushi had asked me for. I could have overlooked propriety and confessed her deepest love. I would not have tried to be funny or clever, just said the words that came from my heart. And maybe I could have added a postscript saying that the letters he treasured had always had a coauthor, another Indian girl at the school. She was the one who had made the jokes he liked and had political opinions he respected. She could still write to him, if it was what he desired.

As I thought this, I was filled both with sorrow for Bidushi and a flash of something else—guilt—at thinking I could remain part of Pankaj's life. I tried to choke back a sob, but was unsuccessful, for Pankaj looked up. He took off his spectacles and wiped his eyes with a handkerchief.

"Sorry, I have bothered you . . ." I trailed off, feeling ashamed.

"You speak fluent English," he said tightly. "And when you came to meet our car, you already knew I was expected to visit. What kind of staff does this school have? Are you a servant—or a spy?"

He questioned me roughly: the way an aristocrat typically did to a lesser. And I knew that I didn't look quite like the other servants, dressed as I was in the good pink sari with a rose tucked in my hair. Now I understood that my wistful dream about confessing my existence in a last letter was wrong. I couldn't risk his learning how close I was to Bidushi.

I switched back to the soft, regional Bengali I'd grown up speaking. "I'm very sorry, Saheb. I only spoke English because I am accustomed to using it here with my betters—I mean, my *English* betters. Not that the Ingrej are better than Indians," I added hastily, remembering our political exchanges.

Pankaj put his glasses back on and squinted through them at me. "Go on, speak English. It seems to be your preference."

My heart beat triply as I struggled to think of what to say to extricate myself from the situation. I had invaded his sorrow, embarrassed him by catching him weeping—and for this he was angry. Trying again I said, "No, no! I am making mistake upon mistake because I am torn with grief, too—"

"Mistake upon mistake. Who taught you that phrase?" There was a strange light in his reddened, sorrowful eyes, something that made me afraid that I couldn't stay a moment longer without giving away the truth.

"I'm very sorry, sir. For reasons of work, I must leave!" I blurted, and once again, I ran from him, stumbling along the stone path, roses all but forgotten.

Mistake upon mistake. I had written those words to him in English, in one of the letters, liking the way the *M*s sounded so close together. But the phrase could be my undoing, if Pankaj continued to remember.

❦   ❦   ❦

INSIDE THE SCHOOL, I wiped my sweating face and hands before proceeding at a normal pace to the infirmary. As I drew near, I heard a surprising amount of noise. As I entered the sickroom, I found Mr. Bandopadhyay was softly chanting a prayer. Instead of participating, the jamidar-uncle was arguing with Dr. Sengupta, who was looking downcast. I imagined how sad she was that Bidushi hadn't improved. The jamidarni-auntie was wailing and being held by Pankaj's mother. So much noise was not good for Bidushi; I was shocked that Dr. Sengupta was allowing it.

With misgivings, I looked toward Bidushi's bed. A sheet had been pulled from bottom to top, covering the small mound of her body. The medicine stand had been disconnected and pushed to the other side of the room. And with all of this, I finally understood why Pankaj had fled outside to weep in private.

Bidushi was gone.

CHAPTER
8

Hissing serpents poison the very air.
Here fine words of peace ring hollow.
My time is up; but before I go, I send out
My call to those who are getting ready in a
Thousand homes to fight the demon.

—Rabindranath Tagore, "Hissing Serpents," ("Number 18"), 1937

It is impossible for a servant to take time for grief. Everywhere, people have their needs. For the rest of that afternoon, I ran dishes from the kitchen to the dining hall with a face that said nothing, although my hands would not stop trembling. I struggled to remember Bidushi's final words. She'd said that she felt cold. Now I wished I had lain down to warm her. It would have been better for her than the bath.

Everyone knew. In the kitchen and hallways, I overheard the other servants debating whether the cremation would be done by a Hindu priest in nearby Midnapore or if the Mukherjees would bring her home. Timing mattered. A corpse should be burned within the day for the soul to escape into the next life.

Miss Rachael was watching me with hard eyes through all of this, and then she came up, smiling with false sympathy, saying that Miss Jamison wanted me in the infirmary. I went quickly, wondering if this would be a chance to pay my last regards to Bidushi. Or maybe the headmistress wanted me to wash Bidushi's body, as that work might be considered too gruesome for Nurse-matron and the jamidarni-auntie.

Upon entering the infirmary, I saw Bidushi's bed was already empty and stripped of sheets. I bobbed my head for Miss Jamison and made a respectful namaskar with my hands toward the Bandopadhyay parents and both Mukherjees.

"I have a question for you about Miss Mukherjee's possessions." Miss Jamison spoke to me in clear, loud English, as if she wanted the others all to understand. "Her fiancé wished for the return of a senti-mental gift he made to her. Perhaps you know it?"

During this address, Bidushi's aunt was leaning forward, her ban-gles tinkling against one another like little bells of warning.

"Yes, there was a ruby she always wore on a gold chain." My speech came slowly, while my mind raced. Since she was deceased, she could not get in trouble. But I could for having known about it.

"Nurse-matron noticed it and offered to put it in the cabinet for safekeeping. Miss Mukherjee refused, and because the girl was doing so poorly, Nurse-matron let her keep wearing it. But now it is no longer with her." Miss Jamison's words dropped hard, like stones in a river.

That morning, I had been desperate to put Bidushi into a state of decent cleanliness. I had stripped off my friend's soiled nightdress without noticing the necklace. Had it been on then? How could it have been lost?

"Maybe the chain broke in the sheets," I ventured, thinking that if a dhobi had found a ruby pendant within his washing bundle, he would not likely bring it forward. But who would be depraved enough to steal from someone who'd died?

"In that case, there would be evidence: a remnant of the chain. It appears that the entire necklace and the pendant were removed by someone," Mr. Bandopadhyay said in the precise English I imagined he used in the court.

"Nurse-matron locked the infirmary door last night at Mr. and Mrs. Mukherjee's request." Miss Jamison moved toward me, slowly, and I had to hold myself from running. "But Nurse-matron found you inside this morning; however did you enter?"

"I came through the window. I did it because I needed to speak to Bidushi and give her a bath." I tried to speak evenly, but the trembling that had affected my hands earlier had spread to my whole body.

"The girl was unconscious," Miss Jamison said. She towered over me, so I had to put my head back to look up at her.

"With respect, Burra-memsaheb, she was a-awake," I stammered. "She heard me announce the arriving people, and she told me she was feeling cold."

"Speak Bengali. I want to hear the lies for myself!" Bidushi's uncle grumbled after his wife whispered something in his ear.

"The jamidar-saheb requests translation," I murmured in a rush.

"Then do it!" Miss Jamison raised her voice. "And, Sarah, I can hardly think of any situation so urgent that you would have broken through a window instead of going to Nurse-matron."

"It was so early that I dared not wake her. Our visitors had arrived outside the school and asked to come inside." I gestured toward the Bandopadhyays, wishing them to nod or somehow acknowledge that I'd helped them, but they remained stonily in place. "I spoke to the men in the stables and the chowkidar who guards the school entrance. Then I went to Bidushi."

"To think this wretch was sleeping in the room with her so many nights, pawing through her ornaments!" Bidushi's aunt said in sharp Bengali.

I could not bring myself to translate those terrible words, so the jamidar, in his stilted English, repeated it verbatim for Miss Jamison, whose face blanched even paler than its normal color.

"Such an incident has never happened here," she answered stiffly. "But I have just learned from the housekeeping directress that Sarah may have coerced your niece to spend money on her before. This likely motivated her misbehavior."

"Misbehavior is not the proper term," Mr. Bandopadhyay shot back in his perfect English. "It is a crime."

"Yes, Mr. Bandopadhyay. Of course you are right."

"It is my son who I grieve for, because he is rather sensitive," the elderly lawyer continued. "He said he sent the ruby as well as some letters. Many letters were found in the dormitory by your Nurse-matron."

Now Miss Jamison looked as if she were regaining some strength. Nostrils flaring, she said, "Letters between our students and any males outside of the immediate family are forbidden. We were never told that anyone was writing to her."

The jamidar whispered to his wife in Bengali, and she gave a shriek. I felt so faint that I had to breathe hard to keep standing. Pankaj wanted his letters. If he had them and saw the words I'd unthinkingly repeated to him today, would he accuse me?

"If the necklace isn't recovered, to have those letters will at least be some comfort for my son," Mr. Bandopadhyay said without looking at me. But in my mind, I was thinking, He wants to know what is in the forbidden letters: the love-filled papers that I long to have as well.

"It is a difficult time for all. You may wish to retire to your rooms. I will have tea sent to you." Miss Jamison's lips drew into a thin line as she spoke. "Sarah!"

I followed Miss Jamison into the hallway, which had filled with a mix of eavesdropping servants and students. At the sight of the headmistress, the servants rapidly scattered toward their proper domains, and the English girls walked off in a more relaxed manner. By the time

Miss Jamison and I had reached the tall Jesus statue in the main hall, all of the listeners were gone, most likely telling stories to the rest of the school.

"This is your chance to tell the truth before God." Miss Jamison gestured toward the statue. "Sarah, you must say where you've hidden the necklace. We did not find it in your quarters."

So they had looked already. I was filled with embarrassment and anger, too. Woodenly, I said, "I'm very sorry, Burra-memsaheb, but I do not know because I did not take it."

Miss Jamison's reply was swift, as if she'd anticipated my response. "Then you will be searched. I shall call Miss Rachael—"

"No!" I said, for the thought of Miss Rachael searching me was as awful as Miss Jamison doing it herself. I could not be a teacher; I could not be Bidushi's ayah; I would not be their whipping girl. "I have nothing hidden on me. I give you my word."

"Your word? The problem is you learned too many of them! If school staff won't search you, the police will. Go to your room and wait. And remember, you are bound for hell."

I hung my head, too overcome to respond. But I longed to say that I wished she would find the true culprit. Maybe a man had crept in the window that I'd left open. Or perhaps the thief was Miss Rachael or Nurse-matron or even the jamidarni-auntie. But how could I say that? I could not accuse with no evidence.

"Aren't you listening?" Her voice cracked with impatience. "Go!"

❧   ❧   ❧

OLD JYOTI-MA WATCHED me pack up my sleeping mat, the composition book and pencils Miss Richmond had given me, and my hair comb. All this I wrapped in a bundle made from my second sari and tied it to a stick she found for me. Then Jyoti-ma whimpered, and I looked up into the doorway of the lean-to and saw my nemesis.

"I always knew that no good would come from you. Next time

they bring a girl from the mission hospital, I will refuse her!" Miss Rachael spoke casually, for she knew there was no need to try to punish me anymore. She had used rumors, spread here and there, to great effect, and finally won her five-year-battle against me.

"I am glad to be freed." I turned my back on her and continued to secure my bundle. Never before would I have dared to speak like this, but everything was finished. She had no more hold on me.

"Free to be a girl of the streets! Very quickly you will find yourself in the only job an unknown female can have."

She was right; I needed money to stay off the street. I thought of my serving maid's stipend: just five rupees a month, but after five years of work, it would be quite a packet. Trying to remain polite, I said, "I'll take my pay, now, if you please."

"Pay?" she laughed. "The thief tries to take more? There is no pay. You've never had it."

I knew what Abbas had told me, and the other servants, too. Tightly, I said, "I am not a thief. If you won't bring it now, I'll go to Miss Jamison and tell her you've seized it."

"I'll tell her you've been getting it each week, just like the others. Why would she believe you? All she knows of you are lies." Rachael's voice was triumphant, and hearing this, I finally lost control.

"Let there be ash on your face!"

The old curse that I spat was too much for Miss Rachael. She rushed forward and pushed me to the hard earthen floor. Then she was hitting my face, and I was striking back to protect myself. Jyoti-ma cringed in a corner, weeping and imploring us to be calm.

"Stop it!" An English voice broke through my consciousness. Instantly, Miss Rachael was on her feet, proclaiming that I'd gone mad and attacked her. I expected Miss Jamison, but to my relief it wasn't she who had interrupted us. It was Miss Richmond, whose hair had escaped its knot, and who was looking flushed in the face, as if she'd been running.

"The dining room staff needs your oversight," Miss Richmond

sternly ordered Rachael, who nodded and disappeared through the doorway, and then she told Jyoti-ma to leave as well. The old woman scurried off, leaving me with the teacher who had changed my life for the better and now had to see me in utter degradation.

"I can explain, Miss Richmond," I said, between gasps, because the fight with Miss Rachael had been fierce. "It is much like *Silas Marner*."

"George Eliot's novel?" Her thin auburn brows drew together. "I don't understand."

"Yes, I am like Silas, accused of stealing something that I didn't— and also the victim of a crime by the ruling class. You know that I loved Bidushi. I would never take from her. Perhaps I could help detect the culprit—"

"I came to warn you that the police have been called." She put a gentle hand on my shoulder. "You must run away from here. Please, Sarah."

Now I felt like vomiting, for I did not know the area at all; I would be caught easily. And I wouldn't be able to ask Miss Jamison about my stipend, either.

"This is the book of Tagore poetry you were translating for me." Miss Richmond slipped it into my hands. "It is of no use to me without your translations. Maybe it will be of some comfort, at your next . . ."

She did not finish the sentence. She did not say *your next home*, or *your next station* because she must have known how very unlikely it was I would find either.

I turned over the small hardcover book I knew so well. The volume was used, and about the only value it could bring would be a few annas, but I knew as I held it in my hands, I could never sell it.

"Thank you," I whispered, and without looking at her again, I left—past the tennis courts, the stables, and the rose garden in which a young gentleman remained sitting where I'd last seen him. I had thought it better that Pankaj would never know anything of my true nature; but now, as I ran, I hoped that he would not believe what they would tell him about me.

As I escaped, my bare feet pounded the dusty path the mali had not yet watered. With each step I was moving farther from the place where I'd learned life's hardest lesson, toward the unknown. No, I realized, it was not unknown. It was the old, large world I had once known; India.

There was only one road down the hill. Eventually, a fork would come, the main road linking to Midnapore, but I feared to take it because of the police. I resolved to take the other road, wherever it might bring me. I did so, but soon the pounding in my head was drowned out by a clattering sound. Some kind of horse-drawn vehicle was chasing me from behind. Oh, for it to be Pankaj: for him to have come after me to say he knew the truth and would take me to Calcutta with him! But the likelier situation was that the police had guessed my route.

Quickly, I veered off the road and into the brush, where I flattened myself to the ground. And then I heard a familiar, friendly voice.

"Come out, Beti. It's only me."

Warily, I lifted my head and saw two feet in well-worn chappals that I recognized. I crept out and found that Abbas-chacha was indeed alone and standing with the horse's reins in hand next to a small cart usually used at the school for moving cisterns and other heavy materials.

"Come," he repeated, in a voice that was strong and calm. "I will bring you to the train. The best thing for you is to go far away to a big city like Calcutta. There, you can vanish."

Calcutta. He was speaking of my dream city; but why? I had never told him I loved Pankaj.

"I know you did not steal." He tilted my chin up with his finger, so I could see into his moist eyes. "You loved that girl like a sister. It's why I've come to help you."

Overwhelmed with gratitude, I tried to touch his feet, but he caught me before that could happen. "No time for that. Get on."

"But, Chacha, how ever will I take a train to Calcutta?"

"You will enter the third-class section and sit down somewhere—and don't give your ticket to anyone except the conductor wearing a uniform! There are tricksters, Beti. How I wish I could take you myself, but I would be noticed missing."

"I have never ridden a train—"

"You will do it. And there you will tell people a new name, and you will find work."

"Yes. And I will never tell anyone that you helped me." I shot a sidelong glance at him, remembering how he'd rescued me from the riverbank, brought me to the school, and listened to my English practice for years. Even though I had not seen him on a daily basis since taking up with Bidushi, knowing he was nearby always had made me feel safe.

"We will stop at my home first. There, my wife will help you change clothing and I will find some money for you." As tears formed at the edges of my eyes, he said, "Just lie down in the back section of the cart and cover yourself with this blanket."

I remained hidden for the half hour or so it took to drive into Midnapore. I realized that I was lying in just the same way as the kidnapped children I'd seen long ago. And while I was not afraid of Abbas, I was worried what might happen if we were discovered. Because of this, I didn't peek from under the blanket at anything, until he stopped. Then I saw that we had come through a gate in the middle of a tall garden wall made of clay and topped with glass spikes. Inside the wall were two huts, one that had a trail of cooking smoke coming from it.

"This is my home," he said, taking the musty blanket away completely as I sat up. "You are safe now."

A water buffalo grazed in the yard along with a few chickens. A pretty, middle-aged woman wearing a flower-patterned sari over her salwar kameez put down the milk bucket she was carrying and looked toward us.

"My wife," Abbas-chacha said to me in an undertone. Then, more loudly, he said, "Hafeeza, your niece is here. It is a good surprise."

"What's that?" With her brow furrowed, Abbas's wife motioned both of us into the large hut. I stood at the threshold, thinking what a comfortable place it was with a smooth earth floor, a swing for sitting, and two cane chairs. High on the wall was a framed paper with curly Urdu writing: the only thing that revealed this was a Muslim home. Suddenly, I felt ashamed for having believed all I had heard during childhood about the Mohammedans being so different.

"Are you mad? Who is this?" Hafeeza looked from her husband to me with concern.

"This is the one I told you many stories about; they call her Sarah," Abbas said. "The young lady she was helping learn English passed away this afternoon. She is quite upset."

"Allah, have mercy!" His wife touched my chin with gentle fingers. "Beti, I know that you loved that girl—and she loved you. You will call me Hafeeza-chachi. I know that my husband has been something like an uncle. But why such secrets about your visiting? You should have come long ago."

"Sarah is in trouble," Abbas said. "The burra-mem accused her of stealing jewelry from her student friend. She said all of this in front of that girl's relatives and the parents of her betrothed, so they all believe it."

"Oh!" Hafeeza said, her lovely almond-shaped eyes widening.

"Of course she did not do it. I have brought her here to quickly give her some necessities and send her off to Calcutta. If anyone asks about a girl being here, we will say it was your niece from Balasore."

"But the girl is not Muslim! If she walks out, anyone can see that."

Abbas countered, "If she wears a burka, her face will not be seen on the train."

"A burka?" Hafeeza regarded her husband curiously. "I do not have any of those."

"Once, my mother gave you—"

"That is long gone," she scoffed, then turned to me. "Don't worry. I'll dress you in a sari and salwar kameez in our fashion. You won't be recognized."

Hafeeza led me to a tank in an area of their courtyard protected by high walls, where I bathed and came back in my wet sari to the hut. Then she brought me in the second room, which had a rope bed, a large steel almirah, and a fine carpet woven with flowers and birds.

"Where do your children sleep, Hafeeza-chachi?" I asked, surprised that the room appeared to be theirs only.

"We were never blessed." Hafeeza's voice dropped an octave, and belatedly I remembered Abbas telling me of this misfortune when we'd driven so many years ago to Lockwood School. "This is a fresh salwar kameez that is small for me. Wear it underneath the sari I'll give you. Now remember, always pull the sari's pallu over your head. That is our Muslim way." She unlocked the almirah and brought out a folded blue sari with golden zari embroidery. It was stunning.

"But I don't deserve this." I turned the sari over in my hands, thinking it the finest garment I'd ever held. Likely Hafeeza had gotten it as a wedding gift years ago.

"I have no need for it anymore. Dress yourself and comb your hair. I can give you a pair of chappals, but they won't fit perfectly. I'm afraid that your feet are larger than mine."

I looked at the leather thong sandals that she held out. I'd seen townspeople wearing such chappals and a few upper-level servants like Rachael and Abbas, but I'd never worn anything on my rough, bare feet.

"Put them on now and practice," Hafeeza said. "You must not fall out of them as you take your first steps into a new life."

BOOK THREE
KHARAGPUR
1935–1938

. . . The moral character of some of the English officers has not been a blessing to India. The majority, indeed, are choice men and many of a grand personality; yet others have disgraced their position, and replied the confidences of the natives.

However, British rule has been an incalculable blessing. India has never before had so just a government in all its history. Never until now has the whole country known peace, since its first settlement. The petty kingdoms, with shifting boundaries, that formerly were engaged in frequent external and internal wars, are now gathered under one stable government, conducted for the benefit of the governed and not for the glory of a single prince. There is a new feeling of security. Every one realizes that the English Government is firm and has come to stay. . . .

Margaret Beahm Denning, *Mosaics from India*, 1902

CHAPTER
9

This heart of mine, a night express, is on the way.
The night is deep, the carriages are loaded all with sleep.
What seems a murky nothing plunged in the infinite dark,
Awaits the frontiers of sleep in lands unspecified.

—Rabindranath Tagore, "The Night Express," ("Rater Gari"), 1940

Good-bye, Sarah, they had told me, with tears in their eyes.

I didn't know it, but that would be the last time anyone addressed me by that tarnished, unlucky name. As years passed, I would meet many other Sarahs, and I always wondered if they felt their name to be a blessing. The servant girl Sarah was someone I was eager to abandon, although I did not yet know who I would become. For this reason, I was relieved not to be asked for any name when I bought the train ticket, just for the money.

I should have been excited about going to Calcutta. But as the monstrous steam locomotive approached, I felt myself shrinking away from it. The engine was almost the height of Lockwood's buildings and roared like a cyclone. The long black snake made of giant metal compartments settled along the platform, and the crowd on the platform surged forward, taking me with them. As I lifted my foot to the first high step, I lost my sandal. I bent to catch it, and this created a jam. Amid complaints and shoves, I managed to clamber aboard and make my way to a third-class compartment with a tiny gap wide enough for me to sit.

An Anglo-Indian man wearing a dark blue suit decorated with brass buttons strode into the compartment as if he did not feel the fierce movement of the train. The many conversations that had filled the compartment were now replaced by shouts from wife to husband for their tickets to give Conductor-saheb. He tore my ticket and placed part of it in his satchel before giving the remainder to me.

After the conductor left, people relaxed and opened tiffin boxes of food and flasks of tea. Bananas were peeled and given out to children. The smell of chapattis and parathas made my stomach rumble, because I had not eaten since midday. A Muslim woman feeding her family gave me a paratha: I thanked her with the Urdu word, *shukria*, and devoured the flaky, spicy bread. As the paratha filled my stomach, my fears lessened slightly. Finally, I was on my way to the City of Palaces. I would find good work—ideally a teaching job like Miss Richmond's, but teaching Indian girls or boys, of course. And one day—if I made something of myself—I would see Pankaj again and let him know me for who I'd become. And if he had never married, the story could end happily, perhaps as romantically as that of Jane Eyre and Mr. Rochester, who had weak eyesight, just like my beloved Pankaj.

The sun went down quickly, and it was harder to see outside the train, except for dots of light that I guessed came from huts with lamps lit inside. After some time, these glowing huts became more frequent, and then many lights shone from overhead as the train slowed and stopped between two very long cement platforms. I was surprised how fast we'd reached Calcutta.

As many passengers stood and groped at the luggage racks for their possessions, I slipped out the doorway. Looking at the platform, I was stunned to see so many Anglo-Indians and Europeans. There were plenty of Indians, too: travelers, friends, and relatives greeting new arrivals, porters, and groups of beggars. What a large city; I felt lost already.

As I disembarked, a one-armed wraith clutching a baby to her hip came right up to my face and called out bibiji, the polite address for a Muslim gentlewoman. I tried to ignore her, but it was impossible; the tears in her rheumy eyes and the sickly baby made me feel sorry. Here was someone worse off than I, and I remembered what Ma said we must always do for lost souls. Reaching into my bundle, I withdrew a paisa that she clutched to her forehead as she murmured a blessing.

"Thank you, bibiji. And do not go with those bad porter men!" the woman said as I glanced about, trying to decide where to go. "I will find a trustworthy rickshaw driver for you."

"No, I'm staying in the ladies' lounge tonight," I said, remembering Hafeeza and Abbas's instructions. "You see, I've only just arrived here in Calcutta, and I know nothing about the neighborhoods."

"Calcutta?" She laughed, revealing a mouth with only a few diseased teeth left. "This is not Calcutta."

"What?" It felt as if all parts of my body had jumped into my stomach—hands and feet included. I was not just shocked but horrified I'd made such a mistake.

"Bibiji was on the train from Midnapore, isn't it? People change here for another train to Calcutta. The train just leaving on the other side is Calcutta Mail, bound for Howrah Station. This is Kharagpur; the Ingrej cannot pronounce, so they say Khargpur."

I fought against my paralysis and turned, intent on reaching the train she mentioned, but the doors were now latched, and a uniformed man on the platform blew a whistle. The train's wheels turned, and a horn blew. In no time, the train pulled away from the platform with a few daring men racing up to cling to the doorway. I could not race to catch it in my difficult sandals. There was enough space on the platform for me to clearly see the sign hanging from the station's roof that said KHARAGPUR.

"But this is not the place I should be!" My shock was turning to panic.

"What? Kharagpur is a *good* place," the beggar-granny said, jouncing her baby. "Here is the longest railway platform in India and, they say, maybe the world!"

I shook my head. This was not the City of Palaces, where I could vanish into safety and a new life. Instead, it was an unknown place in which anything could happen. Already I saw a pair of young, oily-looking men appraising me, a young woman alone with no relatives to greet her.

"Don't cry. Tell the ticket-wallah about your troubles. I will show you his office."

❧   ❧   ❧

THE RAILWAY'S TICKETING manager was Anglo-Indian, just like the train conductor. But he was not as jovial as the fellow on the train. His mouth turned down as I stumbled through my explanation of the ticket I'd bought in Midnapore. When he asked to see my receipt, I tore my bundle apart, but could not find it. Dimly, I remembered the scrap of paper I'd used to wipe my fingers after eating the paratha. I did not have it anymore; likely it had fallen to the train compartment's filthy floor.

The cost of a new third-class ticket was far greater than the amount of rupees I had left over from Abbas and Hafeeza. Feeling like death, I left the ticket window and found that the beggar-granny was still waiting. She had an idea that I should beg alongside her in some rags she would provide. Within a few days I would have enough money earned for the Calcutta ticket; she swore it on her granddaughter's head.

"It's kind of you, but I can't do that. I'm going to be a teacher. I'll start looking for work tomorrow morning." My words were braver than I felt. But I could not think of any alternative.

The granny sighed and thrust at me a scrap of a ticket she'd found on the platform earlier that day. It would allow admission to the ladies' lounge, which only documented passengers could use. I was touched by her generosity, but once inside the lounge, I realized staying over- night would be very unpleasant. On a wooden bench in a hot, smelly room, I found a spot to squeeze in amid many women and children who'd settled in to wait for their connecting trains. I was tired but could not sleep, my thoughts flashing between the losses of Bidushi and Pankaj, my humiliating expulsion from Lockwood, and the terri- fying future.

When dawn arrived, I could bear the bench no longer. I went into the horrifying lavatory and used it all the while trying not to breathe. Then I removed the sweat-drenched salwar kameez. The fine sari I'd worn over it was not too badly wrinkled, so I rearranged it in the draped fashion Bidushi had taught and put on my own green blouse and petticoat underneath. Dressed like this, it would be easier to find work and survive.

After I'd splashed water on my face and combed and braided my hair, I went out to the platform. Here, the beggar-granny reap- peared. She brought me a cup of tea at no cost and recited a list of the names of Kharagpur's various schools that she had gathered from her rickshaw-driving friends. There were so many school names that I left the station feeling hopeful. I would become a teacher in this strange city. But no matter how many schools I visited, very few of their tall iron gates parted. Of the two schools that did, my lack of diploma and references sent me straight out again. Each time I walked away from a school, I felt the eyes not only of the curious children and the stern chowkidars but also of others from my past. I could feel Miss Rachael reminding me that I'd overstepped and Miss Jamison telling me I was bound for hell. I even sensed Thakurma's reproach. If I had stayed with my family, I would not be in such trouble.

I was walking in a groomed, wealthy section of town, and as I turned from one brick-paved avenue to another, I came to a large, lovely garden dotted with plants and trees. People sat on benches, and children sailed back and forth on swings. A short metal ladder stretched up and from it spread a diagonal length of metal that children slid down, laughing with delight. What was this thing?

I found a bench in the shade, where I rested my tired feet and slowly ate a ripe mango I'd picked up from the garden of one of the schools that had rejected me. I sat for a long time, my eyes half closed, longing to be one of the playing children with a watchful mother. But in truth, I knew I was old enough to be a mother myself. I didn't deserve comforting.

Through my tears, I watched families eat, play, and depart. Then came a young Anglo-Indian woman with an English soldier. The soldier carried a blanket that he spread on the grass, and then the young lady opened a basket, from which she brought forth a tall green glass bottle with a cork that popped off with a burst of smoke. As bubbles spilled over the top of the bottle, the man rushed to thrust it in the girl's open mouth.

I watched raptly as the two exchanged the bottle to share in its drinking, lavishing long kisses and caresses on each other in between. I had never seen such physicality; I was shocked but wanted to see what might happen next. The Indian men sitting nearby in the park pointed and made loud, rude comments; the mothers with children turned fiercely away. I eyed the couple's bottle, wondering if it was like the toddy the Lockwood stable workers drank on occasion. Then the girl opened up a newspaper bundle to reveal shingaras, the crisp horn-edged pastries stuffed with vegetables or mince, and my stomach growled with hunger. Under the warm sun, I fell into a half dream; I was feeding Pankaj, and he was looking at me just as adoringly as the soldier did his girl.

❦   ❦   ❦

THE DREAM BROKE when I heard loud English voices. I opened my eyes to see an English military officer shouting at the couple. Swiftly, the soldier got to his feet and put his cap back on. The girl rose in a more leisurely fashion, her skirt rising to expose her thighs before she brushed it back into place. The two went off in different directions, leaving the crumpled newspaper and bottle behind.

Was there food left? I rushed toward their leftovers but discovered the shingaras were all eaten and nothing remained in the large bottle. Dejectedly, I took the newspaper for reading and the bottle to use later on for collecting water. As I put the bottle in my bundle, I felt the nearby people looking disapprovingly, and I realized I must appear like a lost soul.

Quickly, I left the park and walked into a warren of busy shopping streets. I did not have enough money to feed myself through the next two days. What would I do? As my mind slowly turned from hope to panic, I found another bench; this one along the street. Trying to look like I wasn't loitering, I opened the newspaper that I'd saved and began reading.

After a few minutes, a fashionable Anglo-Indian seated herself on the opposite end of the bench. I realized she was the girl from the park. She was only a little older-looking than me but was so different, with a milky complexion, shoulder-length golden-brown curls, and a silk dress with a fluttering hemline that just covered her knees. She wore such thin silk stockings it almost appeared that her legs were bare as they disappeared into high-heeled pumps. She caught me looking and her pink lips spread into a charming smile.

"Excuse me, but do you know if the tram has already passed?" she asked in fluent Bengali.

I was not accustomed to Anglo-Indians speaking to me politely, so I hesitated for a moment. "I don't think so, Memsaheb. I have been waiting here almost half an hour and not seen one, although my head has mostly been in the newspaper."

She switched to English then and asked if I could read all the words in the *Statesman*.

"Of course," I answered in English, my reserve going up. Was she going to tease me?

"Can you read that?" A fingernail, pink as a rose, pointed at a review for the Fred Astaire and Ginger Rogers film, *The Gay Divorcee*. Dutifully, I read to her the details of the "frothy comedy" starring the "king and queen of carioca." I didn't understand the words *carioca*, nor *divorcee*, but I was not going to volunteer that.

"I know the big song from it already—'The Continental'—and 'Night and Day,' which is simply lovely. Your accent is—" She shook her head, so the glorious brown curls bounced. "Where did you go to school?"

I dared not name Lockwood, in case there was anything about me in the newspapers. I decided to use Bidushi's story. In the poshest voice I could muster, I said, "Since early childhood, I had a governess."

"Really?" From her expression I could not tell whether she believed my lie. She said, "My father skipped back to England when I was six, and my mother could afford to send me to school only two more years. Wasn't ever good at it, either. So what's your name, Miss Excellent English? Who are your family and are you already married?"

I scrutinized my interviewer. With her pink fingernails and low-cut dress, she did not appear connected to the police. In fact, she had gotten into trouble in the park for her behavior. Softly, I said, "I'm not going to be married, because I have no family to give dowry. They all died some years ago in a cyclone."

"So sorry!" Her eyes widened in sympathy. "And what's your name, then?"

I hesitated, because I didn't want to give any name that could connect me to Lockwood School. Finally, I said, "Pom."

"Pam!" She nodded with approval. "I have a cousin with that name, but she isn't half as pretty as you are. I'm Bonnie. How old are you?"

"Fifteen," I answered, deciding to ignore her mispronunciation of my name. In a few minutes, I would never see her again.

"Oh, quite grown up! And where are you from, Pammy?"

I decided to confide partial truth. "I come from the south, near the sea. My family died in a tidal wave that hit some years ago. I came here by accident; I was looking for Calcutta. But now I'm searching for a teaching job, although it may be impossible for someone of my background."

"Oh, dear. I live with my mummy and sisters not far from the Railway School, but I'm sure they only take European or Anglo-Indians to teach." She glanced at her wristwatch that sparkled with little crystals where the numbers should have been. Could they be diamonds? "It's already half five. Even if that damn bus comes in the next minute, I shall miss the opening. It's too late now; I will have to go another day."

Quickly, I said, "I'm sorry for your misfortune, Memsaheb."

"Remember, I'm Bonnie," she said, putting an arm around my shoulders. "Come along. It's only a short rickshaw ride home for tea."

"I'm sorry?" I bristled at the unexpected touch and her strange words.

"Come with me for tea, Pam. You're invited." Gently, her fingers stroked my arm, and a shiver went through me because this was so very different from any touch I'd ever felt. Bonnie's caress was a strong, pleasing sensation that made me feel alive.

Bonnie squeezed my hand and pulled me toward a waiting rickshaw, just the way I would have led my young sisters when they needed guidance. I had no words, because I could not believe this wealthy Anglo-Indian girl was bringing me home. But how would I manage tea, having never eaten anywhere but seated cross-legged on the floor?

"But I can't," I said. "I'm bound for Calcutta and a teaching position."

"You can do that later. It's just a cup and a bite, Pam," Bonnie said, as if reading my nervousness. "And don't forget to bring that newspaper. I want to show the other girls how beautifully you read!"

CHAPTER
10

Another element in this population is the Eurasian—a mixture of European and Asiatic blood, representing every degree of intermingling, from almost pure English to almost pure native. This class numbers a hundred thousand souls. They almost invariably adopt the customs of the Europeans and many of them are highly cultured and refined.

—Margaret Beahm Denning, *Mosaics from India,* 1902

Bonnie's home reminded me of the fortress pictures I had seen in history books at Lockwood School. The tall, rectangular bungalow of golden brick had curved iron grates on all the windows and curtains behind that, masking what I guessed immediately were riches inside. She led me through the gate and past a small garden filled with circular beds of rosebushes in many colors: red, pink, white, yellow, and even orange. It was quite a hodgepodge that did not seem to fit the house's stern design, but as I walked up the path behind Bonnie, the sweet and spicy smells of the roses were enticing.

Someone must have been watching our approach because the door opened just as Bonnie set her foot on the top step. "Are we busy?" Bonnie asked a tall chowkidar who was dressed in red livery. He had ushered us into a cool, dark hallway lit by a few sconces in between portraits of beautiful European ladies and Indian maharanis.

"Not at all. Right now, only Mr. Williams has come." The chowkidar took Bonnie's hat and placed it on a shelf in the hall cupboard.

"Tell Mummy I have a new friend, Miss Pamela. She'll be staying to tea." Bonnie stepped out of her shoes, and I did the same, glad for Hafeeza's chappals. If I'd been barefoot, Bonnie wouldn't have considered me worthy of any invitation.

"Where is your mother?" I asked, as it was unusual for a housewife not to greet her guests.

"You will soon meet Mummy—but we must freshen up first. You can bathe in my quarters, and I'll have Premlata, one of our servant girls, bring up a drink. Sweet lime or salt?"

Running my tongue over my dry lips, I asked for salt. Bidushi had bought the special drink for me during our trip to the Midnapore bazar. I wondered what she would think of this fancy house. And then a startling realization came: perhaps Bidushi *was* with me. Her cremation was surely done; what if she had been reincarnated into Bonnie? Bonnie's invitation made it seem as if Bidushi's generous soul had jumped inside, because why would a rich Anglo-Indian ever bring a shabby stranger home for a meal?

Bonnie had a pretty bedroom with a large, four-poster bed covered in a pink-flowered quilt, with white pillowcases trimmed in the same pink. There were two almirahs; hers held a rainbow of beautiful Western clothes. There was a wireless radio on her dressing table and many bottles and pots of cosmetics. On the wall was only one picture: a framed photograph of the starlet Merle Oberon, whom she said was an Anglo-Indian from Calcutta.

I had never heard of Merle Oberon; I had never even seen a film. All these exciting, glamorous ideas whirled through me as Bonnie showed off her very own bathroom, which had a tub set into a tiled floor and water that flowed right into it from a silver spout. The bath and sink water was heated by turning on a geyser mounted high on the wall. Bonnie showed me how to work them and also explained the correct seating for the white porcelain privy similar to ones I'd seen in the students' lavatory at Lockwood School.

Bonnie left me in this lavatory of wonders. When I came out wrapped in towels, she was sitting comfortably on her bed listening to the wireless. Next to her was a folded gold-and-orange-patterned silk sari and a very small matching gold blouse.

"I thought you might like this sari for dinner tonight," she said, smiling prettily. But my senses were on alert. She might have examined my bundle and decided that the two cotton saris within were too worn for me to wear before her family. As I did not want to embarrass myself any more that day, I allowed her to wrap the silk sari and let her comb my hair and place a few bangles on my wrists. I felt shy to be waited on by her, but I sensed there was no way to resist. When she led me to the long mirror set into her door, my reflection was that of a stranger with large eyes, high cheekbones, and full lips, with a woman's body clearly revealed by the sari she had wrapped low around my waist.

"Not bad," Bonnie said, clapping her hands. "If they fit, you may borrow my slippers tonight."

Walking gingerly, because her feet were bigger than mine, I followed Bonnie downstairs to a parlor with windows covered by long, embroidered curtains, even though it was still sunny outside. Ranged across a series of settees and lounge chairs were five young ladies, all quite different-looking but attractive. They wore clothing I'd never before seen: shimmering saris with short blouses, gold-embroidered tunics and flowing pajama pants, and tight, beaded European gowns. For me, it was like being in fairyland, and the girls seemed just as interested in me.

"Look at those eyes—lotus eyes. Add a bit of kohl and mascara and she could be in films," said an Indian girl wearing a green chiffon sari who introduced herself as Lucky-Short-for-Lakshmi. Behind Lakshmi was Shila, also Indian, but wearing a party dress that barely reached her knees. I tried not to gawk at her long golden-brown calves, which seemed to shimmer and, like Bonnie's, did not have a single hair growing on them. The girls repeated my name among themselves, and I heard it changing. Pam. Pamela. Pammy.

"Bonnie says you speak well," said Natty, a golden-skinned Anglo-Indian with a head of thick black curls. She appraised me with cold eyes almost like Miss Jamison's, although she was a hundred times younger and prettier. "Sakina, fetch the latest copy of *Vanity Fair* for the girl to read. I must hear this so-called Mayfair accent for myself."

"Natty is a school graduate, so she thinks she's a genius. Don't mind her," Bonnie murmured in my ear. But I understood Natty's suspicion. They were like the Lockwood girls, just more beautiful because they had Indian blood—but many castes above me, without question. That was the only thing I was sure of in this loud room that smelled of so many perfumes my head was beginning to hurt.

Bonnie brought me to a sink to wash my hands, and then we went to a long veranda on the back of the house, where a table was set with many chairs around it. Three young maidservants fanned flies away from the dishes: crisp shingaras, iced cakes, and square-cut cucumber-and-tomato sandwiches. A brass tureen held a mountain of steaming white rice flecked with onions and spices, and there were at least half a dozen curries in other bowls.

I was so starved that I longed to descend on the table immediately, but these inquisitive young women would not let me move. One had her hands in my hair, undoing the braid I'd carefully made after washing upstairs. Another was lifting the pallu of the sari to examine what she called my figure. I'd always thought that figure was a term from mathematics, but now I realized it meant something else.

"Girls, that is enough! You will have plenty of time to chat up Pamela after the meal."

The high-pitched voice belonged to Bonnie's mother, who had joined us. I examined her covertly. Although she had the same lilting accent as Bonnie, she was darker, something she'd attempted to mask with pink powder. Reddish-brown curls fell around her head like a frizzy halo, and she had jeweled clips holding it back from her face. A short and stout woman, she nevertheless wore a tight long evening dress with a low neckline almost completely covered with sparkling necklaces. Her brown eyes were unusually small and seemed dominated by black-painted eyelashes. I had never seen anyone look like this, not even in the colorplate illustrations of *The Arthur Rackham Fairy Book*.

"Sit next to me, dear heart." The lady took my wrist in fat, strong fingers that were covered in jeweled rings and showed me a chair next to the table's head. I took it as the other girls flopped into their seats, still laughing and chattering. The servants came around to serve each of us from the bowls; despite the abundant offerings, some girls avoided shingaras, and many others refused meat or dal. Bonnie's mother accepted food from every bowl and urged me to as well. I did not want to appear greedy, but I was so hungry that I gratefully accepted every delicacy that the servants brought.

As they feasted, the girls talked back and forth, mostly making jokes. Then an argument broke out about someone called Mr. Evans. The mother interceded, reminding the girls that in a family, everyone shared. Bonnie chimed in that she was still missing her pink suspender belt; could anyone remember seeing it? In the midst of this strange conversation the male butler walked in, bowed his head to Natty, and said, "Murphy-saheb is here."

Natty rolled her eyes, pushed back in her chair with a careless scraping sound, and left. Two others were called for in the same manner over the next half hour. No one returned, even though food was still left on their plates. I worried about it, wishing I could wrap it in papers to take for myself the next day.

"Are you enjoying yourself?" The mother asked, looking from me to my empty plate.

I must have been staring at the leftovers. Quickly, I said, "Yes, madam. I cannot possibly thank you enough for your kindness."

"Bonnie was telling me that you are completely on your own." From her expression, I could tell she expected me to say more.

"Some years ago, there was a cyclone, and I lost my family: parents, grandparents, two sisters, and a baby brother."

"What a difficult lot in life," the mother said. "Tell me, were you ever married? For an Indian girl your age, it is the usual custom."

"Oh, no, madam. There was nobody to arrange anything for me, and I don't want that kind of life. Work is my dream. I am traveling to Calcutta to look for a teaching job."

"So you are independent." Mummy sounded thoughtful. "Now you are amongst friends, all of whom have lost their families in some sense or another. You must not be afraid anymore."

After the meal, Sakina returned, wearing a different dress and carrying the *Vanity Fair* magazine. At everyone's urging, I read a short story by William Seabrook, putting on a posher than posh accent that made all the girls howl. Bonnie put an arm around my shoulder and whispered in my ear that I read so well I should be a wireless announcer. Then she boasted her house had several parlors loaded to bursting with magazines and books, and that she would take me to find some good reading for the evening hours. I realized that I was happy: an emotion I hadn't felt in a very long time.

As the servants cleared the table, the girls rose up slowly; I could tell that they didn't particularly want to leave. I heard some men's voices coming from the front of the house. My first instinct was apprehension; but then I guessed that the lady's husband had come home and brought friends. I wondered what kind of business Bonnie's father did to have built such a fine house. But then I remembered that he'd abandoned her to go back to England. It didn't make sense about Bonnie's mother not having enough money to send her to school, because there was so much fine jewelry and clothing on everyone. And the food! I would remember the feast for the rest of my life.

I lingered on the veranda with Bonnie and her mother, not wanting to say my good-bye. From the garden, I heard the call of doel birds, *chhr-chhr-rr*. This I knew was a kind of warning. I felt the hairs on my arms stand up, reminding me that I had no place to go tonight. My confident speech about going to Calcutta to Bonnie was an empty lie.

As if she'd heard my thoughts, the mother said, "You are very welcome to stay in Bonnie's room tonight. The girl who used to share with her is gone."

She'd said girl—not sister. I mulled this over until I understood what it meant. This was not a family home but a boardinghouse. This was the reason all the girls downstairs did not look like blood sisters. Bonnie had brought me here hoping I'd become a rento, not knowing I was too poor to afford it.

With a sinking feeling, I confessed, "You are too kind to a stranger, Burra-memsaheb, but—"

"Mummy!" she corrected, laughing. "My full name is Rose Barker, but I'm not Mrs. Barker to anyone but strangers. And you are Bonnie's friend, dear heart, not a stranger."

"Mummy," I said awkwardly, hardly believing she had called me dear heart again. "Mummy, I'm very sorry; I don't have money to pay for your hospitality."

At my words, the lady's high-pitched voice rose to a mouse's squeak. "Oh, you have hurt me! To suggest I would charge money when I have invited you to stay at Rose Villa! You are welcome to all the luxuries, and don't forget it."

"But you are overly generous." I hesitated, then went forward. "My dream was always to work as a teacher, but I am of course capable of other jobs. If I could work here—any tasks or chores—I would be most grateful. I could sleep on the kitchen floor or anywhere you might have room."

"To think I would be so cruel!" Mummy exclaimed. "Our Bonnie wants you to stay with her so she is not lonely."

That didn't make sense. I began an apology. "Thank you, but I cannot accept—"

"Thank you," Mummy parroted back, "for your hospitality. Say that, Pamela. It's the only thing I want to hear."

THAT NIGHT, MUMMY put me to bed in Bonnie's room because she said Bonnie would stay up very late. Smelling of roses and musk, she leaned down to draw the mosquito net around me.

After she left, I lay between the soft sheets, thinking how quickly my fate had changed. My best friend on earth had died; yet another girl had stepped forward to comfort me. Who had ever heard of such luck? It was confusing to be taken in by rich strangers. I feared it was all a dream and I would wake up in the railway station's ladies' lounge with an empty purse and stomach. But if this were truly happening, I was the luckiest girl in India: being gifted with food and shelter so I would have a chance to work and earn enough to reach Calcutta.

On the house's roof, a slow tapping began. Within a minute, thousands of goblins were dancing *jhup-jhup* on the roof. My breathing slowed as I filled with the understanding that the garden birds had been calling to one another only because of this. Rain was coming! A sweet, cool rain that would wash away the pain of the last five years and allow me to bloom anew.

PREMLATA WAS AT my bedside the next morning with a cup of tea and biscuits on the saucer. Awkwardly, I took the cup of sweet warmth to my lips, noticing that Bonnie had come to bed, but was still lying fast asleep. Premlata quietly asked if the rain had disturbed my sleep. She said that it was false rain because the monsoon was not due until the next month. She left the room after telling me a proper breakfast would be served downstairs at ten.

Next month, where would I be? And with whom? I glanced at Bonnie, who remained like a lump on the other side of the mattress, dressed only in a thin petticoat. A smell of smoke and something sweet hung around her. She snored gently while I drank my tea, waiting for her eyes to open. She slept on, as if wrapped in the most overwhelming fatigue.

After I'd finished my tea and left the tray outside the door for Premlata, just as the teacher-mems used to do for me, I decided to brave the bathroom myself. Remembering what I'd learned the day before, I lit the geyser's flame and soon had hot water running into the bath. Then I lathered myself with fine soap that smelled of jasmine and watched it bubble away into nothing in the clean, warm water. I was so happy in the warm bath that I whispered to myself some lines from the Tagore poem about a bird taking wing to fly to freedom. The line had meant nothing the first time I'd read it but now seemed as if it had been written just for me.

When I came back into the bedroom, Bonnie was awake and smiling. She showed me a different sari and blouse I should wear that day and helped wrap it around me in the proper fashion of her home, so my lower stomach showed. Then she slipped on a dressing gown and went downstairs with me, where the proper breakfast Premlata had spoken of was being served. Eggs, bacon, toasted thick bread, dal, rice, vegetable curries, baked beans, fruits . . . it was almost as luxurious as the previous night's feast, although we did not sit down altogether; girls arrived sleepily every few minutes, and a few, like Sakina and Doris, not at all. Just as Bonnie and I were finishing up, the front door chimed and the chowkidar said that Rima the beautician had come. She was a young, pretty Muslim lady who yelped at the sight of me. I felt ashamed, as if she thought I looked very rough and ugly, but Mummy laughed and said it only meant Rima was eager to fix me up, if I was willing.

I said yes, not knowing the lady would spread warm wax all over my legs and many other parts; in short, painful bursts my hair came off, so I looked as smooth as the others. Rima told me it was the custom of the house for her to visit weekly to groom all the girls, and I should not worry about the cost this time, as Mummy was paying.

Next, the beautician massaged my feet with oil and cut and shaped the toenails; it was almost like what the barber's wife did in our village, except the beautician painted all the nails with a red lacquer. Then she moved on to my hands. After rubbing them brutally with the same stone she'd used on my feet, she prescribed that I massage every part of my hands, from wrist to fingertips, with almond oil thrice daily.

Lucky-Short-for-Lakshmi—the girl who had been kind the night before—asked if she could teach me something about cosmetics, and with curiosity and anticipation I agreed. I'd seen servant girls at Lockwood line their eyes with ash, but Lucky showed me a black kohl pencil that did the same thing with less mess. Pinkish rouge pressed into a metal case was for the cheeks, and shades of silver and brown powder were for decorating the eyelids. Then there was an array of short fat pens, all colored red or pink or almost purple.

"What is your caste?" Lucky asked while she was using a tiny brush to color my lips. She was gazing only at my mouth, as if that was more important than her question, but I knew this was pretense. If she learned where I came from, she'd have to throw the brush away.

After she'd finished painting my lips, I said, "Nothing. I'm Christian."

"All Indian Christians were something else before." She made a kissing gesture at me and then laughed.

I could not smile back. "Why do you ask me this?"

"I watched you last night. You would not look at the servants—you hung your head every time they came to serve you! Everyone is wondering about the new girl. Her English is Mayfair, but where are the Mayfair manners?"

"I'm sorry." I tried to sound calm, but my insides were quaking.

"I know you are not a Dom," she said, naming the caste of the people who prepared corpses for cremation. "And I don't think you are a sweeper. You're something else: some kind of Sudra."

I closed my eyes, wishing to be elsewhere. She was right that my people came from Lord Brahma's lower half. But Baba had told me that legs were the strongest part and that was our gift from Him. I once agreed with this, but after the way I'd worked hard and been treated unfairly at Lockwood, my feelings were different.

"Don't be frightened." Lucky fiddled in a jewelry box, pulling out earrings. "I am not highly born. My family is from the thatching caste. My father sold me to a temple when I was seven to bring them the blessing of a son."

"What happened then?" As I spoke, she put down the earrings and looked up at me with eyes that were no longer merry. "I never saw them again, so I don't know if a brother was born. And it was very hard at the temple: little food and terrible work. The only good part was learning to dance. When I was fourteen, one of Mummy's friends came to watch our group perform. I was the one he liked best, so he paid the priests to let him bring me here. I was no longer Lakshmi, but Lucky. This name fits me. I feel lucky."

"You are lucky to be living here. My father grew rice for a jamidar near the coast." I decided it sounded more dignified than to say he was a peasant. "I do not dance or have any talents like you, unless you consider speaking English any value."

Lucky put one hand comfortingly around my shoulders and used the other to raise a hand mirror before me. "Your voice does not match your face, Pammy, but both are quite nice. Remember to never let your eyes run away from another person's again. The only time to drop your eyes is when you are trying to appear shy for a gentleman. Even then, you must coyly peek through your lashes like this!"

Why would I look at a gentleman? I wanted to ask but was interrupted by the sound of a car door slamming outside. Lucky slid off the bed and went to look out the window. Through the opening, I saw an English policeman with a fat red face. Panic filled my head and my clean, perfumed body broke into a sweat. They'd caught me.

"I must go!" I was already calculating how quickly I could get my bundle repacked and run down the staircase and through the back garden to the lane behind it. There would be no chance to thank Mummy and the others. No chance to do anything but run.

"What is this? Why are you afraid?" Lucky grabbed my hands in hers and wouldn't let go.

I felt my breath come in short bursts, as if I were already running. "The policeman—please don't tell him I was here—"

"He's not here for you; I swear on everything I own." Lucky dropped my hands. "Lots of nice people are frightened of the police. Just tell me."

I should not have said anything, but Lucky's face was so sympathetic that I confessed that I'd worked at a school where my student friend had died, and the police suspected I'd stolen her necklace. Lucky's painted eyes grew large during the story, and when I was finished, she gave me a tight embrace.

"I shall not tell a soul, but I promise again that Chief Howard is no danger to you or any of us. He's head of the Kharagpur police and is Bonnie's good friend," Lucky said.

"Her friend?" I asked incredulously.

"Very much so!" Her happy smile was back. "Let's go to her room and tell her he's arrived."

☙   ☙   ☙

CHIEF HOWARD WAS the first man I observed arriving at Rose Villa that day. Several more followed him during the hours from noon to three o'clock. Mummy's girls ran up and down the stairway to meet these friends who, from the sound of it, were mostly English or Anglo-Indian. As I sat on Bonnie's bed, trying to read the film magazines the girls had lent me, I found myself distracted by the laughter and chatter below. Why were these men visiting in the middle of the day? After four o'clock came a relaxed period when the girls washed, dressed freshly, and had a big tea, and then: more visitors all night long. I went to bed in Bonnie's room by myself, just as I'd done the night before, but this time I hardly slept.

The next morning, when I found Bonnie sleeping next to me, I drank my bed tea and waited for her to awaken. When she did, my questions were ready. Who were these visitors, and why were so many of them English?

Bonnie looked at me through half-open eyes that still had traces of mascara around the edges. She said, "You'll meet them soon enough. I'd like to take you into town today. We can run a few errands and go to see *Bombshell*."

After breakfast, Bonnie had me dress in European clothes: a blouse with fluttering sleeves and a skirt that left entire lower halves of my legs exposed. I was both excited and embarrassed to see myself in such a foreign costume. She wanted me to wear her high-heeled pumps, but I fell out of them so much that she relented and gave me a pair of glittery chappals left over from the girl who had once shared her room. They fit better than anything else she'd offered.

I had not seen much of the town, so I was eager to go with Bonnie into the bustling Gole Bazar. To my surprise, Bonnie was not interested in any of the shops but went into a building she called a bank. The outside of it was guarded by chowkidars who wore high, stiff turbans and carried rifles with bayonets. Inside was a vast room tiled in black-and-white marble. A counter of polished wood lined one wall, and there were brass grilles separating the Anglo-Indian gentlemen who worked behind them from the queued customers.

"Today is a big deposit." Bonnie's expression was bright as she showed me the packet of rupees inside her purse. She explained that the bank would store her money safely so thieves could not take it. She was depositing one hundred rupees, wiring twenty to her family in Cuttack, and keeping ten for the next week's fun. I wondered what job she had that paid so much, but first I wanted to understand her vocabulary. *Fun* was an English word I had not heard, and when I asked for an explanation, Bonnie laughed and said it meant movies, restaurants, and clothes. She told me that part of the money she was putting in the bank included a fifty-rupee fee Mummy had given her for bringing me to Rose Villa. If I decided to stay at Rose Villa, that payment would be doubled. Why would someone pay for a girl to bring a friend home? I wondered, but these rich people were the strangest I'd ever known.

"Soon you'll have your money," Bonnie said after we'd left the bank. She didn't know that I'd lost every rupee I'd earned through Miss Rachael's keeping it. To have money in a guarded bank seemed better than keeping it with a person.

"I asked Mummy if I could please do some work in the house, but she hasn't given me anything," I said. "Maybe she's still deciding."

After a pause, Bonnie said, "Nobody will *give* you the work. You must choose it."

"Tell me about the work you do. Maybe I could apply for a similar position?"

Bonnie's eyebrows arched high, and she seemed about to say something, then smilingly shook her head. "Let's not think of work now. We have a picture to see!"

At the Aurora Cinema, she bought my ticket and suggested we first visit the ladies' lounge. After we'd done our business in the stalls, we washed our hands at sinks next to each other. Bonnie unsnapped her pink velvet purse and gave me a vial of oil to use for my hands while she repainted her mouth.

"Your hands are not good," she said, looking critically at the quick rub I gave to my palms. "Did anyone tell you?"

"The beautician did. My hands are like this because I've done some housework." I still was being careful with Bonnie; Lakshmi was a safer confessor for me because she was Indian.

Bonnie was still looking worriedly at my hands as we left the ladies' lounge. "Mummy requires hands to be softer. And how are your
feet?"

I'd gone barefoot my whole life until a few days ago, so my feet
were as tough as a water buffalo's hooves. I thought all of Bonnie's
concerns were quite strange, but I did not question them because I
was more interested in the grand auditorium we had entered, with a
stage before us covered with the widest, longest red curtains I'd ever
seen. And then the curtains parted, the lights dimmed, and the screen
became bright, first with words and then moving figures. In minutes,
I had forgotten about Kharagpur and was transported into the world
of California film stars and their elegant houses filled with mirrors
and chandeliers and even small fluffy dogs. How unbelievable and
gorgeous it was—but no more so than my new life at Rose Villa.

❧   ❧   ❧

AT THE PICTURE'S end, I emerged, blinking at the bright light and
the India I had almost forgotten. Bonnie sang a phrase from a film
song in such a clear, high voice that everyone looked. I noticed the
attention she was drawing, but she did not mind. It was as if she
wanted to be Jean Harlow! A thin, dark man who looked to be the
age of my grandfather ran us all the way back in his rickshaw. Bonnie
counted out three annas for him and, when he complained, gave him
one more. She was generous, with a heart as big as her voice.

As we came into Rose Villa, the chowkidar rushed toward Bonnie
with concern on his face. "Miller-saheb was here but is now gone. He
said he will return in an hour's time to see you."

"Damn!" Bonnie's red lips drew into a pout. "I'm going to have to
hurry. Well, Pam, you'd better come up and give me a hand getting
ready."

I was pleased to be of some help after Bonnie's kindness to
me. I followed her up to her room and picked up the clothes she

tossed on the floor when she went in to bathe. I expected Bonnie to wear undergarments similar to what the older Lockwood students wore: brassieres and camiknickers and petticoats and thick pants that reached almost from the rib cage to midthigh. Instead, she had thrown off a suspender belt with stockings, a brassiere, and very small pants, all of which she exchanged for a new set in the startling color of black.

"Take the red dress from the almirah—here's the key," she said to me.

I turned the key, the door swung open and I found a V-necked red dress in a slippery silk I'd learned was called crepe de chine: the silk of China. I was stroking it with pleasure when a shouting voice below made both of us look up.

"Do us a favor and find out what's going on," Bonnie mumbled, her mouth full of hairpins.

"But Mummy said I shouldn't be seen!"

"It's only a lady shouting; I want to know who. Take the back stairs, and if you peep from the landing, nobody will see. Go on, then!" She waved me off, and I tiptoed down the back stairway, trying to keep the wood from creaking. As I crouched on the landing, I could see that the shouting woman was a middle-aged Anglo-Indian woman wearing a plain dress. Mummy was facing her, with her back to me; this meant I wouldn't be seen. I settled down to watch.

Mummy was saying in a friendly voice, "I don't know who you are talking about, Mrs.—"

"Robinson." The visitor interrupted angrily. "Leonard was here again last night; I know from the foul smell he brought home. You mustn't let him in. We have three children and another one coming. I can barely pay the bills, yet here he is, throwing away his packet."

Mummy stretched her bejeweled fingers toward Mrs. Robinson's shoulder, but the lady flinched dramatically. Mummy took back her hand. "Mrs. Robinson, I wish I knew your husband to speak to him, but I don't. Kharagpur has many restaurants and taverns and clubs.

Perhaps one of the cheap places round the railway station might be better."

"You're lying." Mrs. Robinson's screech was like a teakettle on the boil. "I've heard Leonard call out the name Doris in his sleep, and I know there's a girl by that name here. And don't you insult the Kharagpur railways. It's a better business than your horshop!"

I drew back in the darkness, stunned by the insults the visiting lady was shooting like Ravana's evil arrows. Horshop. What did it mean?

"That is too much, Mrs. Robinson." Mummy's voice was as strict as Miss Jamison's. She called out for the chowkidar who came and wrestled Mrs. Robinson out the door; all the while she kept screaming bloody murder. Then there was a banging of the door and a momentary calm. I waited breathlessly in my secret perch until the chowkidar returned.

"She's in a rickshaw," the chowkidar said, between gasps of breath. "I gave him five annas to take her home."

"And you think you deserve to be reimbursed?" Mummy asked in her mouse squeak. "Let this be a lesson. If you ever again admit a wife, I'll have your head!"

I melted back up the stairs and narrated everything about the fight to Bonnie.

"Must have been Leonard's missus." Bonnie stood up, smoothing the dress over her flat stomach. "He's a conductor with the Bengal Nagpur Railway. He comes about every two weeks and spends almost his entire pay."

"But Mummy said to the lady that he never came here!"

"What else could she do? The important thing was to get the ugly bat out before she saw anyone. Lots of railway men come here."

"But why do they come?" I asked, the deepening mystery of the situation overcoming my natural shyness. "Why must I stay upstairs, knowing nothing?"

Bonnie snorted and said, "By now, anyone with sense would know."

Because I didn't belong, I didn't know. Feeling dejected, I dropped my gaze. Then recalling Lucky's advice, I brought up my head and said, "Yes, I am new to this world. I can't know anything unless you tell me."

"Really?" Bonnie laughed lightly, and with a wave of her hand, indicated I should follow her. She rapped lightly on Lucky and Sakina's bedroom door. Lucky answered; she had her petticoat and blouse on, but nothing more. Looking alarmed, she asked, "Don't tell me someone's already here for me!"

"Not to worry yet, dear. Who is in the Lotus Suite?"

Lucky shrugged a slim shoulder. "Natty and a chap from the cantonment, I think."

"Ooh!" Bonnie knelt down and rolled back the flowered carpet on the center of the bedroom floor. Bonnie put a finger to her lips and looked at me with a clear warning. Then she removed a short length of wooden flooring and motioned for me to come behind her. The spying hole was close to a fan set in the ceiling of the bedroom below. The fans whirled continuously, obscuring the view. But I could see part of a very large bed that had its sheets tossed about. I could see a man's back—thick and fair, with some blotches. On either side of the back were bare, golden limbs. They must have been Natty's legs, because it was Natty's throaty voice I heard, calling the man pet names.

I blinked and pulled back, my head spinning from my first sighting of—I could not say what it was, for it was too shocking. I looked behind me and saw Bonnie and Lucky shaking with silent laughter. They were not surprised at all; they did not think it was immoral. Suddenly, I realized that this was what they all did. They were behaving as wives; the men must be paying them for it. No wonder Mrs. Robinson was enraged! It wasn't horshop she had said—but *whore shop*. Was this Bonnie's work—the job I'd innocently asked her about applying for?

"Bonnie-memsaheb? You are wanted for singing downstairs." Premlata's soft voice came from the second-story hall.

Bonnie replaced the wooden piece and rolled back the carpet, then was gone in a whoosh of silk to finish dressing.

"At least it pays well." Lucky was sorting through her jewelry box, pulling out necklaces hung with colorful crystals. "When I was at the temple, I had to do the very same thing, but there was no money paid to me, and I could never refuse anyone. At Rose Villa, bad men aren't allowed back, and we have Dr. DeCruz to keep us from getting sick, and Chief Howard protects us from all other trouble."

"But I can't do that!" I could barely look a male in the face to say hello; how could I be naked with one? And it was not just the doing of it that seemed incomprehensible; it was the embarrassment over something so immoral. That kind of touching was for married people. In my family's small hut, with so many children and grandparents about, I had never caught a whiff of such business going on between my parents. It was a wonder they'd had the privacy to conceive my little brother. And if Pankaj ever learned I'd descended to such behavior, he would burn every one of my letters.

"The men will be pleased that you don't know anything. You must behave that way for a long time." Lucky pulled out a purple silk sari with elaborate gold zari designs. "This is perfect for tonight; some of my customers like to pretend they've got their own temple maiden. They want you to wave incense around their heads and touch their feet: such poor, mixed-up blokes."

They weren't the ones who were mixed up, I thought. It was wrong for the girls to behave as if they were married to these strangers. Yet my friends did not cry about it; in fact, Bonnie had been proud to put so much money in the bank, and I had envied every one of her rupees. I still did.

I realized now that it was good that my family members were dead; they would never know the shame I'd brought to all of them by entering this house of sin. I remembered Miss Rachael mocking me, saying that an unknown girl could do only one job. As much as I'd hated her, she'd predicted the weakness that would bring me, a poor, stupid monkey, into the tigers' cage.

CHAPTER
11

Neither mother nor daughter nor wife are you,
O celestial Urvashi!
In no home do you light the lamp,
when Evening on the pasture alights,
wearily holding her golden skirt.
With halting steps, with throbbing breast and downcast eyes,
to no bridal bed you smiling shyly go in silent midnight.
Unabashed are you, and like the rising dawn, Unveiled.

—Rabindranath Tagore, "Urvashi," 1895

You are a sweet girl, Pamela. And you have the potential to earn more than any of the other girls who are here with me now. Can you guess why?"

From my chair in the parlor across from Mummy, I shook my head. It was ten o'clock the following morning. My eyes were red and tender from weeping almost all night as I debated whether to vanish from the immoral house before dawn broke. I had stayed only because

I was afraid to walk in the night and could not imagine where I would go with the few paise I had left.

Mummy looked at me and began ticking her fingers. "Your English accent is better than anyone's, it's true. And you're quite pretty for a medium-complected Indian. But there's a third thing that you have—actually, that I *hope* you still have—that I must confirm."

The only item of value I'd brought with me was the book of Tagore poetry, but what could that have to do with anything? No, it couldn't be that. Lucky might have told her about the ruby necklace; Mummy might believe I had it and want it for herself.

"You're stiff with fear, darling." Mummy settled herself more comfortably on the settee and patted the space next to her. "Have you never been to a physician?"

I said that I'd been treated by a doctor once, a good Scotsman who'd saved me from cholera. I didn't mention that I'd begged him to let me stay at his clinic as a worker, and that he'd refused. If that had happened, I would not be sitting here, facing such a horrible decision about how to live.

Mummy's breezy voice broke into my regretful thoughts. "All the girls see Dr. DeCruz. After he confirms your innocence and freedom from infection, I will be able to publicize your debut." Mummy explained that if I accepted her offer, I would spend the next month or two learning to dress and make myself up. After becoming presentable, I would be allowed to sit with the girls in the downstairs reception rooms.

"Come, I'll show you." Taking me by the elbow, Mummy brought me on a tour. The first room, still littered with empty glasses and dirty ashtrays, had soft sofas and lounge chairs and an upright piano. It was for Englishmen and had plenty of English books in the cases, too.

As if she'd noticed how longingly I'd looked at the books, Mummy said, "A long while ago, Englishmen had quite a funny name for us: *sleeping dictionaries.*"

I had always loved the word *dictionary*; it spoke both of answers and endless possibilities. But this was a strange-sounding book. I looked at her inquiringly.

"When the first Englishmen sailed over with East India Company, they didn't know a word of any Indian language. How could they progress?" She raised her pencil-thin eyebrows as if expecting an answer, but I had none. "What saved them were women: local girls who became their mistresses, all the while teaching language and good manners so the fellows could speak to the nawabs and get what they wanted. My granny always said that pretty girls built British India through many sleepless nights of hard work!" This she finished with a smirk.

I bit my lip, thinking of all Pankaj and I had written to each other about the unfairness of British rule. How terrible that Indian women helped the enemy succeed. And it angered me that these men had mocked them by using the name of the most important book in my life.

"You can bite your lip the first time you meet a man!" Mummy interjected, interrupting my thoughts. "But not constantly. Come, there's more to see."

Another parlor was for Anglo-Indians, decorated similarly but with a Victrola for playing records instead of the piano. The last parlor had a highly polished swing, sitting beds spread with fresh sheets, and a platform with Indian musical instruments. This room was intended for my race only. Mummy said that, historically, the British would not visit brothels where Indian men went because of suspicion of communicable disease. But I imagined the divisions were also because each group disliked the other and thus could not bear to sit together. I guessed that Pankaj would never enter such a place, no matter how fine the furnishings; it was outside his moral code. There was no danger of his coming here and discovering me, but I hated the thought of losing myself to customers, instead of waiting for him.

Mummy pledged that she would show me to everyone. It would

only help raise my price. After enough suitable offers were placed, she would accept the highest bidder. She promised that I would not be hurt and that the money I would earn from the debut night would be more than most of her girls earned in a month. She would take only half, as was her custom. Room and board would be deducted from my portion, but I could bank the remainder or have her keep it in her bedroom lockbox.

"Most of our girls like the convenience of having their cash in-house; but it is up to you to decide later." I felt her eyes on me, as if she knew how much I wanted the money. "I ask you to stay on with us for a full month after your debut. The first time you are with a man is not a good indicator of what things will be like. It always gets better."

To walk in front of men I didn't know. To be given to whoever paid the most. To have my most private place made public. All of it laid out so crassly made me feel like fainting. Again, I thought of Pankaj waiting in Calcutta, alone with his heartbreak. In a small voice, I said, "You once said that I could leave."

"Of course you may still leave!" Mummy's posture straightened. "Go on your way! Your old clothes have been washed, and you are welcome to take them and whatever else you have upstairs. But what are your choices, Pamela? If you fall into the hands of ruffians, you will find yourself in a situation much worse than this, and for that you'll receive a few annas and no shortage of abuse."

So many times I should have died already: first in the great tidal wave, next from cholera, and then in custody of the police. All of these horrors I had managed to escape through my own actions. Rose Barker was right. I had to put away my schoolgirl dreams about Pankaj Bandopadhyay to accept the only work for which I was qualified.

Mummy's tiger eyes were looking at me sadly; there were even tears blurring their black rims. I did not believe these tears, but I understood that she was offering me my best chance to prosper and never fear a night without shelter. And despite the shame I felt about such business, I had never eaten so well before—or been able to wash

myself so comfortably—or sleep between soft sheets at night, surrounded by friends.

I told myself I was not the same person anymore. The happy peasant girl called Pom had been washed away in a flood, and the servant
girl Sarah had vanished before the police had come. Who was left?
Pamela, the girl everyone thought was pretty and well spoken. Pamela
could earn packets of money to keep in the bank: money that could
take her wherever she wanted to go.

As I said yes in a low voice to Mummy, I knew that I did not miss
being Sarah. But in my heart, I still cried for Pom.

❧   ❧   ❧

AFTER THAT CONVERSATION, things happened quickly. It
started with a visit from Dr. DeCruz. The experience was even more
humiliating than I had expected: lying on a bed in one of the suites
while he poked at me with metal things, looking at the secret place I
had never even seen for myself. The doctor said that I would be subject to such physical examinations from him twice monthly.

"That, of course, is nothing compared to regulations of days of
old." He elaborated that, in the past, prostitutes with symptoms who
were working at the official British military brothels were forcibly kept
in a place called a lock hospital. But his modern medicines could cure
almost anything; he said I should never hide painful symptoms or delayed menses. He also showed me gruesome pictures of men's private
parts, which he explained showed symptoms of various diseases. If
I were wise, I would avoid anyone showing such signs and inform
Mummy.

Dr. DeCruz looked as Indian as I did, but his name meant that
he'd had a Portuguese ancestor, someone who had probably done to
an Indian woman what Mummy's Ingrej customers were doing today.
There was a cross inside his bag, and I guessed he might be Catholic.
I wondered whether it was wrong for someone of his faith to perform

such assistance to Rose Villa. I asked Bonnie about this, and she re-minded me that prostitution was legal in India and the doctor was obliged to serve the needs of the British just like everyone else.

The following day a seamstress came to measure me, and while I stood in Bonnie's bedroom, half dressed and shivering, she, Lucky, and Mummy discussed a series of costumes to be made. There would be pink, yellow, and white nightgowns trimmed with lace, a pretend school uniform, various saris, and a dancing girl's costume with a tiny blouse and full, low-waisted skirt. English dresses were cut for me as well, but I would not be allowed to wear them until I could walk properly in high heels, which I now practiced for an hour daily, making circles around the small veranda and along the garden paths. Every-thing was happening in a way that made it possible for me to think only of clothes and grooming and advertising, not of the upcoming act that would change me forever.

Mummy sat at the desk in the parlor, chewing a pencil while she struggled to write an advertisement that would run in the Kharagpur and Calcutta papers. *Exotic Indian Rosebud has joined the bevvie of beautys in Khargpur. For details about debut, write to Box 247 or tele-phone KH912.* She showed it to me, and despite my misgivings about the whole business, I felt compelled to correct her spelling.

Bonnie and Lucky taught me about French letters, lambskin sheaths that I practiced rolling over bananas until the girls deemed me proficient. I couldn't imagine anything the size of a fruit fitting into me; when I expressed my worries, they both laughed. But then Lucky became serious and warned that some customers would attempt to convince me against using French letters, and I would need to stand firm.

"You have noticed there are no children here," Lucky said. "Hear-ing babies cry and children chatter reminds men of their own brats at home, so they aren't allowed. If your belly swells, you cannot stay here. And then there's disease, of course. The soldiers especially can shoot diseases inside you!"

"Lucky, stop! Pam already saw Dr. DeCruz's pictures. You will be fine," Bonnie said to me. "Just remember that the French letters are kept in the ebony box on top of each nightstand. You don't even have to open a drawer to get one."

Learning my way around the lovers' suites was another task. The beds were larger, and the nightstands next to them were filled with various accessories the girls took giggling pains to explain. And the thing about it was, for my first time—actually, the first dozen times—I was to behave as if I knew about none of these sticks and scarves and feathers; to behave with modesty and fear, as would befit a virgin. I nodded, thinking to myself that surely I would never be bold enough to use the things.

One week turned into two, and inquiries about me kept coming. Every evening, I was dressed in the schoolgirl uniform, with my hair oiled and plaited, but with bare legs disappearing into Bonnie's treacherous high-heeled pumps. Carrying a copy of *Lady Chatterley's Lover*, I would come down the stairs when summoned to the parlor.

This was the hardest part, for it meant facing men who were mostly English: the most terrifying individuals I could imagine. *Blue-eyed devils*, I remembered the children saying to one another in Johlpur. I was supposed to face these devils as they drank whiskey and looked me over with bad purposes in mind. My dreams of discussing great books with Pankaj had faded, just as the sun had set outside the villa's shuttered windows.

The only way I could calm my breathing was when Bonnie was with me. Sometimes, while we awaited being chosen, Bonnie sang film songs while one of the gents played the piano. Her encouragement, whether it was a wink, an arm around my shoulders, or kind compliments, kept me from fleeing. Her singing cheered me into thinking we were playing roles in the cinema—that this was only pretend.

"Our Pamela once attended one of the finest boarding schools in Darjeeling, and her nature is friendly and intelligent," Mummy would say. "Darling, won't you read from Mr. D. H. Lawrence's brilliant book to us? It is so provocative."

And I would read until Mummy would say something like, "Up to bed, now, darling, it's time for you to get your rest. You have a very big event coming up, whenever the right man comes to gently-gently teach you the ways of the world. . . ."

I would stand up and clumsily drop my book to the floor, resulting in one or two men in the room having the chance to watch me bend over for it. At least I couldn't see their faces: that was the only saving grace of this humiliating exposure.

Each night, more men came, and the telephone rang with inquiries as far as Calcutta. Mummy ran a second announcement, saying that bids on the Exotic Indian Rosebud would close in five days' time. My official age had dropped from fifteen to just fourteen; but my lineage had escalated. Mummy claimed that I was the daughter of the concubine of a nawab who had sponsored my schooling until a terrible stroke had felled him. The Englishmen nodded and smiled at the story, showing their narrow yellow teeth. One man even boasted that he'd been to dinner at the same nawab's palace. For Englishmen, image and self-importance were everything; even when talking to a brothel owner.

"What should my last name be?" I pondered aloud to Lucky one sunny September morning when we rode a rickshaw into the Gole Bazar. Lucky was *on leave*, as everyone politely termed the seven-day abstinence for menstruation. Because she had the time, she'd been tasked with picking up the July 1935 *Photoplay* downtown and to bringing me to a cobbler to order my first pair of proper high-heeled shoes.

"That's right; to have a bank account you need a surname. The girls with bank accounts use the name Barker—" Lucky broke off because her attention had been taken by the banging and shouting sounds from a nearby street.

As we'd walked from where the rickshaw-wallah dropped us toward the shops, I heard a dull roar coming from somewhere, but I had not paid mind until now, when the sound was close enough to distinguish as male voices. As their shouts grew close, Lucky pulled me into the doorway of a newsagent, and this made me nervous, too. The shop's grille door was pulled down to the ground, even though it was already noon. Lucky rattled the grille, calling for someone to open it. A small middle-aged man wearing a wrinkled shirt and dhoti grudgingly came to lift the grille open but closed it quickly after we had entered.

"You should buy something after what I did for you." The man's eyes raked us, as I'd learned was always the case when men recognized us. Rose Villa girls did not look like ordinary Kharagpur women, which meant that boys as young as eight and very old men, too, looked boldly and made vile noises.

"Of course. Thank you, Lahiri-babu," Lucky said, giving him a cheeky smile that was all empty promise. Through the bars of the window, we watched the throng of men, dressed in white with matching Congress caps just like the people who had challenged Bidushi and me outside the sari shop.

"Are they Congress Party?" I asked the news-wallah, who was staring out the grille along with us.

"Yes, they are, and do you see the green-and-white flags? That is for the Muslim League. They are together with the Congress Party in political protest as they have done before. A few years ago there was a terrible event at Hijli Detention Camp. At the time, some prisoners were cheering because they had just heard that an English judge had been killed: one who had given a death sentence to a freedom fighter."

"I have heard very little about it; tell me more, please," I said, remembering hearing some vague mention of a prison massacre in one of Pankaj's letters.

"The jailers at Hijli were so angry about the rejoicing prisoners that they shot into the cell and killed two men and injured many others. Most people were afraid to protest that year, but today it seems different." The clerk looked out the window, and his expression seemed almost proud.

"It's better that Natty and Bonnie and Doris are still at home," Lakshmi murmured in my ear.

I nodded, thinking it could be dangerous for English-looking girls to be in town at such a time. With my eyes, I continued to follow the stream of marchers. Not all wore Congress caps; some wore high Sikh turbans or small crocheted Muslim caps. But most were Hindus with tika marks smeared on their foreheads showing they had worshipped before joining the procession. Their signs bobbed up and down: *RE-MEMBER THE FALLEN HEROES. FOR OUR MOTHER COUNTRY, WE STAND READY TO DIE.* Even more forceful than these words were the faces bearing expressions somewhere between elation and violence.

"They're not going to bother Indian merchants," Mr. Lahiri said, as if he'd noticed my staring at the lathi carriers. "I've been hanging a Congress flag for several days."

"Where will those people go with their lathis?" Lucky asked wonderingly. "They might smash something to pieces: hopefully, not the cinema or the bank!"

"They may be going to the Masonic temple."

Lucky and I exchanged glances. We had never been inside the place that had nothing to do with worship. It was the seat of the society of Masons who were all English, many of them part of the railway administration. Indians surrounding their precious building would make them feel trapped, the way I had been when the floodwaters rose up around the tree.

"We should see for ourselves. Look, lots of others are following," I said, noticing some townspeople emerging from their houses to join the wake of the procession.

"Of course we can't go—it's dangerous." Lucky was busy paging through the *Photoplay*. "Lahiri-babu, I will buy this magazine. Thank you so very much for giving us shelter."

"Let's just go a little bit farther," I said to Lucky once we'd stepped outside. I felt like a tremendous happening was afoot, and I felt like I wanted to see a little bit more. I'd never seen Indians standing up to the British; the idea of it gave me a thrill.

"Okay, just a bit," she agreed, her expression dubious. We joined hands to keep from being forced apart. We moved with the crowd into the larger street, passing the bank that was indeed shuttered, its entrance guarded not by one guard but by a line of two dozen guards wearing khaki uniforms and small, round black hats, carrying lathis and rifles. The marchers now appeared to be about three hundred strong. A few dozen police holding guns lined the borders of the street. For the first time, I felt a quiver.

"Go home now. This is your final warning!" A tall officer spoke into a metal cone. A chill ran through me. But a corresponding roar came from the people surging toward the police, pelting them with sandals and rocks. Then, at the first rifle shot, the shouting turned to screams. Now the police had dissolved into the crowd and were hitting the men and boys with lathis. I heard the sound of wood breaking bone, more shots and screams, wails and bellows of anger from all sides. My stomach clenched as I realized this would not be the spectacle I'd hoped for but a dangerous melee.

Lucky pulled my hand so hard I could not ignore it. I finally understood that if we stayed, we would be hurt. As we hurried against the procession's tide, I saw police heading for us. One constable raised his lathi overhead; but his companion shouted something that made him put it down.

"Run home to Mummy, girls. Not the place for you!" the second policeman said to us, with a kind of half leer. My cheeks burned with embarrassment. Too many people could tell our background without our saying a word. I was ashamed of this and also for not being as brave as the people who wouldn't run and were suffering the consequence. I could never be the kind of freedom fighter that Pankaj had written about.

Five minutes later, we had found a rickshaw on the outskirts and were on our way back to Rose Villa.

"I'm not going shopping with you again," Lucky said in a shaking

voice. "My new magazine's torn, I lost a heel, and if that English policeman says something about us to Chief Howard or Mummy, we will
be ruined. Mummy wants no conflict with the British whatsoever."

Lucky warned me not to say anything at tea about what happened, so I didn't. We just passed around the *Photoplay* magazine. By
the next day, however, the riot was public knowledge. The servants
reported that in the downtown section, one man died and three dozen
people, including women and children, had severe injuries. I knew
that we were fortunate to have escaped when we did, but I still felt
like a coward.

❦   ❦   ❦

IN THE NEXT week, Mummy accepted 401 rupees for me from the
Marwari merchant who had bought Doris's virginity years ago. He'd
come in from Calcutta by train and would not leave Kharagpur, he
said, until he'd had his satisfaction. I asked Mummy about the odd
number, and she said plus one was for good luck. But I didn't feel as
fortunate as everyone thought I should.

That evening, while he was paying Mummy downstairs, I took a
hot bath scented with rosewater. My thoughts turned to Bidushi and
our long-ago imaginings of her wedding. I was glad that Bidushi would
never know about tonight. How disappointed she would have been
to learn that the first male hands touching me were not a handsome
bridegroom's but those of a wrinkled old man. And Pankaj! I was sure
he would not remember me, nor would he understand that I would
always wish for him, no matter what I'd become.

Briefly, I thought of submerging myself so I would drown: the
death that by all rights should have been mine five years ago. But I
could not, because the other girls kept coming in to wish me well.
When I was drying off in the bedroom, Bonnie delivered a cup of
warm milk with saffron that she said would relax me. The more I
drank, the dizzier I became. Through the haze, I knew that I should

have stayed in the protest march in town and not come back to Rose Villa. Now it was too late. Almost a hundred rupees had been spent on my clothing and food and such; I could not possibly pay it back to Mummy.

Bonnie took me by the hand into the Lotus Suite. I wore no jewelry, only perfumed skin cream and a transparent lace nightdress. I lay on the bed with eyes tightly shut and did not open them even when the stranger came into the room. But then he made me stand up and dance for him while he slowly clapped his hands and sang. So I had to open my eyes to keep from falling down.

In the room's pink light, I saw a man the age of my own grandfather, but heavy and with a face like a ghoul. How wrong it was for him to use a girl my age; to make me stand and take off the nightdress for the dance. When he finally bade me to lie down, I thought that at least I could close my eyes against his contorted, pockmarked features. But his hands, with their moist, worm-like fingers, were everywhere.

Inside my mind, a horrible film was playing. I was out on the street seeing the enraged faces of the English officers and the Indian constables and protesters. The camera moved closer to show the pursed lips of the little boys spitting at the police and the open mouths of their worried mothers calling them back. And then it showed the townsmen with their lathis, hitting so hard. The fighting had moved inside me: blow after blow after blow; pain and pushing, all at the same time.

"You are only hurting yourself by moving. Stay still!" he huffed into my face with breath that smelled like onions.

I had changed my mind about everything. But as I struggled to get out from under the man, he moved his elbows so that I was pinned in place. All I could hear was *still . . . still. . . .*

I was too weak to fight him. Despite my drugged mind, I understood that I could not escape this man or the other customers who would come after. The same horrible scene would replay each night, in an endless loop.

CHAPTER
12

My trial is hard indeed. Just when I want a helpmate most,
I am thrown back on myself. Nevertheless, I record my vow
that even in this trial I shall win through. Alone, then, shall
I tread my thorny path to the end of this life's journey.

—Rabindranath Tagore, *The Home and the World*, 1919

No longer was I considered a girl. At fifteen, I was a working lady. This was hard for me to understand, because I did not look any older than before, but I was earning thirty rupees a day, on par with the top earners: Bonnie, Lucky, and Natty. This was not because I was any good at my work. Every time I lay down, my mind blacked out. I ran away to the cupboard of my childhood memories, burying myself in the fairy tales, songs, and stories once told by my mother. And I felt that through all of it, Ma was holding my hand. She comforted me from her faraway place and kept me alive.

My mental absence was not noticed by the men. They saw me as new, and that was enough. Five more times, Mummy sold me as a first-time debut. So many men thought they had won the auction that they were truly delighted and did not notice the small vial of chicken blood I used. And as for the French letters—how they pleaded against using them, since I was supposedly innocent. Yet I mustered my courage to dress their members with the sheaths, all the while murmuring praise and endearments. I had caught no diseases, Dr. DeCruz said with satisfaction after I visited him each fortnight. No babies, either.

The one thing I'd caught was sadness. All the money was not enough to make up for the way my heart sank every time a customer sitting in the parlor pointed at me. I understood what it meant, but I didn't know whether he would be straightforward or a game player. Or whether he would be quick or someone who would thrust for an hour or force me to keep my mouth open too long.

The other Roses took pity on me, trying to teach me what I could do to make the man reach satisfaction more quickly. Doris said a woman's best weapon was her tongue—and with Doris's repertoire, the proverb took on new meanings. Natty had a special skill at humiliating gentlemen. She said that the ones who'd gone to boarding schools in England liked that especially.

One skill everyone felt seriously about developing was called woman's intuition. This was the way a woman understood another's feelings through listening carefully and noticing slight physical cues. Just by looking at a man's shoulders or the movement of his eyes or hearing the pitch of his voice, one could determine whether he would be easy or difficult, kind or selfish. Woman's intuition could be used to read anyone, even females: Bonnie explained how she'd known I was desperate for shelter when she saw me slumped on the bench; the *Statesman* on my lap told her that I had advanced English skills.

Just as I'd suspected, the way I spoke English was my greatest asset. In the dark bedchambers on the second floor, customers called me Anne or Margaret and other names of girls they had lost or never had in the first place. Without being told, I understood I was to say that I desired them, loved them, and would be theirs forever. Sometimes, they would stay in bed with me for hours, just talking. That type of encounter was the best, for it earned me a lot of extra pay without a moment of pain.

Outside the suites, I used my intuition to learn more about the secret lives of the others. Beside Natty's bedroom door each morning was an empty bottle of whiskey. Sakina's room was perpetually fogged with a haze of opium smoke. I did not smoke or drink yet, but I wondered if I might need to later on, when the reality of what was happening finally drove the fairy tales out of my mind.

Sometimes I dreamed of Pankaj's sad, handsome face and a grand house with a marble staircase leading up to a bedroom without spy holes or boxes of French letters: just a plain white bed covered with pink and red rose petals. In these dreams, I was not Pamela but Bidushi in a lovely bride's sari, with a ruby hanging from the neck. That jewel remained my lodestone for that which was beautiful and pure.

It had crossed my mind that the loss of Bidushi's ruby was what had taken the life spirit from her. If only Bidushi had lived and I had been able to accompany her to Calcutta as an ayah and live the rest of my life at the edge of her and Pankaj's marriage. Then I'd not be dreaming of the ruby on my neck. The gem would only touch my hands when she gave it to me for polishing, and I would help her to keep from never losing it, in order that one day, it would pass to her firstborn daughter.

My refuge for such imaginings was the bed I slept in at the end of each night with Bonnie. With her on the other side, breathing softly, I could sometimes trick myself into feeling that I was in the hut in Johlpur with my sisters nearby. I felt so close to Bonnie. So when she asked if I'd take a matinee with her and Chief Howard one day, I agreed. It was not that I was eager for her touch, but a prearranged job meant time away from the choosing parlors that evening.

"We sleep together every night, don't we? It will be easy." Bonnie winked as we went together to the Hibiscus Suite with the big red bed and overhead mirror. "Just follow what I'm doing and listen to what he wants. He's really just an overgrown child."

✲   ✲   ✲

MR. HOWARD WAS chief of the Kharagpur police and protected Mummy's business from trouble. And even if the Midnapore police had alerted their nearby colleagues about a jewel theft, I doubted that any description of a young servant girl with a messy braid could be matched with what I looked like now, dressed in fine silk, with glossy hair that fell freely to the middle of my back, kohl-lined eyes, and hands and feet as soft as satin.

The chief arrived in his khaki uniform, complete with pith helmet, lathi, and pistol. In the suite, Bonnie helped him take off his clothing, all the while shooting me looks to do something more than pick at the bedspread. I took his shirt, still steamy and pungent, to hang out on the clothes press as we always did for the customers while they rested. His trousers were of the same material but very long. As I folded them over my arm to bring to the press, the chief called out for me not to remove them from the bed's footboard.

"Bobby sometimes likes me to wear the pants, doesn't he?" Bonnie giggled.

I wished I could speak with her privately. When I'd touched the trousers, I'd felt an object in the front right pocket. It was hard and thin. A rush of fear went through me as I worried it might be a knife. But he would not use a weapon on girls he liked. Mummy had always said her customers were Kharagpur's leading gentlemen. And he had taken it upon himself to be Rose Villa's protector.

As I arranged the chief's uniform, Bonnie finished undressing him, and herself as well, and then gave me a meaningful look. Dutifully, I stripped off all my clothes and went to join in. I should have been familiar with Bonnie's nakedness. But in our bedroom, I'd always kept my eyes respectfully averted. Now she was reaching toward me, making it impossible not to really see her. How very slim she was: much like a classical statue from a history book, with a narrow waist and hips and small high breasts without nipples. I realized as she drew my hands to her breasts that she did have nipples, but very small ones. The thatch between her legs was light, too: an unearthly blond, but I knew this came from a peroxide soak on the villa roof.

How different Bonnie and I appeared reflected in the round mirror: light and dark, curvy and boyish. Day and moonlight. From the way Chief Howard was rubbing himself, I sensed that he liked the contrast. With a happy laugh, he shouted to Bonnie to open his briefcase. With one graceful hand, she drew out a length of gold cloth.

"Sir, you've brought your turban again! Goody!" Bonnie clapped, but I sensed it was only the beginning of something strange.

"She'll know how to wrap it; she's from a nawab's palace," the chief said, pointing a long finger at me. "Tonight I'm playing maharajah with my old wife and a new one."

"Don't call me old, Bobby!" Bonnie tipped up her nose at him, all the while showing me how to kneel on the bed in front of the major so he could play with my breasts as I tied on the shimmering cloth. In a warm voice, she stroked my hips from behind and sang out her lines. "Sir, I am only waiting to serve and give you every pleasure you deserve!"

I hadn't seen Bonnie work before, but I was quite impressed with her musicality. I was having a harder time with the turban. Growing up in Johlpur, I'd never seen anyone wearing a turban except for itinerant holy men. I certainly had never wrapped a man's head with one. But I tried to seem comfortable as I rolled the gaudy length around the man's balding pate, averting my eyes from his face. When I'd finished, the police chief did not at all look Indian, but reminded me of the pictures of wizards in children's books. His eyes twinkled at me and he whispered that my job would be to bring Bonnie to good pleasure. If I could do this, my life would be spared.

"She will service us both, Rajah," Bonnie said, draping a possessive leg over him and giving me a sultry look. What was I to do? I had never trained on women. Her parts were not like his. I could only hope she'd pretend with me the way we all did with the customers.

Bonnie rolled from side to side, arching her back. She murmured, "Touch me as you'd like to be touched, darling! It's as simple as that."

But it wasn't. I'd had some strong feelings when I'd thought about Pankaj and his letters, but I had never imagined being touched in turn. Over the last half year, so many men stroked, pinched, and poked me, I could not match any of these movements with feelings of pleasure. I was frozen as I looked at Bonnie undulating on the bed, and I wondered how to proceed: top or bottom?

In his pretend rajah's accent, the chief said: "Rajah's pet will play, too." He rolled onto his side and then moved his hands and knees to the foot of the bed where his pants lay. I whipped my head around to catch him reaching in the pocket. He brought out an object carefully, but it half escaped from his hand, and I caught my breath.

It was a snake. A short brown one. I was so horrified I could not even say anything. I just clapped my hand over my mouth. The chief was keeping the creature low so Bonnie couldn't see it. In any case, she didn't notice; she was quite involved in chattering to me.

"Be a good pet, Pammy. Fluff my fur and brush it," she said. "There is a little brush in the nightstand, remember. . . ."

I glanced from her to the major, who was crawling determinedly forward, keeping his hand with the snake out of sight. His eyes gleamed at the sight of Bonnie's parted thighs and in the midst of my grooming her, he suddenly lunged forward. The snake's head snapped, and Bonnie caught sight of it coming toward her womanly place. In an instant, her pale face had gone all white and her eyes rolled back in her head. Then she jerked and collapsed on the pillows.

The chief was still laughing and trying to show Bonnie the snake, not noticing her collapse. Filled with fear and sorrow, I gently lifted Bonnie's arm, which fell limply to her side. Then I shouted "Bonnie!" in her ear.

Her lack of response told me death must have been instantaneous, although it was so recent she was still warm. Looking at her, I felt the same hollow feeling in my stomach when I'd seen Bidushi's covered corpse. This was a terrible way to die; and I would not let myself be the next victim. With my heart pounding, I jumped from the bed and ran straight out into the hall.

"Bonnie's dead! Chief Howard killed her!"

At my screamed words, I heard a murmuring begin in some rooms; but I wanted to be sure Mummy downstairs heard, too. I shouted again, "Bonnie's been killed! Chief Howard's snake must have bitten her!" and I heard the sounds of people moving behind the doors, and soon men were running out, half dressed; they were not coming into the Hibiscus Suite, although I'd left the door wide open, but running downstairs, one after the other.

Mummy lumbered up the stairs. "What in hell are you shouting about? Look at you naked in the hallway! No shame!"

I had been so scared I hadn't taken time to dress. Panting, I said, "He killed Bonnie with a snake—"

"Hardly!" said Mummy, walking into the bedroom. Bonnie still lay spread on the bed, unmoving; the chief had his pants on and was furiously buttoning his shirt. He had forgotten about the turban on his head.

"Stuff and nonsense!" he said, pointing a finger at me. "All I brought was a toy. A little pretend snake."

"Show me," Mummy said, and he put it in her hands; now I could see it was made of many wooden pieces that fit together and painted to look like a snake's skin. "Pamela, this is a common toy from the bazar. Any fool can see!"

"Oh. Then Bonnie must have died of—fright." I heard my voice falter and hated myself for having been so stupid.

"Very doubtful!" Mummy slapped Bonnie's face hard; and before my amazed eyes, her head turned.

"What happened?" my friend said hazily, lifting a long arm to her brow.

"You saw a toy, lost your senses, and your little friend caused a near riot," Mummy said briskly. "Every other customer in the house had fled and the most important of all, Chief Howard, has been inconvenienced."

"Bobby, I'm so sorry, but I am deathly afraid of snakes—" Bonnie shuddered. "Is it still here?"

"Take the damn thing with you!" Mummy said, shoving it in my hand. "Go upstairs. Wash yourself. There are other customers waiting downstairs, and if you're lucky, they haven't heard what you've done."

"Come back to me, Bobby," Bonnie murmured weakly. "We can get another girl in for the double—"

"No. The mood's spoiled," he said, and with angry, swift movements, he began dressing himself.

Later on, after the man departed and new customers had arrived, Rose Villa settled into normalcy. In our bedroom, Bonnie slowly drank a whiskey and slipped into a fresh dress. Passing me on her way out the door, she put a hand on my shoulder.

"Buck up." She gave me a half smile. "I know you only did it because of worry."

Relief flooded my tight body, because I was so glad she had survived. That was the important thing to remember, not the shame. "Bonnie, I'm very sorry, but I honestly thought you had been struck dead—"

She held a finger up like a teacher, and her eyes burned into mine. "Pamela, a lot of things will happen here that look like something fearful but really are not. You'll manage it, if you're tough. But do remember: don't tell on the men. They hate it."

※   ※   ※

FALL TURNED TO winter and then spring. I pushed down the shame of the Snake Mistake, as everyone was calling it, and kept working. Enough money was flowing into the house that Mummy continued to treat me well, and after paying her my room and board fees, and making my bank deposit, I allotted myself four rupees per week spending money for clothing and books. I struck an arrangement with a bookseller to return books I'd read for half of what I'd paid. Most of them I gave back: but not the Brontës nor the Austens, not Shaw's *Pygmalion* and certainly not *The Home and the World*, the famous Bengali novel by my beloved Rabindranath Tagore. I lost myself in the plight of the character Bimala, torn between a good husband who loved her and a dashing activist who persuaded her to steal for him without so much as saying a word.

I was mulling over the book's difficult ending when Premlata rapped on the door to tell me that Mummy wished to see me. I was only half dressed in my blouse and petticoat, so I quickly wrapped myself in a sari and went out to the veranda, where she sat with her accounting book.

"A special customer whom you haven't met will arrive this evening." Mummy gave me her most insincere smile. "He's called Mr. Ralph Abernathy and is the acting superintendent at the Hijli Detention Camp. His favorite girl here is Natty, but as you know, she is on leave."

"Yes, I heard." I was thinking of the name *Hijli*. Last fall, the newsagent had told Lucky and me about the slaughter of prisoners there who'd made the mistake of celebrating an Englishman's death. Perhaps Mr. Abernathy had shot one of them himself. I felt even more querulous about this unknown man than I had Chief Howard. "He telephoned that he will be arriving later this evening, so I'm giving him to you," Mummy said. "He does not like to sit in the parlor with others but goes directly to the room. You will meet him there wearing only some good lingerie. And scent is very important. What kinds of perfumes do you have?"

"Just sandalwood and jasmine. Mummy, what about Doris or Bonnie—wouldn't an Anglo-Indian girl suit him better?" I was loath to be anywhere near a prison officer.

"Not in this case. He's been with Natty a very long time, and if he finds he prefers one of the others, well, there will be a catfight the likes we've never had. You're not in that group and"—here she lowered her voice—"he's a bit different, in his tastes. He requires special patience. You've got that in spades, and really, my dear, you have no choice in the matter."

※　※　※

NATTY'S MONTHLY MADE her not only idle but also cross, demanding sweets from the kitchen and back massages from Premlata. I found the girl curled up in bed with a hot-water bottle and *Vanity Fair*. I told her Mummy was assigning me to Mr. Abernathy and begged her to explain what was different about him. Natty rolled her eyes and said, "Prepare yourself for a very long, boring night with the Taster. God help you if you're ticklish."

"The Taster?" I asked, feeling confused.

"Just listen." In vulgar terms, Natty told me how Mr. Abernathy's pattern was to spend upward of an hour laying out food on her body and then eating it with his hands and mouth. He would rarely desire sexual congress—just this ritual. I should know it was coming if he brought any restaurant packages or tiffin boxes.

"Of course he's fat," Natty drawled. "That's why I call him the Taster. I imagine he's dining morning, noon, and night—and at all points in between! Imagine, coming into town to see a girl and not being able to stop chewing one's cud for a bloody minute!"

"What kind of food does he eat?" I could bear a lot but not to be treated like a plate on which hot, oily food was dropped.

"Restaurant food: usually Indian and Chinese. One time he brought English food from his canteen. Beef." From the look in her eyes, I knew she was trying to terrify me, so I thanked her for the information and left.

There was scant time before his arrival, so I quickly slipped down to the kitchen. I resolved that I was going to do this well. I'd satisfy the man, earn my money, and keep Natty from mocking me for failure.

When the Taster arrived an hour later, I was on the side of the bed wearing violet silk camiknickers. I rose, and without even looking at him, bent forward to respectfully touch his feet; but he caught my hands in his, pulling me to stand just inches away from him. He was big, but to my relief, not as grossly heavy as I'd expected. But he'd brought two tiffin boxes.

"What's this?" he raised my hands to his nose.

"Cardamom. Good evening, sir. My name is Pamela." From underneath my lashes, I judged him to be somewhere in his forties. He had likely been in India twenty years or more.

"Of course, I've heard of you. Highest virgin price paid in Khargpur since Natty." He inhaled my hands again. "So what do they have you doing, working the kitchen? You smell like that pudding. What do you call it in Hindustani?"

"Kheer," I replied, my heart thumping at the gamble I'd taken. "Sir, I hear you enjoy a feast, so I prepared one for you."

"Where?"

"It is invisible!" I said, turning my head so he could bring his mouth to my neck and discover the smell and taste of fennel seed. As he undressed me, he found it all: the cloves inside the bend of my elbow, the turmeric on my shoulders, the saffron paste that tipped my breasts.

When I'd sprinkled some parts of my body with spices, I'd hoped to distract the Taster enough that he wouldn't put any of his own smelly food on me. And as I lay passively, letting him taste the hills and plains of my body, it did seem that he'd forgotten about his tiffin boxes.

The Taster was excited, groaning his guesses of the various spices. Privately, I thought that his endurance—or rather, the muscular ability of his lips and tongue—was astonishing. Nothing that Natty had said prepared me for how invasive and disturbing this was. I had thought that by choosing the spices, I'd feel like I was in control; but I wasn't. It was time to take a fantasy trip somewhere else, so I told myself the touch was nothing, that one day, there would be no more men like Chief Howard and Mr. Abernathy with their oddities and perversions; they'd be gone from India, because the freedom fighters would get out of jail and fight them to the death. And I'd help them all I could by telling them the men's names, the weapons they carried on their persons, and the days they came regularly to Rose Villa and could be easily surprised.

But my thoughts were not enough to change anything. And it was my bad fortune that I had intrigued the Taster so much that he decided not to go back to Natty. At first, I was surprised that she minded so much, but she didn't like being shown up, and she was missing the income. To hurt me, Natty played little tricks to show Mummy I wasn't a good worker. It wasn't the case, for I now had a faithful group of about ten gentlemen who were likely to book in advance. It was my almost-English accent and the other language I'd learned of physical deception: making parts of my body rigid, and other parts tremble and quake, as if what these men were doing was as pleasurable for me as it was for them. These talents were almost eliminating my need to compete against the other girls in the downstairs parlors and ensured my savings' growth. I hoped to have enough saved in ten months to escape the life and perhaps enroll myself in a school somewhere, to complete my education and even take the Cambridge examinations that were needed to become a teacher. I could not think that Pankaj would ever accept me, given what had happened at Rose Villa; but at least I could make myself anew.

This was the only thing I was sure of: my ability to make money. Love and lust were other matters. What continued to surprise me, as the months continued, was how different the man's and woman's experiences were. The men all seemed to enjoy themselves very much. Yet I shared none of the excitement in my flesh or mind, and, in fact, there were still occasions that intercourse hurt like daggers, and I would beg

Mummy to let me off the rest of the night so I would be comfortable enough to work the following day. Mummy didn't like it but acquiesced because she did not want to lose multiple days of income from me.

Those few nights that I took leave felt like paradise. If I didn't have something from the bookshop, I'd drop into one of the empty parlors, take a book, and vanish upstairs. It was interesting how many books in the English language had been written about fallen young women: *Clarissa, Tess of the d'Urbervilles, Fanny Hill.* I was the only one who liked these books; the others preferred film and celebrity magazines, or anything about film or fashion in the Calcutta newspapers.

Their annoying habit of cutting out photographs and adverts forced me to rise early to read the entire newspaper before it was cut to pieces. Those days, the news pages were full of a so-called German Problem—something nobody in the house really understood. I had not heard talk of it among the Indian Army officers in the parlor at Rose Villa, so one evening, I decided to ask the Taster as we'd finished and he was sitting up with pillows behind his back, eating a real beef dinner off a tray.

"There will be war here in India before Europe." He spoke while still chewing. "There are too many rabble-rousers in India these days, with the meetings and processions and nonsense."

I wasn't satisfied with the answer, so I said, "How could there really be a war here? Indians have no arms to use."

"Of course they do. The bandits who attack the wealthy jamidars in the countryside steal arms from their treasuries or enough money to buy arms easily on the black market. The prisons are full of thieves."

"How do guns reach the black market?" I asked. One day, I would use this information; I was sure of it.

"They're brought by the crooked native constables, of course, reporting a gun broken or lost—you can't trust anyone." He stretched one monstrous hand to grip me under the sheets. "Ah, here's a fine black market! What is inside?"

I shifted away, laughing as if it were a game. I'd already served him once; I didn't want to again, especially with him in the midst of a beef dinner.

"But why are you asking, my little morsel?" he persisted playfully. "Are you thinking of picking me off?"

"Oh, no, sir," I lied. "Then I would be too lonely. Won't you tell me that funny story again—the one about eating the Christmas pudding all by yourself when you were young?"

"Only if you'll play the Christmas pudding."

❋　　❋　　❋

MR. ABERNATHY HAD been talking about Indians hitting the English; but in the *Statesman* newspaper I read later that spring, I saw an article about Calcutta boys throwing stones at the police. All of them had been dragged out of their homes later that evening, thrashed, and thrown in prison. Their lawyer was pleading that the wrong boys had been wrongly arrested as all named parties were reportedly in school at the time of the attack. And when I saw the lawyer's name, my stomach quaked, for his name was Pankaj Bandopadhyay, Esquire.

Pankaj must have joined his father's practice—and how exciting that he managed to practice law in the area of nationalism, which had been his earliest wish! If Bidushi could have known that Pankaj was well and working in politics, she would have been pleased. I wondered if he had married; for it had been almost a year since Bidushi's death. For some reason, I hoped that he had not. But if he had married—and, in time, had a daughter—maybe I could be her teacher. Then I could fulfill my promise to Bidushi to watch over him.

❋　　❋　　❋

NOW I HAD a personal motivation for getting the day's newspaper before anyone else: to find any mention of Pankaj and his important work. I had Premlata bring it with my bed tea, so nobody was awake to witness my tears when I read that he'd lost the students' case. This was a travesty; still, I was convinced that he would keep on with his important work. As 1936 turned to 1937, he defended many people charged with sedition and civil unrest; only about a quarter resulted in acquittal, which did not surprise me any longer. And then, suddenly, Pankaj's name was not in the paper as pleader, but defendant.

> Calcutta, February 10, 1937. Bijoy Ganguly and Pankaj Bandopadhyay face sentencing today on charges of propaganda, libel, and inciting civil unrest. Mr. Bandopadhyay had represented Mr. Ganguly as a pro bono client until the latter was arrested earlier this week. Calcutta police say Mr. Bandopadhyay knowingly paid for the printing of a Bengali pamphlet designed to incite public unrest regarding the case. The pamphlets were recovered by Calcutta police at Bandopadhyay's Ballygunge residence. Police are also charging Mr. Ganguly for making false statements about maltreatment by the Calcutta police.

I was very upset about the situation, but I thought the girls would laugh at me if they knew I secretly loved a Calcutta intellectual. So I privately kept watching the papers until, one morning, I saw the verdict. Pankaj received a sentence of two years, and Bijoy three, at the Port Blair prison in the Andaman Islands, a small colony a thousand miles off Bengal's coast.

It would have been hard enough if Pankaj were sent to Mr. Abernathy's nearby jail, Hijli. But the high-security prison nicknamed "Black Water" was considered to be a far worse place. Originally created after the 1857 mutiny for the confinement of incorrigible Indians, the prisoners today were almost all Bengali freedom fighters kept in solitary confinement. There were rumors of polluted water, very little or rotten food, flogging, force-feeding, and other cruelties. But nobody knew for certain, because the prisoners could not be visited by anyone. If someone died in the Andamans, any excuse could be made by the prison officials. No one would know the truth.

CHAPTER

13

JEOPARDY: . . . 2. A position in a game, undertaking, etc. in which the chances of winning and losing hang in the balance . . .

—*Oxford English Dictionary*, Vol. 5, 1933

On her deathbed, Bidushi had requested that I take care of Pankaj, that I always ensure he was well. Nothing I'd said or done that wretched day at Lockwood School had helped him through her loss, and my inability to reach Calcutta had prevented me from doing anything that might have kept him from his court troubles. My Princess would have died another death to know her beloved was in prison.

This knowledge of how I'd failed both Pankaj and Bidushi—the only ones whom I'd become close to after losing my family—tore me apart. I wrote him one heartfelt letter, and then another, in an envelope marked with his name and *Port Blair Prison, the Andamans*. But each time I went to drop a letter in the postbox, I changed my mind. I didn't know if prisoners would be given letters, and even if they could receive mail, why would he want to learn what I had become?

He would certainly be insulted to hear from a prostitute. He should never know that the literary voice he'd once adored was now crying with false ecstasy to all kinds of bad men. So I didn't mail the letters but tore them into tiny pieces, and then stopped writing altogether.

🐝   🐝   🐝

I TURNED SEVENTEEN in June 1937, when it was very hot and we were all waiting for rain. The ceiling fans whirled at top speed, blowing out the candles on the cake that was served to me at tea. After we ate, I opened the many small gifts the Roses had given: useful things like cosmetics, stockings, French letters, and skin cream. I was genuinely touched; I'd never had such gifts. For a moment, my thoughts turned to my first days at Rose Villa, when I had been so excited and thrilled by the friendship and luxuries offered unsparingly.

That afternoon, Lucky and Bonnie treated me to a matinee showing of a musical comedy with Deanna Durbin called *Three Smart Girls* that made me laugh very hard and forget my worries about Pankaj for a few hours. But as I came out, I thought about how I'd once thought myself very clever, but really had been more foolish than anyone I'd ever met. At Rose Villa, we separated to bathe and dress and then came down for the evening's work. The girls drifted away from the main parlor, leaving me as the sole choice for a handsome young first-time customer, an army sergeant transferring between regions with a layover in Kharagpur. I knew my friends had meant this to be a favor, but when the man disrobed and I had a good look, I recognized the weeping rash from Dr. DeCruz's photographs. I was so sickened that I did not have to feign the nausea that made me run from the suite.

Mummy was annoyed by my abrupt dismissal of a new client, suspecting it was due to the lazy sleepiness that stemmed from two champagne cocktails I'd had during my birthday tea. She ultimately sent in Sakina, who was too fogged from opium to complain about anything. Sakina had used her mouth over a French letter but still developed such ugly blisters that she was put on leave for a month. Feeling guilty, I asked Sakina if she was angry with me, but she said that I had not made her do it; Mummy had.

The experience with the sergeant confirmed my belief that the younger, better-looking men posed the highest risk to our health. Bonnie and Natty and Doris could not understand my pessimism, for all three of them harbored dreams that handsome army men would enter Rose Villa, fall madly in love, and whisk them away to become mistresses of their very own households. Bonnie's own mother had been set up with her own small garden house and two servants to tend to her. But the soldier had shifted back to England; and with the money gone, the household had dissolved. Still, Bonnie held to her dream of a European knight walking into Rose Villa, falling in love with her, and leaving with her by his side. This was why she sang so much in the evenings beside the piano, as if she were really just a film star playing the role of a singing and dancing girl until she found her husband.

I also dreamed of leaving Rose Villa, but I knew nobody would ever take me away but myself. If only Mummy didn't charge me so much for food and shelter. I'd calculated that it would be another few months before I had enough money saved to buy passage to Calcutta and cover school fees, housing, and food. But where would I stay—and which school would accept me? I had no inkling. Still, I set a goal that by the time that Pankaj was out of prison, I would be free from my own shackles.

%   %   %

ON A STEAMY afternoon in late August, I went to the bazar to exchange some books for new ones. The rains were intermittent that day, making walking only a slightly dampening experience, and I noticed small papers littering the path that ran along the doorstep. I knew these papers were usually political-party messages, but this one had extra large lettering that caught my eye. A public meeting was being called to discuss the situation of the Andamans prisoners. It would be held at 4 p.m. in two days' time at a local school.

A slow, pleasant warmth spread through me as I read the notice more carefully. At this meeting, I could learn more about the prison conditions and any movement toward the prisoners' release. The late-afternoon timing was unfortunate because customers arrived from five-thirty on, which meant I was supposed to be dressed and ready in the parlor by five fifteen.

I promised myself that I would attend only part of the meeting. And even though there was risk of being late to the Villa, my desire to learn more about Pankaj's plight outweighed all of it.

☙ ☙ ☙

AT THREE O'CLOCK Wednesday, I took a short tonga ride to the school on the Indian side of town. The roads here were rough and full of litter, and I felt the people's eyes on me, as if they knew my Rose Villa background—despite the fact that I'd worn my plainest sari and no jewelry at all.

I had tried seeking work here long ago. This time, I went in with a large throng of men and some women toward a main auditorium. Most of the males attending wore white Congress caps, and I remembered the long ago time in Midnapore when Bidushi and I got on the wrong side of Congress protesters. Self-consciously, I touched the sari that I was wearing, hoping it was woven in India. At Rose Villa, nobody thought about such things.

The event was slightly late beginning. The local party leader who quieted the lively crowd with waving hands said that the Andamans report would be given immediately. He said the Andamans prisoners had forwarded a petition to the viceroy, asking to be repatriated to India. The viceroy had not yet responded, and as a result, the prisoners had begun a hunger strike. A ripple of concern seemed to go through the crowd, especially when the organizer said that all the leaders of the Congress Party, and even Rabindranath Tagore, had cautioned the prisoners not to put themselves in such a dangerous position.

"How many have died?" The question was called from the crowd.

"A handful since July 25; but more are sure to go," answered the Congress spokesman with a long face. "The last time there was a hunger strike at that prison, back in 1931, the guards did force-feeding. And that in itself is quite harmful."

It was now the end of August. How could the men still be alive? Did Pankaj welcome death because he longed to be with Bidushi? This thought dogged me as the speaker went on, talking of how prisoners in jails throughout India were striking in sympathy. I would starve myself if it would bring Pankaj back to India, but who would pay notice to the sympathy strike of a prostitute who continued to lie down for Englishmen and take their money? I wanted to leave Rose Villa badly, but I had nobody to turn to who would accept me. As the proverb went, I'd made my own bed and had to lie in it.

GLOOM SURROUNDED ME like a thin cloak as I returned to Rose Villa after the meeting. I had little time to freshen myself upon arrival and decided to wear a dress instead of a sari. I would use my English voice and wear an English costume, for I wanted to share nothing of who I was with my customers that evening. Stoically, I powdered my face peach and painted my lips a garish coral color. I wanted to look ugly, not to be chosen too many times.

"You don't look the same," Lucky said, coming into my bedroom around six.

I slammed the cosmetics box closed. "Why not? Mummy says we should vary our appearance."

"They don't come for cheap tarts—that's why we can't wear red saris or chew paan." She frowned at the ill-fitting floral chiffon I wore. "I haven't seen that frock before."

"It's one of Bonnie's old dresses. She was throwing it away."

"For good reason! Not that necklace; take this one." She placed a heavy circlet of artificial diamonds around my neck, in place of the faux topaz I'd selected. "What's wrong, Pamela? What are you thinking?"

"Nothing," I said sullenly. And it was true. I was so distracted by my worries over Pankaj and the Andamans prisoners that I hadn't taken note that the Taster had arrived early and been waiting since five in the Chrysanthemum Suite's red-sheeted bed; Mummy suddenly realized and rushed upstairs to tell me. This time, I had neglected to cover myself with spices and fine lingerie; and there was no time for it. As Mummy pushed me toward the suite, scolding me all the way, I wondered if he would be disappointed or merely glad to get on with his evening meal. I could smell the food he'd brought even before opening the door.

"Good evening, my saheb." I crouched to touch his feet as usual. When I came up, he pulled me close. His nose moved over my face, and then my shoulder.

"What is this?" he said abruptly. "You didn't prepare for me."

I thought of saying that the scents were so mysterious and faint that they had to be smelled most carefully. But the thought of him behaving like a street dog, sniffing and licking, made me want to deter him as long as I could. So I gave an automatic smile that felt like a spasm.

"I bathed, Saheb. Would you like to as well?" I extended my hand toward the attached bathroom, which he customarily used after he was through.

Suddenly, his manner stiffened. "What did you say? Do you think I stink?"

Pressing my lips together, I shook my head. Of course he reeked. Some men washed up before they arrived, but he didn't. The Taster smelled of meat and all the things he ate, and of sweat and the evils of his prison. And tonight, as he pulled me against him, I inhaled the harsh rye that Mummy kept downstairs.

"Speak, girl!" But before I could think of a better answer, he raised his fist and delivered a blow that smashed my lips open. I was stunned, both with pain and fear. The violence had happened so fast, I hadn't seen it coming and had no chance to turn my head. Now my lips were bloody and my tongue smarted. I saw my smudged coral lipstick on his palm as he brought it back to strike me again.

"You don't smell," I gasped out, but he hit me anyway, and then he pushed me down on the bed and was tearing the flowered dress. Now I cursed myself for wearing something so simple; for I had no intention of being taken roughly in a house that prided itself on its genteel nature. At Rose Villa there were to be no beatings *by men*, Mummy always said coyly, implying that the reverse was acceptable.

"Sir, you mustn't!" I shouted for the sake of anyone who might hear me in the corridor. But my next call for help was cut off, for he had filled my mouth with a greasy piece of mutton that had come out of his suit pocket.

I could not get my hands anywhere near my face without his hitting me, and I could not even speak without fear of choking. So I lay still as he raped me, for that was what it was this time. And the worst of it was, he had moved into me so fast I had not been able to bring out a French letter out of the box for my own protection.

"You will get your—just deserts!" The Taster panted hard as he pumped. It seemed that the liquor he'd consumed made it hard for him to perform. As he fell soft I hoped he would give up the whole business, but he made a growling sound and kept on, slapping at me each time I tried to free myself. If only it were the Lotus Suite, where the others might see through the ceiling spy hole; surely they would rescue me. But we were inside the Chrysanthemum Suite at the far end of the hall, a hellish room decorated with scarlet-colored lights and bed coverings, and on them, my blood.

At last he reached his goal and rolled off me. I spit out the foul piece of meat and wept with pain. The horror of what had happened filled me; I could not go to my imaginary cupboard for rescue. I'd been locked out.

The Taster stood and began to dress. Burping, he said, "No tip for you tonight."

I lay still until he stormed out, slamming the door behind him. Natty was leaning against the wall when I slipped outside, still shaking, a few minutes later. She looked at me with cold eyes: as if she knew but did not care.

"Did you hear him hurting me?" I said, my throat catching.

"I heard something." Her pretty lips pressed outward into a smirk.

"Why didn't you help me?"

Her eyes glinted at me. "If you take on a big customer like the Taster, you've got to handle him right. I tried to tell you that last year."

Now I understood Natty: she had nursed this resentment, all the time, for his dropping her in favor of me. Despite his loathsome practices and what I'd had to suffer.

"He's yours once more," I spat, tasting blood in my mouth. Then I went up to my room to bathe, cleaning every bit he had invaded. As I brushed my teeth, I stared at my face in the mirror above the sink. I did not look like the girl who had arrived at the brothel two years earlier. I had become her ghost.

❧   ❧   ❧

THE NEXT MORNING, everyone agreed that the Taster had misbehaved and should not come back to the house for a while, but Mummy said that too much liquor was the real villain of the story. If I had been at the house on time, he would not have drunk so much rye-and-water. Then, as I expected, Mummy asked where I had been yesterday that I'd come back so late.

"At a film. But, Mummy, I'm hurting down there," I said, too embarrassed to use any of the silly words the others did. "Dr. DeCruz should examine me before I work again."

"I can take you before lunch," said Bonnie comfortingly.

"Not so fast," Mummy said. "I'll give two days off—if it's still hurting, then go. But don't divert me from my questions. You came back late, in a tonga from the Indian side of town."

So Mummy had been watching for me that evening. I shivered, knowing that more anger was unavoidable. I said, "Indians do see films, as well."

"And what did you see? Surely not *Devdas* again?" Her voice was acidic, because she had disapproved of how much Lucky and I had enjoyed this Bengali-language film about a romantic young couple hindered by their caste difference. "Or did you actually go to a certain political meeting? There was a paper about it left in your wastebasket."

"There was a newsreel at the meeting," I said, flustered that she'd caught me so easily.

In a hard voice, Mummy said, "You're not mixing in Congress politics, are you?"

"I'm not mixing anything," I answered defiantly. "I just went for the film."

"The Congress Party and their war for independence will be the death of India. Don't you understand what it means?" Mummy's cheeks flushed red, despite their dusting with white powder. "I have no papers. I can't get passage to England and neither can Natt and Bonnie and Doris. If Indians take over, they could close my villa!"

"Mummy, don't be upset," Bonnie soothed. "Nobody will ever close this place. Remember how well you've been able to attract new clients through the railways. There's always new money coming."

"If India is taken over by natives, the Anglo-Indian railwaymen will be sent packing." Mummy's mouth seemed to pinch inward as she spoke. "It will be a blacks-only railway, and all the trains will crash or be late! The hell if I'll have those types in Rose Villa!"

CHAPTER
14

CHEERIO: *A parting exclamation of encouragement; "good-bye"; also quasi-adj: cheery.*

—*A Supplement to the Oxford English Dictionary*, Vol. 2, 1933

Politics were not good for me.

The more I thought about Pankaj's and Netaji's words, the less I could bear my life at Rose Villa. Freedom, dignity, unity were what was called for—and there I was, lying down for the enemy. Prostitution was more than a physical humiliation; it was becoming mental torture. And although I did not smoke hashish like Sakina or drink like Natty, my low spirits placed me among their lot.

The hunger strike had spread to prisons all over India; Gandhiji gave speeches and Rabindranath Tagore wrote letters about the Andamans, making the starving prisoners international news. It became too much of a black spot on the face of India's government, and in September, what everyone longed for came true: the viceroy directed the prison superintendent at Port Blair to begin releasing its political inmates.

The news relieved me, but I still felt empty. Yes, Pankaj had survived and would go back to his lawyer's life in Calcutta, but I had not yet departed my despicable profession. The only escape I had within Rose Villa were the shelves of old books in each parlor. One afternoon, when I was dusting mildew off the spine of a tattered Rudyard Kipling volume, Mummy came in. I was both irritated and worried, because I hadn't yet groomed myself for the evening; and surely she would notice.

"I have always wondered: How did you build such a marvelous book collection?" I said in the hopes of distracting her.

Mummy grimaced at the book in my hand, as if she thought it was rubbish. "My father left trunks of books with my ma before returning to England. She always said, if only he'd left his papers in the trunk, too. If I had his birth certificate—if only!—then I could prove myself and get a British passport. And then—oh, to be in England with all the luxuries!"

"Did your ma read them all?" I asked, to avoid hearing another one of her fantasy tales about the easy life that lay ahead for her in Devon or Brighton.

She laughed, her face creasing like a fractured pink-and-brown plate. "Oh, no. My mum couldn't read because she wasn't sent to school. I was the first one, and that was only until I was eleven. I once tried reading some of those stories when I was sick in bed, but they're dreadful. Anyway, the books aren't for us but for the customers. Every now and then a man is too shy or has some reason not to go upstairs. So the books can amuse him while his friends are having their fun."

"That's why I'm keeping these books clean. I don't think a gentleman would be impressed with our house if his fingers touched mildew."

"I don't worry about the men, Pamela. I worry about you. After all—you are my favorite."

I looked up at this with surprise, for I had always thought Bonnie was Mummy's special one. Her words could not be genuine.

"Pamela, you are among my top earners, but since the monsoon, your numbers are down. I have noticed that your new customers do not choose you again, and you are coming up with all sorts of reasons to be on leave. Why are your periods so long suddenly? You are only hurting yourself."

"I don't know why they don't want me as much. I'll try harder." I could not address her second point. I was lying about my menses because they had stopped altogether. It was not something I wanted to dwell on. I knew that all my customers had used French letters—except the Taster, the time he'd raped me.

I told myself that nothing was wrong; that it was just the mental tension. Or, if I truly were with child, the baby would slip out of me while still unformed. As frightening as the situation was, I could not bring myself to consult anyone for help. The girls couldn't keep a secret; and Mummy controlled so much of my life that I could only imagine how enraged she'd be.

I'd thought the doctor would find out, but Dr. DeCruz examined me the first two months without noticing anything amiss, and this spurred me to go on with the pretense. When he went for a long holiday to the hills, this bought me even more time. I went to the halal butcher and bought animal blood that I added to my cloths in the bathroom soaking pail so Premlata would not think anything out of the ordinary, during the time I went on leave. In the back of my mind, I knew that what I was doing was senseless; that if I really were carrying, my belly would give me away. But I would rather put things off than face them. A baby would mean the end to everything: my dreams of going to school and maybe seeing Pankaj again.

"I am not quite well," I said to Mummy, as we stood together in the parlor. "Perhaps if I did something different to help you for a while: writing advertisements, organizing all the books in the parlors—"

Mummy interrupted me. "No more books. You've turned lazy and fat, and that's not what the English want. I must see an uptick in your numbers or your days here will end. *Thik hai?*"

"*Thik*," I answered her question with a gloomy *It's fine*. I worked harder to pretend pleasure, and customer satisfaction slowly returned. But as she said, I was getting bigger, and that was a new danger. Instead of going to my scheduled appointment with Dr. DeCruz, who'd returned in October, I sent word to his nurse that I was having a heavy period and would reschedule. And to camouflage my physical changes, I began to wear silk caftans and elaborate necklaces to draw attention to my face, which was always heavily made up.

"Your looks are changing," Bonnie said, and from her expression, I could tell this was not a compliment.

❧   ❧   ❧

ONE WARM SUNDAY morning I lazed downstairs with Bonnie, savoring the brief coolness of the veranda as we drank our tea. Right away the two of us split up our copy of *Amrita Bazar Patrika*, a Calcutta newspaper published in English that I liked better than the *Statesman*. Bonnie was reading the fashion and entertainment page, and I had the first section with world news. I wondered what would come first: a European war or my baby. Both were ominous events that I sensed were unstoppable.

The sound of a tonga caught both Bonnie's and my attention. The mynah birds that had been chattering overhead cut themselves off, too. Customers usually went to church services on Sunday morning, not coming till the afternoon.

Bonnie groaned. "All I can say is, he'd better be very rich or handsome."

I glanced at my watch. I'd bought it recently, a slim Japanese bracelet style that thrilled me each time I checked it. It had been a dent in my savings, but I knew I'd need a watch in order to get to school on time, when I finally began work on my teaching certificate. The time read half eight, which was too early for any client.

"If this is the infamous Rose Villa, you must be the morning roses!" A strangely accented male voice jolted the quiet of the garden veranda.

As the man came into view, I closed my silk wrapper tightly. I was shocked that a sunburned white man in rough clothing as dusty as a laborer's had found his way to the back garden without being stopped by anyone.

"Sir, you are out of order," I protested, disliking the leisurely way the tall, red-haired man was looking both Bonnie and me up and down. Bonnie made a quick gesture spreading her fingers on the table. *He's mine,* it said.

Premlata came running out to the veranda. "The darwan was sleeping, Memsaheb, but he will come soon!"

Although she'd spoken in Bengali, the man seemed to understand her concern. He slung a heavy satchel off his shoulder and stuck out a hand. "No worries, eh? My name is Bernie. Bernie Mulkins."

"Are you a Yank?" Bonnie asked, smiling up at him as if he were a film star. I could not understand why, but her woman's intuition must have told her something.

"No, my pretty lady. Australian or Aussie—as they sometimes say."

"I'm sorry, Mr. Mulkins, on Sundays we aren't open till two o'clock," I said.

"I'm sorry, too." He grinned back at her. "My train came in an hour ago. And the light's so good, I can't wait."

Bonnie gestured toward an empty chair. "You must not have had breakfast yet! Please sit down, Bernie. My name is Bonnie. I'm sure you know its meaning." Then, even though Premlata was just inches away, Bonnie shouted for her to bring a new pot of tea and fresh milk and some biscuits for the saheb.

"You appear to be Anglo-Indian. A lovely Eurasian half-caste." Bernie Mulkins studied Bonnie with lazy, practiced eyes.

"Yes. My friend Pam is not, but that's obvious, isn't it?" And although Bonnie laughed, her words gave me a sense that she was afraid I might somehow poach him.

"Excuse me; I have something to do," I said, getting to my feet because Bernie and his questions were making me uncomfortable, and I was feeling sickly anyhow.

Bernie Mulkins pulled a tattered business card from his satchel and gave it to Bonnie. "I've been traveling India three months now, shooting people. That's why I've come."

"Shooting?" I exclaimed, my eyes going to his heavy bag. Surely it couldn't be full of guns.

"Shooting photographs." Bernard Mulkins laughed. "I take pictures of the people of India—all of 'em, from the wretches in their hovels to maharanis. Down in Calcutta, I heard about beautiful girls hidden away in a villa in Khargpur. I haven't shot any Anglo-Indians yet, so I decided this was a must-see, and having met you two lasses, I'm convinced. How many others like you are in the house?"

Bonnie's eyes were alight. "Do you take photographs for fashion magazines and such?"

"I have, but I'm under contract now to shoot photographs of lovely women for a very special book—"

"Books last forever. They aren't ever torn up or thrown away." Bonnie breathed deeply. "Oh, Pam, you must go wake Mummy."

"She won't be happy to have a visitor so early." And, I was thinking to myself, someone who wasn't a paying customer.

"I think," Bonnie said, her eyes fixed happily on Bernie Mulkins, "once I explain to her, she'll be quite happy indeed."

Bonnie knew Mummy better than I did. Within an hour, she had called everyone downstairs—even the girls still yawning with sleep. We would all pose for Mr. Mulkins before our work started. We wouldn't be paid because we weren't providing the usual services, but he would provide her with a first edition of the book and photographs of all her girls, which would be framed and hung downstairs for customers to enjoy.

※　　　※　　　※

YOU MIGHT THINK that women in our line of work would be accustomed to being naked in front of a stranger; but there is a great difference between a darkened, private suite and daylight's glare in an ordinary room. I was not the only girl who didn't want her picture taken, but Mummy insisted that everyone participate.

"He's well respected, girls. He has exhibited with a famous American photographer called Man Ray." Her voice squeaked as it did when she was most excited. "When his book comes out, you will be known in Paris, New York, and London!"

Nobody had ever taken my photograph before, and I wasn't interested in having a copy; I was bent on staying unrecognized and hidden. Hoping that he'd be so overwhelmed with subjects that he would forget me, I stayed in my bedroom while everyone else crowded about the various places he was setting up for his "shoots." Premlata told me what was happening: each time he chose a girl, he spent a brief period looking at her and then would inspect her almirah in order to choose the right costume and jewelry. To Premlata, this step seemed a waste of time; she said that, in the end, everyone was posing half-naked.

We were supposed to stop by one o'clock, but he was not yet finished. Customers who came were aware something unusual was going on upstairs. When the girls told them, some left out of fear they might wind up in the pictures, though a few seemed to take special delight in watching the photography sessions.

In late afternoon, my turn came to open my bedroom door to Mr. Mulkins and reveal what was hanging in my almirah. I did not pull out clothes for him to examine; I just stood beside the cabinet with my arms folded, wearing one of the faded old saris from my Lockwood School days. I made sure the expression on my face was also unattractive.

"You really don't want to do this, do you?" Bernie Mulkins asked as he studied me.

"It will be a waste of time. I am not photogenic." I had heard girls at Lockwood use this phrase when they despaired over their yearbook photographs.

"And why is it that a girl who chooses a career like yours is too good to sit for a simple art photograph?"

I said that I did not want my face photographed.

"Oh, are you wanted by the law?" He laughed as if he'd made a very witty joke. "Well, I can avoid your face if you like. I shot Natty from behind."

"But you showed her face in the mirror!"

"Who said that?" He sounded aggrieved.

"Everyone. They were peeking through the door."

"The door." He snapped his fingers. "There's an idea. The door could be opened to reveal you—just a glimpse of you, from behind. No mirrors, but maybe—a hand on the door. A white man's hand."

Bernie had the picture in mind: I was to be photographed sitting in a chair that was facing backward. I mentioned that I'd never seen anyone except a drunken Englishman sit in a chair in such a manner, but he waved off my objection.

"It's about light and shadow and angle, love. A glimpse of you through a slit in the door, a hand on the knob. . . ."

But he could not find a willing customer to be photographed. In the end, he enlisted Mummy, because her hands were covered in heavy rings that he declared "imperialistic." Mummy twinkled as brightly as her diamonds to hear this compliment, but in her next breath insisted that he absolutely, positively, not photograph any part of her body and head. There could be no incriminating photographs of her on record, given her undying dream of attaining a British passport.

"Very modest, the two of you," Bernie said, and I turned my head to see him through the crack in the door, posing Mummy's hand. To me, he said, "Head back in place. Hasn't she got lovely curves, Mrs. Barker? No, no, ma'am, please keep your wrist just like that. Don't move."

It was a long time until Bernie declared that he was finished.

Gingerly, I swung one sore leg around to get up from the chair: I didn't even care if Bernie saw the front of me, because I saw he'd put the camera down, and I was anxious to be gone. In the corner of the room lay my silk wrapper, looking soft and comforting.

"Wait a moment, Pamela." Mummy had come through the door into the room and was staring at me with horrified eyes as I slipped on the wrapper. Then she said, "How could you?"

"What's that?" I asked, quickly tying the sash.

"How did you do it?" Her words hit like tiny, sharp knives. "I always ask Premlata about your monthlies. Did you pay her to lie?"

Fear rose in me, as I realized she'd seen my belly. I could do nothing now but tell the truth, because I didn't want Premlata to suffer the same fate I had at Lockwood school. "Premlata did not lie to you. She never knew I put goat's blood in the pail."

"My God." Mummy sucked in her breath. "How many periods have you missed?"

"Only three—"

"Must do the next girl. Cheerio!" Bernie called, his loud footsteps moving swiftly away. "You broke the house rule about French letters, obviously." Mummy paced back and forth. "What do you think our rules are for?"

"I always use them! It could only have happened the time the Taster raped me. He didn't give me a chance—"

"Splendid!" Mummy said sarcastically. "Mr. Abernathy's quite unlikely to marry you. The best we can hope is he'll pay some expenses. If only you had told me right away, I could have taken care of it."

"Taken care? But how?"

"With the help of a dai. So stupid you are, and you're going to stop working immediately! The men will notice your change soon, if they haven't already. It frightens them to bang up against a place where a baby is; they feel it's watching them. And we have no babies living in this house, even if they're still in someone's stomach."

After her last words, my fear was replaced by a small hope. Maybe

Mummy would move me to a rented room. To think of all the reading I could do during the next months! I still would not know what to do after the baby came, but if the prostitution halted, I would surely be free to look for other work. I said, "I see your point about leaving being a good idea—"

"No, you don't see; you are blindly stupid. You are a natural talent who has ruined herself; but damn if you'll ruin my reputation! Oh, what to do?"

CHAPTER

15

INCORRIGIBLE: *1. Incapable of being corrected or amended. Bad or depraved beyond correction or reform: of persons, their habits, etc.*

—*Oxford English Dictionary*, Vol. 5, 1933

What to do?

Everyone at Rose Villa thought differently. Natty told me that the dai Mummy had talked about was very good at pulling out babies before they were born. Then Sakina warned me that a number of that midwife's customers had perished, including her own cousin. Premlata thought I should give up the baby to a temple, because the priests would give me a little money and heavenly blessings. Remembering what Lucky had told me about the duties of temple maidens, I declined.

Bonnie suggested that I burst into tears in front of the Taster, describing my plight, and he might be worried enough about his reputation to set me up in a bungalow in another town that he could visit when he wanted. I told Bonnie that I never wanted to see him again, and I was sickened to find out that Mummy did indeed speak to him about my condition when he was waiting for Natty to be ready. Premlata hid near the parlor door and reported to me that he had answered her with harsh language, saying nothing could ever be proven because I was known to serve half the cantonment.

I was glad not to have any further interest from the Taster, but I continued to feel desperate about the baby. Mummy's rule was fast; she said that I must move out, but she had arranged for a place for me to stay. Wondering what was ahead of me, I packed up my silk moiré dresses, embroidered saris, and high-heeled chappals and pumps with rhinestone decorations. I had room for about a dozen books, so I packed only my favorites and sold the rest back to the bookseller, knowing that I'd need to live on my savings for several months, and maybe longer. In the back of my mind, I was thinking, perhaps this was the best thing. I had wanted to leave Rose Villa, hadn't I?

Mummy had booked a room for me in a place she called a dancing girls' house. She made it clear to the dancing house managers, a sour-looking couple called Tilak and Jayshree, that I must not have my body spoiled by working for them, although I could help by caring for the brothel's young children. They seemed to spill out of every doorway on the day I arrived at the place that reeked of opium mixed with rotting food and human waste. Mummy gave candies to them and cooed that they would soon be getting a baby sister.

"It may be a boy," I objected, because I didn't like how Mummy seemed to think she knew everything.

"Don't say it!" Mummy shook a finger at me. "A girl is what we want. Jayshree will keep her while she's little, and if she's pretty enough, she can shift to Rose Villa and follow in your footsteps. When she's thirteen, you'll be thirty: the perfect age for her debut and your retirement."

Mummy looked so pleased with herself that I dared not contradict her. But the thought that I kept to myself was that I would never allow any child of mine to participate in such a loathsome tradition. My feelings only magnified after spending my first night in the hot, filthy place. I could not believe any children were allowed to be on the premises, with people running around half-naked, smoking opium and cursing. The behavior within its rough clay walls made Rose Villa seem like a cathedral.

I talked to the oldest of the children, a girl called Lina. At nine, she was in her last year before debut, which came much earlier at an ordinary brothel. She was not pretty or well spoken enough for Rose Villa; she would work only at this house. I imagined the prospect would be terrifying for her, but Lina told me otherwise.

"I don't mind, Auntie," she said with a wan smile. "It's better than being rented to beggars at the station, as they did until I was eight."

Lina ruled the weed-choked courtyard where most of the children ran about all day in rags; the tiniest ones were naked and tethered with chains. I managed to convince Jayshree to unchain them for most of the daylight hours and set Lina to playing with them while I washed their clothes and then took each one for a bath and hair-combing. In turn, Lina asked me to properly comb her own hair, and I did so, grimly working out the lice. On all the children, there were lice and other insects, too: ringworms on their scalps, nestled in their food-smeared clothes, and most awful of all, the biting bugs that dug their tiny claws deep into the skin. I could not see them with my eyes, but I recognized the holes they left and how the children cried at the pain. I brought them a cream from Dr. DeCruz that healed the wounds, but the clever bugs still hid in the clothes and bedding. If I had not washed myself thrice daily, I would likely have become infested, too.

Jayshree and Tilak's place was so dirty that the British military were not authorized to visit, which meant their customers were poor Anglo-Indians and Indians. From what the women told me over morning tea, these customers were often rough and unkind. After a week, the horrible sounds I heard at night, paired with the vile surroundings, led me to decide that no matter the cost, I should pay to stay elsewhere. After making an excuse about going shopping in the bazar, I walked through the town, seeking a decent boardinghouse. My polite voice opened doors, but whenever the landladies saw the bump under my sari—and learned no husband would be staying with me—I was refused.

So I returned to the brothel and resolved to walk daily outside and spend time reading in the park, where the air was fresh. But as my stomach became bigger, people on the streets mocked me, the fallen sinful girl.

❧   ❧   ❧

DR. DECRUZ TOLD me I had only a month left until the baby was ready, but each day dragged out like a month in hell. Jayshree wanted more money from me, complaining of my overuse of water for baths and washing laundry. What she asked for was more than I had on hand, so with a great deal of effort, I walked to the bank.

When I gave the bank clerk the savings withdrawal slip, he looked at me sorrowfully. "Miss Barker, I've missed seeing you. Have you forgot that your account is closed?"

I couldn't have heard him right; he must have been speaking of another of the Rose Villa girls. With emphasis, I said, "I'm Pamela Barker. My account is in good standing, with more than five hundred rupees saved."

The clerk looked in his record book again and came back. "Your account is jointly held with your mother, Mrs. Rose Barker. Last month she withdrew the remaining funds. Surely she told you?"

The baby kicked inside, as if he'd also heard the terrible words, and I had to grab at the counter for security. *My God*. Mummy had told me she would either keep the money for me safely in the house, or I could bank it. I'd thought this was a straightforward choice, but now I understood that there was no difference in either method. Girls like Bonnie and Lucky who behaved well could take money out. The ones who displeased her lost their money. Hundreds of rupees I'd had, and now I was destitute, unable to do anything for the baby or myself. I would never get a Cambridge certificate; never even take a train to Calcutta and catch a glimpse of Pankaj Bandopadhyay.

The loss of money felt almost like a second rape. In a daze, I stumbled back to the dancing girls' house. I told Jayshree that if she wanted any money, she would have to get it directly from Mummy. There must have been something about my voice that convinced her, because she didn't argue.

❧   ❧   ❧

SEVERAL DAYS LATER, I had an unexpected visit from Lucky. How alien she looked, with her smoothly lacquered hair, powdered skin, and delicate chiffon sari. I felt a surge of envy, which faded as I remembered what she did each day to earn these luxuries.

"I brought money from Mummy to give those people. They're awful! They aren't making you work here, are they?" Lucky's big eyes, so beautifully painted with mascara and kohl, looked at me with obvious concern.

"I'm not working except for helping with the children, and I've become very poor," I confessed, for there was no point in trying to put on appearances with Lucky. "I have no money anymore. Mummy closed my account."

"How?" Her glossy mouth dropped open, revealing the single dead tooth she always tried scrupulously to hide.

"Remember how we all were told to use the surname Barker when we set up the bank accounts?" I asked. "It means Mummy is the joint owner of each account. The bank lists us all as daughters under her guardianship."

"I have her keep my money in the house," Lucky said slowly. "It's never been a problem for me to get enough for shopping—"

"Because you are behaving the way Mummy wants. But, Lucky,

you must find a way to withdraw your money while you still can—little by little, so she doesn't notice. Hide it somewhere she won't know. You must not lose it!"

"I don't want to cause trouble," Lucky said, and her calm face made it clear she didn't believe she would ever be in my same situation. "But I thank you for the warning. And before I forget to say it, Bonnie sends her regards."

"How is she?" I asked eagerly. I hoped Bonnie would come to see me.

Lucky waved a hand dismissively. "Bonnie is constantly studying new film songs for entertaining in the parlor, if she's not working."

"She comes into town all the time for the cinema! Surely she could stop by—"

Lucky looked down for a minute, then said, "She doesn't care to come to this place. And she's said—that you weren't very intelligent to get yourself in such a situation."

"I see." I thought about the hours I'd spent with Bonnie, sharing her room like a sister. Upon leaving, I'd given her all my newspapers and magazines. I'd believed Bonnie was my friend, but now I understood that she was interested in only what could benefit her.

"The funny thing is, the Australian photographer's been coming around. He's trying to see her without paying, you know, almost like a boyfriend—" Lucky chattered on as if it were the old days. But I had no patience for such gossip.

"Lucky, look around at this filth. Did you see the other women and children here? I don't think Mummy spent more than five minutes here before deciding to leave me. She can't realize how terrible the place is."

"She does know." Lucky's voice was sober. "She says that she sent you here because you didn't appreciate all the luxuries. She did it so you'd come crawling back and never break a house rule or keep a secret from her again. It's supposed to be a lesson to you and us all."

"What's happening to me is a *lesson*?" I shook my head, thinking that Mummy was crueler than anyone I'd ever known, to take not only my money but also my dignity and the child inside me.

"Please let me give you this." Lucky fished into her beaded golden purse and pulled out ten rupees. "It's all I have today. But I will find a way to give you more. Don't worry; you can pay it back later. I can hardly wait until all this nonsense is over and you are back in the room next to mine."

❦   ❦   ❦

BUT ROSE VILLA was even less of a home than Lockwood School had been. I treasured what I had learned at Lockwood, while the skills I'd been taught at Rose Villa I would not share with anyone. How stupidly I had fallen for false kindness, how much I had sacrificed, and how I'd been punished for choosing a life I'd known was wrong from the beginning.

The spring heat had no mercy, pouring through the cracks in the old building's ceiling and walls. The storeroom in which I slept had no punkha on the ceiling nor windows to let in breezes, so I was usually slick with sweat. The baby kicked constantly, telling me he was surely as unhappy as his mother. From the curve of my belly, the brothel women declared that I was having a female, but I disagreed. The kicking and rolling meant that I had a fighter: a boy with the Taster's piggish face. He would be born to a mother without husband or home, in such bad circumstances he would steal as a boy and become a dacoit by his teenage years. My son would be the Oliver Twist of Kharagpur but without a happy ending.

❦   ❦   ❦

ONE NIGHT THE sounds of screeching laughter in rooms nearby seemed even louder than usual; they battered my head like the lathis that soldiers and police had used on the political protesters. I was feeling swollen and tired when I lay down, and it took hours to fall asleep because of the kicking. The baby was late, by Dr. DeCruz's calcuations. But I didn't want the baby to come. I just wanted to be a girl back in Johlpur.

That night, I dreamed myself there. I was standing in a rice paddy. My lost little brother ran along the raised walking edge toward me; I was thrilled to see that he was now seven years old and very handsome. I waited for him, knowing he'd come to greet the child growing inside me, but to my shock, Bhai came up to me and shoved hard. Again and again he pushed against my round belly, as if he were punishing me. And though I cowered and screamed at him to leave me, he would not stop.

Crying out with pain, I awoke to find my legs and the thin bed mat I slept on were soaked. The hard shoving of my dream continued; I breathed through my nose to bear the spasm until it stopped. Then, using every bit of strength in my arms, I pulled myself off the bed and untwisted my wet sari to put on a fresh one.

It was so early that not even the darwan had arrived to the brothel's door; I could not possibly climb the stairs to where Tilak and Jayshree slept—nor did I wish to awaken them. The moon illuminated the street as I walked toward the rickshaw-wallah's stand. My legs shook with effort made all the worse by the anxiety I felt. I knew it was time.

In a rickshaw parked down the street, the thin, wrinkled Bihari driver was curled up in its carriage, sleeping. "Uncle, please," I called to him until at last he stirred. He looked quite worried by my appearance, but quickly helped me into the chair and got himself between the wooden poles.

We reached Dr. DeCruz's residence-cum-chambers twenty minutes later. The building's darwan came grudgingly awake when the rickshaw-wallah left me in the carriage and explained my situation. After some discussion, the rickshaw driver returned to me and gave the bad news that Dr. DeCruz was on night duty at the Railway Hospital.

"The Railway Hospital's a bit far," I said to my driver. "Are your legs strong enough?"

He shook his head, looking worried. "I could take you—but you cannot go inside the place. It is only for Ingrej and Anglo-Indians."

"Dr. DeCruz promised he will help," I said, because at my last appointment, the doctor had adamantly said I was to come to him for the delivery. He assured me that even though my bank account was gone, Mummy would pay to ensure the baby was born in a healthy, safe condition.

With my sharp contractions, the ride seemed interminable. As the baby pushed, I held firm, begging my child to wait. At last, we arrived at the fine white stucco hospital. I disembarked from the rickshaw with the driver's help and paid him with some of the last coins I had. An Indian guard hurried toward me. In Bengali, he shouted, "Not here! This hospital is not for natives."

"But Dr. DeCruz told me—" I could not finish because a new contraction threatened, but I kept walking slowly toward the entrance.

"Go away!" the guard shouted, running alongside me.

"I know he is here," I said, gripping the doorway to help pull myself into the brightly lit building, with its high ceilings and smell of antiseptic.

"But there is no Indian ward. Go away and get a dai now, before it's too late."

But the last pain had overwhelmed me, and I sank to the tiled floor that was damp with rain that had been tracked in.

"What is this?" a sharp Englishman's voice demanded.

"She wouldn't stop, Dr. Wood, she just kept shouting for DeCruz."

"That's the problem with black doctors," the English doctor said in a voice that was miles away. "You get one, you get his people."

There were new brisk footsteps and low-heeled cream pumps with matching stockinged legs stopped nearby. I heard an Englishwoman's voice saying she'd brought her son with a fever. Where was the doctor?

"This way, madam!" the English guard said to the lady, and his boot kicked my shoulder hard, as he departed. I could not hold back a cry of surprised pain, and suddenly, there were two faces near me, those of Anglo-Indian nurses bending to examine me.

"Where did you come from?" the first one asked. "Do you speak English?"

"Dr. DeCruz told me to come." My voice was weak, but I hoped my good accent would make it clear that I truly was the doctor's patient.

"Dr. DeCruz doesn't treat darkies," said the other nurse.

"In town, he does: darkies and thieves and whores," the first nurse whispered to the other. Then her voice became loud and slow, as she spoke to me. "You must leave. It's hospital rules."

To live, I would have to fight. And the only weapon I had, I realized, was my baby's white father. "The baby's father is English," I panted, "a top officer at Hijli. He wouldn't like this—"

The second nurse grabbed my left hand and twisted it. "No wedding ring; no engagement ring, either."

A new nurse came up and spoke sharply to the others. "Stop playing. Chief Howard's wife just came with their little boy and must be seen for his fever."

"I don't know what you expect me to do," the second nurse said petulantly. "She's big as a cow! I can't move her."

"Get the orderlies to put her on a gurney," the new nurse said. "Get her out of the building and into some transport home."

Two Anglo-Indian men in white uniforms came and lifted me onto a gurney. A sheet was thrown over to hide the sight of me. Outside the hospital, the guards loaded me in a tonga. But as I collapsed onto the seat, the driver refused to go without proof of money.

"I have it," I moaned. As I struggled to pull out some of the coins I'd tied into the end of my sari, one of the orderlies reached in, giving some to the driver and pocketing the rest.

❧   ❧   ❧

I HALF CRAWLED into the brothel after being dropped off on the corner. The kitchen maid and some of the children were awake by now and helped me back to the storeroom, where a fresh sari was laid out on the cot for me and I was gently placed down. Someone ran to wake Jayshree, who said to send for a dai. Shortly afterward, a young, dark-skinned woman arrived; her homespun clothing was reassuringly like that of Johlpur, but the dirt in her nails made me recoil.

"You will do everything I tell you, and you will be fine." Her voice was sharp, and the disapproving expression on her face told me she agreed with Jayshree that I thought too much of myself. "The first thing I must tell you is to stop crying so much. The baby won't want to come if it's frightened by your cries. A girl your age I once treated could not push out a hiding baby. Both died."

The dai tucked a rag inside my mouth and wiped my forehead with a cloth. I could no longer speak aloud, so I silently wept and cursed myself for having come to Kharagpur, for having spoken to Bonnie, for having taken the tonga with her to Rose Villa. The dai's hands touched my swollen belly, and I pushed when she told me. On and on it went, in the hot, dark room, with people coming and going to look at me. Children wept in fear, and their mothers snapped at them to get out and leave me alone.

I felt I'd gone mad with pain; that I could not push, but the baby was doing it, not to help but out of hatred. He didn't want this life any more than I did. The pushes grew harder and more violent; finally I saw white lights behind my eyes. The end had come, I realized, as I felt my body tear asunder. And then a scream broke the air, one brighter and higher than my own.

"A daughter! You have a blessing." The dai called out the surprising news first to me and then the women crowding the hallway outside my room. Loud cheers broke out, and I could make out faces crowded at the doorway, eager for a look. The dai called for Jayshree to wash the baby and wrap her tightly in an old sari blouse. Then Jayshree placed my daughter on my chest. All I could see was a bit of dark hair and mottled pink skin. Her eyes were closed but her rosebud mouth moved like a fish's. A girl. I was startled, but not disappointed.

The dai put the baby to my breast. "If she gets color, it will be within six months, nah? But even if she turns brown as cinnamon, she will be fine. Look how she already knows to eat. She will take-take-take all you have."

I could see my baby sucking, but I realized that I could not actually feel her touch because the pain in my lower body was so extreme. I murmured something about it, and the dai said, "You're all right; I'll clean you. Thank Goddess Lakshmi for your blessing, and stop the moaning. Your worries are over and the baby must not be disturbed."

"What is her name?" asked Lina, who had somehow squeezed into the room. She had brought a wrinkled red sari in her hands. I was confused for a moment before realizing she was trying to offer me an auspicious swaddling wrap for the baby, just as my own little brother had been wrapped in red so many years ago. And I suddenly understood that my little brother appearing in my early-morning dream wasn't trying to kill my baby. Bhai was helping her emerge in the world; to have the chance that he lost. And this child, Lina, was trying to help as well.

"I don't know a name," I whispered, because I had only thought of her as a problem or nightmare or millstone. I could not do that now that Lina had brought the red wrap. It reminded me of the joy I'd felt at Bhai's arrival. Surely my newborn daughter was worth as much as him.

"Jayshree will give her house name and Mummy will choose her good name. That is how it is always done," Lina said.

Jayshree and Mummy might give my baby any names they wished, but I would not use those names. My baby would have a very good one. As I sank into a bottomless lake of pain, I promised this to us both.

CHAPTER

16

DESTITUTE: 1. *Abandoned, forsaken, deserted.*

—*Oxford English Dictionary*, Vol. 3, 1933

My baby was thirsty. She needed me to find her and fill her crying mouth. I had to save her. There was nobody else.

I knew this as I ran through the jungle on the same path I'd taken from the rice fields so many years ago. I was soaked to the bone, and the roots and rocks that pricked my bare feet were powerful enough to send pains shooting up into my belly. Then I felt something cold on my mouth, shocking me. I cracked open my eyes to find I was lying in the brothel storeroom where I'd spent the last five months.

"Didi, Didi!" I heard young Lina's voice cry out. "You are awake after all these days. Don't sleep again, take some water!"

"All these days?" I struggled to understand.

"It is five days since your daughter came. You are not well."

"What does the doctor say?" I asked through the fog that threatened to swallow me. I wondered where the baby was. She was so thirsty.

"No doctor is here. The dai gave you herbs. You drank a medicine she made, and she put some herbs in there, too, to make it better." Lina patted the sheet stretched over my body, and I moaned from the deep, strange pain.

I could barely get the words out, I was so tired. "The doctor must come. His office is in Third Avenue. Tell him—" But I was no longer with Lina. Instead, I was walking the red dirt road that Ma and I once traveled with the brooms; it was dusty and hot and every spring and pond was dried up, without water to drink. I walked on slowly until at last, I heard a voice speaking my name.

It was Pankaj. We were standing in the gardens at Lockwood School once again, and he was looking at me with sympathy in his eyes. He knew I was Bidushi's best friend. He held out the ruby pendant on its chain, and when I did not make a move to take it, he pressed it against my chest. The feel of the cold, smooth jewel shocked me, and I took a deep breath of joy.

"Pamela." I heard my name and was back in the storeroom, but with Dr. DeCruz holding a stethoscope against my chest. At his side was Mummy, dressed in a bright purple printed dress, with her eyelids painted like bruises. A stand had been set up beside the bed with a drip bag of intravenous fluid, just as had been done for Bidushi.

"Very good, Pamela! You're with us again." Dr. DeCruz took away the stethoscope and looked at me closely.

"You should have called the doctor," Mummy scolded. "This is just terrible, you and the precious baby girl at risk."

"I was too sick to call. You chose to put me with people who didn't care to call him, either. If it wasn't for Lina . . ." My voice faded as I realized how, once again, I had come close to death. But missed it.

"Yes, it's very good the girl came to me. You have a serious infection, but I think it's under control." Dr. DeCruz said that during delivery, my body had ripped, and germs had passed through the torn tissue and ravaged me fiercely. The damage had been so complete that it was unlikely I could ever conceive another child. For the last four days, I'd been taking medicines through my arm and been treated with special creams. He had stitched me where I'd been torn and given Jayshree instructions not to let the dai come near me.

"And my baby? I haven't seen her," I said, realizing that her calling to me in my dreams might have been real cries from nearby.

"Your milk stopped completely, so she has been fed by a wet nurse," the doctor said. "If you decide to take her back into your care, you must give her a kind of powdered milk that you can mix with water. You must boil the water yourself, if you can't trust the reliability of the people here. This home is filthy; I didn't know such places existed," he added with a strong look at Mummy.

"It was the only place that would house her," Mummy said evenly.

"It has been difficult, but this dear girl has helped me," I said, indicating Lina with my head. "Now that I'm awake, may I have my baby?"

At my words, the doctor's tense expression relaxed into a real smile. "Ah, the beauteous Hazel. Jayshree calls her Chum-Chum but everyone else is saying Hazel because of her golden-brown eyes."

"I came up with it," Mummy said, beaming. "It's the perfect name for a pretty Anglo-Indian girl. Her skin is perfect: tea brewed for a half minute with plenty of milk! I wouldn't have thought, Pamela, you could produce a daughter so fair—"

"Hazel," I repeated, not liking how the word started out like a cough and ended with a dull consonant. "May I feed her?"

"Of course. You should learn this, as every mother must." Dr. De-Cruz turned to address Lina, who had been squatting in the corner of the storeroom. "Girl, go to your kitchen and see that water is brought to full boil. You must watch it bubble for several minutes before you take it off the fire. And the flask must be cleaned with boiling water before the rest of the water is added."

"Yes, Doctor-saheb. I understand!" Lina skipped out of the room, looking excited to fulfill such a task.

Mummy sighed and rose to her feet. "I must be leaving in order to greet tonight's guests. Doctor, when should Pamela return to work?"

"At least three more weeks for healing. However, she would be more comfortable resting at Rose Villa than this place." He looked at her significantly.

"If you came alone, I suppose—" Mummy began.

"Do you mean for me to return there now *without* my baby?" Through my pain, another feeling was emerging. It was protection.

"Of course! That has always been the plan," Mummy said in a friendly way, but with an expression that didn't match. "Hazel can stay here with Jayshree through the early years. After that, you may pay for her schooling somewhere. Literate girls are more attractive. In fact . . ."

I lost the rest of what Mummy said because yellow spots were appearing behind my eyes. I had never been so angry. Mummy must have sensed my distress because all of a sudden she stopped speaking but waved her fingers and swept out.

Lina came in straight afterward, carrying the flask of boiled water in one hand and my bundled baby in the crook of her other arm. Dr. DeCruz chided her for the casual manner in which Hazel was being handled and took the baby from her and placed her into my arms. Then he fiddled with some milk powder and a glass bottle that were in his doctor's big leather bag. He said the drink was too hot; it would have to wait twenty minutes before Hazel could take it.

I could barely pay attention to his lesson in making and serving baby milk because I finally had the chance to examine my daughter. How well she looked. The thin mat of hair I remembered had grown into a robust thatch of dark brown curls. Her pale, plump arms waved in the air as the doctor tapped at them. I thought how perfect her lashes were, surrounding eyes that were lotus-shaped like mine but so much lighter; there was green mixed with the golden brown. I wondered if this color would stay or change as years went on. I wanted to know. I had not wanted this child while she was in me, but now that I'd seen her, I felt as if there was a magical silken cord knotting us together.

The doctor ordered Lina to leave the room. After we were alone, he closed the door and said, "I want to ask you something in confidence. Do you wish to leave your child to be raised here?"

I looked at him, trying to sense if this was a kind of test Mummy had asked him to use with me. And how did he know about my true secret feelings?

The doctor's voice was soft. "Leaving her here is not your only choice. I can help."

My body collapsed with relief, and the words rushed out of me. "Doctor, I cannot keep her with these people. I would rather us both die than that happen!"

"You shouldn't stay here, either, but I know that you won't be able to find any kind of decent home or work for yourself with babe in arms. That is why I want to bring Hazel to a very good home." The doctor reached into his case and withdrew a crisp paper.

It was an official birth certificate issued by the Railway Hospital. On it was typed the name *Hazel Mary Smith, Date of Birth 15 May 1938, Bengal Nagpur Railway Hospital, Khargpur. Race Anglo-Indian.* John Smith was listed as *deceased father, nationality, English.* I was listed as Pamela Barker, *mother born 1920, Anglo-Indian.*

"She is so fair, nobody has to know that you are Indian," Dr. De-Cruz said, when I looked up at him in dismay. "It's only to make things easier for her."

"Who is this Mr. Smith?" I felt confused. "And you know that I did not give birth at the hospital!"

"I typed and signed this all myself." Dr. DeCruz's gaze was stern. "If the document is used outside Kharagpur limits, no one will think to challenge it. The child is obviously Anglo-Indian."

"Where will our home be?" How much I wanted a real home; it was all that I had longed for, ever since the tidal wave.

Stroking his silver-black mustache, Dr. DeCruz said, "I shall bring

Hazel to one of the church homes for Anglo-Indian children in the hills. In these places, Anglo-Indian children receive housing, food, and religious education. She will be cared for until maturity."

The idea of the strange place, so far away, was frightening, but it did not sound as if Hazel would be made into a servant. And at a school, I might be allowed to tutor or teach, especially if I managed to get the Cambridge certificate. Hesitantly, I asked, "May I live and work at this place, too?"

"No. These schools bring up children in a completely English fashion, so they are never confused as to their identity. Hazel is quite lucky to qualify for a place like this. Many of the children get scholarships that lead to higher education and good jobs in the railways and schools and even hospitals."

I shivered, thinking about how my daughter might grow up to become like one of the Anglo-Indian nurses at the Railway Hospital. If she saw me on the street, she would recognize me only as a native below her. Should she ever learn that she was my flesh and blood, she would weep. Pushing down my sorrow, I spoke carefully. "There is so much to think about. I must make sure my baby is getting enough milk and growing strong. She needs my care and cannot travel now."

"And you are still recovering!" Dr. DeCruz said, his voice smooth in the same way as when he prepared me for my life in prostitution. "Take all the time you need to heal, Pamela. When you are of sound mind and body, the right decision will be obvious."

He had spoken of a school in the hills; but what kind of school would take an infant less than a month old? I studied the doctor, thinking that he could do anything he pleased with her. He might be planning to sell or give her to an Anglo-Indian family. Because I would have no further contact with her, I'd never know.

The baby made a rude noise, breaking my train of thought.

Dr. DeCruz laughed. "Hazel may be ready for the bottle now. What do you think?"

"Let me try." I tilted the bottle again, and her rosebud lips fluttered against it a few times. But then she took it, and as she drank, her eyes looked up at me. It was as if she were saying, *This does not make any sense, but I am doing it for you.*

"She's a clever little one." Dr. DeCruz sounded approving. "Now, before she spits on it, I'll take back her birth certificate."

"Here you are." I handed it to him, and watched it disappear into his deep leather bag, thinking that this would be all he'd ever get of the girl he'd named Hazel Mary Smith.

CHAPTER
17

FUGITIVE: 1. Apt or tending to flee; given to, or in the act of, running away.

—*Oxford English Dictionary*, Vol. 4, 1933

There was so much to do for my daughter that I could hardly keep track. Fortunately, Lina helped: reminding me when to take my medicine, bringing water and the baby's milk, and washing the baby's and my laundry. I thanked her over and over, knowing that, without her, both the baby and I would fail. Then a large box from Rose Villa was delivered. It contained baby clothes, skin cream for me, and at the bottom of the basket, one hundred rupees hidden inside a bottle. The congratulations card was from Lucky-Short-for-Lakshmi. I was overwhelmed by the kindness of the gift and hoped Lucky would come to see the baby.

The hundred rupees were more than enough to get passage to Calcutta. But it would not be enough to pay rent for a decent place, to buy food, and to pay for school fees, although how could I even attend school with a baby? I wished so much for advice from Bidushi, because she understood money and knew a little about Calcutta. But now I would have to rely on Lucky. After the first big gift, I waited in vain for her to come. When she stayed away, I realized she must be under orders to do so. Mummy wouldn't like Lucky or any of the girls to feel the kind of maternal yearnings that could lead to a professional mistake.

Out of the money Lucky had gifted me, I paid Lina ten annas each week with strict instructions to hide it for herself. I told her she might want to leave the brothel someday; that to clean houses or care for a family's babies might be better suited to her nature. Lina said nothing but looked as if she were thinking about it.

❦   ❦   ❦

TWENTY-ONE DAYS WAS all the time I had left before returning to Rose Villa. And I found that as much as I had wanted to get out of the dancing girls' house, I regretted the end date coming because of leaving my daughter. I could not leave her with Jayshree; nor did I want to give her to Dr. DeCruz. I avoided thinking about them, instead spending hours memorizing her small face with its sparking green-gold eyes. The eyes had made me fall in love and dream of how beautifully and happily she might grow.

As a girl, I used to hide in an imaginary gold almirah; as a mother, the sanctuary of my dreams changed into a tall white bungalow. In such a home, I imagined that my daughter would inhale only good smells: saffron from rice at the table, jasmine from the garlands twined in her hair, and ink from her school notebook. How different it would be from this brothel, where we were always on the run from the opium fumes that curled their way under my door if people smoked nearby.

As my strength improved, I was able to do more for my child. I bathed her several times each day and, afterward, rubbed her skin with mustard oil until it gleamed. I sent Lina to the bazar to buy the baby tiny cotton smocks, and I made nappies and swaddling cloths from my own old saris. The brothel women called this frivolous waste and said that the baby was too young to hear stories. But she fed beautifully when I recited poems. And that joy she gave me led to my understanding of what her first name should be: Kabita, which meant poem. Her middle name was Lina, after the little girl who had saved us both.

Dear Kabita! Sweet Kabita! I whispered into her tiny pink shell of an ear, willing her to do the improbable and learn her name to hold inside her always.

Twenty-one days shrank to eleven and then to only five. I knew that I could not linger on, yet I knew I could not give Kabita up to Jayshree or Dr. DeCruz. Surely there was a better situation. A bud of an idea grew secretly inside me, just like Kabita had. And just like before, there was no one I dared tell.

I WAS NERVOUS to leave Kabita on the day of my medical appointment with Dr. DeCruz; but I feared bringing her with me would be more dangerous, lest the doctor seize her from my arms. So I kept her home under Lina's care.

As I'd expected, Dr. DeCruz immediately asked for Kabita when I stepped into his chambers. After I assured him she was only home due to a cold, he bade me to his table and swiftly removed the stitches that he had placed. "I did something for you," he said briskly. "I stitched in a way that it appears your hymen is still intact. You can make your debut again before returning to your profession."

I stared at him, not believing it. How could I pretend to be a novice after all that had happened? I was a woman of eighteen years, and my face was not that of a child anymore. Nor did he understand that the baby had changed me, and I had finally gained the strength not to return to Rose Villa. He had thought prostitution was not the life for Kabita: why would he recommend it for me?

Dr. DeCruz was talking about Hazel again and holding out a certificate of relinquishment for me to sign and date. Dutifully, I signed Pamela Barker but marked it for the next day.

"That's a bit of a delay." When the doctor frowned, the edges of his mustache drooped. "You see, I have a nun waiting to escort the baby tonight."

I tried to look sorry, and I said that the brothel would be very busy that evening with many drunken customers, and that Jayshree and Tilak could easily enlist some of these ruffians to prevent Hazel's departure. In a respectful tone, I said, "Could you please come for her tomorrow before noon, when the customers and ruffians are gone? It will be quiet and safe, and I can leave at the same time for Rose Villa."

Dr. DeCruz didn't look pleased, but he nodded. "Very well, then, I'll come tomorrow around ten in the morning. With the nun."

As the doctor stepped out of the room so I could dress privately, he left his instruments on a tray and the folder of papers next to it. I opened the folder, seeing notes about the birth and my health condition going back to the time I'd come to Kharagpur, the relinquishment statement I'd just signed, and underneath it, my baby's birth certificate. The relinquishment I would later tear to bits, but the birth certificate was a different matter. It proclaimed my baby the daughter of an Englishman, something that would give her chances at many schools and jobs: a life better than my own.

Slipping both papers into my bag, I finished dressing and left the room. In the front reception area, I said a polite good-bye to his nurse-receptionist. I had been a model patient. I doubted that Dr. DeCruz would look for the papers until it was too late.

❀   ❀   ❀

THAT AFTERNOON, I went into the Gole Bazar and bought baby frocks in larger sizes, another bottle, and more milk powder. Then I went to a sari shop, where I found two durable cotton saris suitable for an ordinary housewife. Then, in a Muslim shop, I ignored the curious expression of the shop owner and purchased a black burka. I could think of no better disguise for the task I had ahead.

When I returned to my room, Kabita was screaming. Lina handed her to me with apologies, but I told her not to worry. Inside, I felt more confident than I had in years. After I'd settled Kabita, I slid out the suitcase I'd brought from Rose Villa. I packed all the books I still had and the few European dresses and saris that did not seem too gaudy for my future life.

As I'd told Dr. DeCruz, it was a busy night at the brothel: the end of a pay fortnight for the men who worked in the railway yards and workshops. I kept out of sight but heard them laughing as usual. The men trouped upstairs with the women, and it always seemed just as one pair were settled, someone new would announce his entry with shouts at the door. Matters were complicated when Jayshree demanded use of my room for the customer overflow, as she did from time to time.

Kabita and I were banished to the children's sleeping room. I asked Lina and her brother to take my suitcase out to the hallway and hide it under a table with a long cloth. They easily accepted the story I told them about wanting to keep my things safe from the strangers in my room.

I stayed in the room that Lina and the other children shared, telling them stories until they all slept; my words were calm, but inside I was not. Not until four in the morning did I tiptoe downstairs with my baby and her bundle of things. My suitcase was still under the table. I unlocked it to take out the burka I'd bought, and put it over my simple sleeping sari. Now that I was dressed, I went outside with Kabita and the suitcase, closing the door softly behind me. My heart pounded fiercely, for the journey had begun.

The man who had taken me to the hospital was sleeping in his rickshaw as usual, but I decided that I could not risk his recognizing my voice through my disguise. So I waited in the shadows with Kabita strapped to me with a scarf under the burka. When a tonga stopped at another brothel to drop off an early customer, I hurried out and negotiated a fee for a ride to the station. As I rode off, I looked through the narrow slit in my black veil at the slum to which I would never return. How ugly it was: full of women's and children's misfortunes. *But not ours.* I whispered to Kabita that now her real life would begin.

❦   ❦   ❦

AT KHARAGPUR STATION, things were more complicated than I thought they'd be. To reach the platform for Midnapore, I had to climb steps to an overhead walkway, all the while managing the baby and my suitcase. I couldn't manage it without the help of a coolie, who took the case and also saved me a seat inside the crowded third-class compartment.

Even though I could see little outside the small window the burka offered me, I had the sense everyone was looking at me and wondering about my situation. Only after the stationmaster blew his whistle and the train moved did I feel safe enough to uncover Kabita from the heavy burka. Because she was out of her quiet, dark hideaway, she promptly awoke, wet herself, and wailed. I was beset with annoyed looks and criticism from the rest of the compartment while I changed her. When I heard the conductor call for Midnapore, I was very relieved to get away from them.

At the small railway station, I stored my suitcase and took another tonga straight to the mosque, which I thought was vague enough that my path could not be tracked. Outside the tremendous white building decorated with many minarets, I asked the driver to stop and wait until I returned. I disembarked with Kabita, walking around the mosque with a group of women and then melting away from them into a maze of small streets, eventually coming to the one I remembered. A few steps down the street, and I spotted the small walled compound that belonged to Abbas and Hafeeza.

Since the night before, I had been mentally composing the letter I'd leave with Kabita. I dared not write anything down at the brothel that might be discovered; and on the train my hands had been too full with Kabita to write. Now at last was the time to bring out the paper and pen I had tucked into Kabita's bundle. In Bengali script I wrote:

Honored Uncle and Aunt:

Aadab; my most respectful and loving greeting. This beloved girl of mine was born on May 15th of this year. Her father is unwilling to take responsibility. I have no roof over my head to give her, and no means to feed and clothe her. I have brought her to you in the hopes you may raise her as your own.

As you can see, she is in good health. I believe that she will be a pleasant, helpful, and grateful child. She comes with some money I have left for her expenses and education. It is my sincere wish that she might attend school.

I have called her Kabita, but you should give her any name you would like. She takes her bottle six to eight times daily, three spoons of milk powder and the rest boiled water. Your beloved Allah will bless you many times for your kindness to a child whose only crime is being born in a dangerous place to a wretched mother.

I did not sign. I was ashamed of how I'd turned out, even after the help Abbas and Hafeeza had given. And for this reason, I decided not to leave the birth certificate. It was better for them to believe the child was merely fair. I looked down on Kabita's sweet, sleeping face and thought how long it might be before I saw her again. Then I whispered to her the words that I left out of the note: that I loved her. No person would believe it of a woman giving up her child; and I didn't care to try to convince them. Kabita knew my voice, though, and as I whispered it, I hoped she would at least have a brief feeling of comfort.

The property's gate was locked, so I could not bring her in. For a moment, I panicked, but then I noticed a broken-down crate a bit farther down the lane. I retrieved it and climbed up and found that now I could reach over the top of the gate. I hung Kabita in her little sling over the top of the gateposts, so she remained safely on the inside where the right people would discover her. Through all of this, Kabita slept quietly on.

I carried the crate away and sat on it in the shadows of another house, which was higher up the hill, allowing me a good view into Abbas and Hafeeza's home. How quiet it was there. Kabita still slept. The sky continued to lighten, and vehicles, people, and animals came into the street. Finally, a woman emerged from the hut to light a cooking fire.

I barely breathed as the woman turned away from the fire and toward the gate. She moved slowly toward the bundle and then more rapidly; I could see now that it was Hafeeza, under the rough shawl's cover. Tenderly, she picked Kabita up out of the sling, and I heard her croon some words. And suddenly, I felt robbed.

I told myself that I should not feel this way, that I was the one who had willingly left my child for her. Tears still rolled down my face, dampening the inside of the burka. I knew this was the safest place in the world for Kabita. But I couldn't leave; my feet felt as if they'd been buried in sand. In fact, I stayed on the box, quietly crying, until a louder sound broke through: the Imam's voice, through a megaphone atop the mosque. He was calling people to the ten o'clock prayer. This reminded me that in less than a half hour, the train to Calcutta would leave.

As the Arabic prayer finished, I started walking away. As my feet moved, I silently prayed that Kabita would embrace her new life as tightly as I had once embraced her. But for me, it was time to go.

BOOK FOUR
CALCUTTA
1938–1947

*How much Calcutta means to India and the European
domination of the Empire can never be conceived by those
who are unfamiliar with the city and its unusual importance;
who know not the many matters in which she leads opinion in
India; who are ignorant of her abounding trade and commerce;
who have neglected to study their history upon the conquest
of India, with special reference to the part Bengal played;
and who have never visited her for sufficient time to realize
why so much of India's prosperity depends upon the financial,
commercial, and traffic organisations of the city. Calcutta, in fact,
although no longer the capital, is undoubtedly the Indian City
which not only attracts greater attention than any other in every
way, but is regarded as the first British city of the East.*

*—Travel in India, or City, Shrine and Sea-Beach: Antiquities, Health
Resorts and Places of Interest on the Bengal-Nagpur Railway, 1916*

CHAPTER
18

*Calcutta to those who know the place will always be a city of
happy memories, not only by reasons of friends and associations
but because of its many natural beauties. Not the least of it are
sunsets over the Hooghly, lighting up the sky beyond the smoke of
the mills in a gorgeous radiance . . .*

—*Travel in India, or City, Shrine and Sea-Beach:
Antiquities, Health Resorts and Places of Interest on the
Bengal-Nagpur Railway,* 1916

The city was loud but could not drown out Kabita's cry. It rose
above the voices of the touts and the train horns. *You left me,* the
cry said. *You are the worst kind of woman on this earth.*

But Kabita would never be rented to beggars. She would have a
real mother and father. Her life wouldn't be marked by sin and starvation but affection and learning. She would have everything I'd once
had and more. I told these things to the wind, to carry back to my
child in Midnapore.

❧   ❧   ❧

WHILE I WAS sure of her future, I was less so about my own in Calcutta. Howrah Railway Station was steamy hot and full of people hurrying at top speed. With my heavy suitcase, I felt awkward and slow, especially since I had no idea where to go. But seeing clearly would help.

In the privacy of a toilet stall in the ladies' lounge, I abandoned the burka. From the top layer of my trunk, I took out one of the European dresses I'd had at Rose Villa, for I had decided to try my luck at passing for Anglo-Indian. I took the idea from Rudyard Kipling's novel *Kim*; its central character, Kimball O'Hara, was a sunburned English boy who pretended to be Indian so he could live freely. I'd do just the reverse, using my fluent English and knowledge of English habits. I hoped this might land me a proper job typing papers, selling jewelry, or answering telephones: the jobs enjoyed by the young lady characters in American and English films.

Outside Howrah was a confusing jam of rickshaws, trams, tongas, and cars. I boarded a tram headed for Chitpore Road, an area I remembered from newspaper advertisements as known for reasonable but respectable hotels. Unfortunately, I was the only woman dressed in European clothing on the packed tram: a regrettable decision. The entire trip was an exercise in trying to get men to stop nudging my bosom or rubbing against my legs: something I couldn't refuse at Rose Villa but was bent on never allowing to happen again. Quite deliberately, I dropped my suitcase on the bare feet of a man who had grabbed at me and later swung it hard against a couple of pinchers when I disembarked.

A few curses followed me, but the unpleasantness faded as I took in the spectacle of Chitpore Road, a seemingly endless thoroughfare packed with shops selling more things than I ever dreamed existed. And it was not all under roofs: at the road's edge, armies of perfume sellers, brass merchants, tailors, and vendors sold wares. Cobblers strolled with their tools hanging from long poles across the shoulders—as did the peddlers, who sang out the quality of their leather and nails.

With so many colorful distractions, it was hard to catch each one of the hotels. I looked carefully at the posted tariffs before choosing a narrow brick building where I saw an Anglo-Indian gentleman leaving and an Indian couple with two children going in.

The receptionist was an older Anglo-Indian gentleman called Mr. Jones. After he'd finished registering the Indian family, he turned to me. The rate for a single room was two rupees per night; I could afford it, but not for very long. On the register, I described myself as Camilla Smith, daughter of Jonathan Smith, Bombay. I had decided on Camilla in a snap moment for its being close to Pamela, but not quite the same; and Smith because it was a way I could still feel linked to Kabita.

My room on the second floor was small and hot, with a narrow iron bedstead and a moth-eaten blanket. In the corner was a cracked porcelain sink with a tap that eked out a trickle of brown water. I opened the window for air, and instantly, the room filled with the racket of the road below. But the pillow and sheets were clean, and there was no taint of the brothel about it.

Nobody would smell anything of my past, I vowed as I washed my face and looped my hair into a chignon. If I intended to easily pass for Anglo-Indian, I would need to cut it into one of the shoulder-length, curling styles that were popular that year. But at least I had real silk stockings and heeled pumps and a clutch purse into which I tucked the Positions Available section from the *Statesman*. It appeared that there were many good clerical jobs on a street called Esplanade. I drank some water from the sink and decided there were still enough hours of light to look for work.

I went downstairs and asked Mr. Jones how to reach the business district called Esplanade. He recommended that I take the tram. After my bus experience, I spent some more of the money Lucky had given me to ride inside the second-class car. I pulled the bell when my seatmate, a kindly Anglo-Indian lady, advised me it was close to the Chowringhee-Esplanade crossing. I walked the wrong way at first, but then a shoeshine boy corrected me. And finally, I was standing on the world-famous shopping street.

It was impossible not to gawk at the rows of magnificent British office buildings, so tall, elegant, and white. Many had designs carved into them: wreaths and flowers and angels. The famous names I'd seen in newspaper advertisements were here, in stucco or brick: Hall & Anderson, the Army & Navy Stores, Whiteaway Laidlaw, and Chippers Shoes. The thresholds of these institutions were guarded by stony-faced chowkidars who stepped aside for Europeans but questioned anyone else wanting entry. A thought sparked that I could become a saleswoman at Whiteaway Laidlaw, but when I approached the chowkidar, he told me to move on.

This curt dismissal was repeated by the chowkidars overseeing the shipping office I visited, as well as the travel agency and the accounting firm, all of which had advertised their needs. I did not look Anglo-Indian enough, I realized with dismay. Over and over I heard: *No Indians. Position filled. Send a letter. Go away.*

Calcutta could not be conquered on the first day, I told myself. Back on Chitpore Road, I bought an omelette wrapped in a warm paratha from a street vendor. I'd eaten nothing since leaving Kharagpur. I would be grateful for the free breakfast at the hotel the next morning. It was twilight by the time I was back inside the hotel, and I lingered by the reception area to study last Sunday's copies of the *Statesman* and *Amrita Bazar Patrika* for other jobs that might still be open.

A position for a Eurasian or domiciled European file clerk at the Writers' Building caught my attention. It would be exciting to work for a writer, English or Indian—and maybe one day, if I worked hard,

I could rise up from filing to writing. Miss Richmond had liked my translations; perhaps this was something I could offer, as well as filing.

When I asked Mr. Jones if he'd heard of the Writers' Building, his thick eyebrows rose. "The Writers' Building is where the sahebs make their administration. It is so large you cannot miss it: a redbrick building with hundreds going inside and out."

"Make administration" was not something I understood entirely, but I nodded because I did not want to appear ignorant. Mr. Jones said the building was in a place called Dalhousie Square near the Great Eastern Hotel. How grand it all sounded. I hoped I was not shooting too high.

IN THE EARLY morning, the first thing I saw against the window was my bundled daughter. I gasped before realizing that the heap of cloth in the window was the dress I'd washed the night before and hung to dry. The winds had knocked it down so it collapsed on the sill in a mound that looked like Kabita's sling. And I remembered that she was no longer with me.

My darling baby: How was she? Had she had her morning milk, was her wet nappy changed, and was Hafeeza or Abbas holding her? Tears came to my eyes, but I stifled the emotion that rose in my throat. It would not do to cry. I should not disturb the others still sleeping in rooms around me.

The dress that had dropped from the window was still damp and wrinkled, so I chose another one I'd brought, a pink-flowered dress that was a bit spangly. I used my nail scissors to cut off the gold bits. I devoured the hotel's breakfast of tea and buns and then went outside into bright and busy Chitpore Road to find a letter-writing man with a typewriter. When I told him what I wanted, he laughed.

"From the way you speak, Memsaheb, I can imagine you can write a very good letter in English yourself. You do not need my services."

I had never been called Memsaheb before; it made me feel wary that he would charge me more than the illiterate. Resignedly, I dictated to him a letter from Mrs. Theodora Markham regarding Miss Camilla Smith. I worried that he might challenge the letter's topic, but in the end, I was the only one protesting. He had made three spelling errors; I could not show such a letter to anyone. After a brief argument, he allowed me to sit down at the typewriter and do it myself. This spectacle brought about all kinds of laughter from passersby, and he was aggrieved enough to charge me eight annas, double what I'd heard him asking from a previous customer.

It hurt to pay that much, but after my experiences in Esplanade, I knew the benefit of having a typed paper to show the chowkidars guarding the Writers' Building. I also managed to use the letter writer's fountain pen to make a grand signature befitting the fictitious bank director's wife, who had employed me as her personal assistant for two years and was very sorry she could not take me to England with her.

I thought the letter was strong. But when I presented it at the Writers' Building, two chowkidars denied me entrance for want of an appointment. I left to the sounds of laughter and commentary about my English dress and legs. But I resolved not to give up, since I'd tailored the letter specifically to this job, for which there really was an opening. All I needed was to enter the building from another point.

Casually, I strolled around the corner and saw the back of the grand building. Halfway along the ground-floor windows, I saw an office with a desk near the window and nobody inside. I'd climbed so many trees in my girlhood; this would be simple, if only I could find the first foothold.

Speaking warmly, I coaxed two street boys to make a step with their arms for me to use getting up to the window. It was not so bad to get up, and the window was already fully open. I pulled myself through after making sure the room really was still empty. I landed on a desk and carefully slid off it. After straightening my dress, I exited the office into a hallway buzzing with movement.

Well-dressed Englishmen strode from one place to another, as did smaller numbers of Indian gentlemen dressed in copies of the Englishmen's clothes. I looked for a woman to whom I could ask directions but saw none save for one European lady who looked at me with obvious surprise. Based on this, I didn't approach her but spoke to a barefoot peon carrying a tea tray. He told me the office of Mr. J. White in accounting was on the third floor, second door on the left.

When I knocked on the closed door, a voice shouted to enter. I found myself standing in a small room bordered floor-to-ceiling with file cabinets. A young Indian man wearing an English suit was seated at a desk with a large typewriter and stacks of files next to him. He looked past me as if he were still expecting the person who'd knocked.

"I've come to interview for the file clerk job," I said in my best attempt at Oxbridge.

"Who invited you?" The clerk snapped back in English, but with a regular Bengali accent.

"I received a letter." I would have to say it wasn't with me, if he demanded to see it.

"What is your name?" He was looking at a list with a frown.

Another lie. "Camilla Smith."

He looked up at me with eyes that said he understood my game exactly. "That is very odd. I am making all of the calls for Mr. White, and nobody on my list is female. The job is for a male graduate with references."

"I have brought a reference letter as requested." I spoke calmly, pretending I hadn't heard the rejection in his voice.

The clerk took the letter from my hands and held it up to the light. Smiling broadly, he said, "Ah, yes! I recognize this cheap paper. You had this typed by one of the fellows in the Hogg Market, didn't you?"

"Sir, that is not true!" I felt my chest tighten under my uncomfortable European dress. He was taking pleasure in my defeat.

"And how did you come by the name Smith?" the clerk snickered. "Another lie, or was your mother a bad woman?"

As I stood there, shocked by the gross insult to me by one of my own, a portly, red-faced European man in a khaki business suit came through the door. Another one followed him. In a flash, I guessed that one of them could be the Mr. White I was seeking, whose opinion would perhaps overrule the pompous clerk's.

I looked at the second man who'd entered and appeared to be scrutinizing me with interest. He was the younger of the two, with an angular build and a lightly tanned face that made his blue eyes appear piercing yet not unkind. My woman's intuition told me to speak to him first. In a strong but polite voice, I said, "Sir, I have come to apply for Mr. White's filing position."

"Sorry, I'm not your man. But he is." The man spoke easily in the upper-class accent that I was striving carefully to replicate.

The other gentleman looked at me critically without speaking, and I began feeling self-conscious. At last, he said, in an accent that was not as pleasant as Oxbridge, "I didn't expect a woman would come for the job interview."

"The advertisement didn't say woman or man," I protested.

"No ladies were invited," the clerk interrupted. "Sir, she is a pure interloper!"

I remembered the way Lucky had taught me to use my eyes; I made them large for Mr. White. He grunted and said, "Since you're here, I'll look at your reference letter. Ranjit, give it to me."

The clerk called Ranjit handed his employer the letter with obvious disdain. Mr. White skimmed the letter while the second man settled down in a chair facing the desk. I stared at the two men, wondering how much money they earned.

Mr. White cleared his throat and said, "You were schooled in Darjeeling? I haven't heard of this one."

"It's quite small, run by some teachers from England and Ireland—"

"And it seems you have worked as a lady's private secretary. That's well and good, but it's hardly filing experience."

As I opened my mouth to defend myself, a memory of what I'd done for Miss Richmond came forth. "It's filing and much more. I can type correspondence and make translations: Bengali to English and the converse. I cared for all of the memsaheb's books, organizing them completely and protecting them from mildew with regular cleaning. I see that your files are already threatened by damp." I gestured toward the shelves loaded to the ceiling with discolored files and papers bound with red tape.

"Moisture is worrisome," the second man said in his crisp voice. "Mr. White, I hope that my expense report hasn't moldered away."

"Not at all, sir," Ranjit chimed in. "We have many reports to process. It takes time. We do everything according to regulation."

"I won't hire you," Mr. White said, giving me back the letter with a baleful look. "This is a seat of government where men do serious work. Ranjit, show the girl the way out."

I left without a glance at any of them, stepping rapidly down the hall, where it now felt that everyone was staring. My face was warm, and there was a lump in my throat that would turn into a sob if I had to open my mouth. I hurried out through the main doors, ignoring the outraged chowkidars. My attempt to secure an interview had been so humiliating that I vowed on the spot never to apply for jobs with any English organization again.

Yet outside in the sun, after I'd been walking for ten minutes, I was able to restore myself. I'd failed to find work within the Writers' Building, but it was just the second day of looking for work in the city where Rabindranath Tagore wrote, Netaji had crafted his plans for independence, and Pankaj was practicing law. They didn't work for the British; they worked for themselves.

For me to come here, I'd given up Kabita. Failing to find work would mean failing her, for I had it in mind to send as much money as I could spare to Abbas and Hafeeza. So the next day, and the day after that, I began searching for work at Indian businesses, this time wearing a sari and a forced smile on my face. And again I was rejected; sometimes for my gender or lack of credentials or known family, but most often for no reason at all.

It was only at night that I allowed myself to feel hopeless. A week into my stay, as I tossed and turned in the narrow hotel bed, I wondered what Bidushi would suggest. And it seemed that, with a rush of wind clattering the window, I heard a name.

Pankaj. Find him for both of us.

CHAPTER
19

POSH: The suggestion that this word is derived from the initials of "port outward starboard home" is referring to the more expensive side for accommodation on ships formerly travelling between England and India is often put forward but lacks foundation. . . . Smart, "swell," "classy," fine, splendid, stylish, first rate.

—A Supplement to the *Oxford English Dictionary*, Vol. 3, 1933

Number 27 Lower Circular Road, Ballygunge.

This address had lived in my mind since Bidushi had spoken of it years ago. This was the house where Bidushi and I were to live in peace and enjoyment forever. But when I went to Pankaj's residence the next afternoon, it was not exactly as I'd hoped. I had expected a shining white palace: instead, it was a graciously proportioned, lemon-colored bungalow the same size as its neighbors. But it was a very pretty house, with many long windows shielded by ornate grilles. Tall mango trees stood on either side of the front walk that was guarded by a Sikh chowkidar sleeping in a chair.

I walked close enough to read BANDOPADHYAY AND SON, PART-NERS AT LAW inscribed on a brass plaque attached to the fence. I gazed up to the guarded windows, remembering how Bidushi had asked me to take care of Pankaj. It had been my dream, too. But approaching him now? How could I possibly do this? He or his parents could remember me from that awful last day at Lockwood School. Perhaps they'd still think of me as a thief at large and would shout for their chowkidar to fetch a constable. I should not have visited their street at all; but I felt such a longing to see at least a bit of the dream that Bidushi and I had shared in our lost girlhood days.

A long car drew up and stopped at the house. Hearing the motor, the chowkidar I feared came awake in his chair. I walked down the street a bit farther and casually turned at the sound of the opening car door, hoping against hope to see Pankaj.

The car's occupants were three men wearing white Congress caps. Sunlight sparked off the edge of the round glasses worn by the tallest gentleman, who was too old to be Pankaj. In fact, he strongly resembled Subhas Chandra Bose, the new president of the Congress Party. It couldn't be, I told myself; but when I saw his moon-round face, I recognized it from the newspapers. This man was the legend: the honorable Netaji, who had been an important topic in letters between Pankaj and me.

At this point, I lost all pretenses of continuing to walk. I stood there gaping as Netaji walked through the gate the chowkidar opened for him, followed by the others. If I'd been braver, I would have run up and said how much I admired his words and deeds; that he had given me strength during my darkest times. But before I could do anything, a bowing servant boy opened the front door, and they vanished inside.

The car in which the men had traveled moved on to park at a slight distance, underneath a shade tree. I watched it, thinking about whether I dared approach the chauffeur. I walked the few extra steps and leaned in the window where the driver sat reading a newspaper.

"Was that Netaji who went inside?" I asked, still excited from the surprise. The driver looked at me a bit cautiously, so I said, "I admire him so."

"Yes, it is Netaji," the driver said after a pause.

"Why is he in the Bandopadhyays' home? I live in the neighborhood," I added to make my inquisitiveness seem reasonable.

"Strictly a business matter! Bandopadhyay-babu aids with matters for the party." His tone was as starchy as if he himself had picked up fame by associating with the leader. Still, I noted the respectful title he had attached to the surname of the family his employer was visiting. It made me wonder which Bandopadhyay, Esquire, he was talking about. "Do you mean the old gentleman?"

"No, the young one. The old gentleman is dead—died of heartbreak while his son was in the Andamans."

I found this very sad but believable. "And the son is back now, living at home? Married with children?"

"Not that I know about." He scowled at me. "But if you live in this neighborhood, you should surely know all of this."

Pankaj was still alive, free from prison, and working with Netaji! And maybe not yet married. As I walked home, these morsels of information filled me with as much happiness as if I'd had a decent meal.

❧   ❧   ❧

MY MODEST FUNDS were declining more rapidly than I'd expected. Regretfully, I decided to vacate the hotel because Mr. Jones was asking me to make payment every second day, as if he sensed something was wrong. He had given me directions to many of the schools that I had found listed in *Thapar's Calcutta Guide*. But it was obvious to him—and to me, too—that the job search was not fruitful.

"Why not try the telephone company?" he suggested the day I was leaving. "Many of our girls are becoming operators."

The hotel receptionist still believed that my background was

Anglo-Indian and that I could find work based on my fictitious name and accent. But I had learned over the weeks that I was too dark, too shy, and too unsophisticated for any of the teaching and saleslady and secretarial jobs. I understood it, but it made me angry, this haughty professional world with the whites on top, Anglo-Indians next, and sycophantic Indians trying to catch up. I was sick of aping the English. I was in a blue-and-pink-printed sari, with bangles on my wrists and chappals on my feet when I checked out.

"Miss Smith, are you all right?" Mr. Jones's thick silver brows crept together. "Dressing in native garb will not help you in your search. Not unless you intend on being an ayah."

I shook my head. The many memsahebs in the city ensured a steady demand for baby ayahs. But my milk was long gone; I could not be a wet nurse. Nor could I bear to spend time with little children when I had given up my own daughter.

"Perhaps it's best to go back to your own family."

I nodded, letting him take comfort in the illusion. By day, I walked the streets of residential neighborhoods and plucked fruit from gardens for my meals. I drank water from the taps that were on some street corners and, with the funds I had left, I bought chapattis or parathas to eat very slowly. But the nights were awful. I was staying in the Howrah Station ladies' lounge, barely getting any sleep with all the noise and movement around me. And there was the matter of my luggage. I could not safely leave it in the ladies' waiting room while I went about the city looking for jobs; nor did I like taking it with me, even though I'd paid a cobbler to add wheels and a pulling strap. I was beginning to worry that the reason I was not being hired was because of the way I looked lugging the trunk.

The morning after my third night sleeping in Howrah, I looked at my suitcase with loathing. Inside were three saris, two dresses, and a dozen books. I also had some grooming necessities, a waning purse of rupees, and Kabita's birth certificate. The heaviest weight in the suitcase was the books; they were the sole reason I still needed to keep the suitcase. I knew it was time to leave them behind, just as I'd stopped showing my false letter of reference.

To put away the crumpled reference letter was simple, but to say good-bye to my collection of books hurt, for they had been my steadfast companions through everything. If I sold a book, I would no longer have it to retreat into, to allow forgiveness and forgetting. In the end, I determined that I would not let go of the Tagore poems but I would forsake the others—and I had an idea where. That Saturday morning, I took the tram into Chowringhee, disembarked, and walked to Bilgrami's Classic Books of Asia and Europe: a business I'd always longed to enter. Inside, I inhaled with pleasure a delicious odor I recognized as old paper. The shop was small and made even tighter by towering bookcases barely two feet apart. Customers of all races perched on low stools between these bookcases, reading. At the front of the room was a high counter, and behind it sat a very wrinkled old man who was lost in his reading. I had to ring the bell on the counter to get his attention. Out of habit, I asked him whether he had need of anyone to work; he said he did not, but in a kind way that led naturally into my request that he consider buying my books.

"Yes, we do take used books." The old man scratched his chin. "But the condition must be excellent. Perhaps it is best if you give me a list of your titles and their condition."

"The books are already here." Feeling short of breath from excitement, I bent to open the case. In less than a minute, all my remaining life treasures were before him.

He looked at them without touching. Finally, he said, "Show me that leather-bound one."

It was the Tagore volume that Miss Richmond had given me to keep. Now I wished I had already moved it to the purse, so he wouldn't have seen it. He made a slight face as he paged through it and said, "The pages have markings and there is a musty smell. Mold is already there."

"The place I stayed was quite hot."

"Books should be aired regularly and dusted. Otherwise all is lost." He surveyed the shop, where fans whirred quietly, and I followed his gaze. A white man was standing several feet behind me with a heavy book in his arms. The bookseller said, "First, I must help the other customer."

"Of course. Just tell me—are you interested in any of the other books?" I took back the Tagore that I hadn't wanted him to have. "They are quite good books, some in English, the others Bengali."

"I can take them, but not for resale." He waved a hand at the stack I'd made. "There is always a need for paper, to be used in packing or as wrapping. It will be only a few annas, I am afraid."

"You would tear my books apart?" I couldn't hide the alarm I felt.

"Of course. But now, I must help this gentleman."

He would not get my books; they had served me too well to earn such mistreatment. With fumbling fingers I repacked them into the suitcase while the Englishman paid for his book. I felt his glance but did not look up. To him it must have been a joke: a young native woman trying to peddle old books.

I packed up my suitcase, locked the case, and turned it on its side so I could wheel it to the bookshop's doorway. Then I heard fast steps from behind and a voice saying to wait.

The Englishman had his new book in one hand and was reaching to hold open the door. I assumed that he wanted to get outside ahead of me, but then I realized he was only trying to ease my passage. It was an unusual courtesy for a European to extend to an Indian, but I was too upset to acknowledge it with more than a nod.

"Aren't you the one who came to the Writers' Building last week?"

On the pavement outside the shop, I turned around in surprise. The customer in the shop was the second man who'd been with Mr. White; I hadn't recognized him this time dressed casually in an open-necked white shirt and light cotton trousers.

Quietly, he said, "I could never give up my books. Actually, I'm seeking someone to help me with them."

Such problems the wealthy have! I was not interested in engaging in small talk, so I pulled at my suitcase to show him I needed to go.

The man continued, "I transferred here two years ago with a decade's worth of books still in boxes. My book collection needs to be taken out, aired, cleaned, and shelved in some sort of sensible arrangement. It's hard to find someone to do that."

"Why are you telling me this?" My question came out sharply, because I was tired of hearing about good jobs for white people only.

A nervous-looking smile creased the man's angular face. "It seemed you were looking for employment the other week. Unless you are otherwise engaged, this might be something for you."

"But Indian women cannot work in the Writers' Building. That was made clear to me." Remembering how I'd been dismissed, my words came out as small and hard as gravel.

"My library is not there. It's actually housed in my personal residence—"

"Good-bye, sir." I yanked my suitcase and began walking, furious that he thought I could be lured to his dwelling. I had changed my clothes, taken away the cosmetics, put my hair in a proper braid. How could he tell what I'd once been?

"No, no, don't look like that—it's a household position but with no cleaning, just library responsibilities." The man was hurrying after me. "I have been trying to find someone for the last three months. The educated babus all desire their own desk in a proper office, and the servant types don't know the first thing about organizing books. And you can type; isn't that what you told Mr. White?"

At this, I stopped. His eyes were a clear blue, but he had good color to his face; he did not look very much like the white devils I'd feared in childhood. My woman's intuition was telling me to stay. "Yes, I can type. But I don't know why you recognized me—"

"Not many Indian women come to the Writers' Building. Your accent is distinctive. But let me introduce myself properly; I'm Simon Lewis." He reached into his pocket, took out a silver case, and withdrew a card for me. I immediately discovered that his surname was not spelled like it sounded: it was spelled Lewes, just like the name of an English poet whose work had been discussed briefly in Miss Richmond's class.

"Like George Henry Lewes?" I asked.

He smiled, revealing even white teeth. "You know poetry. He was a very distant illegitimate relation, and unfortunately passed on no talents to me. And what is your name again, miss?"

While inside the Writers' Building, Mr. White and Ranjit had both read the false letter of reference with an Anglo-Indian name. But I had a feeling Mr. Lewes didn't care if I was Indian or Anglo-Indian or Chinese, as long as I could type.

Swiftly, I said, "I'm called Kamala. Kamala Mukherjee." The surname came from the girl I'd once wanted to be, and Kamala was a dignified Hindu name that sounded like Camilla, which he had heard. It had a good meaning, too: lotus, reminding me of what Ma used to say about my eyes.

"Miss Kamala Mukherjee, I'm very pleased to know you." He held out his hand to me, and, gingerly, I took it. "I've got the Buick waiting just down the street. Would you consider coming to look at the library, at least?"

Trying to act as if I rode in private cars all the time, I nodded.

I HAD NEVER been in a car before, and the scent of the leather seats and cigarette tobacco tickled my nose, even though the windows were open. The driver he introduced as Farouk loaded my suitcase into the boot, alongside Mr. Lewes's purchases. I was too frightened by what I was agreeing to do, so I sat as far apart from the man as I could.

Mr. Lewes explained his residence, Middleton Mansions, was not a private bungalow but something called a mansion block. The ground floor flat was occupied by an army officer he called the Infernal Mr.

Rowley for the many annoyances that were part and parcel of his behavior. The first and second stories were Mr. Lewes's rented space. He had two and a half bedrooms, the library, a dining room, a parlor, and kitchen, and there was a bathroom on each level. His staff consisted of four male servants, all of whom excepting Farouk lived in a garden cottage.

"What about your wife and children?" I would have expected some female servants to tend to their needs.

"No family yet." He sighed. "It's a good thing. No ayah work for you!"

My forehead broke out in sweat, for the situation was more dangerous than I had thought. No ladies in the house! I would try to schedule my hours for the time when Mr. Lewes was at his job; that would be the only way I could feel secure.

"And where do you live in Calcutta?"

"Right now I am staying near Howrah," I said, for I had reasoned that I could not afford to leave the station for a rooming house until I'd had my first week's pay.

"Oh, that's quite far." He sounded disappointed. "It will be hard for you to report for work during monsoon, when there is flooding everywhere. Well, maybe you can shift closer."

"I thought this was a temporary job," I said. "Unpacking and arranging, isn't it?"

"Oh, the work will likely take you through the end of next year, if you do it properly. Maybe longer, even."

Number 9 Middleton Street was a tall, pure-looking white stucco building; my heart beat faster as I realized it was rather like the fairytale bungalow I'd dreamed of for Kabita and myself. No, I told myself. She had her new home, and this was only a place for me to spend days working. Two similar white mansion blocks stood nearby, with green gardens all around. A gardener was on his knees cutting the lawn with scissors. I stepped out, inhaling this smell of fresh grass mixed with flowering jasmine vines.

As I emerged from the Buick, the rest of Mr. Lewes's staff came out of the house. Shombhu, a thick-bodied Bengali man of about thirty, was the chief of the household staff. His round face seemed to collapse at the sight of me. Behind him came Manik, a thin, sharp-eyed cook from Orissa with a teenaged assistant, Choton. There was an even younger houseboy, Choton's cousin Jatin. Only after all were introduced to me did Mr. Lewes reveal that I was Memsaheb Kamala Mukherjee who might be coming to organize the library. He turned to me, as if I were expected to say something to them: but I was too shy to do anything more than croak hello and put my hands together in namaskar.

"Let's go inside," Mr. Lewes said.

His flat's first floor was dominated by a long drawing room filled with a cluttered jumble of Victorian and modern furniture. One side of the drawing room had three closed doors; Mr. Lewes said they went to a guest room on the left, his bedroom on the right, and a shared bath in the middle. Off the main hallway was a doorway to the kitchen and a second door leading to the library.

This was the most important place. I had anticipated a grand room lined with built-in bookcases, but there were only three book-cases, and all were jammed with books. The rest of the room's space was stacked floor-to-ceiling with wooden crates and cardboard boxes. Between them were a few narrow openings that led to a partners desk with two chairs piled atop it for lack of room. Clearly, there were too many books in the room for the space. There was a smell of old paper, dust, and who knew what else: like the condition of the books in my trunk but magnified.

"A formidable job," Mr. Lewes said, sounding a good deal less cheerful than in the car. "It will take hard work. Patience. It's not just typing but unpacking and sorting and cleaning."

"Do you really have time to read all of these?" I asked in wonder.

"I try. And some of them are so interesting I've written essays about them—a mad hobby, I suppose, because I write so much for work."

"It sounds like a busman's holiday, sir."

"Ah. You know metaphors, too."

"I will do my best with your books," I said, feeling happy to have met someone who felt as strongly about books as I did. "But to put them all away, more bookcases are needed."

"Yes! I've been given the name of a good carpenter but haven't yet made arrangements. That can be among the first of your responsibilities. Just make sure the bookcases aren't so tall that they cover what few windows exist."

I nodded, looking upward at the row of small windows set close to the ceiling that appeared to be opened by a long pole standing nearby. They were so very high that I imagined that even if the whole line of windows were open, it would be hard to feel much of a breeze.

The second floor held a storeroom and another small bedroom with its own bath, probably meant for an infant and ayah. All three rooms were piled up with boxes of books. "You may use the bathroom upstairs," he said, answering the question I had been afraid to utter. I was quite pleased to see it had a tub with taps and a toilet with a pull chain, just as I'd had at Rose Villa. I wouldn't have to wash on the streets again, if I came here each day. I was on my way back to a comfortable life.

"Please come early on Monday, before I leave for work," Mr. Lewes said.

"How early, sir?"

"Six thirty would be fine."

I nodded, hoping that buses or trams from Howrah ran early enough to get me all the way to the White Town by six thirty. Then Mr. Lewes reached into his pocket and took out several bills. Pressing them into my hand, he said, "Consider this an advance. Get what you need, organize your transport, and so on."

Forty-five rupees. My pulse raced at the sight of so much money, given to me without my having done anything. And trusting I'd come back to work. But I did not know if this was money for one month or two. I had to ask.

"Thank you, Mr. Lewes," I said, folding it into my palm. "I suppose it is time to discuss the wage structure?"

"Not quite enough, eh?" Mr. Lewes's eyebrows drew together. "What would you say to fifty a month? With weekends off, of course."

This salary was in line with the office jobs for which I'd applied. Mr. Lewes must have been very rich to offer so much to a house servant. I was so overcome that when I opened my mouth, no words came out. I could not think of how to thank him. But was it too good to be true?

It's fine as long as he doesn't expect more, I told myself after leaving the house through the front door. Mr. Lewes was an obvious bachelor; but with me, he'd seemed respectful and bookish, rather than lecherous. And I was tired of running. All I wanted was to be safely set up in the city, earning enough money to support myself and send something to Kabita.

❦   ❦   ❦

EMPOWERED BY THE cash advance, I searched the rest of the afternoon for a hostel or rooming house. Just like the landlords of Kharagpur, none in Calcutta would take an unmarried girl without proof that I was studying nearby and financially backed by my father. In the end, I found another cheap hotel in the vicinity of Howrah, just one rupee per day. And then I resolved to use some of my money to buy clothes—the kind of softly hued, quality silk and silk-cotton saris that I'd grown to admire.

Mr. Jones at the hotel had once advised that the best shopping was in Hogg Market, the place the Writers' Building clerk Ranjit had cited: the Hogg Market, two large old brick buildings selling everything from lamps to dal to, of course, clothing. The dozens of sari shops lining the floors were decorated with swags of bright silk that seemed to shout with happiness and promise. I let Bidushi's spirit guide me into the best place, and within an hour had chosen three saris of cotton-silk blends that were both stylish and practical. The shop owner assured me the coordinating blouses would be stitched within a few hours, so I ventured deeper into the market to buy a warm shawl for the coming winter. Passing a children's shop, I paused at the sight of the stylish garments in the window. My daughter was growing. For two rupees, I bought a fancy dress and a matching hat for Kabita that I'd mail to Midnapore the next day.

I left the market with a light step, because the fear was over. I had work and money, and would be eating a meal soon. It seemed that out of the darkness, Goddess Lakshmi had emerged to bless me.

CHAPTER
20

BIBLIOPHILE: *A lover of books; a book-fancier.*

—*Oxford English Dictionary*, Vol. 10, 1933

The next morning, I paid a half anna for a ride in the back of a lorry leaving Howrah for the White Town. It was 6 a.m. but already the streets were crowded with every kind of vehicle and animal. I was let off near Chowringhee and Park and ran all the way to Middleton Street. I was there at seven fifteen.

Shombhu, the household's chief bearer, opened the door with a heavy expression. He told me I was very late and should go directly to see Mr. Lewes in the library. Feeling sickened to have erred so soon, I hurried in with an apology.

"It's all right." He met my panicked eyes with a reassuring glance, then went back to the business at hand. "I'll show you which boxes should be unpacked first. You'll need to use a hammer to pull out nails from the wooden crates—can you?"

"Certainly," I said, for I'd seen every kind of tool used in the stables at Lockwood. "Sir, may I ask something?"

"Ask me anything. That's why I waited to see you before going to my office."

"How many books do you have exactly?" The sight of so many boxes was both daunting and enthralling.

He ducked his head, looking almost sheepish. "A few thousand, but I lost count some years ago. The exact number will be discovered by you."

"Shall I make a list of the titles?" I looked longingly at a typewriter on the desk, remembering the pleasure of using Miss Richmond's.

"Yes, as a starting point. You can use it to type up reference cards that will also have call numbers following the code developed by Mr. Melvil Dewey."

The code? I had never heard of this, nor of Mr. Dewey. My stunned expression must have given me away, because he said, "The Dewey decimal system is explained clearly in one of my reference books. But unfortunately, that book still has to be—"

"Unpacked." A giggle escaped me because the situation was becoming absurd. He laughed, too: a rich, warm laugh that seemed to share my feeling. And suddenly, I was at ease. Mr. Lewes seemed to understand it would take time for me to organize.

"Have a good day working," he said, picking up his hat from the edge of the desk and a briefcase marked with the ICS emblem of crossed swords. "I look forward to chatting about what you've found when I return this evening."

After Mr. Lewes went off, the houseboy Jatin came with a tray holding tea and biscuits. "Memsaheb will need strength," he said, coughing from the dust.

"Thank you. And please don't call me that; think of me as your big sister. My first name is Kamala," I added, because as much as I desired respect, I wanted Shombhu and him and the others to feel comfortable with me.

"Kamala-didi, then?" He spoke the words hesitantly.

"Yes, I'd like that very much." I gave him a sisterly smile, but he dropped his eyes.

After I'd finished the good, sweet cup of milky Darjeeling, I tied my handkerchief over my face and set to work on the crates; once they were emptied, I put them in the hallway to be removed and began making stacks of books by subject.

Outside of the many volumes of the 1933 edition of *Oxford English Dictionary* and some other English language reference books and works of literature, Mr. Lewes's collection appeared to be focused on India's literature, geography, history, and culture. Most were printed in English but some of the old ones were in Portuguese, Dutch, and French. There were also many large blue volumes called *The Gazetteers*: massive reference books compiling the events, agriculture, weather, and economies of various provinces from the 1800s up to present.

I was busy all morning until Jatin interrupted me again with a lunch tray. I'd become hungry without realizing it. The mounds of books had utterly distracted me; I had not felt so excited since I'd first learned to read English.

Mr. Lewes found me reading the book on the Dewey decimal system when he returned at six o'clock. I jumped up, feeling guilty that he'd caught me reading instead of sorting, but he was pleased I'd opened six crates. He told me to finish up and come to the veranda for a cup of tea.

After I washed the book dust off me in my little lavatory and had brushed my hair, I went outside to the grand stone veranda with two long teak lounging chairs, one of which was occupied by my employer, who was smoking a cigarette and had a gin-and-tonic on a small table beside him. Where should I go—to the other chair or just stand? I tried to delay the awkward choice by gazing about at the garden, which was beginning to smell of night-blooming jasmine. When Mr. Lewes motioned for me to sit down near him, I awkwardly did. Then he asked how the day's work had gone.

How could I tell him what joy it was to work with my favorite things in the world, that I'd come from the depths of degradation into the most pleasurable, honorable profession imaginable? I could never tell him this; so I decided to ask a question instead.

"Is there any place I should store very large government books, like *The Gazetteers*? There are dozens of them, and they are oversize and will take up a great deal of space."

He drew his brows together in puzzlement. "For now—perhaps the hallway? I suppose you think my collecting them is irrational."

"I don't think that," I said quickly. "It's just that they are not individual books like the others. I imagine there might be many of these *Gazetteer*s all over India on the shelves of various government offices."

"But they're not considered items of value. My guess is almost all *The Gazetteer*s in those offices will be thrown away within the next decade, which makes conservation necessary."

"Why thrown away?" I was curious about the way a collector's mind worked.

"Because of the coming independence. Who will want to keep books detailing the intricacies of British rule once we're out of the country? I may be one of the few people left in the world with such records." He blew a smoke ring heavenward. "Didn't you have trouble reading the minuscule print?"

"Not at all. I hold books like that a distance away." But I was startled that he would voice the thought the British would give up India. Had he no faith in his own government?

"You're definitely farsighted, then. I noticed that when you were trying to read in the bookshop. You will visit my eye doctor on Park Street to have an examination and some spectacles made. Don't worry; he'll put it on my bill," he added, as if noticing my startled expression. "I am nearsighted myself, which means I have no trouble reading but need glasses for distance."

I had not known that my eyesight was poor. I had sat in a faraway corner of the classroom and seen every letter on Miss Richmond's blackboard. Maybe I would be more comfortable wearing spectacles; but the thought of going to a doctor filled me with anxiety.

"You needn't see Dr. Asdourian right away," he said, as if he sensed my feelings. "Just when your schedule allows."

❧   ❧   ❧

AND SO MY days went: I arrived more or less by six o'clock, worked all the morning, and after a simple Indian lunch that Manik made for me, I went out to Bow Bazar, a neighborhood filled with merchants from many countries, with synagogues and churches. It was in this area, filled with jostling people of all races speaking languages I'd never heard, that Mr. Lewes had recommended I locate a furniture maker.

Mr. Chun, a wizened old carpenter originally from Shanghai, was delighted to take my order for bookcases; and I was warm with pride at directing a project. Within a few days, Mr. Chun had sketches of an ingenious design with pegs allowing the shelves to be heightened or reduced according to whim.

Mr. Lewes liked the design as much as I did and chose to have the bookshelves made in mahogany. After we looked over the estimate for cost and drawings, he began giving me ideas of how the books should be arranged. I made notes but then felt duty-bound to give him some bad news: that dozens of his most precious acquisitions had pages falling out or covers that had separated from their broken spines.

"If I had a book press, I could use it to glue new covers to the books," I suggested. "I could also replace some of the cracked spines. The covers that are only slightly torn can be mounted on linen."

"Where did you learn these ideas of book preservation?"

"Last weekend, I visited the Asiatic Society and the National Library and spoke to some gentlemen there about how they care for their books and manuscripts." Seeing his eyebrows go up, I added, "I'm sorry, sir, perhaps I should not have gone without asking your permission?"

He shook his head. "Not at all, and you've made me quite interested. I should like to see some of these examples you're describing."

I went with him to the library, where I switched on the electric light. Although I'd asked Jatin to dust each day, the space still was a musty den. I explained how I had been airing a few dozen books daily, brushing off the mildew in the garden. He looked at the books I had set aside with the worst covers and after leafing through a few, said that he preferred that they be rebound by a professional bookbinder. He must have seen my face fall, for he added, "It is not such a necessity with books that aren't so old. And I'm not opposed to your setting up a book press. You can air the books now, while the weather is fair, and spend the next rainy season working on such repairs."

If he was talking about the next rainy season, it meant I'd still have work in eight months. This was a good sign for me, but I worried again that he didn't have an understanding of the books' conditions. I said, "Humidity will ruin the books if you keep them inside the whole monsoon. They still need air and brushing, as long as rain isn't falling directly on them."

"The only way around the damp weather is air-conditioning. Have you heard of it?" His eyes held the same spark that I'd noticed when I'd agreed to investigate his library.

"Yes. Some of the picture houses and hotel ballrooms have it— but isn't it terribly expensive?"

"As more sophisticated machinery is being developed and shipped to India, the cost is dropping. Air-conditioning has gone into trains and even some private homes in this city."

I nodded, trying not to reveal how decadent and slightly lunatic I thought he was. Cooling books was an extravagance I could not comprehend. Heat could make people very sick or even die: I'd seen that in my village. And it was supposed to be even more difficult for Europeans to bear India's heat.

"Whilst I research air-conditioning, there are some small cedar boxes I had made to protect the oldest and most valuable books. You will find them as you continue unpacking. I saw you have already found the oldest book in my library, the Portuguese sailor's account dating to 1465."

"I was afraid to open that one." I made a face, remembering the fragility of its cover.

"It's good you didn't. But it's one I'd like to have worked on by a professional bookbinder. I don't have a specific name; I heard the best district to find someone is near Presidency College in North Calcutta."

"Do you mean College Street?" I had been reading maps and walking everywhere on my weekends off.

"Yes. But you must be very careful there." His eyes lingered on me overly long, and he added, "It's a hotbed of terrorism."

I nodded, all the while thinking this was another example of irrationality. College Street was where Presidency College and many other educational institutions lay: the city's font of education, bookselling, and publishing. I'd already put it on my list for future exploration, because of all the books I might find—and because it might be a neighborhood Pankaj would visit, too.

CHAPTER
21

People tell me the modern woman is aggressive. I wonder if this is true. But if it is, she has a good reason for it, and her aggression is only the natural outcome of generations of suppression. The first taste of liberty is intoxicating, and for the first time in human history, a woman is experiencing the delights of this intoxication . . .

—Vijayalakshmi Pandit writing in *Amrita Bazar Patrika,*
May 15, 1938

The next morning, I boarded a tram that rattled and pitched its way out of central Calcutta north to College Street. A lively mix of people surrounded me as I looked away from a round baby who seemed to be the same age as my Kabita. It still hurt to look at babies, to remember all I had given up in order for us both to live.

I gazed out the window, trying to distract myself with the view of North Calcutta. People were visible in the streets, sleeping, chatting, washing themselves, scrambling eggs, and frying puris. Children played on the curb, as if blissfully unaware that their homes had no walls or roofs. They did not miss what they had never known.

I disembarked near Presidency College, slinging over my shoulder the heavy bag that held a few memoirs and histories all published after 1900. I hoped to determine the bookbinder's skills before committing older, more fragile and valuable books into his hands. Mr. Abhinash Sen was recommended to me by librarians I had visited at both the Asiatic Society and the Imperial Library. He was supposed to be tops, yet not overly priced.

Sen Bookbindery and Publishing was on a lane off College Street. The reception room was simple and clean, with an altar to Krishna in one corner and a framed picture of Gandhiji on the wall, draped with a fresh jasmine garland. I waited at the counter for some time before noticing a small silver bell. I rang it, and a thin young fellow in a wrinkled shirt and dhoti came out from behind a doorway. I told him I had come to see Mr. Sen with a half dozen books.

"It's Haresh you need. Wait. He shall come shortly." And then the young man vanished.

As I studied the price list for various services that was posted on the wall, the door behind me opened. I turned, expecting to see the missing Haresh but instead found myself looking at a pretty young woman carrying a large stack of books in her arms.

"Hallo! Have you been waiting long?" she greeted me in Bengali.

"Yes," I replied, not hiding my irritation. "If you want books repaired, it may take a while! The fellow called Haresh is not here."

The girl's brown eyes widened. "Oh, that crazy fellow is just across the street having his tea!"

I did not hide my irritation. "Well, he may have all the time on earth to do his job, but I came from downtown and have been waiting twenty minutes already."

"That's terrible! I will scold Haresh when he comes."

I looked at her in confusion, and she grinned, showing dimples on both sides.

"Haresh works for my father. He's good with the books but bad with his schedule. Father tolerates him because he is talented and has been with us so long. I'm the eldest daughter of the house: Supriya Sen."

"I'm Kamala Mukherjee." I spoke hesitantly, for the Brahmin surname, especially, felt like a lie. "I am the clerk for a private library and have brought in some books."

She nodded, looking pleased. "I'm so glad you waited. Kamaladidi, you must come with me upstairs, it will be more pleasant than this room."

"That is very kind of you," I said, surprised she was being so friendly.

"It's time for lunch anyway," she said. "Will you eat with us? It will give you a chance to meet my father."

The last time a stranger invited me to eat with her, it was Bonnie, and that tea had brought on the lowest point of my life. As I hesitated, I saw Supriya's lips tighten. I knew her family name was Sen, which put her in the doctors and writers caste that was just below my pretend caste. Maybe she thought I regarded myself above dining with her.

I smiled and said, "I would like that so much."

Supriya led me up a narrow staircase to the residential quarters. Her mother, Mrs. Promilla Sen, immediately invited me to call her Mashima, or mother's sister. But although I smilingly thanked her, I knew she could never have actually been my kin; her rounded figure, and the thick ivory bangles and fineness of her cotton Murshidabad sari made it clear that she was quite prosperous. There had been nobody like Mrs. Sen in Johlpur.

Mrs. Sen—I had to remind myself hard to think of her as Mashima—bade me to sit down on a cushion and released a stream of questions. From which branch of the Mukherjee clan did I come from? Was I at Bethune College with Supriya? How had I learned about their business, and why was I so thin?

I answered that my people were from the coast of Bengal and

not connected to any of the important local Mukherjees. I'd been educated at a girls' school in the countryside but left early due to the death of my parents. I had come to the city recently and taken a position organizing the private library for a senior ICS officer who also wrote essays about old Indian books. I chose my words carefully. If they learned that I was unmarried, with a child abandoned just a month earlier, they would no doubt throw away the teacup I'd drunk from and send me and my books packing.

"To work for an Englishman must be loathsome!" Supriya said after peppering me with questions about my job.

"Not at all," I said. "I enjoy all the books, and Mr. Lewes is very polite and asks my opinions. It's because he trusts me that I was able to investigate book restoration and come here. Truly, the only ones telling me what to do are the books! They have been neglected so long that they need a friend."

"Then it is like the romantic novel *Jane Eyre!*" Supriya declared. "Only instead of taking care of children, you have books, which are much more interesting."

At this, her mother scolded her, saying the windows were open and half the neighborhood could hear that the Sens' oldest girl didn't want children. But Supriya just laughed and asked me how much I earned per month. When I told, she shot a defiant glance at her mother. "Why won't Baba pay me? I work hard organizing his accounts. Look at Kamala; how lucky she is! I should like to quit this family to become a working lady."

Before her mother could even answer, there was a sound of clattering on the stairs and more voices, female and male. Two young ladies came up along with a little boy in a sailor suit.

Supriya quickly made introductions. "That's my baby brother, Nishan. My younger sister, Sonali—she's the one with specs and the serious expression—always picks him up at the Hindu School for boys on her way back from Loreto House. Now they're home, we can call downstairs for Baba to come and eat. Bina, fetch him!" she directed a young maidservant.

"And what about me?" The other young woman was unwinding a scarf from her head, revealing a long, lustrous fall of hair. "I'm the guest. You should have introduced me first!"

"You are no guest; you are my third daughter." Mashima pinched the newcomer on her cheek. "Kamala, this is our dear Ruksana Ali. Her father is the doctor who cared for us when he lived in our neighborhood. Now he is at Calcutta Medical College Hospital."

"Where Netaji was treated," Supriya said. "Thank God he is off his sickbed and in charge of the Congress Party. Now we will finally have change in India; you mark my words."

"My family supports Krishak Praja, the Farmers' Party," Ruksana said to me. "Its leader, Mr. A. K. Fazlul Huq, could well be the governor of Bengal someday."

"Because he's a Muslim, and there are so many more of you than us," Sonali said mischievously.

Ruksana's eyes narrowed. "Mr. Huq is very good at building coalitions between all religions. And we have our choice. There's the Muslim League party; we like this one better."

"Why be in a peasants' party when you are so far from the country?" Sonali said.

"It's about landworkers' rights. We should all be thinking about it," Supriya interrupted.

Mashima said in a placating tone, "Please, my daughters, don't frighten Kamala with all your politics. She surely doesn't care."

I had been following this conversation closely—how amazing to hear them talking about peasants having a voice in politics.

"Ma, you must vote in the next election," Supriya said. "I worry that our Netaji can't stay in charge of control in Congress. His ideas about modernizing are so different from what Gandhiji advises. There's a division of opinion inside the Congress Party that could ruin everything."

"But the men who will vote whether Netaji stays or leaves are the Congress ministers, not us," Mashima demurred.

"If you support the left-wing ministers, Netaji will get the votes from them to stay president," Supriya pointed out. "Please, Ma!"

"I will vote if Ruksana's mother goes, too," Mashima answered, beaming with the same dimples her daughter had. "Then both sides are fairly represented. Oh, I hear Baba coming! Now we shall eat."

Mr. Sen was somewhere in his late forties and the opposite of his wife: rail thin and short. He was dressed in a crisp white shirt and dhoti and had a certain formality. The kitchen maid served Mr. Sen first and then came to me and Ruksana before offering everyone else the fragrant fish-head dal, fried eggplant with neem leaves, potato curry, and mutton cooked with onions and rice. She ran around next with chapattis just hot off the griddle and urged me to try the home-made mango and lime pickles. Everyone ate as if such a lunch was an ordinary event. For me, it was a real feast made all the more special by the friendly family group.

Afterward, we washed our hands at the small sink in the room's corner. Then I laid the books on the clean table before Mr. Sen, who gently examined them, confirming what I'd thought. Several needed sewing, new spines had to be created for others, and for two, new cloth covers were in order.

"When Haresh works, he works well. But I think he has a problem with tea. He is drinking it across the road many times a day. I have a strict policy, no tea in the workroom! It is too much of a risk for the books," Mr. Sen declared.

"I am very glad to hear it, because my employer's collection is quite special. It must never be damaged." I shuddered at the thought of anything going wrong. "Don't worry, Kamala," Mr. Sen said, looking at me with kind eyes. "And were you saying that you have more books to mend than these six?"

"I believe there might be as many as three hundred needing re-pair, but the simple fixes I can try doing myself with a press. To you I might bring two hundred if . . ." I did not want to say, *if your work is as good as I hope.*

"I will teach you how to do the easy repairs," Mr. Sen said. "Su-priya knows, too. Anyone who is careful can do it. But you were right to bring the difficult jobs here. And with such good business coming in the future, I shall offer you a professional discount."

❦   ❦   ❦

I WAS EXCITED to give the news about Sen Bookbindery to Mr. Lewes; he arrived home late that evening, though, and bathed before dinner. When I finally saw him in the dining room, he had swapped his suit for a white Indian cotton one and tan cotton trousers. In these unconventional clothes, he looked rather appealing, and then I chided myself for the inappropriate thought. I was wearing, for the first time, the new horn-rimmed glasses that his optometrist had made for me. Mr. Lewes noticed the spectacles straightaway and asked if they had changed my reading comfort.

"Oh, yes. But I must tell you about Sen Bookbindery. I met the whole family, and Mr. Sen is just starting with a few books. He seems trustworthy and will be giving a ten percent discount."

But Mr. Lewes shook his head. "Oh, don't listen to that. Indians always say you're getting a discount, when you're really just receiving the inflated Ingrej price."

Automatically, my back tensed. "But I'm not Ingrej, and they are very kind people! I would like to give them the work."

"You don't know the number of times I've seen Indians walk away with a newspaper for a paisa and I'm charged triple." Mr. Lewes's voice was bitter.

"You're right," I said, deciding that he needed comforting. "I don't know what happens to you. But I would be happy to buy your newspapers for you, if you think it would keep you from being cheated."

"That brings something up I've been meaning to ask about." He cleared his throat. "Would you sit down, please? There's plenty of food. Tell Manik to bring you a plate."

I hesitated because the request for me to sit with my employer seemed improper. But the food smelled awfully good. Per his request, I'd asked Manik to make Bengali dishes. He'd come up with tiny shrimp steamed with grated coconut and mustard seeds; spinach cooked with ginger, cauliflowers and potatoes; and a cholar dal with coconut. On the side were parathas and plenty of rice and, in the end, a frozen milk pudding with pistachios. To my relief, Manik had not considered this menu a nuisance; he'd rubbed his hands together and said the whole staff would enjoy eating whatever was left.

"Please join me," Mr. Lewes repeated, and I breathed in the table's aromas with pleasure and sat down in the chair on his right.

"Kamala, you know that I read in the evenings." Mr. Lewes glanced toward the slim pile of newspapers between us. "I believe you review these same papers the next morning?"

"I enjoy looking at the old papers when I take my meals," I admitted. "I hope that's all right?"

"It's fine! But I would like to learn a bit more about the newspapers printed in local languages. Which ones do you think are the best?"

"*The Hindu* and *Bengal Today*," I answered, then hesitated. "But there's also an important Bengali Muslim newspaper called *The Azad* and another Muslim newspaper from Delhi called *The Star*. And of course, most Hindu gentry read *Ananda Bazar Patrika*, the new Bengali paper published by the founders of the English-language paper, *Amrita Bazar Patrika*."

"As you know, I already take *Amrita Bazar Patrika* as well as the *Times of India* and the *Statesman*. I'd like to add these five other papers you've mentioned, but I would naturally need translation assistance. I don't suppose you'd consider reading the papers to me? In translation, of course."

It was odd to have such a request rather than a direct order. It also felt strange to be looked at so intently. Still, translating five newspapers was a lot of work. Warily I asked, "But when could you hear the translations? You leave around seven and aren't usually home before six."

"You could stay a little longer, perhaps eating dinner with me while we go over the papers. It will save you the cost and trouble of finding a meal near your hotel." Mr. Lewes's angular face held an emotion that I'd not seen since leaving Rose Villa: not outright passion but rather a kind of deference that came with asking for their most precious fantasy.

Did Mr. Lewes want me? Over the past month, he had been cordial but had not touched me or said anything out of order. Perhaps his strange expression was solely because he was in love with the written word, something that was quite understandable and would make me feel all right about sharing more dinners with him. I had no intention of any kind of involvement with an Englishman beyond the professional, especially with the reality of Pankaj alive and well in the city.

But perhaps he yearned for a window into reading Indian languages. I remembered being ten years old and seeing my first books at the Keshiari Mission Hospital; I'd envied the nurses and Dr. Andrews for their ability to read and write. Mr. Lewes was undoubtedly struggling with the same longing, believing that Bengali and Hindi could open truths about India that he didn't know. And would this be such a bad thing for an Englishman?

"Yes," I said, smiling to make the uncertainty fade from his eyes. "Of course, Mr. Lewes! That kind of help is something I can easily give."

CHAPTER
22

APPEASE: . . . *2.a. To pacify, assuage or allay (anger or displeasure).*

—*Oxford English Dictionary*, Vol. 1, 1933

By late 1938, the newspapers became the bookends of my day. A newsboy brought them every morning and I looked them over to decide which to share with Mr. Lewes over the evening meal. I'd become concerned by news of the greater world. In China, the Japanese army had taken control of Canton. In Europe, Herr Hitler had annexed Czechoslovakia and then Austria. Would Mr. Chamberlain's document of appeasement only lead to Germany taking more countries? Journalists' opinions were divided. It all seemed so far away, like the mythical stories Thakurma used to tell. But nonetheless frightening.

India had its own brewing war. Verbal battling was on between older congressmen and the young, left-wing party members Sonali and Supriya Sen knew. I translated a dizzying amount of articles and editorials, even some originally in Urdu, which was my weakest language. Mr. Lewes seemed fascinated, asking many questions and making notations of my translations. Despite my desire to remain coolly professional, I was inwardly proud that because of my languages, I had knowledge and skills that he, a Cambridge-educated ICS officer, could not begin to approach.

As October turned to November, the sun sank earlier, and my transportation to Howrah each evening became chancy. I never knew who might come up behind me on the tram and bus or follow me when I disembarked and ran in the dark toward my shabby hotel. My anxiety grew about walking at night, so one evening, as I'd finished reading *The Hindu* and Mr. Lewes looked poised to ask for more, I said, "Sir, it's growing quite late, and the buses become scarce. May I please translate that one tomorrow?"

"Goodness—it's almost ten. How I've kept you talking. Please, Kamala, eat something before you go."

But there was no time to eat the chicken curry and rice that had grown cold on my plate. I stood, telling him that I needed to hurry for the tram.

"Are you still in that hotel?" He frowned. "I've hoped you might find a boardinghouse nearby."

"I can't be admitted to those places," I answered, unable to mask my irritation. "Especially not in the White Town. It would be different if I were enrolled in a college with a father who could vouch for me."

"Why can't he?" Mr. Lewes's eyes were keen. "Don't tell me you had an argument and ran away."

"Oh, no. He's deceased." I was about to add, *in a cyclone,* but cut myself off. If I said that, it might bring him closer to understanding that I was really a peasant. And he would ask me what I'd done with myself for the last eight years.

"I wish I could help you, but I don't think there's a chance in hell I could pass as your father." Mr. Lewes made a regretful grimace. "How much do you pay for your hotel?"

"A rupee a night."

Mr. Lewes shook his head. "Then you're spending thirty to thirty-one rupees a month—not counting the other expenses! That's not prudent. I wish I could pay you more."

"You're not Grindlays Bank."

"Too bad, eh?" He chuckled, and suddenly, I thought back to all the men who had paid for things I hadn't wanted to do; all those filthy rupees I had earned and lost. My cheeks flushed with shame.

"Sir, I really must go." I looked toward the library where I kept my shawl and purse. "The trams are less frequent now."

"I know what to do; I'll send you in the car with Farouk. He can take you wherever you need."

"But Farouk has gone home. He knows you are finished for the evening."

"Damn." He thrust his hand in his pocket, and came out with two rupees. "Will this cover a taxi? Please take it. Not as an advance, but a gift."

Any other thrifty person would have taken the two-anna tram ride and pocketed the bounty; but I was tired, and the shadowy figures lurking along the tramlines were a real fear. Mr. Lewes did not want me to take the tram; I should not dishonor his gift. Despite his being English, he had been nothing but kind to me: as kind as an uncle, although far too young and attractive. Simon Lewes was twenty-nine, I knew from the passport he'd once forgotten on his desk. Surely he would marry soon. I wondered what his future wife would think of my working in his house all day and in the evening sitting at the same dining table as him. If he married, I imagined the schedule would change.

"Thank you, Mr. Lewes," I said. The coins stayed warmly in my palm as I found a taxi at the Chowringhee intersection and took it all the way to where I needed to go.

🐝   🐝   🐝

16

I CONTINUED TO read for Mr. Lewes in the evenings and take car rides home from the driver, Farouk, as the winter holidays came. I knew the Durga and Kali celebrations well, but Christmas in Calcutta was something new to me. Everywhere street posts were swathed with garlands, and lights twinkled around windows and doorways of Christian-owned shops and houses. Fluffy-branched trees from the coast were shipped to Calcutta and decorated with colored balls, candles, and sweets. Many European homes displayed beautiful trees shining in the windows as I rode past them in the evenings.

I thought a Christmas tree would have been nice in Mr. Lewes's flat, but he did not get one, nor did he ask Shombhu to put up tinsel or garlands or decorations of any sort. When I asked him why, he said that he would spend his holiday looking for books in Bombay.

"Actually, Kamala, I'd like to ask a favor whilst I'm gone. Are you able to stay not just the days but overnight in the little room on the third floor? I don't like to leave the place unoccupied, and you might enjoy the convenience of not having to travel and the financial savings."

"I know that room," I said, playing for time while I thought over this proposition. "It even has bedroom furniture. I always wondered who was there before."

"It was left from the last people here. I'll ask Shombhu and Jatin to air the mattress and give you fresh linens; that is, if you're willing."

I liked the idea of staying in the flat. Mr. Lewes thought I was helping him. But I worried that the others would be resentful of my staying inside the house, while they lived in the garden house. I said, "What would Shombhu and the others feel about one of their kind staying inside?"

"You are not the same as them," Mr. Lewes replied sharply. "I shall tell them to treat you as a memsaheb. If I hear otherwise, there will be repercussions—"

"Please don't do that!" I was horrified at the thought I should be treated like a British lady. "I will speak to them about the change myself."

"By all means," he said, looking at me with something new in his expression. "And might you oversee more of the household responsibilities—paying for the groceries that come, the dhobi, and so on?"

"Yes, I'd be happy to, because I'll have no travel time to worry about." I smiled, thinking that while it might appear to Mr. Lewes that he was giving me more work, his absence was granting me time to explore the city, perhaps finding Pankaj, and certainly continuing relations with the Sen family. I had become very friendly with Supriya, and she had invited me to dine with her family for both Durga and Kali Puja celebrations.

Mr. Lewes looked as pleased as I felt, and the day before his departure I moved my possessions out of the dingy hotel and into Middleton Mansions. The small room was very pleasant and already furnished with a narrow iron bedstead and a chest of drawers. I set up a little shrine to Lakshmi, arranged my collection of books, and slept better than I had in years.

Before going away, Mr. Lewes distributed everyone's Christmas bonus: a half month's extra pay. After sending ten rupees to Abbas for Kabita's expenses, I treated myself to a delightful novel by Daphne du Maurier and also a new Bengali-English dictionary, intending it as a gift for Mr. Lewes upon his return. I'd noticed that he hadn't a contemporary dictionary in his collection, and maybe he could use it to learn to read at least the news headlines for himself.

For the first time, I felt independent yet secure. Life became pleasantly casual with Mr. Lewes so far away. Now the radio was kept on all day and evening, and Shombhu felt comfortable enough to sing as he went about his household cleaning. One day, he was crooning an Oriya folk song that was easy to follow as he dusted the furniture. I sang out the next bar; Shombhu was silent with surprise but then joined in. When I came out of the library, he gave me a real smile, and I knew from the spicy shingara pastry Manik sent with my afternoon tea that both of them were relaxing.

I'd also resolved not to ask the servants to do anything extra for me. If Jatin didn't wash the floor one morning, or Manik served left-overs for lunch, or Shombu lounged for two hours with a Bengali newspaper, the house would still be in a fine state. After a week I asked Shombhu whether he agreed that Mr. Lewes's sofas might look better placed facing each other in the room's center; and if the china cabinet in the dining room could be moved to a different wall. And so, without anyone feeling imposed upon, the drawing and dining rooms finally became less cluttered and finally reflected the grace of the flat's architecture.

At Christmas, I gifted Shombhu with a record of popular Bengali songs to play on the Victrola. Manik received a handsome bowl from me, and his assistant, Choton, his very own chopping knife. Jatin was the youngest, so I gave him a ball to throw to his young friends in the evenings when he played with them out on the street. In thanks, Manik and Choton made me my favorite milk sweets; Shombhu gave me a pencil with eraser attached; and Jatin gave me a big bunch of flowers from the garden that I arranged in a glass vase and set on the dining table. We were becoming friends, if not family.

Mr. Lewes was still away in Bombay in early January, so when Su-priya asked me to come with her to a young women's political meeting at a place called Albert Hall, I was excited to go.

"Your sari should be made of khadi; either plain with no border at all, or with a slim green or orange border, the colors from the freedom flag," she coached me. Then with a twinkle she added, "And don't wear gold jewelry lest you be pushed to give it up to the cause!"

Khadi was the rough homespun Thakurma used to weave because we were too poor to buy cloth. How pleased my grandmother would be to know that smart city women sought it out. But to me, it felt like wasting money buying something so plain.

I met the Sen girls and Ruksana at their home and together we set off to Bankim Chatterjee Street. Albert Hall was a narrow sliver of a building that didn't look like anything; but up a steep staircase lay a high-ceilinged room filled with more tables than I could count. The women had clustered at four tables in the back of the room, where Sonali, Supriya, and Ruksana led me. I felt a mixture of excitement at being part of this political women's group but also some apprehension they could see through to my lack of schooling.

Because Calcutta's fine colleges attracted students from all over India, I found myself meeting young ladies from faraway provinces like Punjab, Madras, and even the royal kingdom of Travancore. All of the women had high-caste surnames and studied at either Bethune or Loreto College. We spoke a mix of Hindi and English because of all the regional differences, and to my surprise, my English was still crisper than anyone's. When asked about where I'd studied, I spoke briefly about a small boarding school in Darjeeling that had recently shut down.

"No money for college, I'm afraid," I said at the end of it. Smiling, I added, "How envious I am of you all!"

"But she's working at a real job! I'm the one who's sick with envy," Supriya said, flashing me a smile.

"Pakoras are coming and coffee for all. Will you take coffee, Kamala?" Lata Menon, the group's leader, asked me with a warm smile.

I had never tried coffee, but I nodded. It was supposed to be strong, and wasn't that what these intellectual young women were?

"Very good, then. We need to get word out about Netaji. Please will you help us?" Lata leaned toward me while her sari's starched pallu remained perfectly in place. What control she had!

"Of course I shall—but why does he need help from young women? As president of the Congress Party, he is known by all."

Lata's voice was somber. "There's a movement afoot to have Netaji lose the Congress presidency. The old members think he's moving away from the party's ideals. He could be thrown out in this month's elections. And my goodness, he welcomes the participation of women patriots. He wants equality for us in every way."

"That's a bit controversial, isn't it? And I've read in the papers that some people don't believe India's able to carry off the civil unrest campaign that Netaji advises." I sipped the coffee. Even with milk and sugar it tasted much darker than tea: dark and dangerous.

"People like me!" Ruksana said, causing every head to turn in her direction. "If we disregard Gandhiji's feelings about giving the British another chance, we show disrespect for him. And how can we do that? He is the heart of the movement, the only Hindu activist Muslims tolerate."

"Ruksana has a point," Supriya said, getting everyone's attention with her firm tone. "Perhaps we should make a resolution taking this into account but not disregarding Netaji entirely."

The resolution was made. Like Supriya and Ruksana, I felt the conundrum. I wondered if Pankaj still believed military action was needed to free India. After reading about the impact of violence on Europe, I wasn't sure that patriots using force against the British in India would result in freedom. Still, I kept listening; and it seemed the coffee put vigor in my mind where it had not been before. I did not know the correct answer to reaching independence; but I wanted to work toward finding it. When I agreed to join the Chhatri Sangha group, a cheer went round.

Supriya linked arms with me as we left Albert Hall an hour later. In my ear, she whispered, "I knew you would like them and they would like you! Everyone was most impressed to have a working woman join us."

"I'm just happy you befriended me," I said, swallowing the lump that had come up in my throat. If I hadn't gone to Sen Bookbindery at exactly the time Haresh was out drinking tea, I would not be living this new and exciting life.

CHAPTER
23

A well-known Brahmin doesn't need to wear a sacred thread.

Bengali proverb

When Mr. Lewes returned, he was pleased that I'd saved some money overseeing the household expenses; and even happier about the flat's redecoration. He walked around the drawing room's wide-open spaces, admired the flowers, the polished silver, and Indian prints that I'd had framed and hung.

"Kamala, you have made it a home! I can't imagine how you did so well, but I don't want it to stop. Please don't go back to your hotel." His blue eyes looked deeply in mine.

In truth, I was relieved by the invitation, because I hated the idea of ever returning to unsafe lodgings. And with free housing, I could save much more for my future and contribute to Kabita's upbringing.

After accepting Mr. Lewes's generous proposal, I felt shy offering up the pocket-size Bengali-English dictionary I'd bought as his gift. I handed it over, anyway, with a gilt-edged card offering him wishes for a Happy New Year. He read the card with a smile, but when he opened the book, it faded.

"You shouldn't have," he said, paging through the book. From his odd expression, I realized he might not like it. After all, he owned a mint 1827 edition of William Carey's Bengali-English dictionary, and the 1868 edition of *Hobson-Jobson*. He'd once shown me an essay he was working on about English words that had been invented because of the experience in India: *kedgeree, box-wallah*, and the like.

"I chose it for you because it's *different* from the antiquarian dictionaries," I said. "The pages are strong enough to be turned and in the back are cross-translations of Bengali proverbs and English ones, too. You may want to write about Indian proverbs someday."

Mr. Lewes looked strange; I realized, after examining the way he was working his hands, that he was flustered. "Thank you. It's most considerate. But, Kamala, you mustn't spend money on me again. I can't pay what you're worth."

The dismissive apology fell away from my ears. Thinking about his vast collection, most of which were first editions, I realized he might be someone who cared more about dust jackets and copyrights than contents. Maybe that was why he'd praised the way I arranged his rooms; he cared for the look of things, not substance. And perhaps I'd acted above my station by giving him something. He was not a friend, but a saheb.

As I stood, regretting my choice of the gift, Mr. Lewes closed the dictionary and said, "I know you've made a section for all the dictionaries. Why don't you catalog this and add it to the collection?"

❧   ❧   ❧

AFTER THAT INCIDENT, I did not feel the same inside the library. I felt stifled. I did not pause in my labors to browse; in fact, I did not crack open a book until the day I unwrapped a package from a Bombay bookshop. Inside the brown paper were two glossy new books, one a guidebook by Joseph Summers called *Birds of the Nilgiri Hills* and the other *Female India*, photographs by Bernard Mulkins.

Bernie Mulkins: the lusty, dusty traveler who had arrived at Rose Villa and changed my life. Memories of that hard day returned as I paged through the glossy photographs. Here was Lucky-Short-for-Lakshmi with her face wreathed in cigarette smoke and a melancholic expression. When Bernie had focused his camera, I'd thought he was just after showing her womanly parts, but now I understood what he had also revealed was her loneliness. In Natty's portrait, he had captured another emotion: avarice. Seated at a vanity while making up her face, the mirror showed her beautiful but cold eyes. The picture was so clear that I could make out all the various containers of whitening creams and nail polish on the vanity and a purse spilling over with rupees.

Bonnie had the most flattering photograph; she stretched over two pages with a regimental army flag draped over her hips. She was literally wrapped up in England, but making the kind of advertisement no British company would ever sponsor.

The book held pictures of poor Indian women, too: peasants who worked in the fields wearing saris without blouses and dark tribal women whose faces were only illuminated by the whites of their eyes and the sparkle of their nose rings. He had even photographed a young bride going off to her new household in a cart, her face wet with tears.

It was easier to look at the others' pictures, but finally I took a deep breath and looked at my own. As he'd said, the picture did not reveal my face. Still, I could see the slight widening of my body, the evidence of how I was growing a child. I realized that all I might ever have of Kabita was this, a picture of my body with her hidden inside. A pang struck me, because I so wanted to see her as she had grown. But maybe it would be worse to see her. How could I see my child and leave her again?

Painfully, I dragged my thoughts back to the crisis at hand. Mr. Lewes must have bought the book in Bombay; but from its perfect condition, I could see he hadn't paged through it before the purchase. Still, he might think of looking through it one evening. I couldn't throw it away.

If the book stayed, my picture within it could not. Even if Mr. Lewes couldn't know it was me, I'd surely become obsessed with this physical reminder of my past. Without giving myself time to doubt the action, I took scissors and ran them along the book's inside seam, so the page with my photograph came out. After I'd torn the paper into fragments, I realized I couldn't throw them in the wastebasket, which would arouse suspicion I'd vandalized the collection.

So I wrapped up the pieces in a handkerchief that I tucked in my purse. It was only a short walk to the chai-wallah's cauldron, and as I stood there, waiting for a cup, I let the pieces drop in the fire. By the time the tea was on my tongue, the shreds of my old life had curled into charred bits of nothing.

Still, I could not forget. *Females of India* was in the window of the Oxford Bookstore and was well reviewed in the English language press. As I sat each night translating the newspapers, fear steamed like the cup of tea at my side. What if Mr. Lewes asked whether a package of books had come from Bombay or searched for them himself? If he looked carefully, would he notice that a page was gone?

I had become so anxious that I wished I could monitor Mr. Lewes's movements in the library. When the air-conditioning contractor began banging up the place, I gained the opportunity. I had emerged from my bath one evening and noticed a loose floor tile. As I bent to lift it out, I realized that the air-conditioning workers must have struck hard enough to crack the plaster between my floor and the library ceiling. The break was enough to offer a tiny glimpse into the library below.

As I knocked away more to get a wider view, I recalled the hole in the floor in Rose Villa. The girls had shown me something I hadn't wanted to know about; whereas my desire to watch Mr. Lewes was quite practical. I slipped white paper over the hole so it didn't show, and then placed the tile back. It was very little effort, yet I was sweating from the realization of what I'd done.

Mr. Lewes would be terrribly shocked if he found out about the spy hole. Perhaps shocked enough to dismiss me. It would be my job to make sure he never found out.

❀   ❀   ❀

MY DAILY HOURS in the library became complicated by the workmen, who filled the air with the sound of their saws and hammers. Because of them, I barely heard the telephone ringing one morning, but I got it just in time and found Supriya on the line. She reminded me that I had a finished order at the shop. Then she mentioned an upcoming political meeting at which Netaji was rumored to be making an address.

Thrilled to see the leader in the flesh, I said yes. I would go to Sen Bookbindery first, pick up the finished books, and then stop at the meeting on my way home. Mr. Lewes didn't ask me to account for how I spent my time; he seemed most interested in the hours we spent together, over the newspapers.

I met Supriya, Sonali, Ruksana, Lata, and three others by the lush gardens bordering Government House. What a contrast our plain, homespun saris were to the bright flowers spilling through the wrought iron fence. Nevertheless, the guards watched us as if we were some kind of entertainment. Finding them just as funny, Sonali giggled and waved at them.

"There will be no more waving and joke making," Lata cautioned as we approached the steps of the majestic, Greek-columned Town Hall. "Our group's reputation is very important. Hundreds of freedom fighters will be here; we do not want them to think us silly schoolgirls."

Supriya made a face at me; I knew she thought Lata was too stern. I winked back at her as we entered the wide marble hall. Supriya led our group up the stairs; the second floor was not as crowded, so we went to take positions at the front of the gallery. As other ladies filled in behind us, I remembered my first Congress meeting in Kharagpur. Only this time I was witnessing history, passing binoculars back and forth with my friends to get an intimate view.

Onstage, one Congress politician after another came forward, each praising Netaji and calling for the community to unite behind him. And finally, Netaji strode out, his tall, lean figure dressed in a neat tan suit that almost looked like a uniform. When Netaji saluted the audience, the effect was as if a general had taken charge.

Netaji's words rang out sharply about the needless division within the Congress Party. He said that history had proven already that India would not find its way to independence without leadership from the citizens of Bengal, a comment that made the audience cheer loudly. He declared it was the duty of every man and woman to fight as never before.

As Netaji's voice rolled over me, I became aware that the hairs on my arms were standing. I was in the presence of a tremendous leader. When Netaji gave his blessings on the audience, the room erupted in thunderous applause. People in the hall below rushed the stage, trying to drape jasmine garlands over Netaji's head. Then a young man began steering Netaji off the stage.

Something about the young man struck me as familiar. Still throbbing from the roar of applause, I turned the binoculars on his face. The man had spectacles just like Netaji but had a longer, handsome face with black hair waving back from the forehead.

I had not seen him since I was fifteen, but in the three and a half years that had passed, his features were the same. Here, at last, was Pankaj Bandopadhyay.

CHAPTER
24

KSHATRIYA: *a member of the military caste, the second of the four great castes or classes among the Hindus.*

—*Oxford English Dictionary*, Vol. 5, 1933

Pankaj's time onstage was too brief. As he guided Netaji away from the audience, I realized how attractive he'd become with time's passage—or was I looking at him with my experienced woman's eye? I felt I knew his heart and mind so well, after having written him hundreds of letters—and receiving as many back.

In the infirmary, Bidushi had told me to take care of Pankaj. I wondered how she would feel about my speaking to him. As I moved through North Calcutta pursuing political activities, I would surely spot him again. But should I try to speak? He'd been angry with me all those years ago in the garden. If he recognized me now as Sarah from Lockwood School, he could ruin everything, and perhaps even have me arrested. But if he didn't recognize me—it could mean a fresh start. My tasteful, Indian-woven saris, my posh Calcutta manners, and my circle of intellectual friends placed me in a new league. And Pankaj was free; he was unmarried; and he was too great of a temptation not to think about.

❧   ❧   ❧

ARVASH, THE SPRING season, was almost done. By day, I worked in the lovely, air-cooled library sorting through memoirs: various soldiers' and missionaries' accounts of a happy, exotic India marked by tiger shoots and rajahs' feasts. But the papers I translated for Mr. Lewes at night were so different; filled with stories of anger, of people being arrested for civil disobedience. Netaji had been reelected as Congress president, which made me happy, but no Congress minister except his own brother, Sarat, would serve in his cabinet. Realizing he could not accomplish anything without friends, Netaji resigned the presidency in April. By May he'd formed a new party called the Forward Bloc, an effort to bring all left-wing elements of the independence movement together.

Mr. Lewes was very interested in Bengali opinions of the Forward Bloc. As he listened to my translations and made notes, I wondered if he wished this new, angry India would go away. I imagined his job would have been simpler one hundred years ago, when Indians were too frightened of their rulers to speak up and there was no Congress Party, Muslim League, or Communists.

"A train derailed yesterday. I wonder what the local press are saying about it," Mr. Lewes said one summer evening as we sat down on the veranda. It was just before the rains arrived, and to stay cool, he wore a white linen shirt and thin cotton trousers, with chappals on his feet. I was dressed in the sheerest cotton sari I owned, one that I would not normally have worn around him, were it not for the heat. Sometimes, I caught Mr. Lewes looking at me a bit longer than was seemly, but what he would say next was always ordinary and businesslike, taking away the nervousness that had briefly surged inside.

These were the kind of jitters that I imagined would come when I was able to see Pankaj again, but it had been weeks since the rally, and I didn't know how to ask where he might be without making Supriya suspicious of my motives.

I returned my attention to the news story. "Yes, I saw mention of that somewhere. Thirty-seven dead, and more than two hundred injured, wasn't it?"

"At the office I heard at least forty dead with the number sure to rise." Mr. Lewes took a sip from his gin-and-tonic. "Why don't you read to me what the *Star* reports."

Urdu was not my strongest language, so it took me a minute to locate the story. I read, "The Down Calcutta Mail was thrown off the rails between Chinsurah and Calcutta. Engineers and station workers examining the track afterward found two fishplates had been removed." I continued translating the article, which reported that railway officials had declared it an act of sabotage.

"It's mysterious that this train was attacked," I mused aloud. "I would understand it if an important English figure was on board. But nothing's been mentioned."

"It could be that particular train wasn't the target," Mr. Lewes said. "One train ran those same tracks a few hours earlier that was supposed to be transporting Subhas Bose and his brother. But their plans changed."

It was interesting that Mr. Lewes knew this; I hadn't seen it in the paper. And I wasn't sure what he was implying. Searching his face for a clue, I said, "No Indians would want to kill Netaji."

Lighting a cigarette, he said, "Gandhi supporters couldn't— because of the nonviolence pledge—but Muslims have no such boundaries. And there's no end of trouble in the legislature between the Hindus and Muslims."

But not with Ruksana and her non-Muslim friends, I thought. The young women in Chhatri Sangha listened and learned from one another. "What if the English tampered with the line—that is, ordered some Indian railway workers to do it?"

Mr. Lewes winked at me and said, "Have you tossed aside Tagore in favor of Agatha Christie?"

Stiffly, I said, "I will never love any writer more than Rabindranath. As for Mr. Christie, who is he?"

"*She* is an authoress who concocts very clever detective stories— pleasure reading for trains and sickbeds. But to return to your theory, I find it implausible that our government would order an assassination." He gently blew out a smoke ring, which hovered between us before disappearing. "Do you think other Indians would believe it?"

"I don't know." I felt it was time to change the topic; Mr. Lewes shouldn't know that I was well acquainted with the nationalist movement. "We have a very nice dinner coming. For the first course, Manik has prepared a delicious-looking soup from lau squash and ginger. He wanted me to ask if you'd prefer it warm or cold."

"Who cares about soup? What's your opinion of Bose and his Forward Bloc?" Mr. Lewes studied me like a tiger stalking its prey.

He really wanted to know. Carefully, I answered, "I don't know enough to have a firm opinion. The book Mr. Bose wrote about his ideas is banned, so I really don't know what he believes."

He nodded. "*The Indian Struggle* is censored in India, but it was published in England a few years ago. I'll lend it to you, if you'd like."

"What? How did you get it?" I was shocked that Mr. Lewes would own a book decrying his own government.

"Collectors can find anything." There was a mischievous gleam in his eyes. "Just don't take the book out into public or leave it around the flat where anyone might see it."

"All right," I said, because I did want to read it. "And there is little risk with the servants—it's only Manik and Shombhu who can read and write, and they don't ever come up to my floor."

"As well they shouldn't!" Mr. Lewes coughed. I wrinkled my nose, because I did not like the smell of his cigarettes. I also didn't believe something that made people cough could be healthy, no matter what the advertisements pronounced. As if he'd sensed what I was thinking, he stubbed out the cigarette.

"Thank you very much," I said.

"I smoke too many of them, I think," Mr. Lewes said. "And I've made up my mind about the soup. Please tell Manik I would like it cold."

❧   ❧   ❧

I READ THROUGH *The Indian Struggle* three times. I found the book opinionated but magnificently so. Netaji had written the history of India from antiquity through the present, including details of the brutal tortures and killing done to people who had attempted to protest British rule. Mr. Lewes must have read the book closely, for I saw thick underlinings on many pages, particularly those relating to revolutionaries like Bhagat Singh, and every mention of the words *terrorism* or *revolution*. He had also drawn question marks and the occasional exclamation point in the margins. I did not have to ask Mr. Lewes the meaning of his defacements. It was clear he did not approve of the book.

One evening that Mr. Lewes was away in New Delhi, I took up Supriya's invitation to meet again at Albert Hall. Some guests wanted to speak to the Chhatri Sangha women's group. The monsoon was on, and my tram stopped due to water on the tracks, but I was determined to keep going. Offering to pay double the usual rate, I caught a rickshaw for the second part of my journey. I was an hour late when I arrived at Albert Hall. Supriya and Sonali, who lived close enough to have walked, were already at the table, looking slightly bedraggled as they waved at me to come forward. Then I saw others I knew: Ruksana, Lata, and some men. Men at the table! It was rare for young Indian men and women to freely socialize. Before taking my seat, I stopped at the corner where people were leaving their wet umbrellas.

"I hope we'll get the same umbrellas at night's end," a male voice said in my ear.

"Yes. They're all black, aren't they?" I agreed with a laugh.

"Black as sin! Just as the British say about us."

The man's arch comment made me look up at him as he wiped off his fogged eyeglasses with a handkerchief. It was Pankaj Bandopadhyay. So this was why I'd kept going through the rain; somehow, my woman's intuition had told me I couldn't miss the meeting. My heart raced with happiness. Because I'd not expected to see him again so quickly, nor have him speak directly to me.

"Are you with the Chhatri Sangha group?" Pankaj offered a social smile, clearly not recognizing me as the servant girl from four years earlier. I should have been completely relieved; but the romantic in me wished I hadn't been so forgettable.

I told him that I was a group member and my name was Kamala Mukherjee, which led to him introducing himself. I tried to keep a calm demeanor, but inside, I was jumping with excitement. Pankaj and I were on speaking terms.

"Come, then," Pankaj said. "Let's see if we can find seats. I will buy the first round of coffee."

"Pankaj-da, you're all wet!" Supriya said as the two of us came up. I remembered Supriya saying she knew many activists, but I would not have guessed Pankaj.

"I feel like a bedraggled crow," he said wryly. "I don't know how your friend Kamala stays so elegant. Tell me, did you travel by palanquin?"

"Tram and rickshaw! But I have a good black umbrella." I sat down between Sonali and Supriya, trying to keep from smiling too much. Did he really think me elegant? The others were introduced: a sallow, middle-aged Bengali man called Bijoy, and Arvind, a curly-haired youth closer to our ages but with an accent from another place. I found it interesting that nobody gave their surnames during introductions, and the females added *da*, the suffix meaning elder brother, when they addressed Pankaj. Clearly they already knew him in a friendly way.

"Who else would like chicken sandwiches?" Pankaj asked when the bearer came to take orders.

I shook my head, remembering I was supposed to seem like a proper Brahmin in public. Lata, who really was a Brahmin, also declined, but the Sen girls ordered chicken, as did young Arvind, and Ruksana, who was the gathering's only Muslim.

"What kind of Brahmin eats chicken?" Lata Menon said to Pankaj after the sandwiches came.

"Freedom fighters need strength to fight," he laughingly rejoined. "You know the legend of the Kshatriya caste: a king made those Brahmins eat meat so they'd be strong enough to fight for him."

"Even though you are presumably hoping to be reborn in your same caste?" Supriya said teasingly. All the girls seemed so familiar with Pankaj; it made me a little jealous.

"I don't care about caste; I think of myself as an Indian. I should not even have mentioned Hinduism because religious divisions ruin everything." Pankaj nodded toward Ruksana and said, "I am honored by your presence at this table. I hope you bring more friends from your community to meet with us."

"My group is already here." Ruksana's back straightened, and she gestured toward the Sen girls, Lata, and me. "We ladies usually only work with one another."

"And what have you been doing?" Pankaj scooped up his sandwich half.

Ruksana answered, "We raise funds for the independence struggle, and, of course, we debate politics."

"Yes, that is something we really enjoy!" Supriya said.

"Did you know that some years ago, sisters in the movement did quite a bit in cooperation with men?" Pankaj's quiet voice drew me even closer. "They organized training centers to teach martial arts; they blocked entrances to universities on strike days and spent months in prison. Half a dozen Bengali girls have shot at British officials, including the governor of Bengal himself."

"Are you advising us to shoot guns at people?" I exclaimed, unable to hide my shock.

"We are not interested in becoming bandits!" Ruksana gave him a stern look.

"I am not suggesting that," Pankaj replied hastily. "But over the last thirty or so years, Gandhiji has gained nothing from the English but unfulfilled promises. Netaji has explained what needs to be done."

"Are you with Forward Bloc, then?" I asked, feeling myself grow warm as he turned from Ruksana to acknowledge my question.

"I am holding myself aside so I can continue to work as a barrister for activists," Pankaj said. "I've been arrested twice already, and it hampers my ability to keep others free and aid the movement. So I made a vow to help people within the movement make connections with each other—but I don't hold any official posts."

"That is probably the best idea for you," I said, relieved that he was not at such great personal risk as before. Supriya looked at me strangely, and I wondered if my face was showing my emotions.

"I represent Shakti Sangha, and we are joining Forward Bloc." Arvind spoke in a voice that seemed stronger than his age would suggest. "We are delighted that you ladies have agreed to meet us. As Netaji says, if we wage war for equality of Indians in India, we must regard our women as highly as the men."

"I agree with you!" Sonali said, and beamed at Arvind. As if embarrassed, he dropped the gaze. When everyone's attention had returned to Pankaj, he explained that Shakti Sangha had published many pamphlets with quotations from the speeches of Subhas Chandra Bose and other strong nationalists. It all was being done with a printing press that was constantly being moved from one safe house to another to avoid discovery.

"Something women freedom fighters did in the past was move weaponry to various fighters," Pankaj said. "What they need help with now is transferring the parts of our printing press. It's not as difficult as it seems, for each piece is boxed up and covered with something else."

"Why do you need women?" I asked, wishing I could be part of it and admiring the term he had used. *Freedom fighter* sounded much better than the word the English press used: *terrorist.*

"Lately, the police have randomly stopped men with packages. That is why we hope to shift some of our burden on strong female shoulders," Pankaj said, looking directly at me in a way that made my stomach flutter.

"First, I would like to see what these pamphlets say." Ruksana's expression was serious.

"Certainly, you must see! Unfortunately, we were not carrying materials today; there was too much risk with so many police around the Town Hall. If we meet again, I'll have something for you."

There was silence for a moment, and then a girl called Sulekha spoke in a timid voice. "I am quite interested to participate, but I must first write to my parents about it and receive permission."

Pankaj shook his head. "Letters can be opened by the police. In your situation, it's probably best not to volunteer. And whoever does this would need freedom to move about in the day and sometimes evening, mostly in North Calcutta."

"Sonali and I can help," Supriya said, spooning sugar into a second cup of coffee. "We are always taking rickshaws here and there because of our colleges and schools. And our parents won't bother us about anything. If they found out, they would only be proud!"

"My parents are far away in Travancore," Lata said. "Of course I'll participate."

"That is wonderful. And what about Kamala? She seems to have the ability to travel anywhere without so much as a raindrop touching her." Pankaj looked at me with a warm smile in his eyes.

I felt pleased by the attention but regretful of what my answer would be. Reluctantly, I said, "I can't because I live in the White Town. There are so many English neighbors, always watching from their windows—"

Pankaj's eyebrows went up in surprise. "Is your father in the ICS, then? Where does he stand on independence?"

"Oh, she doesn't dare ask him!" Supriya said with a humorous grimace before I could concoct a stammering reply. I was grateful to Supriya, who must have also realized it was better for Pankaj to move on to another topic than find out I was employed by an Englishman.

Not knowing any of the truth, Pankaj leaned forward eagerly. "Kamala, don't worry, you can still help. You might someday overhear something about the government's plans that could help the independence movement. If you have some information, please come to me."

From his pocket, he brought forward a white card printed on one side in Hindi and the other side in Bengali. The card showed his name, his legal credentials, telephone number, and the address I knew so well. He added, "Don't ever call on the telephone—just come in person. The privacy of telephone connections cannot be guaranteed."

To see him in person. The way he'd said it made me want to faint. To do so meant a terrible risk, not just for the sake of politics—but also my heart.

CHAPTER

25

*"How awfully good of you to come!" she said, and she meant it—
it was odd how standing there one felt them going on, going on,
some quite old, some . . .*

—Virginia Woolf, *Mrs. Dalloway*, 1925

I had Pankaj's calling card!

The ivory card engraved in Hindi on one side, and Bengali on the other, meant Pankaj wanted to see me again. But unfortunately, I did not have anything to say. I knew very little about Mr. Lewes's work except that his office was on Lord Sinha Lane, in a towering building that also housed the police. He also went frequently to Government House, and every few months to Bombay or New Delhi. But I didn't know who he saw in these places, or what they talked about, and I did not want to raise his suspicion by asking.

I felt frustrated that the only type of news I could relate were things like: "Mr. Lewes is having a party and some English people are coming." And that was the truth. My employer had decided to hold an open house to show off his library, which was now fully air-conditioned and filled with books on handsome mahogany shelves, a beautiful Agra carpet on the floor, and plush velvet lounging furniture. As I'd directed Shombhu and Jatin in setting the last furniture in place, I'd feared that my position would end. After all, Mr. Lewes had once told me it was a year's work. But at dinner that week, he told me how he wanted me to expand the card catalog listings, continue overseeing book repairs, and write to bookshops around India to seek titles he was looking for. My work would be mostly self-directed and involve short, special projects.

But this special project—planning a cocktail party—was beyond my knowledge. I quizzed him, Manik, and other cooks in the neighborhood about what the British expected to eat at such affairs; I was surprised to learn the whole event would involve eating small plates of foods while standing, and drinking many alcoholic beverages. Mr. Lewes approved the dishes I suggested and told me what the drinks should be. He gave extra money for me to send Manik and Choton shopping, and then a separate envelope to me with fifty rupees.

"And what is this for?" I asked when I saw its contents.

"A sari suitable for the evening. And a necklace and bangles— whatever you need to complete the picture."

I was taken aback, both by the personal nature of the gift and by the obvious importance of my carrying off the right appearance. Mr. Lewes's insistence that everything be of the highest standard reminded me of a Virginia Woolf novel about Clarissa Dalloway preparing for her own grand house party. Yet this was a straightforward ICS party in Calcutta, unlike Mrs. Dalloway's celebrity-filled one in London. And unlike Mrs. Dalloway, I hadn't invited an ex-lover.

Using the flat's telephone, I rang Mr. Lewes's secretary for updates of names of the growing list; when it passed thirty, Shombhu confirmed my suspicion that Mr. Lewes did not have enough matching porcelain, so I located the same pattern in a small shop in Burra Bazar. New cushions were stitched for the sofas from soft green velvet, and I walked to Good Companions in Cornwallis Street to buy an embroidered linen cloth for the dining table. I supervised floor-to-ceiling cleaning of all the first-floor rooms and showed the gardener, Promod, where to place the prettiest potted trees and flowers from the garden.

On the next-to-last day, I suddenly realized I had not yet bought a sari. I searched Hogg Market until I found a gossamer black silk embroidered with exquisite designs of moons and stars. And then I bought my first items of gold: a series of delicate filigreed gold chains with a cascading bridge of moonstones that settled just about my collarbone, with matching earrings. But enjoying my appearance made me feel guilty; it reminded me of preparing myself for the evenings at Rose Villa and all that came afterward. And this naturally led me to think about the daughter I'd left. With the few rupees left over, I bought chappals for Kabita to grow into and posted them on my way home.

❧　　❧　　❧

HALF AN HOUR before the party, Mr. Lewes appeared in a white sharkskin jacket with his black dinner trousers, but instead of the usual bow tie that English gentlemen wore at night, he had a silk scarf tucked into the neck of his shirt. He looked so dashing I felt that I had to look away.

"After everyone arrives, I will go upstairs," I told him. I was nervous about being amid so many English. They would overtake the flat with their muddy footprints and stinking cigarettes; they would pull out books willy-nilly and spill their drinks. They would laugh and scold and bray until I could not take another moment.

"But I need you to clearly explain the vision and scope of the library. You're the one who knows where everything is. And why are you wearing your specs?"

"To see." Actually, I was trying to be plainer, to be overlooked as I once had at Lockwood School.

back when they're caught? We once had a girl like that one, and I sacked her."

"That's enough, Nancy." Mr. Lewes's voice was curt. Nancy had slid off the desk. Putting her hands on her hips, she gave Mr. Lewes a film heroine's long look. Then she swept out of the room, jabbing her elbow hard against me.

"She was about to have me strung up and quartered! Thank God you finally arrived." Mr. Lewes pulled a pack of cigarettes from his breast pocket.

"I wish you wouldn't smoke in here; it's terrible for the collection," I snapped.

"I suppose you're right." He put the pack back in his pocket. "You are always looking out for me, aren't you?"

Then Mr. Lewes walked right up to me and looked down into my face. I felt a strange current. It was the way the air felt just before the monsoon broke. As he bent down toward my mouth, I realized that he was going to kiss me. I had the oddest temptation to see what this kiss would feel like, but then I stepped back fast and put my hand over my mouth. He stepped back, too.

My head was spinning. I had to do something to break the tension. "You were speaking as if you don't like Miss Graham."

"Her name was not on the list I gave you. She came with friends." Mr. Lewes's face was flushed. "What you saw was an ambush."

I murmured that it was all right, although I was still upset. After one gin-lime, I felt as if I'd gone mad. How many drinks had my employer taken that he was moved to almost kiss me?

Dimly, I heard another voice.

"May I join, sir?"

A short, plump Indian man wearing a dinner suit was hesitating at the door. He was regarding me in the same skeptical manner in which I'd looked at Nancy Graham. Overcome by embarrassment. I longed to shout out to him in Bengali that Mr. Lewes was only my employer and nothing at all had happened.

"Those are only meant for reading." He reached forward and gently lifted them off. I felt a shiver run through me, although his fingers had not even grazed my skin.

"Much better," he said, smiling at me. "And why don't you put them somewhere you might need to use them, like the library desk? But come back quickly; our party starts in five minutes."

He didn't want me to wear the glasses because he wanted me to look pretty. And he had said *our party*, as if I were his hostess. All this hit me like a mistimed thunderclap as the guests arrived: gentlemen in pressed dinner suits and ladies in flowing tea-length and long dresses with puffed sleeves and sweetheart necklines. Of the dozen or so Indian guests, just three were women, all wives of senior Indians in the ICS. They moved slowly with the weight of their ages and their heavily embroidered saris, making me feel like a wallflower in my quiet black silk.

"Kamala—please socialize," Mr. Lewes said under his breath as he passed by with a redheaded girl on one side and a blonde on the other. But the Indian matrons did not break their conversation or even look at me, as if they understood I was only an exalted servant.

Shombhu passed and gave me a sympathetic look. I lifted a glass of sweet lime from his tray; only after I'd tasted it did I realize that I'd mistakenly taken a gin-lime. I sipped it slowly and walked on, trying to seem as if I had a right to be at the party.

"And which babu's wife are you?" The speaker was a very tall, middle-aged Englishman with a narrow rat's face.

"Nobody's. My name is Kamala Mukherjee." I was trying to be politely social, the way that Mr. Lewes would like.

His bloodshot eyes seemed to water. "Then why are you here, Camilla?"

"I work for Mr. Lewes," I answered, noticing the guest had spoken the name I'd put on my résumé that Mr. White had rejected a year earlier in the Writers' Building. Was it a matter of having a bad ear for Indian names or something else? "May I be so bold, sir, as to ask who you are?"

"Wilbur Weatherington." He raised an eyebrow, as if it were audacious for me to ask. "And what is it you do for Mr. Lewes?"

"I organized his library. It was all in boxes a year ago, and now, you should go in and see it for yourself!" I inclined my head toward the library door, wishing him away.

Mr. Weatherington laughed, exposing several rotted teeth. "You can't seriously be a professional librarian. Where in God's name did you come from?"

"I used to work as a tutor at a girls' school—"

"Yes, your accent's all right." His voice was grudging. "Which school was it?"

"Lockwood," I said rashly, for the gin had gotten to me before I could be more careful. "It's quite far; you wouldn't know it."

"A minor school, hmm? I suppose that's why they admit Indians."

What a thing to say! I was so taken aback that as a couple brushed past, I almost lost my balance.

Mr. Weatherington caught my arm, righting me. "You aren't well; you need some air. Come with me to the veranda, Camilla."

"There is plenty of cool air in the library! That is the reason for the party, Mr. Lewes said, to demonstrate the air-conditioning." I spoke fast, because as loathsome as Weatherington was, I could not cause a scene fighting a gentleman guest.

"There are a few houses in Alipore with air-conditioning." Mr. Weatherington's rank breath came near my ear. "I don't think it's healthy for people."

"But it's excellent for books. And that's what Mr. Lewes cares about most!" I was searching about with my eyes, willing him to be nearby.

"Actually, his life mission is the same as mine: to protect the empire." The wheedling tone in Mr. Weatherington's voice was gone, as if he'd realized he would get nowhere with me. "Fetch two more of the potato chops, will you?"

But I did not walk to the buffet table; instead, I slid the plate he'd

given me onto a corner table and walked straight into the library. But there I stopped dead in my tracks.

Nobody was in the room except for Mr. Lewes and one of the women he'd been speaking with earlier. His back was to me, but I could clearly see the blond lady had perched herself atop the desk in front of him.

"Darling, remember Bombay!" she said, leaning forward so the deep neckline of her gown became even more revealing. "You know it can happen again."

Mr. Lewes stepped back. "That was years ago when I was newly arrived and you hadn't yet married—"

"And you still are without a girl," she said, laughingly. "Don't tell me you're all work and no play, Simon. I must change that."

Mr. Lewes coughed and said, "Please, Nancy, won't you come off the desk before you stain yourself with ink? That's a blotter you're sitting on."

The place where I laid fine books was being desecrated. I fumed at both the woman's insolence and the fury I felt at her being so close to my employer. I heard blood pounding in my ears as she suddenly opened the front of her dress, exposing full breasts barely covered by a lace brassiere.

"Tell me you don't want this," she murmured huskily, holding her breasts toward him like a fruit seller offering fat mangoes. It was an act befitting the red-light district, not Middleton Mansions; so vulgar that I gasped aloud.

Mr. Lewes turned and his hands flew up, as if he'd been caught stealing. Blinking rapidly, he said, "Kamala, just in time! Miss Graham has lost a button to her gown and needs help getting it fixed."

He was covering up for what had happened; yet I was unwilling to play along with his lie. Stiffly, I replied that I didn't sew dresses; that was a job for a darzi.

"Honestly!" Nancy Graham buttoned up her tight bodice, which had not torn at all. "How can you let your servants snoop and talk

"Pal-babu. I am very happy to see you." Mr. Lewes sounded relieved by the interruption. "Where is your wife? I hear she's keen on books."

"Mrs. Pal could not attend, but she will be interested to hear about the library decoration and especially the menu. It is much superior to the typical British affair. Tell me, was it catered by one of the Park Street restaurants?"

"Oh, no. I've got a good Oriya cook and an even better personal assistant who concocted the menu. Come, you must meet her. This is Miss Kamala Mukherjee."

I made namaskar with my hands to Mr. Pal, who did the same. But his dubious expression didn't change.

"Kamala, won't you check with Shombhu about whether enough champagne is opened? I thought the drinks table looked a bit miserly when I last stopped by."

Outside the room, I put my hands to my burning cheeks. I could not bear returning to the crowded dining and drawing rooms, so I slipped upstairs to my bathroom to splash water on my face. While closing the taps, I heard the rumble of voices below me in the library. Mr. Lewes and Mr. Pal were still there. What were they talking about?

I shut off the bathroom's light, pried up the broken tile, and lay on the floor, placing my left eye over the narrow crack that opened through the library ceiling. I couldn't see, but I could hear.

"Two thousand, maybe more," Mr. Pal was saying in a low voice. "The papers will give the correct number tomorrow."

"Was it peaceful?"

"As much as you could expect, in such a situation. There were some arrests, and truthfully, sir, those protesters were emotional but not at all violent or riotous. Heavy rain likely kept the worst actors away."

Protesters. They might have been talking about a Forward Bloc rally Supriya and Sonali had mentioned happening today. I'd been invited but was too busy to go.

"Is the poet involved?" Mr. Lewes asked.

"No. He's said to be very upset about the situation, though, and may come up with some kind of written statement."

"That's all we need." Mr. Lewes sighed heavily and asked, "What about the Communists?"

"I made the list you asked for. It's not as long as I would have liked." Mr. Pal chuckled. "Spotting the various faces in such a throng was quite difficult."

"Thanks," Mr. Lewes said, and I could hear the soft sound of a paper unfolding. I had thought he might read from it, but he was silent. At the end he said, "How and when will you next report?"

"Friday next . . . shall we meet in the upstairs bar at the Calcutta Club around seven?"

"I shall be there. But if there's nothing new to say, leave a message with my office canceling."

"It is done."

"Very well, Mr. Pal. And I'm going to unlock the library now, in case anyone's waiting outside. Do have something more to eat before you leave."

"I shall rejoin the group as you wish, sir—but don't think I've stopped working! My ear is always to the ground!" The edge of Mr. Pal's body crossed my spy hole, and I heard Mr. Lewes unlock the door.

My employer bent over the desk. He pulled a key from his pocket and opened the middle drawer. He slid an envelope inside and re-locked the drawer. And then he disappeared from my view, although I heard the library door opening and his voice calling to people to come inside and see the best folios.

CHAPTER
26

DECEIVE: *To ensnare; to take unawares by craft or guile; to overcome, overreach, or get the better of by trickery; to beguile or betray into mischief or sin; to mislead.*

—*Oxford English Dictionary*, Vol. 3, 1933

*D*on't tell on the men.

Bonnie had said it to me when I was fifteen, when the police chief had frightened us with his pretend snake. Englishmen in India could behave with impunity. And we were supposed to allow it. Mr. Lewes was a terrible man. When he'd stood closely to me in the library, I'd been seized by a brief, dangerous fever. But now I felt rage at myself for this lapse and for misreading the intentions of a man who'd stop at nothing to suppress freedom. With his polite requests for my companionship at dinner, Mr. Lewes had manipulated me to gather information. What I'd fed him was allowing his government to keep India under its heavy elephant feet forever.

That night, I longed to break into his desk, find the list, and destroy it. But the rational part of me said to wait. If the list of people seen at the rally vanished, Mr. Lewes might suspect me. I needed only to get into the desk, check the list, and communicate the names to Pankaj.

The next morning, I was in the library at the usual time, dressed to work. I tried wiggling a letter opener in the lock, but it did not work. I put that away and was industriously sorting through a stack of books when Mr. Lewes stumbled in an hour later than usual, still wearing his dressing gown. His face was drawn, and he held a bag of ice against his head with one hand and a cup of tea in the other.

"A good morning to you, sir!" I turned away, thinking he deserved this.

"Not really. I feel like someone threw a *Gazetteer* at my head," he grumbled.

I did not comment, just kept working with my back to him. I wondered if his keys were in his pocket. If I were still a Rose Villa girl, I would go to him and slip my hands into his pocket while I kissed him; I imagined he would like it. But I had come through that hell pledging never to use any of the sordid skills I had learned.

Mr. Lewes sat down at the desk, putting his teacup on the blotter soiled by so many cocktail glasses the night before. "Is that homespun cotton you're wearing?"

"Yes. It's called khadi," I said, pulling the pallu a bit higher over my shoulder to keep my bosom fully covered. "It's all the fashion these days."

"I rather prefer what you wore yesterday evening." Mr. Lewes yawned. "Actually, I haven't thanked you properly for all you did. Except for a few misbehaving guests and my overimbibing, I think it was a good night."

"People enjoyed it," I said, thinking, *everyone except for me*. I had worked so hard to organize it, but then nobody had spoken to me because I was obviously in Mr. Lewes's employ.

"This really is the only tolerable room in the house," Mr. Lewes said, moving the ice from one side of his head to the other. "The humidity never ceases, even this early."

I couldn't stand having him near, not with what I now understood about his character. Coolly, I said, "I'd rather you didn't breakfast in here, as I'm still cleaning up yesterday evening's mess."

He sighed. "I may begin taking breakfast in the garden."

But there is no table in the garden, nor proper chairs on which to dine, I was about to say. And then I had a brilliant idea.

"If you'd like to dine outside, you must have a table and chairs built of a wood like teak that can withstand rain. Jatin can carry out the lounge chairs when you have your drink, but it is not suitable for breakfast or dinner."

"I don't know if I could," he said. "Mr. Rowley wants to know about anything I intend changing in public spaces. He was rather miffed about the air-conditioning work going on."

"It's because he lives downstairs and had to suffer the noise of all the workers putting in the air conditioner. You should have invited him to the party to improve relations."

"I did try, but he doesn't care for mixed parties." At my blank expression, Mr. Lewes added, "That is, parties with more than European guests. I'm sorry, Kamala, but some of my colleagues seem to think it's still the days of the East India Company."

I stopped sorting books and delivered a cool look. "Really? But in those days, apparently the company men at least took the effort to learn the local language."

Mr. Lewes stretched back in his chair. "Not because they were studious; it was because every fellow had his own sleeping dictionary."

"What kind of dictionary did you say?" I asked, although I remembered full well what Rose Barker had told me.

"Sorry. *Sleeping dictionary* was a term used for"—Mr. Lewes hesitated a moment—"their paramours. Every evening, underneath their mosquito nets, company officers learned Bengali and Hindustani from their lady friends."

"How practical," I said crisply. "As you know, you have a modern English-Bengali dictionary to help you, should you like to learn something; but I think not."

Mr. Lewes put down his ice pack. "Kamala, I am sorry if you still believe I didn't like your Christmas present!"

"You have no reason to learn Bengali. Why should you?" I said, thinking, *Not when you have Mr. Pal to spy for you and me to translate Indian opinions.*

"I'm dismal at speaking languages. I studied French and Latin, of course, but when I see the Indian alphabets I just—slow down mentally. I feel like a child." He shook his head, and this made him wince and put the ice on his head again. "Your gift made me feel wretched because you don't spend enough on your own clothing and so on. I wish you'd buy more saris like the one you wore yesterday. You should take yourself shopping next week; I won't have as much for you to do because I'm going to Delhi on temporary duty."

"Oh, that's quite a long trip. What is it you will do there, sir?"

"Meetings. Writing. Perhaps a polo game with some old friends." Again, he yawned.

"Well, I hope you have a relaxing trip. And I am very glad we spoke about the garden furniture. I will know not to bother Mr. Chun about it."

Mr. Lewes passed a hand over his eyes. "Actually, why don't you just go ahead with it? That Infernal Rowley's not my landlord. And go ahead. You may order whatever table and some chairs you think right."

❦   ❦   ❦

MR. LEWES LEFT on Monday morning. I could not stop smiling as I waved him off, because my subterfuge was about to get under way. After giving Manik orders to simplify our menus to ordinary Bengali vegetarian cooking, I hurried off to Bow Bazar. In this old commercial district, the twisting lanes were packed with interesting small shops

owned by Chinese and Nepali and other foreign merchants; I could
have browsed for hours but concentrated on finding Mr. Chun's furniture shop, where I had not visited for some time. Mr. Chun recognized me with pleasure and offered me a cup of delicious oolong tea.
As we sat down on blindingly polished rosewood chairs, I mentioned
that I needed a minor repair to the library.

"Is there a problem with the new ladder? Not the bookcases!" Mr.
Chun's face tightened with worry.

"Not at all," I reassured him. "It's Mr. Lewes's desk. He has mis-
placed the key to the central drawer and is beside himself wanting to
have whatever is inside."

"I know the desk—walnut, two sides for sitting, from England,
isn't it? A partners desk."

"Surely you can fix the drawer—I've heard you can fix anything!"
Woman's intuition told me not to give him a siren's look but that of a
hopeful daughter.

Mr. Chun tilted his head, considering things. "I can remove the
lock plate and put on a new one. But I have no copy of the key, because I did not make it."

"Mr. Lewes insists on keeping the original lock plate. Isn't there
something you can try?"

"I cannot promise to fix it; but I promise to come." Mr. Chun
looked unhappy; clearly this was a prospect of some trouble, and little
financial gain.

"I will be most grateful if you try," I said softly. "And we're also
considering a dining table for the garden and several chairs to go
around. I don't know if you have time for that."

"A new order, you say? Dining set?" The carpenter's eyes gleamed.
"Perhaps—perhaps I can come this very evening. I'll solve every problem and build every thing."

❧   ❧   ❧

THERE WAS A solution, after all. Mr. Chun knew a skilled met-alsmith who could make a new key, but he would need the whole lock plate in order to cut the key to fit it. I agreed, and Mr. Chun removed the lock plate itself and wrapped it in cotton to take to his metalsmith.

"The key will not have the same patina as the old brass," he said, rubbing his finger against it. "But this brass of the lock plate can be polished to match like new."

"Please do not," I said. "Mr. Lewes likes the original finish and it makes the desk more valuable. But tell me, how quickly can the metalsmith work?"

"I will bring it to him tomorrow morning. And Memsaheb, do not worry. I shall tell him that it is an important job to do right away."

❧   ❧   ❧

LATER ON, WHEN Manik, Jatin, and Shombhu had said good night, I barred the door and went into the library. The desk's thin middle drawer looked the same as always, save for the graceful gap where the lock plate had once been. I had some feelings of guilt to be doing this to a man who trusted me implicitly. Then I shook myself. Netaji had said every Indian citizen should work bravely for freedom. It was my turn.

With a protesting squeak, the old drawer pulled out. Inside, I saw layers of papers and telegrams. Slowly, I sifted through all the papers in the drawer, trying to be mindful of the order in which they lay. Mostly they were blurred copies of typed pages on the thin, tissue-like paper that was called onionskin. The pages were reports of various crimes as they were reported in newspapers, including the editorial reaction and letters to the editor about the stories.

I sorted through copies of letters from Bengal's last two governors to the viceroy in Delhi dated each fortnight from January 1935 on-ward. The letters gave reports of strikes, elections, and other notable situations. The theme of each letter was that the governor was well aware of all events in Bengal and was carefully overseeing industry and hunting terrorists. Accompanying these letters were note cards and papers scrawled in Mr. Lewes's handwriting that dealt with the topics in the letters. So he was the true writer—not the governor.

When I was through with the desk drawer, I moved on to search the unlocked drawers on the left side of the desk, and then, the shelves of the library itself. But I couldn't find the list of names. I imagined that Mr. Lewes had already filed a report with the Communist names and discarded Mr. Pal's original list.

I closed up the study and went to my room, but I could not sleep. After tossing and turning for a while, I turned on my small electric lamp and reached for *India's Struggle for Freedom*, which was still in my bedside drawer. Then I was hit with the idea that perhaps Mr. Lewes read in bed, too; and his room could be a place where he stored his lists and other secret information.

One o'clock. With a battery-powered torch, I went downstairs and turned the knob to his bedroom. I had never been in this spacious, pleasant room with a four-poster bed made from mahogany. The same polished wood was used for large cabinets for his clothing, a desk, and two easy chairs. The windows were shut and long linen curtains drawn.

I intended to search the room from top to bottom. Under the small, bouncing circle of light, I saw framed photographs of people in England, including a school with many boys standing in front of it and young men moving a boat with long poles. Mr. Lewes was in the center of this laughing, happy group, a handsome, dark-haired boy barely out of his teens. In the background, I glimpsed the building's spire and guessed it might have been Cambridge. Did he know then what he would become—a suppressor of people's freedom?

I crossed the Agra carpet to investigate a tall dresser. As I slid the first drawer open to find stacks of handkerchiefs, I remembered what Nancy had called me: a snoop. What an ugly word! I moved on to the next drawer, which held his underclothes. I couldn't bring myself to touch such personal items, so I closed that drawer quickly. I carefully checked the other drawers holding his shirts, collars and stays, suspenders, and the like. No papers or anything other than clothing. Then I searched the desk and bookcases and even looked under the bed.

I sank down on the edge of his four-poster, thinking. My eyes drifted over the area I'd originally meant to search: two marble-topped nightstands that flanked his bed. The nightstand nearest to me was empty on top and inside. The farther nightstand was topped by a geography of Uttar Pradesh, a clean ashtray, and a drinking glass. In the cupboard-style compartment below, I found a leather-bound photograph album. I opened it, expecting more scenes of his old life in England, but as I turned the pages, I found the streets and train stations of India. For every picture of scenery, there was a companion picture taken of the same scene, but with a man in it. Some of the men wore Congress caps, or carried Muslim League banners, or had flags bearing the Communists' hammer and sickle. It was apparent by the way these men were looking off to the side that they did not know they were being photographed.

Gently, I lifted the pictures out of the little black edges that held them against the page. On the back, Mr. Lewes had written the date and location and sometimes a name, but more often a question mark. I did not wonder why he'd put these pictures into an album. My only question was whether the men pictured in these political gatherings had already been arrested. The initial shame I'd had at entering Mr. Lewes's room was gone, as was any doubt that I was betraying his trust in me. India mattered more than anything. In terms of gathering intelligence, I'd had a very successful search.

And finally, something to tell Pankaj.

CHAPTER
27

PRIVILEGE: . . . 2. A right, advantage, or immunity, belonging to or enjoyed by a person, or a body or class of persons, beyond the common advantage of others; an exemption in a particular case from certain burdens or liabilities.

—*Oxford English Dictionary*, Vol. 8, 1933

At ten in the morning, I walked at a leisurely pace through Ballygunge, dressed in a purple-and-white-striped sari and carrying a shopping bag in my left hand. The Bandopadhyay home looked as solidly established as it had months before, with the same darwan sleeping in his chair. But this time around, I was not afraid to approach. I tapped my umbrella on the path; the darwan jumped to his feet and escorted me to the large wrought iron door that was answered by a young bearer who ushered me into a parlor to wait.

I perched on a prickly settee and looked around. On the wall directly across me, several of Pankaj's ancestors regarded me with sober, sepia-tinged faces. Lace curtains swayed at the long, open windows that overlooked the street. A large electric ceiling fan stirred the stacks of newspapers on the table, near a framed photograph of Gandhiji standing beside a tall, solemn-looking man. It took me a moment to recognize him as Pankaj's late father. Now I noticed on the far wall, the senior Bandopadhyay's portrait was draped with a fresh jasmine garland. I wondered how recently he'd expired, and how that must have grieved Pankaj.

Because Pankaj's father was gone, I did not have to worry about his recognizing me, but his mother remained. I prayed that four years' time and my fine new clothes and elegant bun were enough differences to disguise me.

I heard a light footstep and saw that Pankaj had entered wearing a kurta and dhoti in fine, cream-colored muslin. Just seeing him quickened my pulse, but the good feeling turned to anxiety when a short, stout woman wearing a plain white widow's sari appeared at his side. His mother's expression was just as measuring as it had been at Lockwood School.

"I have come for legal consultation." I kept my eyes down, pretending to be a shy client desiring privacy. Although Mukherjee was a very common Bengali Brahmin name, I didn't want to speak it aloud in front of her.

"Ma, this is Kamala Mukherjee, from the Chhatri Sangha group." Pankaj smiled at me. So he recalled me only as a well-dressed lady; the servant girl of four years earlier must have vanished entirely from his consciousness.

"You are a Mukherjee?" Mrs. Bandopadhyay came closer, as if to examine my face. "Who is your father? From which town?"

I wished Pankaj had not given me the name. Now my stomach roiled in fear. I opened my mouth to speak, but words would not come.

"There are many Mukherjees in Bengal, Ma," Pankaj said, taking his mother's hand and gently pulling her away. "Miss Kamala Mukherjee is a student friend of Lata Menon's and the Sen girls."

"Oh, the Sens! Such a good family. You are a shy one, Kamala." His mother's face relaxed but only slightly. I was relieved when Pankaj asked her to please return to her room, because this legal consultation, like all others, was private. Mrs. Bandopadhyay went out clutching a shawl around her shoulders but turned her head to give a last searching look.

Pankaj shut the door to the hallway and came to sit in the chair nearest me. "I'm very sorry. Because my mother is a widow, she has little activity and becomes too engaged in my life."

"Oh, it doesn't matter! I found something in my bungalow. Do you have time to look?" I handed Pankaj the album. As he saw the first page of photographs, his eyes widened. He turned another page and then said, "Just a moment. I will fetch gloves to prevent fingerprints."

"I didn't think of fingerprints!" I put my hand to my mouth. "I touched everything."

"Don't worry. I'm guessing that you have not been arrested before and your prints have not been recorded by the Bengal police."

As Pankaj examined each picture, I wondered what tortures he had undergone in the Andaman Islands. And what sort of a person would keep working for his movement when he could easily be arrested again? The answer came to me: the same kind of man as Gandhiji and Netaji and Jawaharlal Nehru. I gazed at Pankaj, and as each second passed, he seemed to be even more impressive. Still, I could not understand why he hadn't recognized me from the garden at Lockwood; Mr. Lewes had been able to recognize me easily that day at the bookstore, although I'd been masquerading as an Anglo-Indian the first time. Well, perhaps that was because Mr. Lewes was a spy by training.

Pankaj finally spoke. "Did your father collect these pictures?"

I felt that I couldn't mislead him any longer. "These pictures have nothing to do with my father. Actually, he is deceased like your own."

Pankaj's eyebrows rose. "But you spoke of your father's position with the ICS—"

"You and Supriya did. I am not free to speak publicly." Taking a deep breath, I explained that I worked as a library clerk for an English ICS officer called Simon Lewes. Behind the spectacles, Pankaj's piercing eyes appeared more interested than shocked, giving me encouragement to continue. I described the conversation I'd overheard between Mr. Lewes and Mr. Pal, and the list of suspected Communists collected at a Forward Bloc rally, and how looking for it had led me to the album.

"Some of these pictures are from Bombay. This fellow looks like M. N. Roy, don't you think?" Pankaj looked up at me.

I moved closer to look at the picture, trying to ignore the enticing scent of sandalwood that came from Pankaj's body. "I have never seen Mr. Roy, so I can't tell you. I don't know much about the movement at all."

"I don't know any of these faces, either," Pankaj turned the page. "All that seems obvious is that they are being watched by the government. Did you find the negatives?"

"No. Mr. Lewes does not have a darkroom or anything like that," I said. "I don't even know that I noticed a camera in the house."

"Then he is likely not the one who took the pictures. Someone else might have delivered them to him. What is your boss's position with the government?"

"His card states he is in the Indian Civil Service. But some of the papers in his desk were on a letterhead saying Indian Political Service."

At this, his eyes lit up. "There are rumors of a spy agency within the ICS. Perhaps they are whom he works for. Can you copy the text of any recent letters he's written?"

"I think so, but—are you going to do something to Mr. Lewes?" Although disenchanted with Mr. Lewes after the encounter in the library, I did not want him harmed.

"I would not dream of it!" Pankaj said. "He is quite a valuable source to us; we want him to stay well and continue working, so we can read his materials. Tell me, is Mr. Lewes already at work today?"

"He's in Delhi, but I'm not sure for how long."

"Excellent," he said, stripping off the gloves. "I'll review the pictures with a few friends as soon as possible. Then I'll send them disguised as a shop delivery to your home. Do you think that would be safe?"

"Very safe." I hesitated, because I did not want this encounter to be the end of it. "I will begin looking for letters to bring to you."

Pankaj's eyes were shining as he looked at me. "Do you understand what you're offering? There's quite a bit of risk."

Since the time I was fourteen years old, Pankaj had been the center of my romantic dreams. He had once cared for me, too. Quietly, I spoke the words that he'd once written to me back in the Lockwood days.

"To take risks in the name of India's freedom is my privilege."

I waited for his eyes to flare with remembrance, but they did not.

🌾   🌾   🌾

MR. LEWES REMAINED in New Delhi for the rest of the week. His absence gave Pankaj time to send back the album, wrapped up in the disguise of a package from the Oxford Bookstore. I was disappointed that he didn't send a note with it saying he'd suddenly remembered who I really was and that we must talk about the past, but I knew now that my best hope was to have him fall in love with the person I'd become. If that meant waiting patiently, I could do it.

Mr. Chun refitted the old lock plate on the desk, presenting me with a perfectly fitting, shiny brass key that I added to the key ring I kept tied to my sari's pallu. The anger that I'd felt at Mr. Lewes for almost leading me into his arms was gone. Instead, I was glad to have learned of his true character before I'd made a mistake. His terrible work had brought me an opportunity I never thought I'd have: it was making me into a freedom fighter—a very secret one, reporting to one of the most important men in the movement.

As the week passed, I built myself a mountain of fantasies: sending information to Pankaj that saved lives, traveling in a burka to bring money to hidden revolutionaries, listening to the Sen girls as they talked about transporting arms with a quiet smile on my face. But then, everything changed.

I was in the garden cutting flowers to make a bouquet when Jatin came hurrying out of Middleton Mansions.

"War!" he said, panting as if he'd run a mile and not merely down one flight of stairs. "England declared war on Germany! What will it mean, Didi?"

I forgot the basket of flowers and went inside and up to the library, where Shombhu, Manik, and Choton were all listening to the wireless. Apparently, Britain's prime minister, Mr. Chamberlain, announced war plans the day before, but now the viceroy had declared India was at war with Germany, too. India's viceroy, Lord Linlithgow, announced this without consulting with any Indian leaders, and already there was angry public reaction. And for this reason, Mr. Lewes had to stay away two extra weeks in New Delhi. When he returned at last, his face was drawn, making him look much older than his thirty years.

"Everyone's raring to fight, but they don't understand Germany's power," he told me over drinks in the garden. We were sitting on Mr. Chun's new chairs that matched the table perfectly; but Mr. Lewes had seemed too troubled to notice.

"How is Germany better off than Britain? Your country has much more manpower, given all its Asian colonies."

Mr. Lewes lit a cigarette, and after taking a long puff, said, "The Luftwaffe—their air force—are unmatched. They'll shoot us to hell and back."

"Do you mean they'll start bombing England?"

"Of course. And should they manage to take strategic locations in Africa and Asia to fly from, or use allies in these places"—Mr. Lewes shook his head, looking somber—"this new war could make the last one look like school games."

❦   ❦   ❦

I WANTED TO speak with Pankaj about Mr. Lewes's thoughts on the war. In a men's shirt box stuffed with rags, I sent Pankaj a message requesting a meeting. I received a message back from him in the same box saying he would see me in a cabin around the corner from the Metro Cinema. I dressed carefully and tried to hide my excitement as we met the following afternoon in the cozy snack place. The first order of business was for him to read my copy of Mr. Lewes's report to the governor on the status of Germans in the city, all of whom were slated for imprisonment. He did so leisurely, with a Lion beer at his side. He'd offered to buy me one, but I asked for tea instead.

"Supriya Sen is quite worried for the welfare of her college's German teacher," I said, taking a sip from my cup of Darjeeling. "She's a working mother who couldn't possibly be spying for Hitler."

"Supriya should ease her mind," Pankaj said, folding the report in two. "The central government will release all of them, I'm sure, once the hostility between England and Germany ceases."

"I don't believe things will cease," I said. Mr. Lewes had slept little since the declaration; he left the flat before I awoke and stayed late at his office every evening. If things were calming down, he would be smiling and behaving normally. But instead, he only seemed more agitated. I had not seen him pick up a novel or any other kind of pleasure reading in weeks.

"Neville Chamberlain is a diplomat," Pankaj said. "He has been chatting with Hitler all along, letting him do some small things in exchange for not doing much worse ones. He can't lead a war effort; he'll find a way to back out."

"I imagine you don't think Indians should fight this war for England." I had read enough about war to fear it; but I also feared what these alien powers would do to India if there was no resistance to their armies.

Pankaj grimaced. "Of course not! If this government becomes consumed with war, it will pay no attention to the idea of independence. I'm outraged that the Congress Party is cooperating. They're supposed to lead us to freedom, not serve as Chamberlain's coolies."

"But what if England does lose?" I challenged. "Then the Germans could take over India as they've already done Denmark and Norway: and who knows what they would do? Have you heard about their actions toward Jewish people in their own country? They are being shut out of jobs and schools and must wear stars on their clothing."

Pankaj pressed his lips together. "Yes, it's immoral. Gandhiji has suggested that those Jewish people perform passive resistance to the leadership: to wear the stars and follow all government directions, but hold peaceful protests. I suppose it might shame Hitler—"

"But you don't believe Gandhiji's ways are working for India," I reminded him. "Why would they work for the Jews in Germany? What does Netaji say to you about the war?"

Pankaj took a sip of his beer and said, "He thinks an overseas war will divert the government from being able to harass freedom fighters. So this could be a good time for us to push the independence movement. And he's believes that it's fortunate for us that the British have finally met a fierce enemy. You know the saying: 'The enemy of my enemy is my friend.'"

"That's surely not a Bengali proverb."

"No, but it may turn out to be the truth." Pankaj brushed back a lock of his hair with his right hand, and I noticed for the first time he wore a heavy gold ring with a square ruby in the center. A ruby the same shape and size as the one Bidushi had. My body froze as I wondered if this was the same ruby that had disappeared so long ago.

"What is it?" he asked.

In a rush I said, "How did you get that handsome ring?"

Pankaj tapped the stone and made a face. "It's a bit fancy for a man, isn't it? Five years ago I bought the ruby from a Parsi jeweler in England. The ruby was set in a pendant that was briefly lost. When it was recovered, I decided to keep it close at hand."

"That's such a mysterious story," I said, thinking about how evasive his storytelling was. "How was the ruby returned to you? Did a bird find it glittering in the dust and bring it back?"

"No, it's a sad story." He pressed his lips together for a moment. "My dear friend who had the pendant died of malaria. When my family and I were leaving the place of her death, I noticed the pendant slipping out from the purse of my friend's aunt. Apparently, the aunt had wanted to keep it for herself without telling anyone! The lady was embarrassed by my discovery and quickly returned it as a token of goodwill between our families. The girl who died was supposed to marry me." At the end of his recitation, his face was flushed, and I saw moistness in his eyes.

"Was she your fiancée, then?" I wondered how much he would confess.

"Yes. I call her my friend, too, because that was how I felt. She wrote me such beautiful, intelligent letters. Almost two hundred of them, before she died."

I was hit with two shocks: first, that he did remember the letters, and second, that Bidushi's aunt had taken the ruby pendant and kept a cool demeanor during my persecution. For so many years, I had worried about the police coming after me. So much ruin had come to me from her dishonesty. Now I wondered whether if I'd stayed at Lockwood, my name would have been cleared. I would never have endured the tragedies of Kharagpur. But then again, I'd still be a servant. I would not be in Calcutta drinking tea with Pankaj.

"What is it, Kamala? You look distressed."

Tightly, I said, "I was wondering . . . if the aunt was charged with thieving?"

"No." He made a face. "At first a servant who was overly familiar was suspected, and she seemed proven guilty when she fled. I felt sorry, but really, there was nothing anyone could do."

"I suppose not," I said, feeling a sharp pain at the way he'd said "overly familiar." I told myself it was better that he never know I was the letter writer. But I yearned to know whether I really stood a chance. Looking closely at him, I said, "What a loss your dear friend must have been. I see it in your eyes."

He looked past me, toward the window showing the busy street. "It has been four years since her passing, so I've become accustomed to thinking of myself as a perpetual bachelor. And remaining this way has freed me to work ceaselessly for the movement. My mother complains that I am married to India, and I suppose it's true."

I remained silent, thinking. Even if he did fall in love, how could a rich Calcutta boy marry someone like me?

A devil's voice whispered, *Nobody in Calcutta knows who you were.* Pom, Sarah, and Pamela were as good as dead. And I wasn't really a Hindu Sudra anymore: at Lockwood, I'd been converted to Christianity. In Kharagpur, I'd undergone a different conversion: learning how to dress, how to speak confidently to men, and how to live comfortably inside an upper-class Anglo-Indian home. Everything that had happened to me—good and bad—had contributed to the making of Kamala Mukherjee. How different I was from the little girl who had desperately clung to a tree with floodwater rising beneath! I steered my own boat. I could build a life rich with ideas, family, and friends—just like the Sens and Bandopadhyays and other members of the educated Bhadralok class.

Take care of him, Bidushi had said on her deathbed.

I resolved that I would.

CHAPTER
28

PROPAGANDA: . . . 2. Any association, systematic scheme, or concerted movement for the propagation of a particular doctrine or practice.

—*Oxford English Dictionary*, Vol. 8, 1933

As I'd suspected, the hostilities between Germany and Britain did not cease. In the spring of 1940, the Nazis invaded France, Belgium, Luxembourg, and the Netherlands. Neville Chamberlain was relieved of his duties as prime minister and replaced by the tougher Winston Churchill, who ordered the British to begin rationing food, cloth, and other materials that would be needed for a long war.

The English newspapers made it seem as if the Nazis would be defeated any day, but this was clearly not the case. And India, so distant from the war theater, suddenly appeared like a safe haven to British families. Into our crowded, apprehensive city, people came. First were the soldiers: brown ones from India and the other colonies, and white ones from England, Scotland, and Ireland. Also arriving were the children of the Raj, those who'd been born in India but sent off to study in England.

That spring, Kabita turned two. She was still much too young to study, but I hoped Hafeeza and Abbas would plan for it. Since coming to Calcutta, I had saved enough to be able to send some money and cloth for dresses. This year I sent paper and pens and the small dictionary I'd once given Mr. Lewes. He had been so unappreciative, and I was sure he would never think to use it. Better for my own girl to have it, for I was sure Abbas would do his best to help her with English.

On the book's packaging wrap, I had, for the first time, written down the Middleton Street address. Since I'd learned of the ruby's recovery, I wasn't fearful of the police. I wanted Abbas and Hafeeza to know my new name and address in the hopes that they would write and let me know about Kabita's well-being. For them to have a way to reach me, if crisis ever came to India.

In our neighborhood, emergency planning was precise. Mr. Withers, the elderly Civil Service retiree living in the next building, became Middleton Mansions' air-raid warden, ensuring all households were supplied with bandages and petroleum jelly. Following his orders, I sadly oversaw the covering-up of our windows with thick brown paper; the loss of light and green views was disturbing. Mr. Lewes secured gas masks for every resident and servant of the entire Middleton Mansions building. I was horrified at the sight of Jatin when he tried his on: it seemed that he was no longer human; that none of us with them were. I did not want to touch the gas masks but I knew that in the Black Town, few residents had such protection, nor were any antiaircraft guns set up to protect them from air raids.

Mr. Lewes was back and forth between Calcutta, New Delhi, and Bombay, involved with others like himself in a vast campaign to ferret out German spies and sympathizers in India. In the library, Mr. Lewes no longer pored over his old books and handwrote the drafts of essays in his elegant longhand. Instead, he set up a machine called a wire recorder. It played back programs the government had given him to study: recordings of German propaganda in which ladies with silky voices coaxed British troops to lay down their arms. There was also counter-propaganda with English ladies speaking German, telling the German soldiers that Hitler was immoral and they would lose their country's freedom forever if they fought. Mr. Lewes wrote similar scripts for the Indian population to hear, as well as pieces encouraging Indian men to join the army, navy, and air forces. The awful man from the cocktail party, Mr. Weatherington, had begun calling on Mr. Lewes some evenings, in order to listen to the overseas recordings and talk about their own propaganda strategies.

"I'll never trust Indian soldiers to fight for us. Remember the mutiny?" Mr. Weatherington, who had passed under my ceiling viewing hole, slapped his hand on the desk, right in front of where Mr. Lewes was sitting. "We must concentrate our efforts on tracing the Fifth Column and locking them up."

"And now that the Germans are imprisoned; who are these supposed Fifth Columnists?" Mr. Lewes countered. "You can't lock up innocent people just because they feel differently about politics. Remember what happened in the Andamans? We wound up letting them go."

"A situation I hold you responsible for, after the so-called human rights reports you made." Mr. Weatherington made a snorting sound. "Don't sulk, Simon. You got an ICE for it: you, the governor's fair-haired boy."

Mr. Lewes was not blond; he was dark. But I knew what the English slang expression meant. It was that he was favored by authority.

And ICE meant companion of the Indian Empire, and was granted by the king each year to a select group of administrators in the ICS and military. I was stunned that the British government would have given out an honor relating to shutting down the Andamans prison—and could Mr. Lewes really have helped? That conversation gave me the impression that Mr. Lewes was not wholly against Indian independence. But I wondered about the freedom-fighting group called the Fifth Column.

The next morning, I wrote to Pankaj requesting a meeting to discuss these new developments. I placed the note under the paper lining in a box of candy and asked Kantu the newsboy to take it to 27 Lower Circular Road. In the afternoon, Kantu returned with a different package from Pankaj. Hidden under the box's lining was a request asking me to come to the Minerva Theatre for the following day's first matinee showing.

I dressed carefully the next day in a lovely green-and-gold sari and went to the cinema, buying a single seat in the upstairs balcony. After the first half hour of *Achhut Kanya*, I slipped out to the hallway where Pankaj was already standing in a dark recess. How my pulse raced to see him waiting there; waiting for me.

"I have some governors' reports for you to read," I said, handing him what I'd translated into Bengali. "But first, I must tell you what I overheard him talking about with his ICS colleague Wilbur Weatherington. They were speaking about the Fifth Column. Do you know of this freedom-fighting group?"

Pankaj grimaced, and I realized I should not have said the name Weatherington aloud but instead used W. "They are talking about Nazi sympathizers who are waiting here, ready to help. Did they speak any names of people they suspect? They could face automatic imprisonment under the war rules."

"I have not heard any specific names. The conversation became an argument in which L said to W that he wished Churchill hadn't spoken against Indian freedom; he thought that it would hurt military recruitment. And W then accused L of ensuring the Andamans prisoners' release. You were in the Andamans when the hunger strikers were released. Do you know anything about why the release came?"

"I was in solitary confinement; if L was there, I didn't know it. But I wouldn't believe that he did anything to change the situation. The ICE is given for service to the empire."

I wanted to know more about the Fifth Column, but I couldn't continue speaking because a second couple came out to the lobby.

Shooting a look at them and then at me, Pankaj murmured, "We should go back to our seats."

"You do that," I said, feeling self-conscious. "I can leave the theater now."

"If you did so, the ticket agents would notice. Take your seat again, and I'll take mine."

I found a different empty seat, and he came in a bit later and sat three rows ahead. Under the straight, white beam that shot from the back of the theater, I could still see him.

In the darkened cinema, the brilliant screen showed the Bengali actress Devika Rani captivating her handsome costar, Ashok Kumar. But I had no eyes for them. All I could do was look at the fine, intelligent head of Pankaj, the Calcutta gentleman who had gone to prison for his ideals and now was making his career defending Indians arrested for sedition. Dearest Pankaj, who had been charmed by my letters and treated me like a gentlewoman! Every meeting we had made me feel closer to him. I was becoming the kind of romantic Supriya Sen would laugh at; not at all the way a female freedom fighter should be.

❦   ❦   ❦

I'D BELIEVED MR. Lewes was too busy looking for Fifth Columnists and Germans to be paying much attention to Netaji and the Forward Bloc. We no longer spent long hours talking about the local news, or even as much time together at all. This change made me uneasy, as if perhaps the feelings he had for me had vanished, or new suspicions had arisen.

It was up to me to improve our connection. One evening, I overheard him speak the name Bose on the telephone. I imagined he was conversing with Mr. Weatherington, who would never use the admiring Hindi word *Netaji*, just as neither of them used Mahatma or Gandhiji when speaking of Mohandas Gandhi.

I went to my room, brushed my hair, and lightly made up my eyes and mouth, the way I had for the cocktail party. Thus fortified, I came back down and asked if he had time for a drink in the garden.

"Yes, that's just what I need!" he said, his eyes warming as he looked at me. "I've had quite a day."

"Good or bad?" I asked as we stepped down from the veranda together into the garden.

"That depends on your perspective," he said with an odd half smile. "Subhas Bose is in prison."

It was all I could do to keep from gasping. Netaji in prison? It would paralyze India's independence movement. I sank down on to one of the teak chairs and asked how the arrest had happened.

"He and his friends were caught on the way to tear down the Holwell Monument in Dalhousie Square. They had all manner of irons and lathis with them." His voice was neutral, as if he had no idea how this news upset me.

The Holwell Monument was not anything Indians treasured. The government had erected the fifty-foot obelisk after the Black Hole incident of 1756 to commemorate a short-lived revolt of the nawab of Bengal's men against the East India Company. The violence resulted in an unknown number of British captives dying of heat exhaustion in a prison cell before the nawab was defeated. The monument was a visible reminder to Indians that sedition was unforgivable.

"You said that Mr. Bose was on his way to Holwell," I repeated, because something about the account struck me as odd. "How did the police know *where* he was going if he hadn't arrived there yet?"

Mr. Lewes hesitated, as if my question had surprised him. "He was quite nearby. And he and his men had lathis and some other tools with them."

"But they had not even touched the monument." I seized on the point he was ignoring. "Could the criminal accusation have been created by the police as an excuse for arrest?"

At my words, Mr. Lewes pressed his lips together. "The police didn't put the tools in his hands; he did that himself. But the city's safer with Bose unable to raise public sentiment against the war. Imagine if the Germans or Japanese invaded and he made a call for everyone to support them!"

He was very good at twisting arguments. I longed to put better ideas in his mind in order to sway his colleagues in the government. Remembering that he had spoken several times as if he believed Indian freedom was sure to come, I said, "Have you ever thought that if India was immediately granted independence, all these internal security risks would evaporate? There would be only goodwill from Indians toward the British."

Mr. Lewes gave a short, incredulous laugh. "You talk about risks evaporating. How can that be, when we would all be gone, including the military?"

I protested, "There are plenty of Indian soldiers who already know the work—"

"The experienced British officers who've been leading the Indian Army, Navy, and Air Force for decades would all be let go. In their place, a fledgling, all-Indian army would have to hit the ground running. Could they successfully protect you and me and everyone else?" The hesitation that had been in Mr. Lewes's voice before was gone; he spoke rapidly, waving his hands to emphasize his point. "Absolutely not."

I settled back in the chair, wishing I could oppose him with more conviction. "You speak as if Japan or Germany is planning to attack India. We have no indication that that's true."

"Absolutely they want India; if those two countries aligned, we could very easily be lost. I'm certain that war will come here. And if we don't stand up to fight, there will be nothing left for our children."

Our children? Surely it was figurative language that Mr. Lewes was using, but the way he was looking at me, it seemed like something else.

"Sorry," he muttered. "You have the right to a different opinion."

"Nothing to be sorry for," I replied, trying to shake the mood that had swept over like a sudden cloud of rain. I could never have any more children. And he could not fight fairly. These were the only things to keep in mind.

%   %   %

THROUGHOUT THAT FALL and winter of 1940, I lived with my ear at the spy hole, trying to gather news about the government's intentions toward the imprisoned Netaji. Mr. Weatherington continued to visit one or two evenings a week. In the desk drawer, I found carbon copies of letters from Netaji to the Bengal home minister, Mr. Nazimuddin, revealing that Netaji had started a hunger strike. The hunger strike had saved the Andamans prisoners; but as weeks passed, nothing in Netaji's situation changed, except his letters took on the tone of a man resigned to dying. I told Pankaj about it, and he was just as worried as me but said that for Netaji to begin eating would show capitulation. It was a game of wills, and he was certain Netaji was intelligent enough to win.

Netaji's trial was scheduled for early December, but the prison doctor declared he was too weakened by the hunger strike to stand before the judge. A new trial date was announced for a few weeks hence, but he remained in such wretched condition that the doctor again forbade the trial and shifted the famous patient to the Calcutta Medical College Hospital.

The suspense was overpowering: many nights I lay awake, worrying whether Netaji would survive. And then, a few weeks before Christmas, the situation took a stunning turn. Netaji was taken by ambulance from the hospital to recuperate in his parents' home. From listening to Mr. Lewes and Mr. Weatherington's conversations, I learned that the provincial government feared if Netaji died while in police custody, riots would sweep Calcutta and possibly the whole country.

"Come with us to a get-well rally outside Netaji's home," Supriya urged when I was having lunch with them one day. "People will chant prayers of support in order to irritate the police who are constantly watching the place."

"I wish I could, but I can't jeopardize my job." I'd already told Supriya that Mr. Lewes worked for the government but had carefully left out what exactly he did. The only one I trusted to know about that part was Pankaj.

"How will Mr. Lewes know?" my friend protested. "You have gone to many political meetings without dire consequence. Ruksana wore a burka and transported two guns underneath it last week for the Strength Brigade."

At this, I felt myself stiffen. "Why do they need guns?"

"Self-defense against the police, of course!"

"Does Pankaj-da encourage this?" I remembered his telling the Chhatri Sangha group that he worked as counsel to the Strength Brigade and other freedom fighters. Not as a fighter himself.

"No, but—" She paused. "You look like you're about to cry! What is it about Pankaj that has made you so upset?"

Flustered, I said, "I only asked what he thought."

"And he was asking about your family and where you came from. I did not tell him a thing!" Supriya said dramatically.

"He should ask me those things himself." I wondered whether Pankaj was investigating me for reasons of politics or because he shared my yearning.

"How would Pankaj have a chance to ask you questions?" Supriya persisted. "Have you seen him outside our group?"

I felt stymied, not wishing to lie to such a good friend. "I noticed him at the cinema once and said hello."

"Who was he with?"

"Some fellow! We weren't introduced," I said. "Why so many questions? Is Pankaj Bandopadhyay always on your mind?"

"Goodness, no." Supriya's hands flew to her face. "What I care about is freedom! Speaking of which, there is a Chhatri Sangha meeting tomorrow afternoon right here! At least come to that."

By now I knew Chhatri Sangha was on the list of suspicious organizations watched by the government. I couldn't possibly risk Mr. Pal or someone similar lurking nearby and telling Mr. Lewes I'd been there.

"I shouldn't do that, either," I said, watching Supriya's face fall. "It's a watched organization."

Supriya looked at me ruefully. "I understand. Your job could be lost, isn't it?"

Feeling embarrassed, I reached into my purse and gave her the remainder of the last month's salary that I'd planned to bring to the bank. "Yes. I'm so very sorry to miss it. But you can give this for me."

"What a packet!" Supriya looked at the thirty rupees in awe. "How shall I say you'd like them to be spent?"

I thought for a moment and then said, "Words are what will win our struggle. You could suggest they put the money toward paper and ink."

❀   ❀   ❀

IT WAS A very different Christmas from the previous year's. Mr. Lewes didn't go to Bombay this time, wanting to conserve money. Still, he asked me to arrange for a Christmas meal. At a Chinese market in Bow Bazar, Manik found a duck and roasted it; Mr. Lewes pronounced it delicious, but its tough, oily meat stuck in my throat.

Because he still gave everyone their bonuses, I went about my usual business of giving small, useful presents to Manik, Shombhu, Choton, and Jatin, and wrapped up for Mr. Lewes a trio of mango chutneys that I'd made earlier in the year, remembering that I couldn't spend money on him. He thanked me profusely, and the next morning, on Boxing Day, a gift box appeared outside my bedroom door. Inside was a plum silk sari with a gold border, and enough matching fabric to make a blouse.

As the smooth, obviously foreign-milled fabric slipped through my fingers, I felt patronized by the expense of the gift and embarrassed to have such a luxury. Because commercial sea traffic had stopped, the shops were empty of imported clothes and toys. I knew the situation in Europe was absolutely bleak, with bombings and shootings and families torn apart. They were probably not even thinking about Christmas goods, just everyone's safety. And in Asia, it was even more frightening, because it was close, and the Japanese had seized Korea and China. The stories about the brutal murders of civilians and the raping of women and children gave me nightmares; one night I even dreamed the Japanese came to India and were looking for Kabita. It brought memories of what had happened in the brothel that I'd thought were suppressed, but were in fact always there, waiting.

IN THE SECOND week of January, when I came downstairs for breakfast, I was surprised to see that the newspapers hadn't yet arrived. After I was done, I walked to the newsstand. Kantu was working alongside his father, handing out newspapers to a long queue of customers.

"Why didn't you deliver to our flat today?" I asked him when I finally reached the busy counter.

"Netaji has vanished; everyone wants to read about it! The newspapers were delayed getting to us, and then these people came." He gestured toward the crowd. "All the Bengali papers are sold out, but you can have the English one."

I walked away, my head bent over the *Statesman*. The account confirmed what Kantu had said about Netaji no longer being at home. But what an exciting, mysterious story! Apparently Netaji had told his family weeks earlier that he wanted seclusion in his bedchambers in order to meditate. A curtain had been put up around his bed so that nobody could observe or trouble him. His meals were left just outside the curtain. All the time the plates came back empty, his family believed he was keeping well. But then one supper tray stood untouched. His worried mother drew back the curtains to find his bed empty.

Mr. Lewes was already at his office. I imagined he was hearing the news there, if he hadn't heard already. Book sorting could wait. I tucked the paper under my arm and took a tram to the Sens'. Of course they already knew; in celebration, Mrs. Sen served everyone sweets. After wolfing down several shondesh, her son, Nishan, jumped around the room shouting *Jai Hind*, the freedom-fighting call.

"Our Netaji outfoxed the police. It's unbelievable because constables were posted on both corners of his house, night and day!" Supriya was beaming.

"Maybe he's still inside the house, hiding somewhere." I could not imagine he would be safe anywhere in Calcutta.

"Impossible; his mother would have found him!" Mrs. Sen interrupted. "It can only be that he wore a disguise to pass by the police and escape the country."

"Do you really think he's gone away?" I felt oddly anxious. "He's not the kind to desert us and the freedom struggle."

"The struggle isn't over!" Supriya squeezed my hand in reassurance. "He will fight for us from abroad. The trick will be getting to Europe. He can't possibly have made it yet."

"Yes," I said, thinking. "No ships are traveling the seas, except for military ones, and they are unlikely to provide him passage!"

"He cannot go by water, then," Mrs. Sen opined. "It must be by land. Nishan, fetch your globe. We will dream up a route!"

※   ※   ※

THE SENS WERE not the only ones imagining Netaji's travel itinerary. In the days that followed, Mr. Lewes and Mr. Weatherington spent many late nights discussing the escape. Their theories were quite different: Mr. Weatherington suspected Netaji had hidden on a fishing boat and was sailing for Japan. Mr. Lewes guessed he had been carried by tribal people into the snowy hills of Darjeeling, and from there would trek into Nepal and then China. But both were proved wrong when British intelligence sent the Bengal government a copy of a decoded Italian telegram reporting that Netaji had reached Kabul, Afghanistan. He was believed to be hiding there while he plotted a route to Europe.

I felt calmer knowing that Netaji was safely out of India. Those feelings changed, though, when I saw a government memorandum calling for his assassination by overseas spies working for the British. Some spies were searching for the escapee within Kabul, while others were setting themselves up along the borders of countries they thought he might pass through on the way to Europe. The name of one country, Turkey, came up as the place with the most concentrated intelligence efforts. I knew I had to tell Pankaj, who might know how to send a warning to Netaji's helpers.

I met Pankaj in the same cabin that we had gone to before. But this time I took the beer Pankaj offered. I told him everything I'd overheard and recited the British memorandum from memory. He did not make notes but listened silently, his eyes never leaving my face.

Pankaj drank the last of his beer, and indicated to the waiter that he wanted a second one. In a low voice, he said, "I'm not sure if I can communicate such news out of India, but I will try. Good work, Kamala. Very good work."

"What about speaking to someone in Forward Bloc? Who is his closest friend?"

"I would speak to his brother, Sarat, if the police hadn't clapped him in prison already. Maybe Sarat's son can help. I know that Sisir is sympathetic to the movement." Pankaj paused. "I really shouldn't say anything more. I worry that I'll put you at risk."

If he worried about me, it meant that he cared. I took a deep breath and said that I'd heard from Supriya that he had been asking about my background.

"Ah!" Pankaj smiled wryly. "No secrets can be kept within the Sen family. That is why I would never have recruited Supriya or Sonali for the work you are doing!"

"But Pankaj-da—why were you asking the Sens about me?" The beer had made me a little bold. I kept my eyes on him, not wanting to miss his reaction.

"Oh, you heard!" He blinked behind his spectacles. "It's only that I was surprised not to have known about you until recently. You seem familiar, somehow. Your name—there are many Mukherjees, but I wonder . . ." He shook his head. "I won't say it. I do not believe in reincarnation!"

Now my heart was beating fast. He felt something! He had caught wind of my old letter-writing voice. Softly, I said, "Do not doubt all the old beliefs. They have been passed down for a reason."

"So, who are your parents, then? Where were you raised?" He spoke cheerfully, as if he wanted to know. But although I ached to confess that I was his lost soul mate, I suddenly felt Thakurma's hand smelling of mustard oil press itself across my lips, urging caution. This was not the right time.

"I come from the coast, a little town nobody's heard of because it was swept away in a cyclone. My family died, leaving me to fend for myself." To test him, I added, "I cannot compare with the college girls in Chhatri Sangha or anyone else whom your mother is considering."

At my words, Pankaj sighed and said, "I've told my mother that I am not looking for a wife. I am only committed to the dream of a free India."

I should not have said the last bit about his mother considering brides; I sounded overly bold. Hurriedly I added, "Yes, you've spoken of your love for India before. I did not mean to imply—"

"I understand," he said with a half smile. "I barraged you with questions and you tried to answer. But you must know what I intend for my life."

He was warning me off. After a few more minutes' conversation,

I bade him good-bye, putting down my half-full glass of beer that suddenly tasted too sour. As I began to make my way downstairs and out of the cabin, I glanced back. Pankaj was watching me with a haunted expression. And despite the idealistic words he'd said to me, I did not entirely believe them.

CHAPTER
29

MISSIONARY: *1. A person who goes on a religious mission;* esp. *one sent to propagate the faith among the heathen.*

—*Oxford English Dictionary*, Vol. 6, 1933

When I was a little girl in Johlpur, my father once brought me into a deep part of the river. Suddenly, he flung me from his arms. I sank underwater and then came up coughing, moving hands and feet in an effort to get back to my father. He held his arms outstretched and praised me, explaining that the waving, kicking movements were exactly right. Treading water was the first lesson of swimming, and the most important one if I was ever caught in water that was too deep.

For the rest of 1941, I felt as if I was treading water: staying alive, but not getting anywhere I wanted. Gandhiji's strength was faltering, Jawaharlal Nehru was locked in prison, and Netaji was unable to do anything for India from outside. But at least he was alive. Pankaj told me he'd passed on my information, and Netaji did not go to Turkey.

From Afghanistan he trekked and rode on horseback to the Soviet Union, where Germans helped him travel by train to Moscow and then by air to Berlin. This information, gleaned from listening in to Mr. Lewes and Weatherington, made it clear that Netaji was safe from the British, for the time being. But I did not trust where he'd gone for help.

"You must understand he's using a clever strategy," Supriya explained when we talked about it one afternoon over coffee in Albert Hall. I'd decided it was safe enough to go because I was just with Supriya, and not with an organized group. "Our independence movement in India is too weak at the moment. It cannot combat British opposition. We need help from the outside to win."

Netaji had been in Austria before but not Germany. I hadn't thought he would work with the Nazi party, which he had criticized in the past. However, since April 1941 Netaji had sent communications about his desire to organize a free Indian government, suggesting that treaties could be signed by Italy and Germany guaranteeing India its independence at war's end.

"I do wish Netaji had stayed with the Russians," I said. "Their government has always been helped by the Indian Communists, and they have every interest in helping India become free."

"But the Russians are strong anti-Fascists," Supriya said. "They will side with the English if Germany threatens them—and Netaji knows that. He had to go to the Nazis. There was no other choice, and fortunately he will prevail."

I wanted to shake Supriya for her belief that everything would go Netaji's way: that he could control the Axis powers to do his bidding. I asked, "But what do Germans think of our race? Look at what they are doing to non-Christians in their country and beyond—"

"Don't worry so much! It will be a completely free India." At my dubious expression, she added, "We will repay the Germans for their assistance, so we won't be beholden. Netaji said so himself."

I wondered how Supriya was receiving information; did Pankaj say such things when he visited the Chhatri Sangha meetings I was avoiding? Since our last conversation, it seemed that a barrier had come between Pankaj and me, perhaps caused by my personal questions. The feeling reminded me of the glass window between the front and back seats of Mr. Lewes's Buick: clear enough to see through, but too thick to allow listening. In the car, I liked the protective wall, but with Pankaj, I wanted it opened, so we could resume the connection we'd once had in our letters.

I finished my coffee and ordered another. Some boys from the Strength Brigade came in and were toasting to Netaji's long life and eventual return as the first premier of independent India. Supriya joined in their cheers, but I found myself unable to. I recalled something Thakurma had said about the unburned dead: the poor souls who could not be cremated and were stuck where they were, unable to move into their next lives. That was what it felt like for me, being unable to celebrate or mourn, just waiting somewhere in between.

❧   ❧   ❧

THE TIDES OF war were rising, and there were no trees high enough to shelter anyone. The Japanese attacked the American Navy base called Pearl Harbor in Hawaii; and within weeks afterward, their army had flooded Hong Kong, Singapore, Malaya, and Burma. It was not just British colonies they were after: in succeeding months, the Japanese conquered the American Philippines and the Dutch colonies of Borneo, Indonesia, and the East Indies. How could such a small island nation accomplish so much, I wondered, and then I remembered that long ago, the tiny island of England had conquered even more. And now they were running like packs of dogs out of their colonies, toward India.

One evening in spring 1942, Mr. Lewes was alone in his study, playing a broadcast on his wire recorder. He repeated it several times, then opened the door and called for me.

"This broadcast from the propaganda ministry of Japan has a familiar Bengali voice," he said, as I joined him. With a shiver of pleasure, I recognized the deep, strong voice of Netaji. Over a crackling background, the leader assured his audience he was very much alive and said that he'd taken charge of Japan's Indian prisoners of war. They'd been freed to serve under his command in the Indian National Army.

"From today, your mind, might, and money belong to the Indian Nation," Netaji proclaimed. "Friends, you have the honor to be the pioneer soldiers of the Azad Hind Fauj. Your name will be written in gold letters in the history of free India."

The Hindi broadcast went on and on. Mr. Lewes sat at the desk, watching me listen. I realized that my expression might be giving away my solidarity with Netaji, so I hastily concocted a frown. At the recording's end, I asked if he would require a translation. He said, "I already have a transcript, but I'd like you to check it for accuracy."

"Of course." As I looked over the paper he handed me, I kept my face still. Netaji had done the unbelievable: made the army he'd always said was needed. And these Ceylonese and Singaporean and Malayan soldiers had new weapons, food, and uniforms coming from the Japanese. They really might succeed.

"The translation is a fine one," I said, after quickly skimming the Hindi and English transcripts.

"Hmm. That's not like you, not to find something amiss." Mr. Lewes's eyes didn't move from me.

Is this a test? I wondered and decided to distract him. "Sir, what do you think this Indian National Army's chances are?"

"To take India? That army is a strong propaganda tool, but I'm not sure whether the Japanese will trust the INA's abilities enough to bring them along on the fight. So far, it's just friendly promises." Mr. Lewes paused, then added, "I'd like to think the INA can't get through to India. But I don't really know."

"If your country had granted us independence two years ago, Netaji would not be heading that army."

"'You said *your* country." Mr. Lewes sounded incredulous. "You speak as if it isn't your empire, too!"

I could not hold back a bitter laugh. "Of course it's not. You have the right to enter any of the colonies and can sit in any train compartment, join any club, and live in any building. You can walk into Whiteaway Laidlaw without being questioned. Your people made money off my father's back and—"

I had spoken of my father. I pressed my lips together, feeling horrified. I was almost telling the secret. Giving myself away.

"Kamala." Mr. Lewes reached out and put a hand on my shoulder. It was broad, warm, and strong, making me jump inside. "I'm sorry there's discrimination. British India is changing too slowly, but as I've said, war makes things hard." He paused. "I miss reading the papers with you. But the wire recordings are just as interesting to hear. Perhaps we should make it an evening radio hour. What do you think?"

"Perhaps another time. I'm not quite myself tonight. I'm sorry." I tore away from his touch and dashed upstairs at double speed, without looking back.

❧   ❧   ❧

THE NEXT MORNING, I worked in the library, my mind filled with thoughts of the previous night's conversation with Mr. Lewes. I'd started spying because I'd been shocked by the nature of my employer's work, but war had turned the situation on its head. War could never be glorious—even though it was better for Netaji to be involved in the freedom struggle than away from it. Yet I suspected that if the Japanese did prevail, they would not really leave India to Netaji.

My feelings about Mr. Lewes were just as mixed. A few months ago, it had been easy to hate him; now, not so easy. He had used the word *discrimination* as if he thought it was wrong, and he missed reading the papers with me. I wished I could tell him that I'd enjoyed that time, too—before understanding I was being used for informational purposes. I told myself now that his suggestion of a radio hour was just another way for him to do some work.

The encounter made me nervous about the prospect of spending more time alone with Mr. Lewes in the library. This was the place where he'd almost kissed me. How dismayed Pankaj would be about what had almost happened.

I had no mind for cataloging, so I set to dusting, going methodically book by book. As I worked, anger rose in me at myself, for thinking of Mr. Lewes's attraction to me when I knew the selfish nature of Englishmen through my hard years at Rose Villa. I had a daughter to support, so I couldn't ever lose my job. Nor should I halt the important spying work I was doing for Pankaj's organization. I had to keep everything the way that it was; but this would be as difficult as my own feelings for both men.

I was dusting violently, to match my turbulent feelings. When I reached the maps section, I was dusting so hard that some of the feathers from my duster broke off. While I was chasing after these feathers, Mr. Lewes poked his head in the door after work.

"A good time for a break," he said, as I hastily put the duster behind my back. "The rain's stopped. Won't you come to the garden with me? There is something we must discuss."

Discussing in the garden meant that he didn't want the house staff overhearing. But what did he have to say that was secret? Would he address me about the violent dusting I'd given his treasures—or was it my rash speech the night before?

Trying to appear calm, I followed him outdoors and sat down next to him in one of the teak chairs. Then I rang the bell for Jatin. When the boy came, I asked him for cauliflower phuluri and two gin-limes. Mr. Lewes raised his eyebrows at my finally taking an alcoholic drink for myself, but I looked back at him with a falsely confident smile. I would brazen my way through whatever happened; I could not appear frightened.

When the drinks had been brought and we were once again in

private, Mr. Lewes said, "You may have heard that the government has begun reassigning houses and larger flats to incoming refugees from the other Asian colonies. Because of the refugees, bachelor ICS officers with good houses are being asked to bunk with other men in chummeries. That's all well and good for the young fellows, but I've got my library, and . . ."

Suddenly, I understood that I wasn't being reprimanded; he was trying to apologize to me about losing the flat. No longer would I have a roof over my head. And without the library work, there would be no money to send Kabita. Pankaj would not see me, either, if I couldn't spy for him. These desperate thoughts flooded me as I stared at my employer, who looked as downcast as I felt.

Fumbling for words, I said, "I shall vacate my room whenever you need it. After that, I will still arrive each day to pack up the library, because surely that room will be needed—"

"No! I have a scheme that can keep our whole household together. I'll volunteer the spare bedroom to a refugee. I think that if I offer straightaway, I have a lesser chance of being thrown out later."

I took a sip of the gin-lime cocktail: bitter and sweet, as it should be. "But there is my bedroom as well. Surely the Housing Office knows that your flat has three bedrooms."

Mr. Lewes waved a dismissive hand. "That's really just a hidey-hole. No one could fit there but a small child."

I had fit there quite neatly. I adored my room, which I'd decorated with a few pictures and the calendar the Sens gave me each year. I even had acquired a small slipper chair and matching footstool that Mr. Chun gave me as thanks for providing so much business. I wondered if I could take this furniture with me; but to where? Sounding braver than I felt, I said, "I will find someplace."

Mr. Lewes put down his drink with an exasperated-sounding clink. "Kamala, do you wish to leave this household?"

"Goodness, no!" My answer came fast, for it was true. But so many times before, I'd lost my home; I did not dare to hope.

"Let me speak to the Housing Office, then. And don't think twice about our conversation last night. It was—refreshing. Good for me to hear." Mr. Lewes was looking at me with a smile in his eyes, so intently that I had to drop my gaze. He didn't understand that if someone joined us, it would no longer be acceptable for me to dine at the table or read the newspapers first. And I would have to be much more cautious about intelligence gathering. But if I could stay—I'd be safe. At least for a little while longer.

❧   ❧   ❧

WITHIN A FEW days, the Housing Office decided to give the spare room to a senior inspector of the Malaya police and his wife. Then, when Housing learned there were two accompanying daughters, they were reassigned to a large bungalow. A week passed, and then the Housing people matched the spare room with Rev. John McRae, a Scottish clergyman who had escaped Burma and was recuperating at Presidency Hospital.

Mr. Lewes thought that an elderly cohabitant would likely be quiet and spend time sleeping, that he would not be much work for me. But I knew how stern religious men usually were; that was what worried me.

On the next Sunday evening, I felt my heart sink as I looked out the window and saw a wizened old man in a black suit hobble to the front door with a bamboo cane. Behind him was a liveried driver who was unloading one small suitcase from the church's car. I would hide my anxiety from the clergyman, I pledged to myself. When I got close enough to see the old minister's face, though, that resolution flew out of mind.

Reverend McRae was not white. He might have been once, but his skin had been so darkened by years in Burma that he did not look like any type of European. In the end, only the brightness of his blue eyes and his strong Scots accent gave away his origin.

"Miss Mukherjee." He bowed as he took my hand gracefully between his long, gnarled fingers. "I am very grateful for your hospitality and will try not to be an imposition."

Stunned by his courtesy, I managed to reply, "It's no imposition. I manage the household and library, and there are others to help with your every need."

The reverend's eyes widened. "I have not been inside a library for more than fifty years. I cannot imagine how many good books must have been written in this time! Perhaps you will take me through your library someday."

"I will be glad to," I said, charmed by his enthusiasm. "Now, please come inside. I'm very sorry about the stairs."

He let me take his arm as he slowly mounted the grand stairway, telling me all the while it was nothing like the mountain hiking he had done while leaving Burma. Inside the flat, I introduced him to everyone. As I'd expected, their eyes widened at the sight of the dark Ingrej. "*Kala-saheb!*" they murmured to one another, grinning. Black saheb.

Shaking my head, I corrected them. "No. You must not call him nicknames. He will be Reverend McRae or Reverend-saheb."

I did not know why I felt so protective toward Reverend McRae. All I understood in those first few minutes was that I did not want him to experience even a moment of secret disrespect. He had been through so much suffering; this was his time to heal.

After Mr. Lewes came in, we sat down to squash bisque, tiny potatoes steamed with peas, and a thin dal. There were parathas stuffed with fenugreek, a sweet mango chutney, and a mountain of rice. Reverend McRae sampled everything in very small portions, saying our food was much fancier than what he'd been eating in his Burmese village even during the best harvests. I didn't mention that I'd ordered an especially mild and simple menu; that would have shocked him.

Mr. Lewes sat at the table's head, with me on his left as usual, and the reverend on his right. It felt natural to be together this way, and the conversation became personal. The reverend explained he had spent the last forty-two years in Burma and had not initially evacuated with the other British. That was why he was arriving months after everyone else.

"I had thought that to stay with my people would keep them safer: that perhaps I could negotiate for them with the Japanese officers."

"Will you tell us about it?" Mr. Lewes leaned forward, showing his interest.

"Each day, I went to the commanding Japanese Army officer, trying to encourage him to tell the soldiers to lay down their weapons. But they would not; and then I found out that some of the village's young women had been taken away. I rushed to the hut where they were kept. I must have put my hands on a soldier." The reverend shut his bright eyes for a moment. "I don't remember being stabbed. Apparently some old friends rescued me from the pile of dead where the Japanese soldiers threw me. The village's healer secretly treated me with herbs in a jungle hideaway. When I was recovered enough to walk, I traveled the jungle and eventually came to the Black Road and continued until I crossed the border."

"Not the main road?" Mr. Lewes inquired.

"That road was designated for the English only." The minister's voice rolled with disgust. "I chose to walk with the Burmese."

"Reverend, we are honored to have someone of your character stay with us. Please understand that you are welcome to remain as long as you like." As Mr. Lewes spoke, I could see from his expression that he was moved.

"I hope to return to Burma, but I know that with my age, and what happened, it is not likely the Church will send me out again." The Reverend McRae gave me a half smile. "But now I am in India, where there is need. I hope to learn some languages so I can take up work here."

"*Some* languages? How ambitious!" Mr. Lewes chuckled. "I've been here for years and have very few words of Hindustani and Bengali, as Kamala can tell you."

I quickly turned to the reverend, hoping that Mr. Lewes's use of my first name had not shocked him. I said, "I will gladly help you study, Reverend. I could teach you Bengali, Hindustani, and Urdu; I also have a smattering of Oriya language."

The minister bowed to me and said, "Thank you, Miss Mukherjee. I shall make some explorations in the faith community, and then I will perhaps learn which language is the most useful for my mission work."

Our lives took on a pleasing new pattern. Each morning as I worked on my usual library chores, Reverend McRae went out to pay his respects at a variety of places and told us enjoyable stories about it over tea. He might breakfast with Quakers on Monday, drink tea with Methodists on Tuesday, and spend Wednesday with Hindus discussing the works of Swami Vivekananda. Thursday might be a Catholic relief services meeting, Friday evening a Jewish Shabbat, and on Saturday afternoon, a Parsi gathering. His denominational home was Saint Andrew's Kirk near Dalhousie Square, but he was usually only there for a short time on Sundays.

After a light lunch, the reverend napped. In late afternoon, he revived for tea and his hour-long Bengali lesson. So it was through a mix of English and Bengali that I learned more of his escape through the jungle. He was even helped by a Japanese soldier who had given him water and told him which landmarks to watch for on the way to the evacuation route.

"God's light shines within each person," he said to me. "Remember this! It is never an entire people who is cruel; it is merely individuals who exert their will on others."

I'd grown up thinking every Britisher was a blue-eyed devil; and certainly the nurses at the Railway Hospital where I had tried to give birth, Miss Jamison, and Mr. Weatherington fit that horrific model. Miss Richmond, though, had given me literacy and the opportunity to stay inside her classroom. Now I understood that she'd been as interested in helping me as she had Bidushi, but had been tied by

Miss Jamison's rules. The reverend had offered true friendship and new ways of looking at the world. And while the outline of Mr. Lewes appeared to be a lock-stock government man, I knew by now that his core was not.

But if there really was a light in every person, I wondered, why were there armies—and why did the world appear so dark?

CHAPTER
30

Wherever you fear a tiger,
that is the place where day ends for you.

Bengali proverb

QUIT INDIA!

In red paint, the two words were slashed on the high white walls that ran around Middleton Mansions. They filled me with a private thrill—but also worry. The words could be read as a personal warning to the thirty-odd Europeans who lived in the mansion block buildings. And even if Mr. Lewes and the others wanted to leave India, all passenger travel was off, because of war activity on the seas.

I overhead Shombhu telling Jatin to remove the message as quickly as possible, but when Jatin went outside with a bucket of water and cloth, Mr. Lewes stopped him.

"If you are seen taking the words away, it could be dangerous for you," Mr. Lewes said, putting a hand on his shoulder. "Let the message stay. It doesn't hurt my pride, and sooner or later, the letters will fade."

The Quit India movement had begun a week earlier at a meeting in a Bombay park, where Gandhiji addressed a group of Congress supporters. He said everyone had been patient enough, waiting for the independence that Britain always said was coming but did not. He announced he was writing to the viceroy, demanding that Britain quit India and offer unconditional freedom. If his request wasn't met, he promised that he would direct the nation's population in a dramatic resistance plan.

By the next morning, Gandhiji and his wife, Kasturba, were arrested. And one by one, his followers began their own protests and were put in jail. Within a week India's penal system was packed with activists, including all the Congress Party's legislators. But "Quit India" had become a national slogan.

It was more than shouting and painting. Factory workers went on strike at steelworks, cotton mills, and the ports. Protesters cut telephone lines. Schoolchildren boycotted classes. Almost immediately, Calcutta's police began beating up the protesters, many of whom were only waving flags or blocking streets. Reverend McRae was as upset about the police violence as I was; he wrote a letter to Governor Rutherford about it. I couldn't understand why he was not frightened for himself, because protesters screamed the slogan directly at Europeans walking in Calcutta's streets; although only rarely were they touched, heeding Gandhiji's order for nonviolence.

I found it hard to stand by and not join the Sens for at least a few of the protests. But just as Mr. Lewes had done with Jatin, Pankaj warned me.

"You mustn't get caught up in anything," Pankaj said, during one of our covert meetings in the cabin. "Kamala, you are too valuable to risk being arrested."

"But everyone's involved," I protested. "If I do absolutely nothing, I'll stand out as a nonpatriot. Can't I at least wave flags with the Sens outside of Whiteaway's and the other English shops?"

"What if you're arrested? You cannot imagine the techniques being used on so-called suspects. And if your employer ever finds out that you've been carrying information from his desk to me, it could bring down many people in the movement."

I supposed he was right. I nodded and said, "This action is like nothing Indians have done before. I overheard L telling W that it's sent Churchill around the bend. Unfortunately, it may mean the prime minister won't ever allow dominion status to be granted."

"So what are we to do? Sit on our hands at home, or give our bodies to be blown apart in the war?" Pankaj rapped his fist on the table. "As I've said, your spying now is at its highest value. But be careful. You are walking a line between life and death."

Maybe Pankaj spoke so strongly because he sensed it might be the last time we'd communicate. A week later, the Calcutta police arrested Lata Menon for gathering money to be used in antigovernment protests. Pankaj Bandopadhyay signed on as her lawyer, and in his initial court appearance, shouted so furiously that the judge ordered him arrested for contempt of court. Now both Lata and Pankaj were incarcerated in the Fort William prison.

Lata was not a close friend, but the idea of her locked in the women's ward of a prison was just as distressing as Pankaj's plight. I could have been jailed many times over for the things I'd done; all Lata had done was gather jewelry from other women who wanted to help the cause.

I knew that I couldn't visit the prison because a record of visitor names was kept, but I was so worried for Pankaj and Lata that I went to the Sens' every week for updates on their situations.

"Don't worry so much! Pankaj is from a prominent family, and Lata is a known Brahmin," Mrs. Sen said, as she set out tea and biscuits in her pleasant sitting room. "They will be placed in the superior prison block away from common criminals. There they have cots for sleeping."

"I hear the cots have bedbugs," Supriya said with a grimace. "I can't imagine either of them standing it."

"I suppose Kamala could ask her saheb if anything can be done to get them out." Mrs. Sen gave me a questioning look.

"Ma, that is wrong!" Supriya said. "How can we ask a white to free us from the whites? Think of Pankaj having to grovel to a European—he would sooner die."

Mrs. Sen protested, "But he must be a good man. He spends so much on bookbinding and pays Kamala fairly—"

"I agree that he should not be asked," I said. "We've got to think of another way."

Because I couldn't visit the prison, Mrs. Sen suggested that I write letters for her to bring—they did not have to be signed with my own name. Lata's letter was easy to write. When writing to Pankaj, I strove for a tone that couldn't be faulted if Supriya and her mother were to see the words.

> *My Dear Older Brother:*
> *I am saddened by your absence. The sun is hot, warming the earth to a steaming point; we await the rains. I imagine it is ten times worse where you are. Please tell me you are able to walk outside sometime and look at India's sky. Through the cell windows, can you hear the koel birds sing at night? I do—and I think their voices speak for you and your fellow inmates. You are not with us now, but you will be again. Your spirit must remain strong, so you can fly again. The rest of us continue watching and writing and dreaming of the future. Your loving little sister*

Two weeks later, a letter came hidden in a sari shop box. It was from Bijoy Ganguly, the Strength Brigade member I'd met a few times and hadn't particularly liked. In tight, cramped Bengali, Bijoy wrote that Pankaj had requested that he tell me not to write to him in prison, because the letter about birds had been suspected as activist code. Pankaj had endured questioning for several days and sent a warning for the Sens not to visit him either in order to protect themselves. The postscript was that Pankaj wished all my future intelligence go to Bijoy.

I was horrified that the letter had been misunderstood and caused trouble for Pankaj. At the same time, I was relieved that Pankaj understood the letter came from me yet hadn't sacrificed my name. As he sat in his cell, remembering the words I'd written, would they give him hope for our future—or, as Bijoy had suggested, would they only remind him of trouble? No matter how much I thought about the situation, I could not divine the truth.

❧   ❧   ❧

AS THE HOLIDAY approached, Reverend McRae went out to the countryside to help deliver services at churches with absent ministers. For Christmas Eve, Mr. Lewes went to Saint Paul's Cathedral for the services, and I stayed home with the Agatha Christie novel he'd given me. Sometime after I'd shut out the light, I was awakened by wailing sirens. My head rang with the sound and my heart raced in fear, for I knew what the siren was signaling.

This was actually the second Japanese bombing attack; the first had come earlier in the week, when several silver spots had appeared in a clear blue sky and the sirens had let loose. I had been in the garden airing books and had gone with the servants into the shelter of Mr. Rowley's storeroom, where we sat together with his servants for a miserable hour. It was terrifying because there were so many likely targets nearby: the Red Road airstrip, Victoria Memorial, Chowringhee and Esplanade and Government House. And Middleton Mansions was a tall, distinguished-looking series of buildings easy for a pilot to spot as a likely home of the British.

And now: Japanese bombs on Christmas Eve. What a cruel and symbolic present for Calcutta's English people.

"Air raid! We must hurry." I called the words out as I came downstairs wearing my wrapper over a nightdress. My employer was still dressed in his suit from going to the cathedral and was carrying the heavy wire recorder out of his library. He directed me to carry his two ICS briefcases downstairs.

Jatin and Shombhu arrived from their garden cottage, holding electric torches to guide us down the blackened staircase. Manik went to the kitchen for a jug of water and steel tumblers, and Choton carried the first-aid kit, matches, and gas masks. In this organized fashion, we trooped down to Mr. Rowley's flat where the shelter lay: but no matter how hard Mr. Lewes pounded the flat door, there was no response.

"He's gone for Christmas!" I said, remembering what his servants had told me as they'd packed to go to their homes for the break. Now I wished I'd asked them for the flat key, because we had no way in. I explained all this and then remembered the garden trench the servants had dug months ago as an alternate safe hiding place. As we hurried into the garden, a horrible smell hung in the air, indicating that someone recently had used it as a latrine. Shombhu and Manik were especially repulsed, blaming the condition on drunken soldiers. Whatever the case, nobody wanted to climb down into it.

Mr. Lewes suggested that we take shelter along a windowless, narrow section on the building's eastern side. The three menservants clustered together, taking up most of the short space. Mr. Lewes gallantly offered me the space near the wall's edge, putting himself between the servants and me. He must have intended to be courteous, but my body's right side was pressed against him in a decidedly improper closeness.

"Those cases you have in your arms are heavy," Mr. Lewes said, his breath brushing my hair. "You can put them down." What he said was sensible, but as I bent down, my hips brushed against him in a very personal manner. He stumbled back a pace, as if he was as embarrassed as I. When I came up, I could smell the Pall Mall cigarette that he still smoked each evening, overlaid with gin-and-tonic. And then there was the scent of him: his core.

"Can you hear the people shouting?" Jatin asked excitedly. "They are saying a bomb fell on Chowringhee!"

"Really? I'd think that if there was a hit, it would have been louder!" Mr. Lewes said. "What do you think, Kamala?"

"I don't know," I said, trying to distract myself from the way my hips fit so snugly against his thigh. I should have been thinking about Pankaj, I told myself; but I could not stay focused despite my fear.

Suddenly, Mr. Lewes shifted out from behind me. Taking a brief-case in each of his hands, he spoke breathlessly. "I must go to the Control Room."

The desire I'd felt had also touched him; I knew a man's physical signs. Of course he could not remain in such an intimate position. My heart pounded with the realization that he did desire me for more than information, despite what I'd been telling myself. And I was shocked, too, that I felt sorry at his shifting away and that I was thinking this even while my heart belonged to Pankaj.

"Mr. Lewes, how will you reach this Control Room?" I blurted, anxious at the idea of his going off through a blacked-out city with bombers overhead. "You won't find a taxi or rickshaw under these cir-cumstances!"

"I will make it." His voice was faint because he was already half-way across the garden. "Bring the wire recorder back in when it's all clear, and don't worry. I have a feeling we'll all survive the night."

CHAPTER
31

*The ordinary woman had perhaps been so busy that the veiled
newspaper warnings of famine had not penetrated to her; but
perhaps that was natural when the authorities kept repeating,
"There is plenty of rice. Plenty of rice." Perhaps there was plenty
of rice, but in that case, who, women were beginning to ask, who
were these people flocking into the towns and the city? Men and
women and unclothed children, all with scarecrow legs and arms
and ribs, and strange sunk eyes and swollen stomachs? Why did
they settle in swarms on the pavements, round the rubbish bins,
sleeping there through the nights, covering the streets with filth
and cess? Why did no one come to move away? Why, rather
did more and more come every day?*

—Rumer Godden, *Bengal Journey*, 1945

The Japanese bombings of December 1942 and January of 1943
didn't create too much visible damage, but they left a giant cra-
ter that no one could ignore: fear. Thousands of Calcuttans fled the
city for their old family villages in the countryside. Choton, Manik's

kitchen assistant, defected, as did Mr. Lewes's chauffeur, Farouk. It took me two weeks before I managed to hire a reliable driver, Sarjit Singh, but I could not find a kitchen assistant for Manik. He said he would rather use Jatin, who was eager to learn cooking.

With the household down one person, Mr. Lewes seemed all the more present. Often, I felt his gaze, but I pretended not to notice. He had not come physically close to me again; and he was much less talkative. Perhaps he was reminding himself it was wrong to feel what he did, or he had developed some suspicions about my behavior.

One afternoon in February, he pointed out a package addressed to me in the hall. I knew right away it was from Bijoy Ganguly, but I took pains to casually open it in front of him, showing him that the book I'd ordered for myself had finally arrived. He never saw the Bengali letter tucked snugly in the book's center, requesting a meeting the next day.

Reverend McRae was also very observant of my actions. One evening at dinner, he commented, "Miss Mukherjee, are you not in charge of the menus?"

"Yes. Is there something you would like me to request for tomorrow?"

"No. I was wondering how is it that you buy our rice. I haven't seen you carry as much as a turnip when you come home from your jaunts."

Reverend McRae's room overlooked the street, so of course he could see me. I had not thought of it before, but he must have noticed me returning from Sen Bookbindery and my other excursions.

"The rice vendor comes by cart, and he drops it off to all his customers on this road," said Mr. Lewes, cutting into a slice of roast chicken. "It's an efficiency that Kamala established for our household."

"My friend from the Scottish church in Dacca says there are some shortages of rice this year. Was the crop poor?"

Mr. Lewes finished chewing and said, "There was slightly less rain this past monsoon, but the rice crop certainly wasn't ruined. What are you hearing, Reverend?"

"That there are serious rice shortages," the reverend said. "Apparently each village in the countryside has a man who controls the price, and the prices are rising out of reach of many peasants."

"The luckiest peasants in those circumstances are the ones allowed to grow and keep a bit of that rice for themselves!" I said, remembering my father's situation.

"But the landowners are demanding more rice from the poor peasants because government needs it for the soldiers. That is hard, isn't it?" the reverend said in his soft burr.

"It's necessary." Mr. Lewes's voice was defensive. "Since the Japanese took Burma, India is the only source for rice for all our soldiers in the Asian theater. It's being stockpiled for their safety."

"But what of the Indians? There are many more of us than the soldiers," I said as Reverend McRae nodded in agreement.

"The rice shortage is only in Bengal, not nationwide," Mr. Lewes answered, but he looked uncomfortable under both our gazes.

Reverend McRae's comments had made me curious. On my next outing to Hogg Market, I spoke to the various men seated amid huge sacks of rice. They seemed relaxed, but the prices they quoted were much higher than what I saw on our twice-monthly rice bill. When I returned home, I went into the kitchen, where Manik was making chapattis, and asked whether our rice seller's price had risen.

"Much higher: thirty-two rupees a maund. Because of those thievish rice merchants, rice costs almost twice what we paid in January." Manik slapped the dough hard against the board. "That is why I'm not buying rice these days, just using our stores. We will buy again when the price returns to proper level."

"Manik, I know you are being careful with Mr. Lewes's money, but you must keep buying rice," I countered. "As the days pass, it may become even more expensive."

He frowned and said, "If I buy this week, the bill will be very high. You and the saheb will scold."

Trying to sound reassuring, I said, "I will only praise you to Mr. Lewes for your caution. And to save money, we don't really need to eat white rice; we can take brown."

Manik sucked in his breath. "But only peasants eat such rough rice. Burra-saheb and the Reverend-saheb cannot!"

Soon I learned that brown rice now cost the same as white, but was more available. I cringed at the high price but knew we were fortunate that Mr. Lewes's ICS salary and Reverend McRae's stipend were enough to cover it and the rest of our usual expenses. Indian city workers who regularly received rice as part of their weekly pay were only getting half their usual allotment. Prisoners had still less; but Mashima told me a group of friends was bringing Pankaj, Lata, and the other jailed activists home-cooked food to supplement the meager prison fare.

And as the reverend said, peasants had no rice at all.

"Bodies are rotting in fields and ditches." Reverend McRae's voice was sober as he narrated the story about his recent foray into East Bengal. "When I asked my driver if there was a disease running through the place, he said, 'It is called the hunger.'"

Manik had made a pillau that evening: brown rice baked with cinnamon and cloves and flecked with morsels of chicken, red pepper, and potato. It was delicious, but I lost my appetite. All this rice we had, when so many people had none.

"The peasants were all walking in the same direction as my car," Reverend McRae said. "That is, toward the city. Their hope is they can find rice there."

The next day, when I was walking in Little Russell Street, I noticed an old woman huddled against the curb with a child, close to the corn roaster's stand. The woman's body was so thin I could see the outline of her bones, and her eyes were sunk into her skull as horribly as a ghoul's. I would have thought she were dead, if her hand hadn't slowly moved to touch the thin naked child, who, from the length of her tangled reddish hair, must have been a girl.

I asked the corn-wallah how long the grandmother and granddaughter had been lying in front of his stand.

"They are mother and child," the vendor corrected me. "They came from the countryside a day ago and could not move any farther. At the end of the street, there are three more people like them."

"I shall buy some of your corn to give her," I said, reaching into my purse.

"They cannot eat ordinary food. Their stomachs became so small they can only digest phan."

He was talking about the starchy water that was left over from boiling rice. It had been served to patients at the mission hospital where I'd once stayed. I said, "In a hospital, they can get phan and the care they need."

He shook his head. "Strong ones find their way to hospitals, but this pair has given up. It's too late."

"Which hospitals will take refugees?" With a flash of pain, I remembered how I'd been turned away in Kharagpur.

"Almost all of them these days: but the hospitals are full."

"I will make sure they get in. Somewhere." I cast a last look at them and went off along Gorachand Road, passing more lying in misery, and some obviously dead bodies covered with flies. A cart piled with bodies rolled past me and stopped next to one of these corpses. A pair of men came down and slid a cloth underneath the body to lift it up into the cart. They were as fast as if they were hauling sacks of grain. A rush of sorrow came up from my belly, choking me. The City of Palaces was turning into the City of the Dead.

A waifish woman walked beside me, begging for phan. Recognizing her accent as that of the Midnapore region, I told her to come with me to the hospital, for perhaps there she could get a serving. As we walked, I thought that if I'd stayed in the countryside with Kabita, the two of us would have starved.

We waited a long time to gain admission through the door. Inside, a sea of people lay on the floors. It took some time to get the attention of a Bengali nurse who appeared close to tears from the chaos around her. I spoke about the mother and child in Little Russell Street as well as the woman beside me.

"We cannot take this woman, nor the others you mention," the nurse said. "Try another hospital."

"But you will serve tomorrow?" I persisted.

"Don't come back." Underneath the anger in her voice, I caught a whiff of desperation. "There is not even enough for the patients we have."

I led the woman to another hospital, which didn't let us in, and then we caught a tram to Entally and visited the hospital there. The peasant woman was given phan but she wasn't allowed to stay. I related to the nurse in charge the location of the exhausted mother and child. She said that the Calcutta Municipal Corporation would send an ambulance, but by this point I was uncertain it would happen.

Before leaving, the Midnapore woman I'd brought bent to touch my feet. I accepted her thanks but quickly turned away, not wanting her to see the tears in my eyes. I had done so little. And now there was a tremor inside me, thinking of what she had said about the shortages near Midnapore. Was Kabita starving? Her parents had known my address for almost two years, but I had never heard anything from them, not even as the money and gifts I sent Kabita continued. I did not expect thanks, but I longed for a word of their health and well-being.

I had only enough money left in my purse to afford passage in a crowded bus that took me as far as Chowringhee. From there I hurried back to the puffed-corn vendor. A legless man occupied the spot where the woman and child had huddled. I stepped away from the whine of his accordion playing to ask the corn-wallah if the ambulance had come.

"No. But the corpse cart did." He shoveled more corn into his pan as he spoke. "The fellows took them along with all the other poor souls going down to the ghat for burning."

"But they weren't dead." I swallowed hard, unable to believe it.

"If not already dead, they were hours away from it. You saw their condition. They had no chance." He shoveled and shoveled, not looking up, but I'd seen his face and knew he was hiding tears.

❧   ❧   ❧

THAT NIGHT I dreamed of the starved woman and girl turning from flesh and bones to flame to ash. At three in the morning, I went downstairs to the library and found a book about a nineteenth-century Indian famine. Feeling desperate, I read until I could stand no more, then put my head down on the blotter and slept.

"Kamala, what on earth?"

I awoke to find Mr. Lewes's hand lightly tapping my shoulder.

"Sorry. Is it morning?" I looked up at him, realizing how much my head hurt. I was struck with a longing for him to run his hand up from my shoulder through my hair, pressing away that pain.

"Where were you yesterday evening? I was quite worried." Awkwardly, he took his hand away.

"I returned around nine yesterday and told Manik I wasn't hungry." I decided to say what was in my heart. "Sir, I must take leave for a few days."

Mr. Lewes settled down on the other side of the partners desk. "Of course. But may I ask you why?"

"The famine is so terrible. I must find out if some family members are all right."

"I thought your parents and siblings were deceased?" As he spoke, his brows drew together in concern.

I hesitated, then said, "These are not immediate family, but I still care very much for them. They stay in Midnapore."

"I see." Mr. Lewes was silent for a moment. "Would you like to telephone them first, to make sure they are in? You can also find out what's helpful to bring."

I shook my head. "They don't have a telephone; I'll just go."

"Take some of our rice with you. Midnapore's not far; Sarjit can drive you."

I did not want anyone coming who could carry tales about where I'd been and what had happened. Trying to smile, I said, "That's very kind, but there is no need to take your car when I can ride a train."

"There's nothing to be thanked for. We British are the ones who made India's famine." And with that, he walked away quite fast; but not so fast I couldn't see him wipe his hand across his eyes.

🐝 🐝 🐝

IT WAS A journey I thought I'd never take again: three hours to Kharagpur before switching to the smaller train for Midnapore. I booked a window seat in a second-class compartment, and I stared out at the rice fields, wondering again about the rice shortage. Mr. Lewes, after being initially so defensive about the famine, was now blaming himself. It was obvious that he didn't personally have involvement with supply policies, but he wore the shame of his country on his back. And this made me respect him a little more.

In Midnapore, I was anxious that I might not remember the way to Abbas and Hafeeza's place, but after seeing the mosque, the memory in my feet took over. I turned down this lane and the other one, seeing that the grimy buildings and landmarks had not changed. Even the bits of glass on top of the wall surrounding Abbas and Hafeeza's small compound had remained. But the name painted on the gate had changed to Khan.

It was unlocked, so I took a deep breath and passed through and on to the main hut. A weary-looking young woman answered, one hand holding a baby on her hip.

"*Salaam Aleykum, Bibiji*," I said, using the polite Urdu words of greeting. "I am looking for my friends Abbas and Hafeeza."

"Oh! I live here now; they have been gone four years," she said, tenderly stroking the baby's hair. "Letters still arrive for them now and again, but I just send them back to the post office."

My letters had never come back; perhaps because they'd been opened by someone at the post office who took the money and gifts. Now I had an answer for the lack of news. In a subdued voice, I asked where they'd moved.

She bowed her head a moment, then said, "I am very sorry to tell you that Abbas-babu is dead. He was so kind. May Allah grant him a place in Paradise."

"Dead?" The word choked my throat. Abbas could not have been much older than forty when we parted, and he was a vigorous man.

"He was mortally injured at the mill where he worked. It has happened there before—the British owner pushes the men to the breaking point. When workers are tired, they move more slowly. He stumbled and fell—"

"But that can't be him." I felt a flicker of hope. "The man I'm seeking worked as a chauffeur at a school."

"Abbas-babu lost the driving job after some trouble with the school. He worked at the mill because nobody else would take him." She interrupted herself to shush the whimpering baby.

I felt numb, realizing the unauthorized transport Abbas had provided for me to escape Lockwood might have been the reason he'd lost his good position. "What of his wife and child?"

"Don't worry, they went to live with relatives in the countryside. I don't know where exactly."

At least she had said *they*. It meant that Hafeeza had kept Kabita.

"Can you tell me which of the neighbors were closest to her?"

"I think the ones next door. You can ask."

But nobody on the street remembered Hafeeza saying which town she was going to. She'd sold the hut and almost everything she owned for too little money, as she was deeply distracted over the loss of her husband. But she still had the daughter, called Zeenat, who was both fair and intelligent. I was not the first one who had come looking for them, the lady next door said with a curious expression, as if wanting me to explain myself.

I did not do that. I asked my questions up and down the street, sharing a little rice with each household. I received gratitude, but no useful information. I felt like a hole was opening up inside me, knowing that the money and gifts I'd sent had not been enough to keep them in their home. Now I could only hope that they had survived.

CHAPTER
32

A poor person seeks food, and a rich person seeks appetite.

Bengali proverb

I was too distraught to remember much about my trip back to Calcutta, but as I tiptoed into the flat close to midnight, Mr. Lewes stepped out of the library, rubbing his eyes.

"How are your relatives?"

Too upset to fabricate anything, I shook my head and went to my room. In my bed, with the covers pulled up over my head, I finally let myself weep. I cried for Abbas, who had saved my life twice over and taken in my daughter. And now Hafeeza and Kabita were gone; whether they were dead or alive, I could not know. All the old feelings of losing my family in Johlpur came back to me. I no longer felt like competent, confident Kamala Mukherjee; instead I was poor, broken Pom.

But as I'd learned long ago, a servant had no time to grieve. I did my best to mask my raw emotional state the next morning. It helped that Mr. Lewes left early for work, so I did not have to respond to any more of his concerns. I ate alone, worked on some book repairs in the library, and after lunch, tutored the reverend in Bengali. Then I went out to the streets, walking for blocks, looking closely at every pair of female refugees. My mind returned to the shrunken woman and daughter who had disappeared from Little Russell Street before I could help them. What terrible irony if they had been Hafeeza and Kabita, coming to my address for help. The little girl's hair was reddish brown; maybe it was not just from malnutrition but from Anglo-Indian coloring. If her eyes had opened, I could have seen whether they were specked with green like my baby's. Would I have known my girl? Could I ever know her, with so many years between us?

The next morning, Mr. Lewes stopped me in the hallway. "Kamala, we must speak. Obviously, something has been quite wrong since the time you went on leave."

"I'm fine," I protested, although I'd barely slept. "It's the others who aren't."

"Which others?" He kept his eyes on me.

"Throughout this city, scores of thousands are dying from famine." Irritation at his lack of understanding swelled inside, made me bold. "Haven't you noticed?"

He nodded. "The government can't admit there's a famine, because then they'd have to provide relief. And they say there is no rice to give."

"That is absurd!" I snapped. "Rice is being loaded on ships to soldiers. And the Bengalis in the countryside who grow it can't take a handful home for themselves and their families!"

Mr. Lewes leaned against the library's doorframe, studying me. "It's always so difficult. I've been in India over a decade now and have seen malaria, cholera, flooding come again and again to devastate the people. Misfortune strikes India, time and time again."

But he had not really seen it. He had not clung for his life in a tree and watched corpses float by. He had not suffered cholera twisting his gut, nor dissolved into malarial shaking and delirium, nor seen anyone he loved die helplessly. He could display compassion, but he could not understand.

Abruptly, I asked, "Has your driver arrived?"

"Of course. Do you need to go somewhere?"

"You have always said you like to see all the sights of India. Won't you let me show you some places in Calcutta?" I spoke in a firm voice, making my question not really sound like one.

"I would be happy to go about with you. But I hardly think now's the time—"

"There's no traffic now. It will be easy."

Mr. Lewes looked at his watch and said, "As long as I'm to Lord Sinha Road by half ten for a meeting."

How had I dared to give orders to Mr. Lewes? A demon must have invaded me. But Mr. Lewes would not fight. In short order, we were in the car. This time, Mr. Lewes settled against the far left side, his face resolutely turned toward the window. It reminded me of how I'd been on my first car ride with him to Middleton Mansions, trying to separate myself from him as much as possible.

In Hindi, I told Sarjit to drive us to the section of the Maidan where the refugees had planted themselves. More than a thousand were there; the green lawn had become a sea of distended brown bodies.

When we arrived, the chauffeur came around to open Mr. Lewes's door; my employer made no movement to leave.

"What's wrong?" I asked. I felt angry that we had come into the midst of the people yet would remain spectators.

"I understand that you wanted me to see that starving people have filled the grounds. I have noticed. It's a wretched vision." His voice was clipped.

"I'd rather we didn't remain behind glass looking at them like an exhibit!" I got out of the door Sarjit had opened for me and walked around to stand by the left passenger door. Reluctantly, Mr. Lewes emerged. I pointed toward the white wedding cake of a building that was the Victoria Memorial and said, "Let's go this way."

Today, nobody gawked at the oddity of a white man and brown woman walking together in public. Those who huddled under ragged blankets were too locked in their own misery to look at anything. As we came closer to the people, an unmistakable smell wafted toward us. Mr. Lewes held a handkerchief to his nose as I spoke quietly, pointing out the signs of starvation. So many bellies were distended, rounding up tightly against gaunt rib cages. And the eyes were the worst, lost deep in their sockets, looking out at the world without a bit of hope or expectation.

When we were in the car again, I directed Sarjit to take us up Central Avenue and then into North Calcutta, over to the Howrah Station area and finally, east to Entally. At this hour of the morning, traffic was still light; the car moved swiftly, revealing block after block filled with collapsed corpses and near-corpses wandering in vain.

As we pulled up to Lord Sinha Lane, Mr. Lewes finally spoke. "Thank you for the tour. I agree that it's awful. I wish the government had money to do something more."

"Money won't help them," I said. "All they need is rice. But none of them have the sticks to build a fire, nor the pot to boil water in."

"Of course rice can be distributed. There must be some people giving aid—"

"No feeding kitchens have been organized yet by the government or English citizens." Unable to hide the sentiments of most Bengalis, I said, "Is Mr. Churchill trying to punish Bengal for the Quit India movement, or does he think that if the population shrinks, it will be easier to rule?"

"That isn't fair," Mr. Lewes said sharply. He pulled out a cigarette, and struck his lighter uselessly against it. "The governor is considering relief measures, but they will be hard on everyone. I know that even *our* household has been hoarding maunds of rice—which is exactly the problem."

I swallowed and said, "Yes. I've come to understand that my buying so much rice last month was wrong. I want to do something to make up for it."

Mr. Lewes's cigarette finally caught light. He took a deep inhalation and then said, "Perhaps we can donate some of our rice. I can look into the official channels."

"How many hundreds will die today if we wait for official channels? These people need to drink phan today. All I can think of doing is serving phan to anyone who comes to the garden. Manik could help me with the cooking."

He looked at me for a long moment. "If you serve thirty people today, they will tell others, and tomorrow there will be two hundred. The day after, five hundred."

"Phan is made with eight parts water to rice," I said, remembering the recipe my grandmother had taught me. "A maund weighs eighty pounds and will stretch for several days. And in those days, we will certainly save some lives." I paused to ensure he was still paying full attention. "Have you ever saved a life before, Mr. Lewes?"

After a pause he said, "I'm afraid not."

"Well, I haven't, either. Here is our first chance."

❦   ❦   ❦

THE REST OF the day, I was busy. I instructed Manik to use our two tallest pots for boiling rice and convinced Mr. Rowley's servants to lend me a third. Then I had Sarjit drive Jatin to the wholesale market to load up the car with as many clay cups as he could buy, and I telephoned the Sens.

Mrs. Sen did not have a pot to spare because she was making phan daily as part of an effort organized by the women's section of the Communist Party. As usual, though, she had some controversial political news. "Netaji sent a message to the government, offering to drop one hundred thousand tons of Burmese rice over Bengal. But the

Britishers would rather see half of Bengal die than accept help from the enemy!"

"Yes, I heard," I said, because I'd seen a memorandum about it in Mr. Lewes's desk. Apparently, the British suspected the Japanese planes would drop more than just rice on Bengal.

"So you are making your own rice kitchen, Kamala. That is a great thing. Would you like Supriya to print a leaflet about your address and the feeding time from noon till two? Someone will distribute it on the Maidan. That is not too far from you."

"Yes, but there will be no set feeding time. I want to feed anyone who manages to find our place, any time of day—"

She interrupted me, sounding exasperated. "Kamala, you don't understand! All the other rice kitchens are on the same timing. Otherwise people will travel throughout the city to take food twice a day and use up what little supply we have. Or they will camp out on your property permanently."

I did not like what Mrs. Sen said, but it seemed that following the rules would mean a more manageable system. So with reluctance, I agreed.

The first day, only those staying nearby came. Reverend McRae and I oversaw the tureens, giving each person a generous scoop that filled the clay teacups. Afterward, people sat on the grass, digesting. Some vomited, and others lost control of their bowels. Two constables stopped by to see if I had a permit for such a nuisance to the neighborhood. I gave each a rupee and thanked them for their concern. They straightened the sign I had put on the gate as they left.

I had feared people might battle one another to get phan, but the lines remained quiet and orderly. Tragically, one woman died at the end of the line, so by midafternoon, the undertakers' cart came to Middleton Street. The next day, nobody died. And two hundred came. The clay cups were all gone, so people were using leaves or even their hands to cup the gruel. I wished I could tell Pankaj about these people and the way it felt to serve them, but I did not dare write to him again.

As my days serving rice continued, I noticed something curious; almost all the refugees were children and females. One woman explained it best: she had left her husband in the country because he could eat leaves and worms. Her children could not. I had not talked to peasants in a long time, and I felt my old country accent coming back. Reverend McRae's Scottish Bengali made the children laugh. But there was a problem: our rice could not last forever. I worried aloud to the reverend about the supply, and whether I would have to offer phan only to newcomers to the city. There was less than a week's store left, by my calculations.

"How can you refuse one person over another?" he asked.

"I can't. It would break my heart."

"Then all who come to you are meant to receive." His blue eyes glowed like unearthly coals against his weathered skin. "That is why you created this kitchen, isn't it?"

His optimism frustrated me; it was unrealistic. "But I do not have enough rice, as I have been saying!"

The reverend's voice was gentle. "If you pray, you will receive. God's angels will bring the message of how this will be."

I resisted the urge to roll my eyes, because I had never seen a winged being in Calcutta except for bats in the garden. And while I deeply respected the way Reverend McRae related to his Christian God, I could not see him as different from the Allah who had led Abbas to rescue me, or Goddess Lakshmi who had guided me out of poverty and into the comforts of Middleton Street. Did the reverend understand that it would be to all of them I would pray? Somehow, I didn't think it mattered.

❧   ❧   ❧

THAT EVENING, I did not share my anxiety with Mr. Lewes, although I imagined he would be concerned if he knew that twenty maunds were almost depleted. After dinner, we all went into the library to listen to a classical music broadcast. Mr. Lewes stretched out on the settee with a book on his chest. Reverend McRae sat snugly in a wing chair reading a book of essays by Swami Vivekananda. I slouched at the desk, ostensibly looking over the day's papers but thinking of only one thing: rice.

The flat's bell shattered this peaceful moment. I jerked my head up to hear Shombhu opening the door a flight below us and then a stamping of feet upstairs. In the next minute, Mr. Weatherington strode into the library with Shombhu anxiously following in his wake, making an apologetic face at Mr. Lewes.

"You left quite early today. An official document came in a half hour later and I've taken it upon myself to bring it." Mr. Weatherington glowered at the whole room.

Mr. Lewes put down his book, looking as irritated as I felt. "Reverend McRae, may I introduce Mr. Weatherington? Who would like coffee, and who is for tea?"

Mr. Weatherington pointed a bony finger at me. "I heard about an Indian woman luring refugees into the White Town. Seeing the condition of the garden outside, I know who it is. Shame on you!"

"I'm not ashamed at all," I answered in a cool voice, but inside I was furious. He would not ruin the last days of the rice kitchen; I could not stand it.

"The rice kitchen was both our ideas; and with Reverend McRae's assistance, it has served thousands of meals." Mr. Lewes came up to stand behind me. He put a hand on the back of my chair, which had the odd effect of making me feel like we were touching.

"Running a place like this out of a good residential establishment could get you evicted by your own landlord," Mr. Weatherington said, watching us closely.

"If you make a fuss about it, perhaps. But I'll know it's your doing."

I cast a glance backward and saw my employer was staring hard at his colleague. It was as if the polite English veneer was gone and something tougher had emerged.

Mr. Weatherington must have noticed, for his voice rose as if in self-defense. "That's not my intention, Simon, but I wish to remind you that Calcutta is India's war production center. You must return to saving India from the Japanese, not saving it for the huddled masses!"

"I'm giving up my car for the war effort. What about you?" Mr. Lewes coldly scrutinized his colleague.

"Oh, no," Mr. Weatherington huffed. "I don't believe in empty symbolic gestures like giving up cars or setting up charities in high-rent districts. Nobody would allow it in Alipore."

I realized now that I despised Mr. Weatherington as much as the worst individuals I'd known: Miss Rachael who'd told lies about me, Mummy who'd sold me, and the Railway Hospital nurses who had almost killed Kabita with their kicks. I hated him, but I wouldn't give him the satisfaction of seeing me upset.

Mr. Lewes still hadn't taken his eyes off his colleague. "What is this really about, Wilbur?"

"I honestly don't know. You tell me!" Mr. Weatherington lifted up his briefcase, unlocked its clasp and took out a sealed envelope.

"Good night," I said, beginning to rise in my seat. I knew what the argument was really about: Mr. Weatherington's jealousy of his colleague, the one he thought the governor preferred.

"Don't go, Kamala. This is news you may need to hear." Mr. Lewes had opened the paper and was reading it over swiftly. "Yes, exactly as I'd hoped!"

"What in hell are you saying?" Mr. Weatherington sputtered. "Don't reveal privileged communications!"

"Actually, Kamala and the reverend are involved." Mr. Lewes leaned down, and I felt his breath against my skin as he put the letter in my hands. "The Relief Control office will send us rice. A dozen maunds per week for an unspecified time."

Mr. Weatherington's mouth worked for an instant, as if he had a hundred objections to raise. But he only made a sharp exhalation, then stormed out of the room and downstairs without as much as saying good night.

"Praise God!" said Reverend McRae, smiling from the wing chair where he'd watched the whole drama unfold. I thought it was about the letter; but perhaps Mr. Weatherington's departure, too.

"Did you know this wonderful thing would happen? Is it your doing?" I had risen to rush over to the reverend and clasp his hand.

"Nothing to do with it, Miss Mukherjee. I'm as happily surprised as you are!"

I glanced back at Mr. Lewes, who was still standing behind my vacated chair and suddenly understood. He must have done it. Slowly, I read through the letter written on engraved letterhead and signed by the governor. It was just as Mr. Lewes had said. Within two days, we'd receive a regular supply of rice each week, free of charge.

Everything had happened as the reverend had predicted. But there was still one thing that troubled me. Although Mr. Weatherington clearly was the bearer of good news, I could not consider him any kind of angel.

*In wartime practically everything is either rationed or off
the market altogether. But it is surprising how comparatively little
these shortages inconvenience one by now. In fact, some are
positively a blessing in disguise. Food for example. There are no
luxuries, of course, and quite apart from luxuries, most of one's
old favorites have vanished. It is months, years in fact, since I
have made close acquaintance with a genuine mutton chop.
Substitutes too are everywhere and most of what one eats,
it seems to me, 'tastes' different. But there is 'enough.'*

—Calcutta's controller of rationing, Lord Elton,
Amrita Bazar Patrika, Jan. 30, 1944

Angrily, I crushed up the page with Lord Elton's editorial. The pompous aristocrat didn't know how few Indians would ever see a mutton bone, let alone a mutton chop. Nor did he seem to understand how pitifully scant the permitted amounts of rice, flour, and sugar were. Mr. Lewes and Reverend McRae obtained their ration cards easily, but I had to visit the ration office several times in order to get the cards for Shombhu, Jatin, Manik, and myself. After experiencing how difficult obtaining a card was, I guessed thousands of Calcuttans might not get ration cards. And what of Kabita and others in the countryside, where there were no ration cards at all?

As Mr. Lewes had pledged, he gave up his car. His driver, Sarjit, was quickly hired by an American colonel come to town. This was the way of the times: because American military officers earned far more than their British counterparts, many neighborhood servants were looking for new bosses. I thought Shombhu and Jatin would stay, but I worried about Manik. The rice kitchen, plus his usual cooking schedule, was much more than he'd had to do before.

"Take rest this afternoon," I said to Manik at least several times a week.

"But who will make dinner then?" He looked at me glumly.

"I shall!"

"You do not know about kitchens."

I could have told Manik that as a girl, I'd crouched on a mud floor sorting stones from lentils, but that would shock and confuse him. I held my tongue, thinking about the many lies, spoken or not, that had become part of me. I did not want to mislead Manik, but admitting humble origins could lead to everything falling apart.

It was easier to concentrate on rice. My mornings were filled with getting the pots gently boiling enough rice for the four to five hundred who came daily. After serving and clean up, I took a brief rest and gave Reverend McRae his Bengali lesson. Then it was time to welcome Mr. Lewes home for dinner and to read him the newspaper translations, which he'd asked me to resume since he began closely monitoring local information about the famine.

These days, all he talked of was the hunger. He had even convinced some colleagues in Delhi to direct national funds toward relief in Bengal. Despite this, he remained worried about the distribution system ordered by Governor Casey, who insisted two-thirds of the rice must stay in Calcutta, although there were ten times more deaths per week in the countryside. As Mr. Lewes doggedly continued, I began understanding why he was doing so much. The new governor, Mr. Casey, had decided to run his office differently than the other governors before him. He had even stopped sending fortnightly letters to the viceroy.

"It's unheard of," Mr. Lewes said one evening at dinner with the reverend and me. "The secretary of state is very much against cutting the flow of information about Bengal's status at a time such as this. He is so perturbed he wrote a letter about it."

"Do you think it's because Mr. Casey prefers the telephone to writing?" I asked, thinking that if letter-writing duties were stripped, Mr. Lewes had lost half of his job.

"Of course not! He's stopping regular correspondence because he doesn't have a bloody notion of how to explain his mismanagement of the famine and labor unrest. It's the same reason he won't let hospitals reveal to the newspapers how many have starved to death."

"Oh, that's why there's so little in the papers—"

"Indeed." Mr. Lewes grimaced. "If Casey only communicates when he wants, he can drop mentions of glorious schools being built and new animals installed at the Alipore zoo. He can shine praise on every church in town!"

"Leave the poor clerics out of it. We are not all admirers of Mr. Casey!" Reverend McRae protested.

Hoping to coax a laugh out of both of them, I said, "Mr. Casey should write some reports of popular films at the Metro Cinema and good drinks at Firpo's. What splendid letters he can write for himself! He doesn't need—"

He doesn't need you, I had been about to say. But in an instant I remembered that although Mr. Lewes had brought up Governor Casey's unwillingness to write letters, he hadn't mentioned that *he* was the one who had been writing them. And nobody could know about this without having seen the drafts and final copies in Mr. Lewes's desk.

At my words, Mr. Lewes had abruptly stopped smiling. My stomach dropped, as I feared that I'd given myself away. But it turned out that I was wrong, because all Mr. Lewes did was ask whether Manik could bring him another gin-lime.

The fall pujas passed without my seeing the Sens; I sent a letter, feeling bad that I had no time to go. I vowed that I would go to them at Christmas, as had been my custom. But Supriya beat me to the punch, surprising me on an early December afternoon by coming into the garden herself. My spirits jumped when I noticed her standing in the corner of the garden; I smiled and motioned to her to sit down at the table on the veranda. After the feeding time ended, I hurried over to greet her.

"Kamala-didi, I hope you are not annoyed that I came without calling," Supriya said, reaching up to give me a hug. "But you are very overdue in picking up these books! Baba said if we kept them any longer, they would be in danger of becoming lost."

"It's my fault," I said, smiling at her. "Let me wash my hands before touching those books. How is everyone?"

"Quite well. Baba and Ma are allowing Sonali to marry Arvind Israni; the wedding is next month. You must come: Baba is designing the most beautiful invitations. The thing that is funny is Sonali's name is changing; her in-laws want to call her Sonal. My little sister will become Mrs. Sonal Israni. How grand that sounds."

"Does she mind?" I asked, thinking if Supriya knew how many times I'd changed names, she would be very surprised.

"Of course not! She is only too happy to be permitted her love marriage."

Love marriage! I thought of my dream of a union with Pankaj, and the happiness inside me began to fade. I said, "Please come inside, and I'll have Jatin serve your tea while I quickly bathe."

I left Supriya in the drawing room to look at some art folios on the coffee table. I went up to my room and after a quick bath, changed into a fresh sari. I returned and was pleased to see that Manik had already brought tea in the best silver service and a china plate of crisp cauliflower phuluri.

Supriya was walking around, looking here and there when I returned. In a dry tone she commented, "This place could belong to a maharajah! I didn't know Mr. Lewes was so rich."

And she did not know, either, that it had been a dreadful hodge-podge until I'd decorated it for him. Feeling strangely proprietary, I said, "It's just a two-story flat. A Scottish minister is staying here, too, because of the war."

Supriya giggled. "But it is your place; it fits you! Look, you are so beautiful in that jamdani sari—and are those moonstones in the necklace?"

My face warmed with embarrassment. "My sari is old; you have seen it before. Eat something."

"It's not only the sari, it is you looking like a candle has been lit inside!" Supriya insisted. "Clearly, the rice kitchen fulfills you. Tell me, how many maunds are you serving a week?"

"About a dozen. We somehow manage to give to everyone who comes."

"I don't think that you will run out of food." She sighed. "Actually, I came here to say good-bye."

"Why? And where are you going?" I relaxed a bit, because Supriya's attention to the flat could have been due to her tension about bringing such news.

"I'm following Netaji!" She grabbed my hands in hers and squeezed them.

"Don't joke like that!" I whispered, shooting a glance over my shoulder. The kitchen door was closed, but I imagined that the men had set up their work close to the door to overhear us.

"Why?" Supriya teased. "Is your church minister sleeping? Or is Mr. Lewes home?"

I shook my head at my impulsive friend. "Supriya, let's go upstairs to my room."

Once she had followed me upstairs, admired my bathroom, and examined the novels on my nightstand, Supriya sat down next to me on the bed. She said that she was not joking about following Subhas Chandra Bose. Apparently he had taken charge of the Indian National Army in Singapore and was forming a women's regiment. She would leave to join them the next day.

For a moment, I forgot to breathe. I was shocked by both the danger she was running toward, and the idea that she could cross India's border. I didn't think it could be done. She would fail, she would die. When I regained my breath, I asked, "How will you possibly go?"

"Tomorrow I will travel by train to Assam, and from there, I only have to cross the river into Burma. People living in the jungle know all the secret ways; Pankaj has told me exactly who to find. I will be safe."

"I thought you weren't supposed to visit Pankaj in prison?" I had not forgotten how my error in writing to him had made life difficult for all of them.

"Pankaj-da was released two months ago, and Lata as well. I'm surprised you did not know." Supriya gave me a guarded look. "I suppose you've been so busy."

"Oh! That is wonderful news." But the relief I felt was tempered by doubt. Pankaj had been free for two months and not sent me any messages? Perhaps he was still angry about my mistake in writing to him—or was he trying to protect me from police who might be following him? *Yes,* I decided; that had to be it.

"Pankaj-da's friends gathered documents showing ties to the Communists, and as you know, the Communists in prison had to be freed because of the new British alliance with the Soviets," Supriya continued. "Lata was freed for another reason: poor health. But don't worry too much; her parents are fattening her up at home in Travancore. I don't think they'll let her come back to join the wild freedom fighters of Calcutta, though!"

Supriya was being so light-spirited that it was hard to remember that she was on the edge of self-destruction. I asked, "What does Son-ali think about your going?"

Her merry expression abruptly vanished. "I daren't tell her for fear she'll tell Arvind or my parents. The best thing is for me to run off and leave a letter behind explaining. I'll say that serving him is my dharma; that is an idea Hindus understand."

I'd left my village home for an hour's walk, never to see my family again; her journey would be even more risky. But I couldn't tell her not to go. Reluctantly, I warned, "Think carefully if you really want to do it. If you change your mind, it may be impossible to return."

"Oh, I will definitely return to India!" Her eyes were once again bright and hopeful. "The INA will come through Burma into India and free everyone from British rule. Sometime next year you'll see me marching down Chowringhee in dress uniform!"

"If that day comes, I will salute you," I said, trying to hold back tears. She was reckless and brave: everything I could never be. She also had the advantage of Pankaj's help. If he believed that she could make it to the INA, she would.

"Don't tease me." Supriya's eyes were wet. "All I want, dearest Kamala, is your embrace."

And we did, holding each other tightly enough to meld into one.

🐝   🐝   🐝

BY MID-DECEMBER, FAMINE deaths were declining, but I was still busy feeding peasants. Mr. Lewes suggested that I take a break from the kitchen one weekend; he was willing to serve the phan himself, with Reverend McRae on hand to help. I was pleased by his offer because I wanted to visit the Sens to find out whether they'd had news on Supriya's journey. I'd added her to the daily prayers that I always made for Kabita, now nearly six years old, at the little Lakshmi shrine in my bedroom.

Lately, I'd had a dreadful feeling that Kabita was alone in the world, without even Hafeeza. The idea had no basis; it had come to me in a dream at night, and I was filled with as much terror as if a man with an ax had been standing at my bedside. But in the morning, I rationalized things. If she was alive, it meant she was a survivor like me. Perhaps she had found bread for herself, or was eating jungle plants. She could have found help from a rice kitchen or orphanage. All I could do was hope that my prayers would carry her through the difficult times.

The Saturday morning was bright and clear as I walked to the tram en route to see the Sens. My city had changed. Trenches had been dug in Park Street and Chowringhee. Calcutta's worn tongas and carts and buses looked like battered toys next to massive military vans and lorries. Most private cars had been taken by the military; one could see their drivers patiently waiting outside the cafés. The Allied military elite dined at Flury & Trinca's and the Golden Slipper by day and slept in the Great Eastern and Grand Hotels at night. How ironic that our city, once the jewel in Britain's crown, was the only Asian metropolis she had left—and the ones able to afford her pleasures were foreigners.

As the tram I rode took me away from the White Town, the affluence vanished. Here the streets were packed with the rural poor, hands cupped for rice. This made me worry a little about how things were going at our rice kitchen. Mr. Lewes might frighten the refugees with his sharp, blue eyes; or he might be scared himself by their overwhelming suffering. On the other hand, I had no doubts about the capability of Reverend McRae. He would manage the feeding without a problem.

The door to the Sens' building was locked with its grille pulled down. Ali, the darwan, was sitting on the stoop, chewing paan.

"They are all at the wedding!" he told me with a smile that split his wizened face in two.

"The wedding? Is Sonali marrying today?" I was stunned, because I had not received an invitation.

"Today is the second-to-last day of ceremonies at the temple, Kamala-didi." He spit paan neatly on the walk. It formed a blot that looked like blood; and for some reason, this made me shiver.

"What good news," I said, trying to shake off my feeling of sadness.

"You should be there already!" Ali chided. "Did you forget?"

I shook my head. I had never known the exact wedding date. Maybe I'd stayed away from the Sens for so long that they'd forgotten me. Yet another loss of people I cared about, I thought, turning back the way I'd come.

At dinner that evening, I had no appetite for the fish mollee and rice on my plate. Mr. Lewes was full of lively stories that evening about the various people he had served.

"I think our accents left something to be desired, but we were somehow understood." Mr. Lewes nodded at the reverend sitting across the table.

"What did you say to them?" I asked.

"*Dekha ho bey.*" He pronounced the words slowly but badly, in his elegant Oxbridge accent. "I believe that it means, see you tomorrow?"

"Thank you, but I shall be on the job tomorrow," I said. "I am so grateful for what you did today."

Mr. Lewes had the determined look that I knew well. "But it's Sunday—after church services, I could serve them. You could go out again with your friends."

"What friends?" I reached forward to push my plate away, accidentally bumping my hand against that of Mr. Lewes. It felt electric; and I pulled away, fast.

Exhaling, he said, "You went somewhere today. I'm guessing you saw the people you bring sweets to on puja days."

Was he jealous, or merely suspicious? I could not tell from his voice. Stiffly, I said, "The Sens are the ones you're thinking of. And yes, they might have sent a letter here. I am wondering if it might have been lost. It would have been a large envelope."

"You once received so many letters and parcels, Miss Mukherjee!"

Reverend McRae said in his warm burr. "But now it's dropped off. My post has, too. The war has interrupted delivery."

My private mail wasn't mailed from overseas, but hand-delivered from a bungalow in Ballygunge or the Hindu College. War wouldn't affect it. I felt nervous that the reverend had brought this up in front of Mr. Lewes, who surely understood that I had no post coming from overseas.

"Kamala, I'm sure I haven't seen anything, but you should also ask Shombhu, who sorts it. If you don't trust his answer, I will ask him myself."

"That isn't necessary," I said quickly. "I trust them like my brothers." Now I felt desolate, for if nobody had seen the large envelope, it must never have come.

※   ※   ※

MR. LEWES DID not even go to church on Sunday. He appeared in the garden before noon, dressed in shirtsleeves and canvas trousers with an apron around his waist.

"I hope Manik won't mind my small theft," Mr. Lewes said, turning up the ends of the apron to show them off. "On which side of the serving station do you want me?"

"How about the right as usual?" At the dinner table, Mr. Lewes sat at the head and I was close on his left. In the garden, he'd subjugated his authority to me; it felt funny.

"Don't think of moving that tureen; it's too heavy." Mr. Lewes went up the steps to load one of the tall brass tureens into his arms and came down carefully to rest it atop the rack I'd set over a paraffin candle.

"It's almost time," I said, looking at the people already queuing outside the gate.

"No bowls for them to use, ever?" he queried.

"They use their hands, as you've seen, or leaves from the trees." I inclined my head toward the mango tree, which was almost completely stripped of leaves and fruit. It had given all it could to the refugees, just as we had.

"I want to try phan."

Shrugging, I said, "It's just like the congee people eat when they're ill. It's not at all delicious."

Mr. Lewes went over to the mango tree and brought back a leaf. I dropped a spoonful of phan onto it, and he brought the leaf to his mouth. After a moment, he said, "It's rather bland. I wonder if it would be tastier with salt or sugar."

"There's a sugar shortage, if you hadn't noticed!" I shook a finger at him, almost enjoying the way he was asking my advice.

"How about jaggery, the Indian sugar?"

"They are grateful for what we give. There's no need to do anything extra."

"But it's Sunday lunch! Where does Manik keep his blocks of jaggery?"

"Third cupboard from the door, upper shelf. Use the round-topped silver key." Smiling at his generosity, I untied the key ring I always wore from the waist of my sari and gave it to him. He returned a few minutes later with two cups of the golden-brown jaggery, which melted easily into one tureen of bubbling phan.

"This sweet pot is the one I'll serve from; tell the children," he said, as I went to open the gate and welcome the refugees in. I told them, and the young ones rushed to be in Mr. Lewes's line. I was surprised how well he did; speaking the few words of Bengali I'd taught him. *Please take some. It's sweet. Come back tomorrow.*

Fortunately the adults were satisfied with the plainer phan. As I served them, they asked in Bengali who the saheb was. I realized then that they thought the property was my own, and he was the guest. During a slow moment, I told Mr. Lewes about the humorous misunderstanding. "I was worried you might frighten them, but it turns out they are only concerned whether you are the governor or my husband!"

"If you told them I was both—what would they say? Tell them," he said with a laugh.

"I won't lie to them!" I couldn't say how much I regretted all the stories I'd told.

When the last refugee had eaten and trailed out the gate, I hung the CLOSED sign and prepared to take the empty tureens inside. But Mr. Lewes had already done the tureens and was blowing out the paraffin candles.

"The work is done. Thank you." I ran damp hands over my hair, which was escaping its bun. I rarely thought about how disheveled the work over steaming tureens made me; but today, I was embarrassed.

"You're very welcome. And you're lovely," he said, reaching out to take one of the curling wisps. My heart started hammering, as he held it for a moment. This could not be. Rapidly, I brought up my hand over his, to get him to release my hair, but all he did was put his other hand over mine. He stepped closer to me; so close that I could smell a hint of smoke and jaggery mixed with his scent.

We had never shaken hands. But today we had used our hands toward the same goal. What had happened in the garden was so unusual, that his holding on to my hand with both of his seemed like an extension of the dream.

From our joined hands, a shiver traveled up my arm and into my brain. This was the same feeling I'd had the night of the Christmas bombing, and the time before that at our cocktail party. As Mr. Lewes pulled me against him, I wanted to let the shivering continue: to lift my face to his, which was lowering with eyes closed.

It was too romantic; I felt as if I were in the cinema, watching the characters of a young Indian woman and an Englishman standing inside a walled garden bordered with flowering trees. They were so close; it was clear that they loved each other. But hanging over the wall was a chorus of mocking Indians and Britishers, ruining it.

This moment was dangerous, I realized with a jolt. It could undermine everything I'd worked for and ruin him, too. Panic flared within me; I turned my wrist, and his hands were gone. And so was I, fleeing through the garden and out to the street.

CHAPTER
34

When you are wise, you will know how much paddy makes rice.

Bengali proverb

When I'd taken the library job, I'd privately vowed that if Mr. Lewes ever touched me, I would leave. But now I couldn't imagine leaving Middleton Mansions and the life I'd built. Nor did I want to leave him. I felt—no, I couldn't let myself remember what I'd felt in the garden. Desire. Affection. Reassurance. All in the space of his holding my wrist.

Trying to calm myself back to a normal state, I retreated to Bilgrami's Classic Books, where I'd once gone hoping to sell my own treasured texts. It was still the closest bookshop in the area, and even though the windows were covered in blackout paper, inside it was neat and serene. I made my greeting to Mr. Bilgrami, who knew me well by now, and carried a stool over to the section where the children's books were. I leafed through a few new boarding school novels. Angela Brazil and Enid Blyton's innocent girls, caring only for each other, their teachers, and field hockey, took my mind off the crisis. I remembered what my ideas of love had been like when I was at Lockwood. Pankaj had ruled my head and heart; now I was confounded by what had almost happened with Simon Lewes. That was his first name. I'd never said it aloud, but now I whispered it.

Simon.

Several hours later, I walked very slowly home, dreading what lay ahead. But he was not in the flat. I found a key ring on the hall table with an envelope. Inside was his monogrammed card, scrawled with a few lines of his handwriting.

I have gone away for a while on business. I don't know the return date. My apologies for this and everything else.

He had not even signed his name. I went into the library and curled up on the settee, reading the lines again. He was apologizing because he'd understood what had happened was wrong: the fru-ition of every cliché and stereotype about British men and Indian women, something we both had fought against so hard and for so long. I did not believe he had a business trip, because he'd never spoken of it. I wondered now if he would stay away until his emotions had calmed, or was he waiting to see if I would do the proper thing and quit working for him?

"The saheb went away on business yesterday afternoon. Delhi or Bombay, I imagine," I told Jatin when he came to my room the next morning with bed tea. I was acting as if I was telling him news, but what I was really doing was fishing for information.

Jatin did not disappoint. As he put down the tray, he said, "That is strange. My cousin-brother saw him yesterday evening."

Trying to sound calm, I asked, "At Howrah Station?"

"No. My relative is a waiter at the Calcutta Club. He said saheb was at the gentlemen's bar upstairs, drinking too much whiskey. He could not have been traveling."

I'd heard that the Calcutta Club had bedrooms for its members. A cold feeling descended on me as I realized that my intuition had been correct. He did not think we could live under the same roof after the kiss. Yet he felt unable to dismiss me.

The following day the telephone rang. I answered and Mr. Lewes spoke without introduction. In response to my murmured greeting, he asked to speak with Shombhu. Feeling sick with worry, I gave the head bearer the phone. After a minute, Shombhu put down the receiver and said that the saheb had asked him to pack a second suitcase with a week's worth of clothing and have it dropped off at the office.

"He's going to Delhi, just like you said to Jatin," Shombhu reported. "He does not know for how long."

Delhi, my foot! I thought. Mr. Lewes was such a creature of propriety; he would not let anyone think he was staying away from his flat for any reason but business. And then Reverend McRae decided to leave the flat, too.

"But why?"

"I'm invited to Dacca to help with famine relief there," the reverend said over dinner on Wednesday, the third night since Mr. Lewes's disappearance. "They're very hard hit there. I'm sorry I won't be able to lend a hand in the garden for a week or so."

"Please don't worry!" I reassured him, although the prospect of losing the reverend's company made my spirits sink even lower. "I'll ask one of the ladies who come regularly to be my helper for this time."

"That's a grand idea, empowering them to help one another. I may share this concept in Dacca."

"First, let me see how it works."

"Yes, yes, of course! And it's a shame Mr. Lewes isn't here—he would enjoy helping on the weekend. I think the rice kitchen's made him into an even better man. Don't you?"

I nodded, all the while knowing that Mr. Lewes would never return to the garden with me. But I would spend time there; and after the reverend departed, working with so many people kept me from feeling lonely. But when I cleaned up afterward, and I looked at my hands, I remembered him touching them. I thought then: If only I had waited for the kiss. He would have left me anyway; but I would have known what it felt like.

As the week continued, my longing turned to anger. If Mr. Lewes really wanted me to leave, he should have sent a letter. But I didn't want to go. Not because I felt duty-bound to spy on the British; but because if I left, the rice kitchen would close. The peasants' needs were more important than a botched moment between two privileged people. And what of my lost little Kabita? If I had her with me, I would not be thinking of such selfish matters.

This attitude renewed my strength; and I began smiling and laughing genuinely again, as I spent hours with the people I was coming to know as well as those I'd grown up with in my small hamlet. And so the rice kitchen ran on until Friday. The feeding began as usual; at noon I was ladling phan with the assistance of a patron who'd become a friend: the Smiler, as I privately called the always-beaming woman of about thirty years, who had been prematurely aged by starvation. The Smiler had brought her five children to Calcutta, all of whom had survived the sixty-mile walk and were finally beginning to get flesh back on their bones. She told me that her smile had started the moment they'd entered the City of Palaces and had their first serving of phan.

"What is that?" the Smiler inclined her head toward the street, and a heavy, grinding noise.

"Soldiers, probably," I said, looking past the gate as a long army lorry stopped right in front of the mansion block. From the sound of things, more lorries were behind that one.

Then I saw Shombhu running: uncharacteristic movement for such a stately man. He was followed into the garden by four constables and a dozen Indian Army soldiers. Trying to appear calm, I put down my ladle and asked the men their business. Instead of answering me, the soldiers shouted at the peasants to turn around and board their trucks. When people refused to leave, the soldiers picked up their lathis. And now my anxiety turned to full-blown, heart-pounding fear.

"Stop it! What are you doing?" I cried out to the constable who seemed to be the boss of the group.

"We are obeying government orders." He shoved a thin paper with smudged typing at me. Dimly I saw the words *relief* and *resettlement*.

"But this is an official government kitchen! These people are supposed to eat every day during these specific hours—"

"Everything has changed," the constable said. "Rice kitchens in the city are closed. The government has made feeding camps outside of Calcutta."

At his words, an image flashed into my mind; the work camps that the Nazis had built for Jewish captives. Not here, in India—I couldn't stand it. Shakily, I said, "This is the residence of Mr. Simon Lewes. You cannot send away his guests without his permission."

"Guests!" the constable said mockingly. "This vermin?"

"I want your name." My breath came in short bursts because the constables carried lathis, and the soldiers had guns. I knew they could hit me just as they'd hit the female students blocking streets as part of Quit India. But the constable and his men turned away and joined the soldiers herding people like goats into the lorries' open beds.

I couldn't stop them. But maybe someone else could. I hurried inside to the library and went into Mr. Lewes's desk, where I knew he kept the governor's letter stating we would receive a free rice allotment to dispense as we liked. But that letter was gone, as was almost everything that should have been in the drawer. Mr. Lewes must have taken his papers to keep on working at the Club. He would not be there at midday, so I rang the office to speak with his secretary, Mr. Branston.

"Is Mr. Lewes there?" I asked, my breath coming so fast that I could barely get the words out.

There was an intake of breath, and Mr. Branston said, "Madam, who are you?"

"Miss Mukherjee. I'm his library clerk, calling on urgent business." In a few sentences, I explained about the rice kitchen being shut down and the peasants being forcibly taken away. If I couldn't reach Mr. Lewes, I needed to reach someone in Government House who knew about the established feeding program we had.

"Mr. Lewes is in Delhi," Mr. Branston said. "So there's really nothing I can do—and no, I don't think you should speak to the governor's office about it, because it was Lord Rutherford who authorized the kitchen, and now Mr. Casey is in charge."

Mr. Casey, who Mr. Lewes had said was too disconnected and made poor decisions about everything. Branston was right; the governor wouldn't help any more than he had.

Only five minutes had passed, but the scene in the garden was worse. The constables were beating the last stragglers into the third lorry, although I saw a number of boys and girls running away from them and down the street. I was briefly cheered by this before realizing that these fleeing children would lose their families, just as I'd lost mine.

For me, approaching the remaining lorry was hard. I had to fight back the terrible old memory of the Brahmin-saheb with his cart packed full of tied-up children. I reached up my hand to the Smiler, who was no longer smiling. In a choked voice I called, "You will have rice where they take you. Hold on to your children. Hold on, don't let them go!"

"Ma, don't let them take us!" someone called to me.

"I tried, but I can't—"

Another voice implored, "Ma, stop them!"

But I could not. The driver put the first lorry in gear, and the people who had been standing inside the lorry beds fell against each other. The vehicle rolled on, followed by its companions.

Somehow I stumbled back to the garden, barely able to see through my tears. Shombhu and Jatin were still picking up the pots that spilled onto the grass. Everywhere clods of grass had been kicked up, and the gate was hanging off its hinge.

"Terrible people, those so-called police!" Jatin took the broken gate in his hands. "If the saheb were here, it never would have happened!"

"You're right," I said, wiping my hand across my eyes. "But not everyone will miss the peasants. It's been a lot of work for Manik, and the neighbors hated it."

"Didi, please! Don't cry so. Go rest yourself."

I shook my head, because I imagined the lorries would take the quickest way out of the city and dump the peasants in a remote spot. Or would they pack them into a prison, perhaps sending them somewhere like the Andamans?

"Please take a rest, Didi," Jatin repeated. I looked into his eyes, which were also tearful, and something unspoken passed between us. I had grown to love the boy like a brother; the little one I had never gotten to care for. I pulled Jatin to me for an instant, and he hugged me back, understanding.

I went upstairs and bathed, desperate to get off the dust and sweat and memory of my failure. I brushed my teeth and put on a nightdress because I knew I would be unable to eat.

Night couldn't come fast enough to put an end to the wretched day. I lay on my bed, watching the sun move across the ceiling, making shadows that bounced as the fan blades passed around. I wondered if what had happened to us had also happened at other rice kitchens, and if Mr. Weatherington had anything to do with the shutdown.

Tortured by my circling worries, I could not sleep. The tall clock in the downstairs hall chimed midnight, and then one o'clock. At two thirty I went downstairs to make myself a cup of tea. By the light of the lamp I carried with me, the kitchen seemed so large and bare at night. As I stood waiting for the kettle to boil, I heard a creaking at the front door.

Initially, I was frightened; my next feeling was rage with myself for having neglected to bar the door, which was my duty when Mr. Lewes was away. I turned off the stove quickly and went to the kitchen door with a cast iron pan in one hand and a meat cleaver in the other. Obviously it was a clever thief to strike when both Mr. Lewes and the reverend were away. But he did not know how strong I could become when it was needed. I breathed deeply, preparing myself for the fight.

The burglar dropped something with a heavy thump. Then he began walking toward the kitchen, where I belatedly realized my lamp might have attracted him. Not wanting to wait for his attack, I gave a deathlike cry and sprang forward with my weapons.

"Kamala!" Mr. Lewes had snapped on the light and was staring aghast at me.

"Oh! I'm sorry, sir!" I was still shaking, although I understood the danger I'd feared was gone. What remained was the strangeness of his coming home so suddenly, and of not knowing what might happen next. I repeated, "I'm sorry. I didn't know you would come tonight."

"My train was delayed. And while I was waiting in the lounge, I heard that Casey ordered the rice kitchens to close. Did it happen already?" Mr. Lewes looked at my face and said, "I'm the sorry one. Sorry I couldn't tell you first—"

"The people did not want to go." I slid the knife back into its block. "The soldiers hit the peasants who protested. It was just like . . ." I was about to say, *Just like the street protest in Kharagpur,* when I remembered he shouldn't know that I'd witnessed that. "Do you think Mr. Weatherington inspired the governor to shut things down?"

"I doubt it." Mr. Lewes sighed, and I noticed that his tie was askew and collar open; he looked hot and thoroughly rumpled. "The governor's been saying that the peasants are not Calcuttans; they don't have housing or jobs in the city, and never will. He claims that they have created a massive instability. So he finally acted on it."

"Taking people against their will is kidnapping. It's like what Hitler is doing to the Jews of Europe—"

"These camps in Bengal are for feeding, not killing."

As Mr. Lewes leaned against the counter, looking sadly at me, I suppressed the urge to run my hand along his cheek, where the evening stubble I'd never seen before had grown. Instead, I asked, "Has the governor said whether our peasants will have to remain in these feeding camps?"

"My friend said the plan is for them to be freed when the rice harvesting is under way and they're nourished and strong enough to return home. It might be only a few months."

"You make it sound almost humane, but I can't bear it." Tears were starting at the corners of my eyes. "The peasants were torn away from here, and I'll never see them again. Everyone always leaves. Even you—"

As I wept, I saw the army lorry, but now it was loaded with all those who had vanished out of my life: my beloved family; sweet, laughing Bidushi, and brave Supriya. And curled up in a basket was the one I'd been stupid enough to give away: Kabita.

Suddenly, I felt arms around me: banyan branches, big and strong. "I left because I was confused—but I won't do it again." Mr. Lewes's voice came softly in my ear. "Kamala, I wasn't sure how you felt. I will not leave you again."

I could have pulled away as I'd done twice before. If I had said, *Sir, let me go*, he would have stepped back. But his fingers were stroking my tangled hair, sending shocks into my head and down my spine. I could inhale his essence mixed with tobacco and gin—except that no alcohol was on his breath this time. He was under the influence of nothing but his own emotion.

At Rose Villa, I always turned my head as such moments approached. But that was not what I did tonight. Tonight, as his mouth closed over mine, I kissed him back, opening my mouth so he could taste the neem and cardamom mixed with my longing. And with gentle fingers, I reached out to touch the warmth of his skin.

CHAPTER
35

TRAITOR: 1. One who betrays any person that trusts him, or any duty entrusted to him; a betrayer.

—*Oxford English Dictionary*, Vol. 11, 1933

I stretched awake, feeling the gentle rolling air from the ceiling fan play across my skin. The room was quieter than usual, with only birdsong coming through the window instead of the usual street noise. *Why is it so cool?* I wondered, pulling the cover up over myself. The sheet felt different, too: fine and soft. My eyes opened to reveal that I was not tucked in my own small bed, but in Mr. Lewes's spacious bedroom on the first floor.

With a rush, everything came back: how he had come home in the middle of the night; how I had cried; how we had kissed each other endlessly in the kitchen until we went together in his room. I remembered how in his room, lit only by the small lamp, he had unfastened my nightdress, and I stood before him in just my skin.

I had not expected this to happen. For so long in my life, this part of the human experience had been almost forgotten. *No,* I corrected myself. During my years at Rose Villa, I had never traveled to such a country of affection and sensation, all of it mixed up so I could not tell one from the other. I hadn't ever believed that sex could be more than a game of pretending or that a man would take time and care with his caresses. But having felt the climbing rush and the explosion, and the sweet comfort of lying together for hours, I finally understood.

The bathroom door opened and Mr. Lewes emerged, still tying his dressing gown. His smile began with his eyes and stretched all the way to his clean-shaven jaw. "You slept late today. Tut, tut."

"That was not my intention, sir." I could not help but beam back at him, because I would never again worry that Mr. Lewes would be upset over anything I did.

"Last night you called me Simon. It sounds so much sweeter to my ear." He came back to his grand bed, lifting the mosquito net to slide in beside me. I said his name tentatively, then said it again, laughing, as he rolled on top of me.

"Twenty-one steps," he said into my neck.

"What, sir—I mean Simon?"

"Twenty-one steps is the distance between my bedroom door across the drawing room and into the hall and up the stairs to your room. Several times over the last years, I have found myself standing upstairs. And then I counted how long I could bear to stand outside your closed door."

I pulled myself up on my elbows and looked at him in surprise. "I never knew you were upstairs. I always felt so safe!" If he had ever done it in my first few years in service, I would have shot out of the house the next morning and never come back.

"I only went up when you were outside of the house, and I was dreaming of you," Simon said. "I thought this kind of thing must never happen, because you were my employee, because I could never jeopardize things and make you run away. I told myself that what I loved about you was your intelligence, your keen sense of organization, your sensitivity to all who live in the world. Nothing else."

"Sir, that is—" I had been about to say, *that is the nicest thing anyone has ever said to me,* but was interrupted by a crisp knock at the door. It could only have been Shombhu with the bed tea.

"How does he know you're home?" I whispered.

"It must have been the suitcases I left by the door!" Simon whispered back. "We've been caught. I don't see any way around it."

Knowing that he was right, I suppressed my urge to dive under the covers. But what would Shombhu think of me? For five years, I'd lived in the house and conducted myself as properly as a school-teacher. And now, I'd thrown propriety to the wind.

"Saheb? Are you feeling fine?" Shombhu was desperately rattling the doorknob as if his locked-in employer was in danger. "Saheb, did you not request tea for half nine as usual?"

"I'll speak to him," I said. I'd already decided the next minutes were crucial, in terms of how the staff would react to the situation and treat me. Because of what I'd done, I might never recover their respect; but I could try. Without hesitation I called out in Bengali, "Thank you for coming so promptly, but please go back to the kitchen and bring a cup for me as well."

A stunned silence hung on the other side of the door, and then I heard Shombhu's feet moving swiftly back toward the kitchen.

"I will open the door for him." I slid down from the high bed and went to the divan to dress in my discarded nightgown.

"You are remarkable," Simon said.

"The way Shombhu reports my reaction to the others will determine how everyone will behave—" I broke off the explanation when I realized Simon's eyes were not on me but the white linen bed sheet flecked with a few rust-colored drops.

I had almost forgotten the small surgery Dr. DeCruz had done. He had sewn me up to be resold at a good price, without my consent. And the irony was I hadn't taken money for what I'd done—I never would, again.

"My God," Simon said in a low voice, "I didn't know. I didn't mean to—"

"Of course you meant to. I did as well." As I sat down on the bedside, I realized I was telling the truth.

During my girlhood reveries, my imaginary guide to the land of counterpane had always been a handsome, intelligent Indian man. Pankaj was the natural hero to take on such a role; but he had not wanted it. As I thought of the way Simon and I had been with each other over the last five years, I realized how blind I'd been. My desire to be the perfect nationalist had kept me from understanding the great connection between us. My old dreams of Pankaj were like a schoolgirl crush out of Angela Brazil: one-sided and immature. Whereas what I felt coming from the man in bed with me was so powerful that it was almost frightening. And this time, I would not run away.

The knock came again, and I opened the door to admit Shombhu, who had composed his face into normalcy and gave me his usual morning greeting.

"Where would you like the tray?" I called over my shoulder to Simon, and from the bed, he mutely pointed to a tea table by the window. Shombhu nearly tripped in his haste to get the tray to this strangely distant place. Behind him was Jatin, carrying a basket with a freshly ironed and folded sari and blouse that must have been just delivered by the dhobi. Jatin was grinning, but a sharp look from me made him drop his eyes.

"And what is your breakfast wish, sir?" Shombhu asked.

Simon paused and said, "Sliced fruit and two eggs poached with toast and tomatoes, please. What for you, Kamala?"

I asked for my usual Indian breakfast: a chapatti, some vegetables, and fruit. Then I turned to the man who had become my lover. "Would you like to eat on the veranda? The morning is quite beautiful."

"Yes," he said, looking at me. "Now it is."

"Sir, I— Your clothing for the day—" Shombhu shifted from foot to foot, and I realized that he must have always dressed Simon.

"I shall take care of the dressing by myself. From now on"—Simon's voice grew stronger—"I shall do this."

❀   ❀   ❀

OF COURSE I helped Simon. He had not dressed himself for quite a while, so he was clumsy at first. But after all was done, he rolled up his shirtsleeves when I went to bathe in his gloriously large tub. I found my guard slipping away with the slick lavender-scented soap on his hands. And then his shirt came off, and the rest of his clothes, and he was in the bath, too. It was the room farthest from the kitchen, I told myself; nobody would know anything except that I was taking a bath at the wrong time of day, and in the wrong room.

But then I stopped worrying about what anybody thought, because Simon was making love to me with only his hands and his mouth, and again the strange physical electricity built and exploded within me—although his mouth covered mine, so no one could hear me gasp.

"I love you," he said, as we broke apart to take deep breaths. "I love you, Kamala."

As he spoke, I realized that nobody had ever said those words to me. With my family, and later with Bidushi, the feeling of love was there; but so obvious it was never said aloud. But this was different, being with someone from the West, who made bold pronouncements. I knew what was in my heart, but it was still too hard to say.

We made it to the garden well after ten. Breakfast was brought out promptly along with the newspapers. As Simon read the *Statesman*, I searched *Ananda Bazar Patrika* for mention of the rice kitchen closings. There was nothing. When I looked at Simon, he shook his head.

"There can't be any coverage because the censorship is still powerful."

"I will always remember them," I said.

"Yes. I should have served them many more times; that is my only regret." He gave me a wistful smile. "It's an odd time to bring it up, but we need to talk about the lawn. I promised Mr. Sassoon that if he'd allow the kitchen, I'd leave the lawn better than before."

I glanced around at the pitted, trampled space where, for a half year, thousands had come for daily sustenance. It looked as bad as the Maidan. "I will speak to Promod about restoring the lawn so the landlord won't be upset. The air raid trench won't look so bad if we border the near side with plantings. You might like to have some more shrubs and flowers for arrangements."

"We might like it," Simon corrected gently. "Would you like it, Kamala?"

And with this short conversation, I knew the peasants would never come back. Part of me would always mourn their absence, yet I would celebrate the gift they had made in bringing Simon and me together.

❧   ❧   ❧

AFTER SIMON WENT off to Lord Sinha Road, I gave Promod careful instructions about the garden; I'd heard about a nursery just outside the city where farmers sold blankets of healthy grass that could be laid down to replace the old. I said I would go with him, because I wanted to consider all the flowers and shrubs myself.

Then I returned to the library, where I had been absent for much too long. A memorandum about improving efficiency of Howrah Station transportation lay on the desk. Simon must have forgotten to take it to work with him; but it didn't look like an emergency. This paperwork appeared as well intentioned as almost everything else he'd brought to the government's attention over the last year. I could have opened the desk to look for something political, but I realized that I didn't want to.

I couldn't spy on Simon anymore. He had changed so much

as he began seeing the abject failings of his government. When I watched him ladling phan and speaking warmly with the peasants, I sensed he'd undergone a personal transformation; and I had, too. I loved him, even though I was still too shocked by the change in my world to ever say it to him. And what would my freedom-fighting contacts think? I realized that I hadn't reported in more than six months to Bijoy Ganguly, the man Pankaj had supposedly wanted to become my contact. I'd been too busy with the rice kitchen for spying, and in those months, Simon had been concerned only with famine deaths, ambulances, and hospitals. I'd communicated this in a message I'd sent three months earlier to Bijoy. But now that the rice kitchen was finished, I would probably be expected to make political reports.

As I sorted through a small stack of books I'd left on the library table, this new worry supplanted my happiness. Simon and I could not possibly keep our liaison private. By afternoon, Jatin's cousin-brother who worked at the Calcutta Club could be talking about it, and so would Manik's cooking friends in ICS households throughout the neighborhood. Simon's good name would be ruined; and I could not allow myself to think of what could happen if my Indian friends found out. Our love affair was impossible—but how much I wanted him! The war between my heart and head felt almost as violent as what was happening in the outside world.

❧   ❧   ❧

I WAS TOO restless to stay inside; in early afternoon, I took a tram to North Calcutta, where I would hunt for a fine first edition of Michael Madhusudan-Dutt's poems to add to the collection. As I walked, I noticed that the absence of peasants made the established Calcutta beggars visible again. They seemed busy gathering up wooden boards and bowls and scraps of cloth: everything that the peasants had to leave behind. If I'd jumped up in the lorry with the peasants, I would be with them. I would not have slept with Simon, and I would not be facing this difficult decision about my loyalties.

As I browsed the various bookstalls, I listened to the chatter of the students around me; they were talking about war news, mathematics examinations, a Communist meeting that evening. After an hour, I could not concentrate on finding the book. I wanted to go into Albert Hall for a cup of coffee but decided against it, lest I run into Bijoy Ganguly, who might demand an intelligence report.

The Sens' house was just around the corner from the bookstalls. I'd been foolish to remain hurt about not receiving a wedding invitation: surely it had been some kind of postal error, and Mrs. Sen would be glad to hear from me about why I'd been absent. But first on the list of topics to discuss would be Supriya. Because of eavesdropping operators, I hadn't dared to make a telephone call to them about her. But I was in North Calcutta, so there was every reason to visit.

In the vestibule, the Sens' darwan, Ali, welcomed me cheerfully and said to go upstairs. I called out a greeting as I knocked. To my delight, the door was opened by Sonali.

"My goodness! So long." She pulled me to her in a tight embrace. She smelled different now, of sandalwood, and I saw the telltale red marking of sindoor parting her hair.

"All my best wishes for your marriage; I'm sorry I couldn't give them earlier," I said. "What luck I have to see you here today."

"I come quite often; we live a few miles away near the Nakhoda Mosque," Sonali answered with a smile.

"Yes, in these modern marriages, the ladies travel freely as they like!"

A cheerful masculine voice came from the parlor; in an instant I recognized it as Pankaj's. Despite my detached thoughts about him earlier in the day, I felt warm. This chance meeting, coming so soon after my union with Simon, would tell me whether I truly had grown out of the crush.

"Do come in," Sonali said, waving me ahead of her. "Pankaj-da is visiting. He had some news of Supriya. Ma is in the kitchen; I'll tell her to pour another cup of tea for you."

Pankaj was sitting on the low bed covered with red cushions; he looked much thinner and grayer than before. It even seemed that on the right hand he held outstretched in greeting, the ruby ring was looser. So far, I felt badly for what prison had done to him but nothing more.

"My goodness, is it really Kamala? You have been keeping extremely well."

"Hello, Pankaj-bhai." I was dressed simply, but I knew from Simon's mirror that my skin had an extraordinary glow, and my eyes were clear and sparkling. "I'm so glad that you are out of prison. I must apologize for having caused trouble for you."

He smiled easily. "All in the past; it's better not to speak of it at all. We are only here chatting about Sonali's wedding. I don't think I saw you there?"

I shook my head, not sure how to proceed. And then Mrs. Sen came out of the kitchen, but she was not bringing tea, just facing me with her thick arms folded across the middle.

"Hello, Mashima," I said, feeling uncertain.

Mrs. Sen's color rose as she looked steadily at me. "I should have liked to invite you, but my husband would not allow it because of Supriya's letter!"

"Oh?" Mashima always said what she meant, but this time she was confusing me. "Did Supriya write to you from Singapore? I can't imagine how, with the censors—"

"I am talking about the letter she left before going off on that mission! She wrote that she'd received your blessings, and we should keep you apprised of her progress. My question is, why? Why would someone I treated like a daughter send my firstborn on such a deadly journey?"

My hands flew to my face as I stuttered, "I d-didn't send her. I warned her to think carefully, because of the danger—"

Mrs. Sen roared, "Then you should have run quickly to warn us so she could have been stopped!"

"Ma, please!" Sonali said. "Everyone in the locality can hear you. And nobody can stop Supriya when she wants something—you know that."

Mrs. Sen shook a finger at me and said, "This year, we lost two daughters: one to marriage, and the other to Netaji! Now all we have is our little boy, who will likely give his life for India if the situation continues to be so deplorable!" She shot a pained look toward her son, Nishan, who didn't look up from the sailboat he was building in the room's corner.

"Stop, Ma!" Sonali interjected. "And, Kamala, I apologize. We are very emotional, all of us."

"The important thing is that your sister is doing well," Pankaj said firmly. "As I told everyone earlier, I heard Supriya's voice on a radio broadcast. She is full of joy about the mission and will make us all proud."

"So you've heard her speak!" I said, not surprised that Pankaj possessed one of the radio receivers that Japanese spies had distributed within India. Mr. Weatherington would have been wild to know this.

Pankaj got up from the bed and went to touch Mrs. Sen's feet. When he came up, he said, "Mashima, if you blame anyone it should be me; I was the one who told her the route to get out of India. And I helped her with provisions and contacts along the way."

Mrs. Sen blinked and then said, "Is it true?"

Pankaj nodded, and from his face I could tell he expected to be verbally battered as I just had been. But that did not happen. Mrs. Sen gave him a half smile and said, "If you told her the way to go, this meant you saved her life."

Pankaj could do no ill, it seemed, but I could. Blood rushed to my face, and I did not know what to say.

"Kamala, I wish I could ask you to stay for tea, but my husband will be coming up to join—and he is not ready to forgive. Supriya's letter upset him very much." Mrs. Sen was looking toward the door.

"Don't worry! I will talk sense to them!" Sonali whispered as I gathered my bag to leave.

"I'm going as well. I shall walk with you to the tram." Pankaj stood up, a lean shadow of his former self, and after touching Mrs. Sen's feet again, followed me out.

"That was too difficult!" I said as we emerged from the building. "I now understand why I wasn't invited to the wedding."

"I missed you there. And I've also missed your reports that Bijoy would forward to me." Pankaj was keeping a quick stride, as if we were just like anyone else walking toward the tram station.

Trying to push down my nervousness, I said, "You should have let me know your concerns through a letter or word of mouth. I've not sent new reports in some time because I've been running a rice kitchen."

"So I've heard. But L is still living on the premises and working for the ICS, isn't he?"

"Yes," I said, realizing that now was the right time for me to explain the change in situation. "He's stopped searching for freedom fighters. He's only interested in the famine. If you knew all the things he'd done—getting free rice for the peasants, improving ambulance transportation—you would be amazed."

"You sound as if you're expecting applause." Pankaj looked at me skeptically.

"He's been through such a change," I said. And as the words came out, I was back in the garden with Simon, remembering the pleasure of working together, and then the passion that rose so unexpectedly and could not be put down. "I spied on him before, yes. There once was every reason in the world to hate him. But it's different now."

"Just because our enemy says he pities the starving poor doesn't mean he's a new man!" Pankaj sighed. "He's British, isn't he? What is this nonsense you're talking?"

I could not bear to reveal what had happened; but for Pankaj to hear the story elsewhere would be worse. Slowly, I said, "Another thing has happened to him. He's fallen in love."

At this, Pankaj exhaled loudly and gave a merry laugh. "Perhaps this explains the behavior change! So he finally met a memsaheb, eh? Is she a pretty young member of the fishing fleet?"

"Neither. She isn't English." I swallowed down my fear and said, "Actually, it's me."

"You?" Pankaj stopped short, and behind the gold-rimmed spectacles, his eyes widened. After a pause he said, "That must be hard. But be strong. I suppose it's for the best."

"What do you mean?" I was utterly confused by his reaction, but Pankaj had started walking quickly again, with almost a bounce in his gait.

"If he falls in love, he may want an affair with you . . . or even marriage." Pankaj's voice was calculating. "The latter would be the better situation, of course. As his wife, you will learn so many more secrets. He will take you to restaurants and clubs where you will gain information from his friends. Kamala, my hat is off to you. Now you can delve deeper into the Indian Political Service than anyone."

"But I just said he isn't hunting freedom fighters! I can't report on him any longer."

"Don't tell me you're in love, too?" Pankaj shot a bemused look at me. "Ah. What a quisling!"

Quisling was the surname of the Norwegian administrator who had helped the Nazis easily conquer his country; since 1940, it was about the worst insult one could use. Shakily, I said, "I will never reveal anything about the movement—and you have no right to call me that ugly name."

"If you marry him out of our own desire, it's only because you're immoral." His expression was tight. "You could have been so much more of a woman, someone like—"

"Supriya!" I finished angrily. "Yes, you admire her for following your directions to go overseas. But you didn't want me to do things like that; you didn't even want me to participate in street protests!"

"You were not needed there; and you're not needed now." Pankaj's tone was frigid. "Honestly, I don't think I can bear receiving another feverish note from you or tolerate the sight of you making eyes at me."

"You think that I make eyes at you?" I repeated, feeling a slow burn start inside. Had I misread the times he had flirted with me, had complimented me, had gazed into my face? No, I had read him correctly then. The woman's intuition that I'd honed at Rose Villa told me this.

Narrowing my eyes as I looked at him, I said, "You did care about me, Pankaj. You are only speaking rudely because you've been usurped. But it's been years. Ten years of waiting, for naught."

Pankaj stopped walking. He turned away from me for a minute. When he faced me once more, his expression was grave. "Ten years?"

"Yes; first we wrote letters to each other, and then you met me first when I was fifteen! But I was poor and invisible to you then, and after that you became so self-involved that your eyesight didn't get any better."

Pankaj was quiet for almost a whole minute, then spoke. "You say ten years—I suppose it could be true that you were somehow in league with Bidushi. There is something familiar about you."

I waited for him to mention Lockwood, but he just shook his head and said, "You know that it could never be; my mother wouldn't accept it."

"What does she think about me?" I challenged, even though I knew the answer could be devastating.

"She didn't think it right that you came to our home uninvited, and she knows that a woman sent a letter that got me in trouble at prison—and guessed it was you. She doesn't like that you have no known relatives in the city." He added, "When I marry, my bride will be approved by her, because we will live following my mother's directions as long as she lives."

"You said you would never wed." I remembered how I'd wanted to change his mind.

Pankaj shrugged. "I was grieving for a very long time. But I realize that everyone around me is marrying. I don't want to become a middle-aged man left by myself."

I was irritated by his callousness, as well as my own stupidity at having wasted so much time longing for a pen-and-ink caricature of manhood. Feigning warmth, I said, "Pankaj-bhai, I know just who you should marry! Your mother might even approve."

"And who is that?" He looked at me expectantly.

"India!" I flung my arms as wide as the world around us. "She's not available yet, but any day her parents will set her free."

"Very funny, Kamala!" He grimaced. "But really, you mustn't go with Lewes. It would be a tragedy."

I realized with a start that Pankaj was so upset that he'd forgotten and said the name aloud instead of the code word L—and that he wasn't the kind of hero I'd once believed him to be. I gave him a cold look and said, "The tragedy would lie in continuing any associations with you. Good-bye, Pankaj."

I saw a tram pulling into the stop and jumped aboard without checking its destination. I didn't care that I had to switch at the next stop, because Pankaj's shocked expression as I told him off was worth it. How could I have admired him, the man too weak to make a choice for himself? And even though I'd told him outright that we'd met earlier, he still couldn't admit when—perhaps because the thought of a servant coming so close to his Brahmin self was too unnerving.

Pankaj had never been in love with me, nor I with him. Instead, we'd been a relationship of words—written and spoken, but naught else. Love, on the other hand, was a language that operated without words. No dictionary could explain it any better than the heart.

CHAPTER
36

RUMOUR: . . . *3. A statement or report circulating in a community, of the truth of which there is no clear evidence.*

—*Oxford English Dictionary,* Vol. 8, 1933

It was too quiet at home. Jatin was not at the door to help with my bags; Shombhu was not singing as he set the table for dinner. Uneasily, I walked up the stairs, hoping nothing had gone wrong.

As I bent to step out of my chappals, I felt a hand slide gently over the strip of skin between my sari and blouse. A lingering caress, that reminded me of the night before.

"Simon!" I said, turning around with surprise. "You're home so early. And where are the servants? It doesn't smell like anything's cooking for dinner."

"I gave everyone leave. I thought I would take you to one of my favorite restaurants. They serve magnificent Chinese food on Park Street."

I shook my head; as much as I didn't want Pankaj's words to have impacted me, they had. "I'm a little tired."

"I'll draw the bath," he said, striding off toward his chambers.

"Simon, really, you mustn't—" I saw the bed. It had been turned down properly, but rose petals were scattered across the coverlet and pillows.

"What's wrong?" Simon inquired genially. "Isn't that the Indian tradition for lovers?"

I was stricken with embarrassment. "Who did this?"

"Shombhu or Jatin, I suppose. Manik contented himself with using the last of the jaggery to bake us a cake."

"Oh, no!" I sank onto the chaise and put my face in my hands.

"Sorry?"

Everyone would know. I wouldn't be Miss Mukherjee, the library clerk, but Simon Lewes's mistress. "Sending the staff away early would have been enough to bring gossip! The fact that they've decorated the bed is even worse."

"I think they're happy, Kamala. Happy for both of us, hoping this is a start of a new way of living." Simon crouched in front of me and took my hands in his. "Like I am. But from the way you're talking, I'm not sure what you think."

Pankaj had sad it would be a tragedy. And despite my defensive protestations, the sick feeling in my stomach told me he might actually be right. Stiffly, I said, "We were both very naïve. You can't imagine what will happen when it gets out that you're with me; you won't be received socially, and your career will crash."

"Both things have already happened!" Simon said, smiling. "Do I look frightened? Come, your bath is full. I won't disturb you. I'll just make tea."

"Tea?" I almost jumped out of my skin. "You can't know how!"

"I went to Cambridge. There I learned how to turn on a hob."

I lay alone in his bathroom, in soft light, with the window open to the koel birds. From time to time, they chirped; I listened for their warning calls, but they did not come. They seemed to say, *Life is good; this man loves you.*

Afterward, I wrapped myself in his dressing gown. The tea was waiting on the second nightstand that I remembered searching years before; the one with nothing inside it. But now I saw a small pile of my lingerie, my hairbrush and the novel I'd been re-reading upstairs, *Tess of the d'Urbervilles*.

"I brought it down for you, but I don't recommend it," Simon said. "I prefer novels with happy endings."

"I gather that's a warning." I took a sip of the tea; it had a strange flavor, but it was good. "What kind of tea is this?"

"It's not proper Indian tea. There's a splash of rum in it. We English make it when someone's tired. And Kamala, just because there are rose petals on this bed, it doesn't mean we have to. But . . ."

And now I noticed something lying next to my book that had not been there before: a French letter still in its paper covering. The sight of it caused me to catch my breath. Just like that, I was fifteen again and facing a customer.

His eyes went to the nightstand. "It's a precaution that I should explain. I don't think you noticed I used one last night—"

"No," I said, looking straight at him. "I don't want to touch that thing; I don't want it near me."

Simon spoke hesitantly. "It's about planning . . . planning for when children are conceived—"

"No. Just come to me." I was certain that I could not fall pregnant, and I knew his health was good. More than anything, I did not want what happened between us to have any relation to my past.

Simon looked at me, and his expression seemed to lighten. He said, "As you wish."

That night I made love straight from my heart, gripping him, turning him, kissing him in places nice women could not know about. I did what I could to bring him to joyful release, and I did not hide my pleasure when it came to me. Afterward, it felt so quiet, lying next to each other with sweat cooling our bodies and the koel birds calling to each other in the garden below.

I could have moved to pull down the mosquito netting, since dusk had passed, but I did not. I wanted to stop the clock in the hallway from chiming another hour. I always wanted to be in this bed, with this man. I sighed, and he rolled onto his side in order to face me.

"What is it, darling?"

"Not wanting time to pass on," I confessed. "Staying exactly here with you, in this moment."

He stretched out a hand to touch my hair. "It can stay like this forever, if you'll have me."

"But I do have you. Right here." I ran my hand over his hip.

"That's not what I mean. Kamala, I want to marry you."

I was hot and cold, all at once. This was why he had given in so easily about the French letter; he assumed we would become husband and wife.

"You needn't be dramatic," I said, because this proposal had caught me off guard, and I wasn't sure what to do. "It's gone on for centuries, these liaisons between English men and Indian women. You've read enough books in your library to know that it rarely ends well."

"You're wrong about that!" Simon chuckled. "Job Charnock, the founder of Calcutta, married an Indian widow. They brought up five children. Lord Ochterlony had an Indian wife and after she died, another. While I cannot make you first lady of Calcutta, you are already a very important one. You'll fit in perfectly as my wife, Kamala. If only you'll have me."

Simon thought I was a high-born Brahmin with an elite education. I had an accent like his own and could decorate a house, drink alcohol, and discuss books. But I was not anything close to a lady. If he knew, he would not think me marriage material. I told him, "Your examples aren't realistic. The fact that I lived under your roof for so long, working for you, will make society regard me as your sleeping dictionary."

"What rot! I don't need another dictionary in the library, or anywhere else." Simon took my face in his hands. "You are the most incredible woman I've ever known, in any country. But you must tell me the truth. I don't want to trap you if marriage is something you don't want. Perhaps you truly abhor my English soul."

In the week he'd been away, I had castigated myself for not having allowed his kiss. Now I'd had his kisses and a great deal more. It was up to me to decide whether seizing happiness was worth the risk.

"Kamala," he said with a catch in his voice. "Answer me. Please."

Decisions. I had taken the jungle path instead of the main road; it had saved my life. I had signaled to many boats, and finally found one that took me. I had gone with a falsely smiling girl into a terrible house, but finally escaped. I knew that accepting Simon's proposal would be as twisted as all my other life passages, leading to an outcome I couldn't assume would be permanent or even happy.

But how I wanted it—wanted him. I paused to take a deep breath, because I knew that if I used the word that was so frightening to me, it could never be retracted. Softly, I said, "No. I don't abhor your soul, because souls don't have caste, color, or creed. I want to marry you. I love you so very much. So much that it—"

Hurts, I would have finished, but he had covered me with his body, and I could no longer speak.

❧   ❧   ❧

IN THE LIBRARY, I found a worn book about event planning for colonials in 1800s India. Written long before automobiles and refrigeration, it made our era seem magnificently convenient. But organizing a wedding in 1944 wasn't a simple matter. Because of the war, most Calcutta churches were tightly scheduled with funerals and memorial services. Military weddings were prioritized first. Simon was already a member of Saint Paul's Cathedral. This should have been enough to secure a date, but it wasn't.

I suggested that we marry in a court, but Simon was against it.

"It wouldn't be fitting, not when I'm a member of Saint Paul's. I'll keep trying to find a slot there and you can look into a Hindu temple. There are even more of those around."

But temples were out of the question for the likes of us. And it seemed that Simon was becoming an outcast within the British establishment. As we were discussing it over drinks one night in the garden, he finally addressed the trouble.

"It's the rumor mill. Some wags are saying that I made you pregnant. In any case, our living arrangement has become a liability, despite the fact that we have a reverend on the premises. I suppose the groundwork that Weatherington laid is playing a part."

"What groundwork?" I asked, feeling a sense of dread.

"He sent me a memorandum shortly after he met you at the party—all kinds of nonsense about it being a risk to keep you as an employee."

"Why? What kind of nonsense?"

"I don't remember the exact words because I threw the letter away. He wrote something about my head being turned by beauty and taking security risks. He said that a Brahmin's daughter wouldn't be allowed to work for an Englishman." He looked at me. "But, of course, your father's deceased. You have to work."

"Yes," I answered, relieved that Weatherington hadn't come up with anything more concrete—like my relationship with Pankaj Bandhopadhyay.

"The churchwoman was asking for documentation of your Christian conversion, your parentage, all sorts of nonsense."

"I see." I put down my glass, thinking. "I'll never be able to find that for her. I've got an idea, though, of someone who might marry us without causing so much of a fuss. I'm surprised we didn't think of him before."

"Reverend McRae?" Simon asked slowly. "It would be wonderful to have him involved. But as you know, I'm not Church of Scotland—"

"Let's just ask him. He's so happy about our engagement."

Later that evening, when Simon and I brought it up over dinner, the reverend laughingly accepted. He said that he had been sitting on his hands waiting for us to ask him, and he did not care a whit what our faiths were. Without even needing to see the church's calendar, he offered us a date a few days hence.

"I can hardly believe this tremendous problem has been solved," Simon said the next morning, as I tied his cravat for him. "Now, of course, comes the reception planning. Tell me, Kamala, how much time will your relatives need in order to organize a trip here for the event?"

I shook my head at him. "You know that my family is deceased. I told you that before."

"You went to see people last year in Midnapore, remember? I want to meet them." His eyes looked at me hopefully; I glanced away, ruing his sharp memory, while I concocted something that I hoped would finish his interest in my family background once and for all.

"After I lost my parents and siblings, my paternal uncle could not afford to support me. This meant that I had to leave school before completing examinations, and I came into the workforce. During the height of the famine, as you recall, I visited them. They were well, but they did not invite me in. That's why one of the reasons that I was sad for a while."

"They didn't let you into the home?" Simon's voice was deadly quiet. "That's unconscionable. Of course you won't invite them. But what about Mr. Sen and his family? You always seem happy after returning from their place."

I shook my head, thinking about how the Sens wouldn't have me for meals anymore because of Mr. Sen's anger at my role in Supriya's defection. "I think I'd prefer a private ceremony. After all, your family won't be present, either."

He shrugged. "Only because there's no sea travel between here and England."

"I can just imagine what they will think of your marrying an Indian!" I knew what they'd do: go into mourning or disown him. Perhaps both.

"Oh, but they're not marrying you. I am." Simon picked up my left hand and kissed it.

He didn't sound especially nervous about the repercussions of our marriage, but I was. Indians would call me a traitor for sleeping with an Englishman. They'd say my political beliefs had all been for nothing. And then they might ask one another: *Who is Kamala Mukherjee? She hasn't attended enough rallies and protests or done anything. Who are her people?*

Once again, I'd be cast out of a community. But this time, I would still have a home, with a man I prayed would never know my truth.

CHAPTER
37

Oh, give me land, lots of land under starry skies above,
don't fence me in.

—Cole Porter, "Don't Fence Me In," 1934

At midday on December 1, I walked down the aisle at Saint Andrew's Kirk feeling like a horse wearing blinders. It was just the veil, I told myself: a tiny piece of netting that made everything on the outside unclear. Along with the veil, I wore another strange garment lent by a lady the reverend knew: a long ivory wedding dress, its bodice embroidered so heavily that it was impossible to see how my chest was rising and falling with anxiety.

Besides the invisible organist playing in the croft above, there were just ten others in attendance: Reverend McRae, Mr. Lewes's old friend Mr. Pal and his wife, four of Mr. Lewes's other friends and Manik, Shombhu, and Jatin. Although it was a small group of witnesses, I feared I'd collapse or, at the very least, make a mistake in the choreographed ceremony or somehow give away my fears about the marriage itself.

"In these difficult times," the reverend said, "the greatest hope for the world is the bonding of people who are unafraid to love each other, regardless of culture, creed, or origin . . ."

Bonding: this word cut at me like a knife. I could not tell Simon about Kharagpur or Lockwood or Johlpur. I felt close to him, but would I ever really be, with so many unread chapters in my past?

Reverend McRae's voice wove back into my consciousness: he had already segued into the vows. I heard the words *love, honor, and obey until death do you part*. Whose turn was it to respond? Simon, so crisp and dignified in a gray morning suit, was looking at me with concern. I realized it was my turn. I'd gone over the vows with both of them before, and I'd seen plenty of English marriages in the cinema. I knew my lines.

"I will." And as I spoke, I privately vowed that this would be my final life chapter. Lewes would be the last name I'd carry; that despite my fears, I would never run. And so it was done. In less than an hour, I completed the transformation from the fictional Kamala Mukherjee into the genuine Mrs. Simon Alston Lewes.

Once it had happened, I immediately felt better. I was a cheerful, relaxed bride serving tea and cake in the Kirk's reception hall; and then I changed into a smart blue silk sari, and the two of us departed in a borrowed Morris. Shombhu, Jatin, and Manik threw handfuls of jasmine petals, not rice, because of the rationing.

The desk clerk at the Great Eastern Hotel called me Mrs. Lewes when Simon and I checked in; and then we were alone, in a vast suite where the bed was decorated not just with rose petals but also gold and silver leaf. Simon had arranged for a gramophone to be there, and as we undressed, it was to the romantic strains of Lena Horne. Briefly, I recalled my old dream of a wedding night with Pankaj; but now I couldn't imagine it.

"Maybe this will be the time," Simon said as we lay down to-gether. "Wouldn't that be magic?"

I didn't answer, because I felt a pang of guilt that Simon's dream would always remain just that. Clearly, my passionate husband was hoping for a child, because he'd already spoken about reorganizing our flat and hiring a bilingual ayah. I couldn't tell him that I'd lost my fertility in a terrible childbirth and that I would never want another child; the pain of giving up Kabita still weighed heavily on me. All that Simon would learn, one day, is that we couldn't conceive. He would likely be devastated; and I would comfort him.

Tonight, though, I put those thoughts away. I kissed Simon gently on his neck, then across his chest and arms. I asked him to lie down, and then I took control. Tonight I wanted to celebrate being a wife. Watching Simon's eyes widen at the sight of me moving sensuously over him, I knew that he was enthralled; and that I should not hesitate to make love the way I wanted. For me, sex would never again be linked with money or force; it would only be for pleasure and love.

❧   ❧   ❧

THERE WAS NO chance for a long honeymoon because of the war, although we did spend a week in Bombay, where we were able to hire a touring car that we drove by ourselves into the Panchgani Hills, Simon teaching me to shift and steer until I was almost as skilled as he. Now that we wore the respectable cloaks of the married, we were slowly meeting people who were tolerant of women drivers as well as mixed unions: a population that included some Anglo-Indians, a few ICS couples and Reverend McRae's friends, who seemed to span all faiths and nationalities. We dined in Park Street restaurants and at the Calcutta Club, which had been founded by Indians and British together. On the surface, Mrs. Simon Lewes was charming, the opposite of a stereotyped shy Indian maiden.

But was Mrs. Lewes happy? With her husband, certainly. But everything else was unsettled. I knew that my opinions about the Indian National Army and the path of the war were too dangerous to be expressed. And I still yearned to know what had become of Hafeeza and Kabita, although I should have simply closed those poignant chapters in my life book. How far I'd run from my past, but now I longed to have just a page—a paragraph—even three words saying, *We are well*.

Reverend McRae offered to leave the flat, now that we were married and might like more privacy. Simon and I both protested, knowing that there was little suitable housing available and not wanting to cast out a man who'd become like a father. As a compromise, the reverend shifted to my old bedroom upstairs, insisting the large spare room where he'd been would be a safe, close-by place for our first child. Simon happily accepted this change, but I found the reverend's acknowledgment of our need for evening solitude embarrassing.

I could understand why my having a baby would seem logical to the reverend, since my new role of ICS wife was hardly taxing. Because I was Indian, not English, I had many fewer social invitations and expectations than the English wives of Simon's colleagues. Instead, I managed the household as always and looked for other things to do, like volunteering for Reverend McRae's orphanage. Speaking Bengali with the children and teaching them their letters was only a substitute for my doing the same with Kabita, but it passed the months.

※   ※   ※

SPRING OF 1945 brought a good rice harvest, which meant the refugees were released from their camps and went back to their villages, for the most part. And then, it was monsoon, supposedly the most romantic time of the year; but this time, marked by the war's fiercest battles in the Asian theater. The Japanese bombed Assam and the INA fighters crossed over, but the Indian Army and the Americans pushed back hard. Simon did not sleep through many nights but spent time in the library, pacing as he listened to faraway reports on the wireless.

One morning in May, Kantu did not bring the newspapers, which signaled to me he was too busy at the newsstand to come. Instead of going straight down, I switched on All India Radio and heard the news that Germany was surrendering. I found myself crying with relief at the liberation of the concentration camps, and the end of killing everywhere.

"Asia's almost done, too," Simon said to Reverend McRae that evening as we all enjoyed a champagne toast. "The Japanese are retreating in Burma. Everything's collapsing like a house of cards."

I wondered whether Supriya was in Burma or Singapore or yet another place. I worried for her safety because the Allies were taking every INA fighter they could catch as a prisoner of war. Would she do something drastic like shoot herself rather than be taken prisoner? I knelt before my Lakshmi statue, now set up in the parlor, praying that she would know that there was honor in surrender; that it would ultimately bring her back to India to continue the freedom struggle.

On August 6, the Americans dropped their secret atomic bombs on the Japanese city of Hiroshima, and three days later, Nagasaki. We heard about the mushroom clouds, the unbearable heat, the unknown thousands presumed dead. There were no photographs yet of the destruction, but I created these images for myself.

"How could they bomb like that?" I said to Simon as we lay in bed the night of August tenth. "This wasn't targeted bombing of soldiers, it was the mass murder of innocents."

"If there were a land war, double the people would have died," Simon said, taking me into his arms. "I hate war, too, Kamala, but this is the only way it could end."

Emperor Hirohito addressed the population of Japan on August 15, telling them he had ordered his government to surrender. Three days later, Netaji bade good-bye to his Indian National Army and escaped to Saigon aboard a Japanese military airplane bound for Tokyo. The plane stopped overnight in Taiwan to refuel and add more passengers. But this load of people and luggage was too much. As the airplane struggled to rise, it crashed and its most famous passenger was caught up in the fireball. Netaji died from the burns in hospital, according to the surviving INA officer who had been his companion for the flight.

I wasn't sure whether to believe it. Some were saying this was a lie told to help wrap up the war; that Netaji had safely reached another Asian country and was gathering strength to come back to India. Others suggested that the Russians had taken him prisoner for his role opposing the Allies during World War II. What an irony that would be, given Netaji's strong relations with Indian Communists before the war. Each time a new rumor came out, I drilled Simon.

"You're correct that there are some inconsistencies in the report of the plane crash; but when you have Netaji's friend confirming his death, what more is needed?" Simon grumbled one Sunday morning at breakfast. "Naturally, our government is accused of lying about the matter. If you add in the unrest over the INA veterans, the situation becomes untenable. Did you know that more than forty Europeans were murdered across India in the last fortnight?"

"I'd heard bits and pieces, but not that number." I toyed with my fork, not wanting him to sense how worried this made me about his own safety—and how sick I felt at the turn of the freedom movement. "How can it be? Gandhiji and Jawaharlal Nehru have never sanctioned physical aggression."

"It's true, but they can't control violent types. I heard through a police source that some bastards knocked down Reverend McRae near the orphanage where he volunteers. If the orphans hadn't rushed in to surround him, he could have been killed."

A new tremor ran through me. I'd not been at the orphanage in the last week, so I hadn't known. "But that's awful! He never said a word about it to us!"

"He wants freedom for India, so I imagine he doesn't want to publicize anything that would work against it." Simon sighed. "This mad violence has turned into retaliation against any European—when the only ones they should really be angry with are me and my colleagues."

"Be quiet. I don't want you hurt, either." I paused, thinking of how to explain the mixed feelings I struggled with. "I believe it's true that the INA veterans aren't getting fair treatment after what they've been through."

"Your opinion," Simon said shortly. "Mine's different."

"Actually, I'm thinking about going to hear some of them speak at Deshapriya Park next week."

Simon drew his brows together in concern. "That may not be a sound idea, Kamala. The police only issued a permit for the event because they worried if they didn't, there would be terrible unrest in the city. But the event could turn to a riot—you know what the climate's like."

"The particular speakers are not of the inflammatory sort; it will be led by Mr. Nehru, as well as Netaji's older brother, Sarat Bose, and some INA veterans," I said, hoping to smooth the furrow that remained between Simon's eyes. "I will be in the ladies' section, of course. Please, Simon. I must be there."

"Then you should go." Simon's voice sounded flat. "I won't hold you back from what you believe in like some medieval husband, although I could send someone to be nearby to help you if something goes wrong. But I think for me—a white man—to be present would just add a spark to tinder."

"Please don't have anyone watch me," I said, remembering Mr. Pal's spying. "That will make it all the worse! Like I said, I'll keep to myself in the ladies' section."

"Do be careful." Simon sounded wistful. "You know that you can't be replaced."

"I appreciate your devotion," I said, stretching my hand out to hold his. "I love you so much, Simon. And I will definitely take care."

CHAPTER 38

Only a diamond-cutter knows a diamond.

Bengali proverb

The crowds in Deshapriya Park were huge, with almost as many women as men in the audience. I found a good place inside the women's section. There, as chatter flew from one to another, I learned something very exciting: that one of the INA veterans speaking would be a Bengali female, Captain Supriya Sen.

So Supriya had survived and made it home. I was elated that my friend was back and hoped her parents could forgive me. Maybe with war over, life for us could be like the halcyon days before—or even better, with freedom so close at hand.

My optimistic thoughts only increased as the program began. It certainly was thrilling to hear Jawaharlal Nehru and Sarat Chandra Bose speak, knowing that once again, I was present in the middle of history being made, in India's most important city. When my old friend finally took the stage, dressed hat to trousers in her old INA uniform, the crowd went wild. Women around me were screaming and throwing flowers. I thought of saying, *I knew her when she was just a college girl!*, but the women's section was full of those who knew her; from Loreto College, from the temple, from the bookbindery. She was known, and she was loved.

"People have been saying that what we did was hard." Supriya's clear voice, amplified by a megaphone, finally silenced the crowd. "But it was not. Each day we spent training under the hot Singapore sun and then trekking into Burma was a beautiful one for us. We worked together, every woman bearing the same load as a man. Muslims and Hindus broke bread together. We spoke the same language, and because of this, we became a family. We did not fight each other, because there was only one battle that mattered: for India's freedom."

My eyes became moist as Supriya, standing straight and proud, declared that even though the INA had not freed India as planned, the support for them shown by almost every Indian, including those working for the police and government, proved the British had lost their hold.

"The liberated India Netaji promised us is here; our minds are free!" Supriya's joyful words were followed by thunderous applause. Ironically, Pankaj Bandopadhyay escorted her offstage, just as he'd done for Netaji all those years before. Then he returned and put the megaphone to his lips.

"Our sister Supriya is as brave as Durga and Kali put together," he shouted to the audience. "I would have gone myself were it not for my commitment to keeping so many of you out of jail. During this time, the INA entrusted me with a radio receiver that allowed me to spread her broadcasts from Singapore and then Rangoon. I can tell you with all certainty that she has been only too modest about her accomplishments . . ."

It had been almost a year since we'd had our upsetting good-bye. I watched Pankaj, feeling strangely unemotional. I would have thought I'd tremble to see him again—either with anger or with awakened heartbreak. But the famous lawyer-activist didn't seem as attractive as I recalled, and his speech wasn't as compelling as Supriya's. I didn't like the lecturing tone when he told everyone to remember how well the INA soldiers cooperated, and that this should be used as a strategy for further freedom fighting. Supriya had already shared the same message, albeit more powerfully. Furthermore, Pankaj's stress on continued Hindu-Muslim unity didn't suit the crowd. Some Hindus spat, and a rumbling grew in the Muslim League section. I knew from talking with Simon, and reading the papers, that Muslims wanted to have their own country when independence was granted. I wasn't happy about this, because I wanted one India with everyone included, but it was clear that they didn't share my hope—and with Lord Mountbatten having close Muslim advisers, it seemed likely their view would be respected.

After the speeches were done, I flowed out to the street with thousands of others. I thought about how I'd been so sure that I loved Pankaj. As I'd thought before, it was more like a schoolgirl fascination with a flamboyant actor. And while I'd spent a lot of time at the Minerva and the Metro cinemas during my spying days, I had come around to feeling that I liked books better than films. Simon was safe and solid: a long novel that I was in no hurry to finish.

Open cars holding freedom fighters and the INA veterans were slowly passing; I saw Supriya, but she was looking the other way, stretching out her hands so people could touch them. I wanted to speak to her, but I imagined it was unlikely to happen in such a crush. Then, all of a sudden, Sonali Sen Israni was at my elbow with her husband, Arvind.

"Didi!" she said, tucking my arm into hers. "I'm so glad to find you. You must come to the party at my parents' house."

"I'm not sure it's a good idea. Your father—"

"Baba isn't angry anymore. He is so proud of Supriya that he tells everyone that he sent her off with his blessings! Please forgive him for being so cross with you! Won't you please come back with me?"

"Yes, we can toast to your marriage as well. I'm very happy about it," Arvind said, with a grin that made his young face look even more boyish.

"You know?" I asked, not understanding his reaction.

"Yes, Pankaj told me some time ago. He hadn't known that your husband did so much to shake up the viceroy and government about the famine. Mr. Lewes cared so much that he even sent a very long letter that was published in the *Guardian*."

"The Manchester *Guardian*?" I stopped dead, causing some people behind us to bump into me.

"Yes, apparently his letter was quoted at a Parliament hearing in which some Labor politicians argued that Britain hadn't effectively governed India." Arvind gave me a pilot's thumbs-up. "Congratulations, Kamala. You married your own freedom fighter!"

"All you ever spoke about were his books!" Sonali added with a laugh. "You kept quite a secret about his character, didn't you?"

As I clasped her hand, I thought about whether Simon really had changed. Could this act, so quietly performed, exonerate his past doings with the Indian Political Service? I recalled how he'd confessed that he'd been passed over for a promotion. Perhaps his sending the letter was why. I was touched that he had not boasted to me about the letter. Maybe my husband was like a jasmine flower: tightly closed all day, but blossoming at night.

❧   ❧   ❧

SEN BOOKBINDING OVERFLOWED with well-wishers, and their table groaned with sweets, luchis, and so many curries. It was almost a prewar spread; I could only imagine that many friends had pooled resources for Mrs. Sen to offer such a feast. I was anxious, though, that the lady might not want me to take anything, because she might still be angry at me for not warning her about Supriya's defection.

Supriya was laughing and chattering with a circle of admirers when I came in; but she rushed over to me and said, "If it wasn't for this woman, I would never have served."

Her words warmed me, but I shook my head. "That's not at all true!"

"Oh, but it is! Nobody in my family can keep their mouth closed; I could not keep a secret about going, so I told it to Kamala. If she had told my family, they would have shouted about it from the rooftops, and I would have been arrested at Howrah."

Pankaj always said that he would not have asked Supriya to do intelligence work; he'd said that the Sens could not keep secrets. The irony was that he would never know that keeping too many secrets had trapped me in a place I could never exit. As I thought about this, Mrs. Sen came out of the kitchen, wearing her usual white sari with a red border. Supriya's mother had her eye on me and hurried over to catch me in an embrace.

"We have missed you," said Mr. Sen, coming alongside his wife and nodding at me. I saw he'd become grayer over the war years; what worry he had endured. "There are too many people about this place today, but you must come next week for lunch. No need to bring books."

"Masho, that is kind of you." I felt myself tearing up because I was so relieved to be accepted by both of them.

"Kind, nothing! I want to know how you like marriage." Mrs. Sen twinkled at me. "And your mother-in-law? What does she expect of you?"

"I like marriage," I said, feeling suddenly shy. "And as of now, there is no mother-in-law. She's in England, and we've never met."

"Perfect marriage!" laughed Sonali.

Mrs. Sen pinched Sonali's cheek. "Don't let your husband hear you!"

"He won't. He's chatting up Pankaj."

I had noticed Pankaj holding court across the room when I'd arrived; he had nodded toward me, and I had nodded back, but certainly not made any effort to speak with him. But now I saw him weaving his way through people toward our group.

"Hello, Pankaj." My heart was beating fast; I had no idea what he intended to say to me.

"My dear Kamala!" Pankaj's tone was solicitous. "I've been meaning to tell you I'm so very sorry about the last time we spoke. I didn't know the whole story."

Was Pankaj sincere? It didn't even matter, because I now viewed him as someone fettered by his mother and social obligations. Pankaj was brave when it came to incarceration, yet he seemed terrified to follow his heart's desire. He was so very different from Simon—who really was the perfect husband for me, as Sonali had suggested. Feeling generous, I said to Pankaj, "That's all right. Do not think about it any longer."

"How well you've been keeping." His eyes glanced over my figure, and I wondered if he was looking for a sign of pregnancy. "You are still enjoying Calcutta?"

"And what about me?" Supriya interjected. "Nobody asks me in that tone: How was Singapore? How was Burma?"

"Ha-ha!" Pankaj said, his expression becoming livelier. "Do you mean you didn't lounge under a coconut palm, Captain Sen, with a battalion of men serving you tea?"

Supriya blushed and said, "Don't be silly. I was a captain in the women's regiment. We trained in both combat and defense missions. Netaji was most impressed with our unit—but the bloody Japanese would never let us get off the ground!"

"What was it like working with the Japanese?" I asked, and then the conversation was off in a diverting direction. Supriya talked about how an armed women's unit had arrested some robbers during a street incident in Burma; and how they had escaped the bombing of their dormitory by minutes. And Supriya had marched for almost a hundred miles on the retreat from Burma. Pankaj seemed to hang on to Supriya's every word, as did the others. Supriya must have been an excellent officer, for her manner of speaking was both friendly and inspiring.

I left the party shortly afterward with good wishes all around. The political talk left me somewhat encouraged, although Simon had told me that Britain would not give up India until the INA trials had been completed.

As I turned into our street, I looked toward Middleton Mansions with pleasure. The rainy season had turned the new grass a rich emerald green, and the borders of striped crotons and cascading bougainvillaea showed the garden was truly being restored to its lovely former condition.

I knew that Simon and the reverend were planning to see a long American film, so I was surprised to see someone standing near the front door. As I drew closer, it was apparent he was a tall Indian. His profile seemed vaguely familiar; then, as he moved slightly, I saw the back of a lady, much shorter and stout, wearing a pink day dress with a matching fancy hat. The lady's shoulders were bent as if she were leaning down to speak to someone much smaller.

They must have heard me open the gate, because the man and woman whirled about to look at me. And then I had to steady myself, for I recognized the woman's plump face with its heavily rouged cheeks and small, mean eyes.

It was Rose Barker from Kharagpur. And the man with her was Hari, one of the Rose Villa darwans. They had come to my house. And even if I ran from them, they would find me again.

My hands gripped the gate so tightly that the wrought iron spikes cut into my palms. I was so terrified that I could not bring myself to go forward, nor were my feet able to run. As I stood helplessly tied to the gate, the third visitor spun around to look at me. She was a child.

A young girl.

Suddenly, my hands weren't frozen anymore. I pushed forward on the gate and walked toward the girl; it was as if there were a cord between us, pulling me to her. The child looked about nine; but I quickly realized that was because of what Mummy had done. Her hair had been rolled into big curls, and her tiny mouth was painted pink. Heavy mascara and kohl rimmed her eyes, which were lotus-shaped like mine, but an unusual greenish brown. I had never forgotten those eyes.

She was Kabita.

CHAPTER
39

All power on earth waxes great under compact with Satan.
But the Mother is there, alone though she may be, to
contemn and stand against this devil's progress.

    The Mother cares not for mere success, however great—
she wants to give life, to save life. My very soul, today,
stretches out its hands in yearning to save this child.

—Rabindranath Tagore, *The Home and the World*, 1919

Good afternoon." My words flowed mechanically as I inclined my head toward her darwan. "Hari. It has been a long time."

There was no point in pretending I didn't know them. They had seen the way I gripped the gate and come forward as if in a dream. Behind my cold face, though, was the secret place where my joy had surged. Kabita was alive and standing in my garden. And she was regarding me with such curiosity, the way I used to gaze at Bidushi's elegant mother.

My lost child. My little girl. My love.

"Where are your servants? Nobody was here to let us in!" Mummy said in her plaintive whine.

She thought I would invite her in and serve her like a guest: what madness! I was grateful that Simon and Reverend McRae were still out at the film. They would never know about her, and neither would Shombhu or Jatin or Manik, because it was their day off. It was awful that she'd come to see me, but at least it was on a Sunday.

"Hazel, this is Mrs. Lewes." Rose pushed the child forward, and she fell into a wobbly curtsy. "I always thought you'd do well for yourself; but this is more than I expected."

As Rose's tiny eyes raked over my moonstone necklace, ostrich purse, and handloomed silk sari, I remembered when she had me take off my clothes so she could judge whether I was worth hiring. But this time, her eyes did not linger on my breasts. She was looking at my rings.

"I'm sorry, but nobody's home to make tea. I can't very well bring you in—" I smiled apologetically, playing the part of an elite lady. "Let me bring you somewhere comfortable."

"No!" Rose said sharply. "Not after four hours on the train and a hellish tonga ride of more than one hour! I must sit down."

Feigning enthusiasm, I clapped my hands. "Let's have a treat at Flury and Trinca's, then. It's just around the corner. Have you heard of it?"

"As long as it's not far," she grunted.

She moved more slowly than I remembered; all those years of overeating and drinking had taken a toll. I wrangled all of us into a tonga and told the driver where to go. As we rode, I prayed that the driver didn't understand much English, because Rose Barker was talking.

"The girls saw your picture in the Sunday *Statesman*, opening a home for old men—how funny, given your past!"

The society page photograph had been taken with Reverend McRae, when I had helped him open a nursing home for the elderly poor. I'd wanted to drum up donations, but now realized it had been a mistake to stand before the camera's lens.

"So you found me—but what about her?" I inclined my head toward Kabita, whose eyes were fixed on the spectacle of Park Street.

"Oh, we found her much earlier. But it took hard work!" Mummy pinched Kabita, who yelped. Ignoring this, she said to me, "After you ran from Kharagpur, I asked Chief Howard to interview the girls on any possible thing they might remember. We tracked you to a school in Midnapore and learned about the school driver who'd been like an uncle to you. He lost his job on suspicion of aiding and abetting."

"That was wrong of them." I felt hollow knowing that I really had ruined his life. I shut my eyes, not wanting to see Rose's smug expression.

"I found only the wife with Hazel in Midnapore, because your driver-uncle had already died at his next job—terrible accident, I'm sorry to say. Mother and child were very poor, so I gifted them with money each year."

Just as I'd been doing. With help coming in to them from two donors, it may not have seemed obvious to Hafeeza that I was Kabita's birth mother. Perhaps she'd thought Rose Barker was the more generous and kind benefactress.

"They were grateful to me indeed," Mummy said, as if picking up on my bitter thoughts. "Naturally, Hafeeza sent word to me when she decided to move to her brother-in-law's home. I kept sending money, of course, so I could keep a connection to Hazel. And how tragic that Hafeeza died from dysentery—it is like that with the poor, isn't it? Half of that household died—but not our Hazel. Her uncle was very glad for my offer to house and school her."

Hafeeza dead! I didn't know whether to believe it until I looked to Kabita and saw the way her lips trembled. A lump rose in my throat as I remembered the odd feeling I'd had in 1943 that something had gone wrong. Trying to keep my voice steady, I asked Kabita in Bengali how long ago her mother had passed. She couldn't have liked the way

Rose was talking about her as if she were as dumb as the mangy horse pulling the tonga.

"Two summers ago," she whispered.

Few words meant less of a chance of crying; I knew this from my own life. Gently, I asked, "And are you now living with Mrs. Barker?"

"Yes." Now her tight little face relaxed. "It is very lovely there. "I sleep in the room with the nicest auntie. She has a funny name: Lucky-Short-for-Lakshmi!"

"Lucky is my business partner now, but still learning. She will be well prepared after I leave." Rose's hand, an age-spotted, bejeweled spider, closed over Kabita's tiny one. "Hazel is our little bud waiting to blossom. I wanted you to see her while she is still innocent. She will be too busy to travel later."

A fresh wave of fear and rage roiled inside me. Kabita was being trained to join the Roses, just as Mummy had always wanted. I couldn't let this happen. I would have to flee with her now—

No. If I grabbed Kabita out of the tonga with me at the next intersection, Rose Barker could call out to the constable directing traffic that I was stealing her fair-skinned child. Kabita would be afraid as well. And even if I did manage to get the two of us back to Middleton Street, they'd know where to come for her. And Simon would see all of them, and my whole past would become clear. These awful scenarios and a few more were racing through my head by the time we'd reached the famous confectionery. I dreaded going inside, but I could not leave Kabita.

"Stay outside," Rose said roughly to Hari, reminding him of the servant he still was, despite wearing city clothing. And this positioning was strategic: if I ran out with Kabita, he'd be there to catch us.

Mummy was impressed with the sugary cakes in the display case. As she jabbed her finger toward the most lavish-looking ones, I bade her to follow me to a table, where we ordered several along with a pot of Darjeeling. Sitting down, Mummy kept Kabita closely at her side.

I leaned over toward Kabita from my place on the table's other side. "Please try the Black Forest cake. If you don't like it, I'll give you my palmier. Did you know that palmier means hand in French! Just as we call this our palm." I lightly tapped on her pale pink palm, but she recoiled. I drew my own hand back, knowing I'd tried for too much; it would take a while for her to trust me.

When the cakes arrived, Kabita stabbed at them with the fork I imagined she was still learning to use. But an expression of rapture slid across her small face. She liked the Black Forest cake as well as the palmier and the rum ball.

"You haven't asked much about the girl," Rose Barker said, licking whipped cream from the side of her mouth. She'd polished off half a piece of Black Forest cake very quickly and was eyeing an unclaimed raspberry tart. I was so unnerved by the situation that I couldn't eat a bite; I was on the verge of retching.

I did not want to talk about Kabita as if she were invisible, so I tried for something innocuous. Feigning a smile, I said, "Are you only calling her Hazel?"

"Of course! It has always been her good name."

"My mother called me Zeenat." Kabita spoke uncertainly, casting a glance at Rose, who frowned. Obviously she was not planning to sell her as a Muslim girl.

"I can call you that if you like," I said quickly. "Are you seven years old, then?"

"Yes. Mummy gave my birthday party," she answered in her halting English. "The aunties gave me three dolls and such pretty-pretty dresses."

The thought of them being able to spoil her—when I could not—made me jealous, and also angry about their techniques of manipulation. Reminding Mummy of her old policy, I said, "She will remind men of their own children, and make them feel guilty. She is too young to stay at Rose Villa."

"But Hazel's excited to earn her own money—aren't you, darling? All the more dollies and sweeties for you." Rose Barker turned her sickeningly sweet smile from Kabita to me. "It's because of the Independence. The English are leaving, and everyone says Indians prefer their girls very young. Her debut will be next year, I think."

I had brought my teacup up to my mouth; now it dropped, spilling tea across the table. "No," I whispered, staring at Rose. "No!"

Kabita gave a small gasp, put down her fork, and looked toward Rose. This made me want to collapse, but somehow I kept breathing.

"Hazel, it is time for you to visit the little girls' room. Pam, tell us where it is."

"In the back. I'll take her—"

"No. You stay; the waiter will show her." Rose inclined her head toward the door in the back of the room; obediently, Kabita went.

I looked back at my enemy. Resisting the urge to plunge the cake knife in her throat, I took a deep breath. "That's not a ploy, I hope, where she goes off with Hari."

"No chance!" Mummy's tone was brisk. "I wanted to speak privately. Now that I've seen you, I'm guessing you'd like to keep Hazel; but for me to release her would cost thousands in unearned rupees. I don't think we can afford it; however, my business partner has a tender heart. Lucky thought I should ask what you wanted."

So this was the game. Blackmail. I shook my head and said, "You can't keep her. I'll go to the Calcutta police—"

"Who will certainly telephone Chief Howard in advance of coming to Kharagpur. And you can imagine what he'll tell them about you!"

"Wait. I won't—" I broke off, belatedly realizing she had tapped my current fear as easily as she'd tapped my old ones a lifetime ago.

Rose smiled sweetly, as if anticipating my reaction. "Here is what I can do, my dear. I can give you the chance to pay me for those lost earnings. Then you can keep your daughter."

"What are you talking about?" I felt my head spinning with anger and some confusion. "I don't earn money anymore. I'm a wife."

"A society wife." She wiggled her fingers as if in awe. "Your husband must have oodles of rupees and pounds of sterling. Investments of all sorts that a wife has a right to."

I shook my head. I could hardly spring the news about Kabita and follow it directly with a request for money. Somehow, I would have to shut down the blackmail plan before it went any further. Struggling to sound calm, I said, "My husband earns a government salary. He's not wealthy enough to blackmail—"

"I am not trying to blackmail! I will not see you again because I'm going home at the end of the month."

"That can't be true. You never had the papers to get a passport," I reminded her.

"I had help. Just look." She opened her purse and withdrew a passport the same dark red as Simon's. Inside was written her name, Rose Barker, and a visa permitting emigration to Britain. "With my earnings, I shall buy a little boardinghouse by the sea. But I need more money for the ticket." Again, her eyes fell on my rings. "Those are very pretty. Are they the most valuable things you own?"

I nodded, although it was not true. The most precious things in my life were my new husband and my long-lost daughter.

"Perhaps you can't afford my offer." She raised her hands in a gesture of mock surrender. "If I'm forced to bring Kabita back to Rose Villa, it will cost you three hundred for the time I've kept her so far— and the inconvenience. But if you decide to take her home tonight, I will forget that I ever knew you—and so will Bonnie and the others. It will cost a thousand, though—after all, I'm going to England."

This financial scheme was ludicrous. A thousand was more than twice the debut price I'd been sold for at Rose Villa and significantly more than the cost of a first-class sea ticket to Dover. I could not let her dominate me this way; I would have to muster the strength she was stealing from me.

"A sea ticket is six hundred rupees," I said. "That I can give in exchange for leaving Hazel here and getting on with the rest of your sordid life."

Rose's thin eyebrows arched into horrible, high moons. "The best bargain I can make is seven hundred fifty—the extra covering Hazel's expenses since June."

"Done," I said before I could doubt myself. "But I don't have such an amount in my purse now. It is Sunday afternoon. The bank won't open until tomorrow morning at ten."

"But you can't take her without paying." Rose Barker ran her tongue over her lips and said, "I've got it. You will put us up for the night, then . . . let's say the Grand Hotel or the Great Eastern."

Both luxury hotels were expensive, but the Grand was unthinkable. And Simon had an account at the Great Eastern; I could charge a room there and come up with a story about a tea party with other women volunteers. Reluctantly, I said, "I can get a room for you at the Great Eastern."

"I trained you very well," she said, looking again at me. "Who would think an Indian peasant would ever be inside this fancy tearoom, eating cake so prettily with a silver fork?"

She was trying to make me feel inferior, but since I had no respect for her, it didn't work. "That's enough," I said. "Does Hazel know I'm her mother?"

"She thinks you are another auntie. I never said you were her mother because I didn't know your intentions."

"Yes." In the half hour we'd spent together, I'd had no time to address the impossibility of my situation. What would I do after getting Kabita? I could not simply bring her home and explain she was mine. After all, Simon thought I'd been a virgin until he'd touched me.

Kabita arrived at the table and was looking covetously at the remains of the sweets on her dish.

"Sit down and finish," I said to her. "And there will be more tasty food tonight. You two will be staying at a very nice hotel." I glanced sidelong at Mummy and asked, "What about Hari's accommodation?"

"Now that I have a good agreement with you, I'll send him back on the late train," she said with a yawn. "But don't try any tricks; I expect you by noon tomorrow."

CHAPTER
40

RESPONSIBLE: . . . *3. Answerable, accountable (to another for something); liable to be called to account. 4. Morally capable for one's actions; capable of rational conduct.*

—*Oxford English Dictionary*, Vol. 8, 1933

I crept in two hours later to the flat, which smelled reassuringly of sandalwood, spices, and tea. How lovely the place was, with its tall windows that were finally free of their brown paper coverings, allowing a glimpse of the night-blooming garden and cool breezes to pass through. Inside, soft lamplight spilled over the fine carpets and well-polished mahogany and rosewood furniture. It was a home into which I'd be proud to welcome my daughter, if only I could.

"Good God!" Simon's words burst forth as he emerged from the library, a book still in hand. "You look awful, darling. What happened at the rally?"

"Not much. It was a peaceful meeting." I was startled by his reference to the day's big event. Both the rally and the Sens' party seemed a lifetime away.

"Come in," he said, waving his hand back toward the library. "Shombhu's still out, so I'll make the gin-limes. I want to hear all about Deshapriya Park. Something must have happened for you to look like death warmed over."

"No, it really was fine." I tried to force my expression into normality. "Some very good speeches were given and there wasn't any violence."

"What did they say?" Simon said from the drinks cart, where he was mixing up the cocktails.

In the last two hours, my world had shifted so dramatically, I could no longer recall what anyone had said at the rally. I paused, trying to remember. "A female INA veteran spoke and, of course, there was Panditji, as people are calling Nehru. He could be a strong leader."

"You don't seem especially keen to talk," he said. "Why is that?"

I twisted my hands, knowing I needed to help Kabita, that this was my best chance. "Actually, something else is weighing on me; and it has nothing to do with the rally."

"Oh, darling, I'm sorry. Please tell me." Simon gave me a gin-lime and joined me on the velvet settee.

Settling into his embrace, I said, "Chatting with an acquaintance at the rally today, I heard news about my cousin's daughter, a little girl whom I've always adored. She is in need of schooling, and there is no money for it. I would like to send her to a good school in Calcutta and oversee her care."

Simon's face had been warmly concerned; but now his eyes narrowed. "Who said this to you?"

"A cousin," I said helplessly.

"And how old is the child in question?"

"About seven, I think."

"Ten years of school then, plus college." His voice was as tight as his expression. "Do you realize you'd be paying the people who forced you to leave school? The family who wouldn't even give you tea when you visited them two years ago?"

Now I regretted those lies I'd told about my trip to Midnapore.

"The money's not for the family themselves; it's only for her to go to school. I shall pay the tuition directly to the school, so there's no question—"

Simon shook his head. "I don't mean to be hard, but I have a bad feeling about this. I think they're lying to you. If you take responsibility for the girl's schooling, you'll soon be paying for all her brothers and sisters and cousins for years to come."

"What do you know about it?" A leaden feeling was spreading inside me. "It's not any of the other relatives asking our help—just the mother of one girl."

"Kamala, I won't give a single rupee to people who were cruel to you. And that's my last word on it."

I would not beg from him. I knew that if he would not support a young relative, he would certainly not support an illegitimate child. Flooded with disappointment, I said stiffly, "I should not have presumed I could ask you to spend money on anything I cared about."

"It's not like that at all; we share money and consult each other on major expenses." Simon's fingers were jumping on the little mahogany tea table, tapping out a tense staccato rhythm. "At least you asked about this matter first. I like to make these decisions together."

Together was the wrong word to use. He alone vetoed or approved; this was the way of all men and their wives. And despite my love for him, this was not fair.

Simon suggested supper at a Chinese restaurant in Park Street. I told him to go on his own, because the gin-lime had given me such a headache that I needed to lie down.

As I crept under the covers, I cursed myself for how badly I'd handled the situation. If only I had never created the fictitious cruel family in Midnapore; if only I had not lied. I wished I could rewind my life the way he could with the speeches on his wire recorder. Then I would never have stepped off the train by accident in Kharagpur and would have gone on to Calcutta as planned. Simon would have found me two years earlier and hired me to work in his library. In time, we would have fallen in love without pretense; we would have had a child together, and there would be no question where she belonged.

Would. Should. Didn't. Cannot. These verbs formed a mocking nursery rhyme that sang in my tired, aching head. When Simon returned from dinner, smelling of alcohol and smoke, I kept my back turned to him, and breathed evenly until he fell asleep.

I had told lies about Kabita in order to stay married. Simon and I were still together; but I did not know if it was worth what I was about to give up.

❧   ❧   ❧

SIMON LEFT EARLY the next morning for a day trip to Jamshedpur, and I began the task of finding money and shelter for Kabita. Only a few hours remained before my meeting with Rose Barker. Schools opened before the bank, so I began by telephoning the ones I'd heard Supriya and her friends mention the most favorably. Unfortunately, fall term had already started, which meant Loreto House just down the street was full, as were Saint Mary's and La Martiniere. I'd need to look outside of Calcutta.

I dreaded sending Kabita to some faraway place where I would have no knowledge of her treatment. And how would I afford boarding school, with what I had to pay Rose Barker? My bank account totaled less than four hundred rupees and could not be replenished as Simon had stopped paying me a salary once we'd become engaged. There were two hundred and ten rupees in the housekeeping expenses purse that I kept locked in the study; but if I used that, there would be no money to pay the servants or tradesmen. The only way to raise money was by selling my personal belongings. I remembered how little my books were valued, and used clothing would only fetch paise from the rag collector. I looked at the rings Rose Barker had admired. The engagement ring symbolized promise and the wedding band devotion; two ideals I never wanted to break, but would have to.

At ten o'clock, Hogg Market was just opening up, and I went straight to the jeweler who had once sold me my favorite moonstone necklace. He beamed at the sight of me, but his excitement faded when he realized I wanted to sell and not buy.

"Just look at this beautiful treasure," I said, turning my hand before him. "A Golconda diamond solitaire set in twenty-two-karat gold. Of course, you may inspect it yourself."

After he'd scrutinized my engagement ring under a magnifying glass, he offered two hundred rupees.

"But it cost us fifteen hundred at J. Boseck last year!" I had not dared bring it back to that jeweler; how much he had smiled at the way Simon had searched for the very best piece. He would ring Simon if I came trying to sell.

"Yes, but the times are hard!" the jeweler said firmly. "Nobody who comes here has even five hundred to spend on a nice wedding set. This is not a fancy foreign shop but an honest business."

I went to six jewelers before I found someone willing to take the engagement ring for four-fifty, the wedding ring for seventy and would give me acceptable-looking replicas to replace them. The man paid the cash immediately and said he'd have the rings copied for me by early evening.

At Grindlays Bank, I withdrew the rest that I needed from my bank account. Paying for school would come later, but I'd worry about it when the bill came.

At five minutes to twelve, I entered the Great Eastern Hotel. Going up the grand staircase, I thought how different this felt from my wedding night. Still, it heralded a different kind of beginning: my relationship with Kabita. I had gathered the money; I could take her; and this made my feet move faster.

Rose Barker opened the door, fully made up and dressed in a long purple moiré gown with high-heeled pumps to match. Kabita sat on the bed, wearing the same flowered frock as the day before, kicking her short legs aimlessly. She did not acknowledge me with either a look or word. I felt guilt, because I'd never asked if she wanted to become mine. I hadn't, because I was sure she would refuse. She had suffered too many losses to want to move on to yet another place.

I went to the desk and began counting out the rupee notes on its polished surface. Kabita was silently crying, long black rivers coming from her made-up eyes.

"Thank you very much," Rose said, flipping through the bills. "No tricks now. Don't interfere with my new life in England."

Her defensive words startled me. I might have misjudged the situation. Perhaps she understood Simon's stature, or feared that when he brought me to England one day, I would seek revenge. In England, she would be an aging lady without relatives around to support her; we would be ex-ICS, with Simon's mother, siblings, and cousins established in West Sussex, part of a powerful social class.

"Don't fret about England," I said casually. "Let me tell you that I expect the same: no contact ever. I'm taking care of the bill downstairs. Your room must be vacated by one."

I picked up Kabita's small carpetbag and waited for her to follow me. Slowly, she slid off the bed and went to Rose.

"Good-bye, Mummy," she said in a low voice. From the way she stood, I could see she was expecting a kiss or hug.

But Rose did not even turn to answer; she was too busy counting rupees.

CHAPTER
41

As is the tree, so is the fruit.

Bengali proverb

If we are quick, we can catch that tonga," I said after I'd taken Kabita outside. There was an arcade over the pavement, shading us; but beyond that, the sun shone down on a traffic jam. The despair I'd felt moments before was gone. Kabita was alive. She was mine.

"Are we going to your flat, Auntie?" Kabita's green eyes looked up at me hopefully, and I realized that she wasn't as frightened of me as I'd thought.

"No. Unfortunately, I don't have room for a little girl to stay with me." Each word felt like a bullet coming out of me and into her; and from the way the light left her eyes, I knew it hurt.

"But your flat building is very nice! And you are going to raise me with all the luxuries. That's what Mummy said!"

"Please don't worry." I found it ironic that she had already learned one of Rose Barker's catchphrases. "Right now, we are finding which lady friend of mine will keep you for a few nights."

"Oh! Is it a house of aunties like Rose Villa?" Her tiny brows drew together.

"No, it's not. But first I have an idea—have you ever eaten ice cream?"

At Magnolia, I could have spent all afternoon watching her rapturously consume her first ice cream. But so much had to be done. As I dabbed at her face with a wet handkerchief, getting rid of the eye makeup and ice cream drips, I explained that I was searching for a nice school where she would sleep in a soft bed at night and spend her days studying and playing with other girls her age. But first I would take her to College Street. Because of Supriya's and Mrs. Sen's school ties, they would surely have ideas of the very best places for a girl to study.

It was soothing to climb the stairs and have Mrs. Sen open the door with a pleased cry, all the tension of the last few years erased. "You've come back to see us! And who is your young friend?"

"Mashima, she is my dear niece from the countryside. She goes by Zeenat," I said, squeezing Kabita's hand. At the sound of this obviously Muslim name, Mrs. Sen raised her eyebrows; I ignored this and asked whether Supriya was home.

"Yes, but still sleeping. She celebrated very late yesterday; Arvind and Pankaj and some others took her out to the coffeehouse. But I will wake her, since you are here."

Kabita and I were urged to sit on the wide, comfortable bed in the reception room, and Mrs. Sen's maid went into the kitchen to make tea and warm up leftovers from yesterday's big party. I needed to talk with Mrs. Sen and Supriya without Kabita hearing. Handing my child some of Nishan's storybooks, I said I was going to the lavatory. Instead, I went into Supriya's bedroom, where her mother was helping her dress. Both looked at me in surprise.

"I'm sorry to interrupt, but I needed to speak to you alone. My niece came to me unexpectedly. She's lost her parents."

The sari that Mrs. Sen had been holding slipped through her fingers. "Oh, the poor child."

"Yes," I continued. "Her father died in a mill accident, and her mother was felled by dysentery. I took her as my ward because her uncle couldn't afford to keep and educate her."

"What a terrible tragedy; but how lucky she's got you." Supriya gave me a warm look. "I suppose she's moving right into Middleton Mansions."

"I wish I could host her; but I can't." I watched the Sen women's eyes widen with disbelief. "It's a complicated situation with my husband and the reverend both staying there; the ideal place for her would be a boarding school, but I can't find one in Calcutta that isn't already full."

"What? Why can't she attend day school and stay with you?" Supriya asked.

"And what kind of school would be best?" Mrs. Sen chimed in.

Before I could answer, Supriya spoke again. "She is very fair-skinned—fairer than you, Kamala! And why is her name Muslim?"

"Her late father was Muslim," I said carefully. "And as you know, so many Indians are light-skinned: the Kashmiri, the Punjabis, the Parsis—"

"But she is Bengali. I wonder—" Supriya broke off. "Sorry. I can't say it."

"Just speak!" I said.

"Is Mr. Lewes her father?" Supriya asked.

Mrs. Sen slapped her. "Shame on you!"

As Supriya rubbed her cheek, I struggled to put together my response.

"Simon is not the father; if he was, it would be much easier!" I forced a laugh. "Don't you remember that I came to Calcutta seven years ago to find work? Zeenat is a bit older than that. I last saw her as a newborn baby."

"I was not saying she was *yours*," Supriya protested. "I was only wondering if some secret offspring came from Mr. Lewes's past. Englishmen are known for not cleaning up their messes."

Mrs. Sen began brushing Supriya's hair in long, thorough strokes. "Don't be silly, she is obviously Kamala's niece. Look at the similarity of their eyes. And I have some ideas about boarding schools for her, but they are not inside Calcutta."

"I can't afford the expense of a Darjeeling school." Nor could I bear the distance.

"I'm thinking about Chandernagore, just an hour up the river." Mrs. Sen put down the brush and began braiding her daughter's hair. "I graduated from an old convent school there called Saint Joseph's. I will write to Mother Superior about your niece. Perhaps she qualifies for an orphan's scholarship."

"But are the teachers and girls kind?" I hesitated. "I mean to say, I was at a boarding school where Indian students weren't well-treated. There was not much mixing."

Mrs. Sen kissed her daughter's head as she finished the braid. Then she turned to look at me. "I have attended some old girls' teas; the current atmosphere and students are very nice. You will both be pleased."

I was overcome by the Sens' interest in helping and also their offer to keep Kabita with them until it was time to travel to Chandernagore. I had not even had to ask—they offered. What true friends they were to me.

The three of us emerged from the bedroom, arms linked; Kabita enjoyed the delicious snacks and tea, which were served just as Nishan came in the door from school.

"You will stay here tonight. They are the kindest family in Calcutta. And I shall be here before ten tomorrow morning to take you shopping."

"Thank you, Auntie," she said, and gave a quick embrace before running to the table to join Nishan, who was setting up the chessboard. To her, it was a playful time with new friends. For me, it was the beginning of another end.

🌟   🌟   🌟

IT TOOK SEVERAL telephone calls to Saint Joseph's to arrange Kabita's admission. Her tuition was scaled to cover the remainder of the year, and she received a fifty-rupee scholarship, which was wonderful for me, as my total cost was just twenty-five rupees. This meant I could afford tuition and the uniforms and other supplies she needed. The thought of her growing up away from me hurt; but I couldn't see another way.

That week Simon worked very long days, which were a blessing for my schedule. Each morning, I went by tram to the Sens' house to pick up Kabita. I had a list of tasks: having her uniforms made, swinging tennis rackets, and learning to tie oxford shoes. We ate in various European restaurants so she could study European table manners and how to behave. For fun we saw films at the Metro Cinema and shopped for books in College Street. Several times we crossed paths with English and Indian women who knew me; I introduced them to my niece Zeenat visiting from the countryside.

As we grew to know each other, Kabita's pinched little face relaxed. To her, I was the mysterious auntie who would listen to every tale she told, but offered no stories of her own. I did not say a word to her about Simon, because the more time I spent with my child, the angrier I became with him. At home, I maintained my normal, pleasant demeanor. I told Simon that I would be traveling with a group of volunteers working on an education progam for orphans. He thought it was an excellent idea and offered a financial contribution that I gladly accepted.

"Godspeed to you," Reverend McRae said as he saw me off at the flat door early that Friday morning. "As you take your place in society, you will be one of the very few who will still connect naturally with the general population, speaking to them like a mother or sister. My only advice is to think carefully about which particular cause you shall undertake. It's easy to spread oneself too thinly."

I felt guilty about his approval and resolved to do something charitable upon my return. I would need to prevent my restless mind from circling back to the reality of this second abandonment. As Kabita and

I boarded the train to Chandernagore, I could barely lift her small bag; it felt as if my arms had become paralyzed. I felt wretched that keeping my life with Simon meant sending her away. Kabita didn't seem to want to go, either; she dragged her feet, scuffing the new black oxfords.

"Why are you taking me away? It's nice staying with the Sens and going about the city with you!" As the train rolled on, my daughter nestled into my side, smelling sweetly of coconut oil and cake.

"I'm very glad you like them," I said with a lump in my throat. "Perhaps you can stay again with the Sens for the summer holidays."

"Supriya-auntie is a famous fighter—did you know? She said that on the school holiday, she'll teach me how to use a gun."

We were not even out of Calcutta's limits, and I had to warn her. She was on her way to a new school, a new life with Europeans who would not approve of the Indian National Army.

"Kabita, you mustn't talk about that outside of the Indian community," I said. "The ladies in charge of your school will be French and English. They won't like girls who are excited about guns."

"Kabita?" As my daughter repeated the name I'd let slip, her expression was curious.

Hurriedly, I said, "It means poem. Your ma loved the poetry of Tagore. It's your second name."

"I didn't know that." Kabita sounded pleased. "Kabita. But it's a Hindu name, isn't it?"

"Actually, we should speak about your school name. Would you prefer to go by Hazel? Many of the girls won't know the name Zeenat." I'd registered her as Hazel Smith, because that was the name on the birth certificate that I'd carefully kept for her.

"Hazel sounds hard." Kabita's voice trembled. "And I don't want to go to that school after all. Can we give back the uniforms and shoes? Why do I have to change places again?"

"Darling, some changes are for the best. And I will always see you for the holidays—"

"But I don't live with you. Or anybody." Again there was quiet despair in her voice.

I could not confess that I was her mother; not in this train compartment only a half hour left before arrival. And it was such a loss. To Kabita, I would always be the auntie who gave ice creams and clothes and paid for her school. Nothing more.

"I will visit as much as I can," I promised, stroking Kabita's hair. Since Mrs. Sen had washed out the shellac from Rose Villa, Kabita's hair had revealed itself as a silky brown mass with gold strands running through. Kabita flinched, so I put my hand back in my lap. I would not let my heart run away with her. My golden girl would remain the treasure I always dreamed of but could not keep.

CHAPTER
42

Where I am, I am not. I am far away from those who are around
me. I live and move upon a world-wide chasm of separation,
unstable as the dew-drop upon the lotus leaf.

—Rabindranath Tagore, *The Home and the World*, 1919

As the days passed, I mourned Kabita's absence. I paid to use a shop telephone to call her during her free period. Because she seemed happy to hear from me, each Friday afternoon I rode the train to visit her. I waited in the visitor's parlor with a book until she skipped in, full of chatter about her new friends, drama class, and chorus. The nuns said she was settling in, although she was frank in her dislike of Latin, maths, and English food. This inspired me to bring a tiffin box packed with a vegetable curry, dal, chapatti, and always on the bottom layer, a sweet that I had made with my own hands. I served the remainder of the batch at Friday night dinner.

The sweets had quite an impact on Simon. He was always affectionate on Friday evenings and when I was going to see the French gynaecologist, because it was almost a year of marriage and I'd not yet conceived. I dutifully recorded the doctor's name, knowing I'd never go, because any examination would reveal I'd given birth before and was too damaged to succeed again. Simon was so keen for a child that he even spoke to me about adopting one of the unwanted babies that had come from unions between the poor women of Assam and the American and European soldiers; but I could not fathom the idea of any child other than Kabita.

I may have been barren, but something was growing inside me like a small, hard seed. It was resentment. I felt that Simon had separated Kabita from me; although I knew that the lies I'd told had led to his decision. But what other way was there, for me to have survived?

🌼   🌼   🌼

AS THE HINDU pujas and Christmas approached, I fell into a happy reverie, determined to bring it all to Kabita, and trying to plan what I could give without spending unduly. One Friday afternoon, I went to see her, determined to learn her wishlist. But instead of coming to the arms I held open for her, she settled herself onto a small ottoman, her ankles crossed so her thin legs stood up like butterfly wings.

"They've brought us tea!" I began pouring her cup.

"No tea for me." She looked away.

"A biscuit then?"

"No thank you, Mrs. Lewes."

I was surprised by her fierce refusal, and the way she would not meet my eyes. I said, "When we first met in Calcutta you called me Auntie—it was so much friendlier. Is something wrong, dear?"

Kabita wrapped her arms around herself, and with her head tucked down, mumbled, "Why didn't you come last week?"

"Darling, I sent a telegram explaining, didn't you receive it? The regular train was canceled, some sort of trouble with political protesters. I couldn't take a later one and be home in time to—" I broke off, leaving unsaid *in time to convince Simon nothing was amiss.* "But I'm here now, and we have lots of fun ahead of us."

Kabita shook off my promise with a scowl. "We shouldn't be apart. Why did you buy me if you don't want to be with me?"

How I wished she had never seen the money go from my hands to Rose's. Awkwardly, I said, "I was not buying you. I was saving you, bringing you back to me—"

"Back to you? I'd never seen you before in my life!"

I could have kept lying to her. But if I lied now, how could I ever tell her later? I remembered all the mistakes I'd made lying to Simon. I began cautiously. "I believe you know that Hafeeza and Abbas cared for you from a very young age."

"So it's true what Mummy said?" As she spoke, her lips trembled. "That I wasn't born to them?"

If I lied to her, I could have soothed her mind forever; but I would not have been able to live with another lie. Hedging for time, I said, "Tell me what Mummy said about it."

"Mummy said that my mother was a very naughty lady who wouldn't keep me." Kabita paused. "But I think she had a good heart. The lady sent Ma letters with lovely things like hair ribbons and shoes and money. Ma said she loved us both."

I coughed and said, "Did you know, I have a story, too?"

"What?" Her face relaxed slightly, because she was used to me telling her fairy tales and reading books aloud during our visits.

"I was born a poor little girl from the countryside. My whole family died and your baba saved my life. He helped me find work at his school where I was a servant who cleaned floors and pulled fans."

"You were a servant?" Kabita's eyes were incredulous.

"Yes. They called me Sarah. Later on, others called me Pamela. Kamala is the first name I chose for myself."

Kabita shook her head. "But your parents must have named you when you were born! That is your name. What's that?"

This startled me so much I almost couldn't respond. In a rush, I said, "Oh, I've grown so accustomed to being Kamala that I've no need for another name. I've had to make many changes throughout my life; more than any woman should have to do." I swallowed down the sob that threatened and said, "The hardest change, of course, was giving you up."

Kabita shook her head disbelievingly. "What?"

"I mean . . . I was your first mother." I put down my cup, because my hand was shaking so hard. "I kept you with me for the first month and a half in a horrible, hot little room. Mummy knew about you. She wanted to keep you for her own selfish reasons, and the doctor wanted you sent to an orphanage. Because I had no home to shelter you, nor money to feed you, I brought you to Hafeeza and Abbas, the best people I knew."

Kabita seemed to shrink into herself, like a young butterfly crawling back into its cocoon. In a muffled voice, she said, "But you are rich. You live in a mansion. You should have taken me, if I really am yours."

She was right, absolutely right. Tears started in my eyes as I confessed, "My husband would throw us both out if he knew."

Kabita's head shot up, and she looked at me with eyes full of hate. "That's a lie."

"No, really, he thinks I'm—I'm better than I am—"

"No, you're lying. You have told too many lies. I don't want you to be my mother."

With that, she had done me in. I had fooled many people, but this girl, nearly eight years old, could read me like a book. Tears flowing freely, I sobbed, "You make me feel that I should never have come."

"You're right!" Kabita cried. "And I don't want to know your first name or anything more about you! I hate you now and will forever!"

※   ※   ※

I WEPT ALL the way home on the train. A worried-looking woman offered me a crusty shingara as consolation. It filled my mouth with a taste like paper; I knew nothing would ever taste good to me again. Automatically, I thanked her and ate it, but I could not taste any flavor.

I had calmed down, but when I got into the flat and saw my reflection in the mirror, my eyes were red and my face puffy. I turned to see Simon, who'd come from the dining room with a drink in one hand. His gin-lime; he'd been drinking more of them in the past few months. With an off-kilter smile, he said, "Sorry—I started eating dinner. Where have you been?"

"The orphans' home." This was a project with which I'd helped Reverend McRae right after getting married, when I was looking for useful things to do. I used the orphanage as my regular excuse for Friday afternoon visits to Kabita.

"The air must be bad outside; you look wretched. At least you made it back in one piece. We will have our anniversary celebration another time, I suppose."

I'd forgotten that this date was the anniversary of one year of marriage. Now I was filled with guilt on top of my existing misery. "Simon, I'm so very sorry! I was so busy with the volunteer work I simply forgot."

"Never mind that. I have something for you." Simon handed me a smallish rectangle wrapped in silver paper. Not a jewelry box; good, because I was still feeling guilty about the rings. Inside the pretty paper I discovered a book bound in plain red morocco. Inside was a sea of empty pages. The only words were stamped on the corner of the front endpaper: Sen Bookbindery and Publishing, College Street, Calcutta.

"Paper is the first anniversary gift, isn't it?" I smiled mistily at him, remembering what I'd learned from the English book about wedding planning.

"Yes. It's a diary," Simon said. "I visited their shop and saw they had quite an assortment of specialty books. I thought an empty book to write in is what you need."

"Important men write about their lives in diaries: I hardly have anything to record." I could not say that I was afraid to put down a single honest word without crying.

"But women have kept diaries, too: There's so much that you hold within: it's my hope that this diary may help you find your voice."

I thanked Simon and said how happy I was he'd finally met the Sens—for this, at least, was true. As I began a stumbling apology for not having his gift ready, he waved it off.

"You don't need to give me anything." He paused. "Well, the one thing—but that's up to the doctors and God, isn't it?"

He would not get his newborn baby. I would not have the love of my daughter. The marriage I'd run to, because I wanted to follow my heart, would never result in a family. It would not be a happily ever after. All this I thought about as we lay back-to-back, instead of in each other's arms.

CHAPTER
43

REVELATION: 1. The disclosure or communication of knowledge to man by a divine or supernatural agency.

—*Oxford English Dictionary*, Vol. 8, 1933

I went back to Chandernagore the next week with the hope that Kabita had softened. But Mother Superior said she refused to see me, even though she was being punished for the rudeness of it. I asked the nun to please release her from detainment and returned to Calcutta feeling sad yet still determined to keep visiting until my daughter's anger faded. It was a wretched holiday. But for every Friday that I made sweets and traveled to her school, I had another rejection. And in between each visit were six long days in Calcutta, a city besieged by its own unhappiness.

1946 brought the long-awaited trials for the Indian National Army. The British had decided not to press charges against soldiers who'd joined, but to bring to trial a few INA officers whose actions were considered treasonous against the Government of India or who'd committed war crimes. The first officer to face charges, Abdul Rashid, was sentenced to seven years' labor for physical atrocities against his own troops. Students in Calcutta reacted to the decision by rioting, which led to a violent police counterreaction. A day after the Calcutta riots Bengal's Chief Minister H. S. Suhrawardy gave a powerful speech about injustice. His audience became so inflamed that they rushed straight at the police cordons and more blood flowed. It did not matter what Mr. Rashid had done to the soldiers under him; it mattered only that he was Indian and that those who had convicted him were British.

The morning after the second riot, I sat at the dining table having breakfast and reading the papers with Simon. At the end of my translation of the article about the events, Simon sighed heavily.

"What are you thinking, darling?" I asked.

"That I don't believe in happy endings anymore."

"Certainly not after reading something like that," I said. "And to think there are still two trials left to go."

Jatin walked in with a silver tray holding two more pieces of toast, each browned to our individual tastes. He smiled as I took mine and waited for Simon to take one; but Simon pushed his plate away. Jatin looked at the uneaten eggs on the plate in consternation.

"Go," Simon said to him; unusually short, I thought. When Jatin had departed, Simon turned his tense gaze on me. "You were out of town last Friday. Where were you?"

It wasn't like him to question my activities. Keeping my eyes on the newspaper, as if the articles were very fascinating, I said, "Last Friday? The orphans' home, as usual. Why?"

"Think again." Simon pulled the newspaper from me. "You never work there on Fridays."

Now I looked into his face; from the intensity of his eyes, I could tell that he knew. Simon said, "You were seen at Howrah Station last Friday afternoon. One of our agents followed you again to Chandernagore, the place you've visited the last five Fridays."

"You spied on me?" I was suddenly cold.

"It was Weatherington's operation. He gave me the report." Simon steepled his fingers and looked at me over the top. "Never my idea; but it was worth it to have the truth at last."

It was so very quiet in the dining room. No noise from the kitchen, garden, or street. It felt as if the world had stopped and all that existed was the blood pounding in my head. I began, "There are orphans in Chandernagore."

Simon held up a hand, stilling me. "As you know, Chandernagore is still French territory, outside the reach of our government and police. Radicals hide there. You are always seen carrying a tiffin box to Chandernagore and back; obviously there's something else inside."

"It's just food—Manik can tell you, he washes it each time. I don't know how you can look me in the face and accuse me of such nonsense!" Despite the confident words, I felt my stomach churn.

Simon looked at me steadily. "I know about the second desk key you carry; I found it on the key ring, that time I helped you with the rice kitchen. That's why I went away. I needed time to collect myself."

I'd given him the key ring so he could go into a kitchen cabinet; and then, after he'd left to stay at his club, I'd found he had cleaned out his desk. He had taken the papers to protect them from me. Slowly, I said, "I remember that day. I thought you went away because you were afraid of the emotion you felt."

"Emotion brought me back," he said, his eyes shining as if they were on the brink of tears. "I was helpless in my feelings for you. You fell into my arms when I returned; you said that you loved me. I told myself this meant my fears were wrong. But bad memories keep surfacing. You knew that I'd written the governor's letters. And you've always been frank about your political feelings."

I was silent for a minute, realizing there was no way the story could come out well. "I'm sorry, Simon. I have looked inside your desk, but not for several years. And things have changed. India's becoming free. There's no need to punish freedom fighters."

Simon shook his head. "You're lying to me about Chandernagore, so how can I believe anything you say is genuine?"

"I don't know how to convince you—"

"Bring forth witnesses from this so-called orphans' home in Chandernagore. Not just for last week, but all the weeks beforehand. They'll make sworn statements before a judge. And they'll consent to official interviews."

I would not sacrifice my daughter to being questioned by him and Mr. Weatherington; to have her life upset by British investigators. Kabita might tell them that I'd given her away—that she was my out-of-wedlock daughter, putting the final ugly brushstrokes on Simon's ghastly picture of me. Stiffly, I said, "I visited that town for a reason entirely unrelated to politics. But I really can't talk about it."

"I gave you a good job, then my heart and all my worldly possessions. Wasn't that enough?" Simon exhaled hard. "Why would you steal secrets from me? Who took your information, the Nazis or Japanese?"

"Neither, and please listen to me!" I reached out to touch his hands, but he jerked them away. "Don't let Wilbur Weatherington kill our marriage. It is his thoughts you are mouthing, not your own. You are angry now, of course, but the moment will pass."

"Really, Kamala?" His voice was mocking. "Just as you've changed from spying to loving at a snap of the fingers?"

"It wasn't just me changing," I said. "It was you. You became a *good* man. You started seeing India as a country with people deserving the right to own the food they grew on land that they'd lived on for thousands of years. And you were so clever and kind that I fell in love with you. I had not expected it to happen, but it did."

Simon stood up from the table. Looking down at me, he said, "Well, I don't care about India anymore, except to get away from it—and from you."

CHAPTER
44

Even though you like me not,
as I have heard you don't,
On you I shall ever hang
Like an iron chain fastened to your feet.
You are the captive wretch whom my prisoner I have made by
Tying my heart to yours with a knot no one can undo.

—Rabindranath Tagore, "Rahu's Love," 1884

February passed into March; the winter rice crop had been harvested and the famine had officially ended. Beneath my chappals I could feel the earth warming, readying itself for the summer heat. But Simon and I lived in our own Antarctica.

Simon moved into the second bedroom, the one where he had once hoped his offspring would sleep. He was off at his clubs again morning and night. Clearly, he didn't want to be near me at any time of the day. And what hurt all the more was that by losing my husband, I realized how terribly much I did love him. I was not lingering in Middleton Mansions because I had no choice; it was because I wanted to win him back. I'd lost hope for Kabita, who had never loved me in the first place. I was not willing to lose him, too.

When Reverend McRae returned from his travels, he noticed Simon's absence at the dinner table. I could not possibly tell him the whole story, so instead gave the partial truth: that Simon's feelings were not the same as when we'd married. I also confided that I'd noticed a sea ticket order left in the library—one-way passage in Simon's name.

"One way, and for just one person?" Reverend McRae's forehead lines wrinkled even more deeply. "Did you tell him you would not go to England?"

"No, I didn't say that. I would prefer to stay in my country, especially with Independence coming, but I do not want our marriage to end! But maybe I shouldn't be surprised by the ticket; over the centuries plenty of Englishmen have repatriated without their Indian wives," I said, recalling what Bonnie and Rose had told me about their own fathers leaving.

I expected Reverend McRae to probe what might have been said between us to cause such a rift, but he did not. He moved the conversation on to different topics: the current political climate and how the homes for indigent elderly and young orphans were faring. Before he went upstairs, he said, "I should know better than to offer advice, but I have just one thing to say. If you are going to be on your own, you must prepare to work. It's a very good antidote to sorrow as well."

It seemed the minister was suggesting that I needed to provide financially for myself, because Simon was preparing to divorce me. This was depressing information, because Reverend McRae was closer to understanding the human condition than anyone I knew. Yet he had spoken of an *antidote*. How I liked the sound of that word, which I'd learned many years ago meant remedy. Using references from my volunteer work, I was hired as a health assistant by the Calcutta Red Cross. My salary was modest—just fifty rupees a month—but I had a full-time position traveling daily with a doctor or nurse to slums throughout the city. Those who I served called me Nurse: another erroneous name that hardly mattered. What was important was having something to do that reminded me of what Dr. Andrews, Nurse Gopal, and Nurse Das had done for me years ago at the Keshiari Mission. Now other people's problems took precedence over my own. I worked five long days a week and did not try to see Kabita on the weekends because now I knew Weatherington was watching me; I couldn't risk his forcing a confrontation at the school.

When monsoon came, the days I spent with the Red Cross became chaotic. Cholera and dysentery were spreading, and too many of the roads were flooded to get to those who were stricken. Most of my working hours were spent sitting in the Red Cross van next to Ishan, the young driver who searched in vain for passage into the slums. Often I told him where to go, because after eight years in the city, I knew the roads well. I remembered the pleasures of driving during my short honeymoon, but neither Ishan nor Doctor Haq thought it safe for me to take a turn.

In the evenings, I returned home to wash and eat dinner with the reverend, if he was free. Simon stayed out until late and upon returning, always sat on the veranda with a drink and his cigarettes, for he had returned to his old habit of smoking, and we no longer shared reading together. If the rain had ceased, I would sit a few steps down from him in the garden, surrounded by the fragrance of night-blooming jasmine, with my diary on my lap. I had begun to write in the diary, although I could not bear to describe any present events. Instead, I escaped back to my days in Johlpur, with the rain drumming on the tin roof of the hut I shared with my family. At evening's end, I went to my room and cut out the pages I'd written to put them in an envelope addressed to Kabita at her school. She could not understand the woman I was now, but I hoped she might feel kinship with the girl from long ago.

In July, the Calcutta Post Office went on strike, cutting our city off from the rest of the world. Reverend McRae went on a relief trip to Burma, making life all the lonelier. Simon had received his Buick back from the army, none worse for the wear, and had hired a new driver, Ahmed, by himself, although I had managed all the staff hiring in the past. I didn't particularly like Ahmed, or the fact Simon was using him for long drives in the evening, when he might otherwise have spent time with me. Still, I wrote. I stamped and dropped the letters into pillar-boxes until the boxes were so full they could no longer take anything. Then I stopped writing, for I could not bear the risk of Simon finding anything.

At least the newspapers were still being published and delivered to us daily. They came in the hands of Kantu, the same messenger who had grown from a young sprite to a mature eighteen years. Somehow, he had learned to read in this time, and it always heartened me, though I did not always agree with his opinions.

"Bad articles in this one today!" Kantu grumbled, handing me *Amrita Bazar Patrika* at the doorway. "Check your copy of the *Star*, Memsaheb. The writers are better."

The planning for independence was going full swing, with a projected handover early in the next year, 1947. Kantu did not want Mr. Nehru to be in charge of the first Indian government; he thought Muslims would be shortchanged. But his mood improved when Mr. Suhrawardy, the Bengal home minister, declared that on August 16 a strike day would be held to protest inequitable treatment of Muslims.

Direct Action Day was immediately a hot topic. Bengal's former home minister, Mr. Nazimuddin, proclaimed there were many ways the Muslim League could cause trouble. In return, the Congress Party leader, M. N. Roy, warned his followers that Direct Action Day would certainly mean violence and to prepare for it.

Rumors about what might happen spread through the public. Manik said he'd heard Muslims were rushing to metalsmiths in order to buy long knives and sharpen the ones they already owned. And one day, when I was riding with the Red Cross, I saw a group of

Hindu men struggling with a heavy bag. Out rolled what looked like a grenade. It was caught up so quickly I thought I must have been imagining it; for how could ordinary citizens have military weapons? It couldn't be. I would not allow myself to think Hindus were preparing their own attack. I told myself it was all for show; nothing would really happen, because the police had stopped so many INA riots with force. The same quick response would stop violence before it started.

On the afternoon of August 15, a line of military lorries carrying soldiers left town. I sat inside the Red Cross van next to Dr. Haq, one of my favorite doctors in the organization. But today he was frustrated, for we could not cross the intersection due to the long column of military vehicles crawling along the Barrackpore Trunk Road. Eventually our driver, Ishan, stepped out. He returned saying that the army regiment had received orders to evacuate to Barrackpore.

"Why would the military leave town on the eve of Direct Action Day?" I asked uneasily.

"Hundreds of police were injured during the INA riots last fall and winter," Dr. Haq reminded me. "The government is sending the soldiers away for their own protection. And the British are worried that if they deny Mr. Suhrawardy his holiday, there could be another anti-European backlash."

"But it's our army. They're supposed to keep us safe!" I watched the exiting line of lorries with dismay.

"That is the kind of story what we've been told all our lives, but this is clearly the government wanting to keep out of an Indian matter."

"I did not know you were so cynical, Dr. Haq," I said, my eyes moving from the long procession of trucks to the slightly built man sitting beside me.

"I am much older than you. I lived through the Hindu-Muslim riots in 1919 and 1925, and those were quite terrible." He sighed. "Now the question is, how we will we manage to work tomorrow? There is no doubt we will be needed."

CHAPTER
45

DANGEROUS ATMOSPHERE CREATED BY LEAGUE GOVERNMENT

*By 31 to 13 votes the Bengal Council on Thursday rejected
an adjournment motion which sought to discuss the Bengal
Government's declaration of August 16 as a public holiday.
Mr. Haridas Mazumdar (Hindu Mahasaba), who moved the
motion, said that he failed to understand why offices, workshops,
and banks would be closed, and why those people of the province
who did not subscribe to the creed of the Muslim League
would be made to join in the hartal of the 16th forcibly.*

—*Amrita Bazar Patrika*, Friday, August 16, 1946

At ten in the morning, the English language newspapers lay flat
and unopened on the dining table, evidence that Simon had
not read them. I hoped he hadn't gone to work on the strike day, but
I didn't know his plans anymore. This made me lonelier than ever,
but at least I could ask the staff his whereabouts. Ahmed was still
sitting in the car parked in the drive. He said Simon had walked to

Lord Sinha Lane and had said he wouldn't need his services that day.

"Burra-saheb said I could use the car for my errands as I wished today. Memsaheb staying home because of the Direct Action holiday?" The young driver smiled ingratiatingly at me.

"What is the errand? No shops will be open."

"Actually, the rally at Ochterlony. I have never seen Minister Suhrawardy speak. I would very much like it." Ahmed twisted his driver's cap in his hands as he spoke.

I knew he was being honest with me. Many Muslims would want to hear the speech. And if I made Ahmed stay in on a government-granted holiday, he would bear a serious grudge against me. Feeling resigned, I asked him about the speech's timing.

"Three o'clock, Memsaheb, but I am most grateful to leave at noon, to get a close position."

"You may go, but I don't know why you want the car. Ochterlony Monument is inside the Maidan."

"If I walk, angry Hindus might catch me." He looked pointedly at the dot of red kumkum I always wore in the center of my forehead. "They are setting up road barricades to keep Muslims away."

"All right, but you must return by five." As I spoke, I noticed he was grinning and nodding, but not with the normal expression of gratitude. It was as if there were some great joke to which he was privy—or that he was getting ready to tell somebody else.

I waited all morning and into the afternoon for the Red Cross van to pick me up, as was the established plan. The telephone didn't work; I imagined the operators were staying out, and perhaps the Red Cross workers had decided to as well. The dead telephone gave me another worry. If Simon wanted a ride from his office, he might not be able to ring home.

But that was a moot point, because five o'clock passed without Ahmed's return. Then it was six. Manik presented me with a cup of tea and asked what to make for dinner.

"I'm not hungry. Take a holiday from cooking!"

"Ever since the February riots, Memsaheb has become as thin as a broomstraw. It is not good."

I forced a smile on my face. "I'll eat a little, just to please you. But nothing fancy. What are you making for yourselves to eat?"

"Potatoes with greens, channa dal, and rice. It's a small meal because the vegetable-wallah stayed away. There's a bit of curd and sugar. I can make a sweet from it."

"Please make mishti doi. Mr. Lewes will enjoy it when he returns. Oh, I will be glad when this day is over!"

Manik raised his eyebrows and said, "I will be, too. I heard that you let Ahmed take Saheb's car to see Suhrawardy. How can he go off with those who are plotting our murders and return expecting me to give him rice?"

His emotion was understandable, but it filled me with indignation. I said, "We have always expected our staff to cooperate without prejudice; and please remember that most Europeans prefer Muslim cooks. Mr. Lewes chose you because of your ability and character only. Please think that way about your working brothers."

"Character? You think Ahmed has good character?" Manik sputtered, then wheeled about and left the room.

I was shaken by Manik's effrontery and hoped that what he said about future killings would not come true. An hour later, I recognized the sound of Jatin's footsteps on the stairs. When he came into the library, he was dripping with sweat and breathing hard, as if he'd run.

"Didi, Bow Bazar is burning!"

"Tell me," I said, pouring him a glass of water from the crystal pitcher I kept on the drinks trolley. Jatin flinched at my serving him from one of the best crystal tumblers, but after I urged him to drink, he did. His friends were reporting that Muslim thugs had come into the city from the countryside to destroy Hindu property and life, and that they were encouraging others in Calcutta to join them.

"It's a good thing that Reverend McRae is in Burma right now," I said, thinking about the vulnerability of his orphanage in the Black

Town. It housed children of all faiths; I prayed the building was locked. "Did your friends say whether the police are acting to stop it?"

"Not very much." Jatin breathed heavily. "They cannot keep up with so many different eruptions. These bad types may be traveling everywhere. And what of Ahmed and the saheb's car?"

"Not yet returned."

"Well, curfew is on now, so he should not be driving," Jatin mused. "Maybe he will come back tomorrow colored black from fire and red with blood!"

I did not want to believe Ahmed would join the rioting, but I did not know our new driver very well, and in such heated times I couldn't expect everyone to remain sensible. Shombhu came in with my dinner tray, and after chiding Jatin for using the good glass, asked me when the saheb was returning.

"Perhaps he went to the Control Room," I guessed.

"I only hope he doesn't walk in the city tonight," Shombhu's voice was ominous. "He has no car and the taxis and rickshaw drivers are not to be trusted."

My stomach twisted as I imagined Simon being accosted on the street, having his briefcase yanked away or worse.

"You miss him, Didi, don't you?" Shombhu looked at me sadly; he and the others had noticed the months of silence between us. I told Shombhu that I would dine from a tray in the library to be near the telephone.

At least All India Radio was working. The news broadcaster said that police had contained the riots at Bow Bazar, but there were riots at Sealdah Station, complicating the efforts of thousands to flee Calcutta by train. And fires were burning along Lower Circular Road in Ballygunge, where Pankaj and his mother lived.

Around ten, the radio reported that military orders had been given for the soldiers in the Worcester and Green Howard regiments to report to Howrah to contain the riots. I thought of the English saying: "better late than never." I supposed this was the way Governor Burrows and his people operated. I continuing listening to reports mixed with incongruous popular music until I fell into a restless sleep.

Suddenly, I heard something. My eyes flew open and I saw that Simon had stepped into the room.

"Thank God you're home!" I exclaimed before remembering that we were not speaking to each other.

"It's six thirty. Have you been here all night?" Simon's voice was hoarse.

Sitting up, I nodded, and he came and sat down on the other side of the partners desk, where my untouched dinner tray was. He was wearing the same suit he'd had on the previous day and looked exhausted. I asked if he had been in the Control Room.

"Yes." He rubbed at his bloodshot eyes. "I came for a wash and something to eat before going back . . . and to see that you were still here. The Buick and Ahmed were gone, so I feared the worst."

"Ahmed took the car yesterday morning. He'd said you would allow it, if I had no need to go anywhere."

Simon gave me a pained look. "Never would I have agreed to that. What if he went to the Direct Action rally?"

Swallowing hard, I said, "I let him go. I believed what he said about your orders, and thought it would be impossible for me to keep a Muslim servant inside on a Muslim holiday. Now I'm so very sorry."

Simon was silent for a moment, then said, "Well, he lied to you to begin with, and it's not your fault the city's gone mad. Only neighborhoods full of Christians and Europeans are safe. You won't believe what they're finding—" He broke off, and I turned to notice Shombhu standing in the open doorway with a tray that held a plate of biscuits and two cups of tea. Simon thanked him and closed the door. In a low voice, he said, "I don't want them hearing too much, lest more rumors spread. When the troops went in last night, they couldn't see much of anything except for flames and mobs. But now that the sun's up, they're finding corpses."

Despite the warm tea going down my throat, I was chilled to my core. "I've heard goondas came from the countryside to stir up trouble."

"Yes. The Muslim League managed to draw hundreds of extra food ration cards for these newcomers as well as special coupons for petrol. Nobody in government bloody noticed!"

"But surely it's not just them. Ahmed told me that Hindus were placing barricades around the city to interfere with people getting to the rally."

"And Hindu merchants have stockpiled American pistols and grenades. Others including gang leaders are supposedly paying men ten rupees per corpse, five rupees per wounding."

I wondered who had set the price, valuing life at so little. "But the Calcutta police are stopping it, aren't they?" Although headed by the British, the constables were largely Indian, and while most of them were Hindu, the ranks also included Muslims.

"They're being blocked. Mr. Suhrawardy has set up shop inside the Control Room. He's working to convince the police to stay out of the Hindu neighborhoods where violence is reported."

I did not think I'd heard Simon right. "He's keeping the police away? How could he do such a thing?"

"As he is the Bengal home minister, he argued that it is his right to direct police movement. I went from one police administrator to another trying to convince them that safety should rise above politics until Weatherington had me thrown out."

"I can't believe what is happening to everyone," I said slowly. "It's as if they've lost their souls."

"I'm returning to argue Suhrawardy has no place there, and if Weatherington bans me again I'll go to the army." Simon set down his empty teacup with a rattle. "While I'm bathing, will you please tell Manik to make me a quick breakfast? I may be busy for quite a while; I know I should have something inside me."

"You're going out again? Simon, I don't want you to be hurt." I longed to put my arms around him, but was afraid of being pushed away.

"No Europeans have been attacked in the rioting. Our neighborhood is quite safe because there are very few Muslims or Hindus here. You must not leave here, and tell the servants the same."

Simon left within the hour. He said good-bye quickly, without a touch or kiss. This first bit of communication in months would have felt like a triumph except for the context of the situation. Too many people were still likely to die.

I paced the library, feeling the tall walls of books that had once protected me press in like the sides of a tomb. The radio continued with the news announcer describing violence, burning and looting from Bow Bazar, where Mr. Chun's shop was; to Jorasanko, Rabindranath Tagore's hometown; and College Street.

College Street! I sat down weakly when I heard this. The Sens' home was in a row of mostly Muslim homes and businesses. Their building sign with an obviously Hindu name would mark them. Sonali was away living with her in-laws, but Mashima, Masho, Supriya, and Nishan were probably home. The fears I'd felt before turned to dread that they might not survive.

The sound of a vehicle stopping outside gave me a rush of hope and I ran into the front hall. Perhaps Ahmed was back with the Buick. But when I peered down the stairway, I recognized the slight figure of Ishan, the young driver from the Red Cross.

"You made it!" I exclaimed, thinking Ishan looked in a dreadful state, with a wet face covered with smudges of dirt and a wild look in his eyes.

"I'm sorry." Ishan bent over, burying his face in his hands. "So sorry, madam."

"What happened?" I hurried downstairs to him.

"It's Dr. Haq. I picked him up in Ballygunge. On Lower Circular Road, there was a bonfire. I tried to reverse it to get away but then men came running and surrounded us. I cannot tell the rest!"

"Speak," I implored him, because if Dr. Haq was in danger, we needed to help him quickly.

"The goondas stole Red Cross armbands out of the back and put them on. Then they took Dr. Haq. They would have taken me if I hadn't proved that I was Hindu. I begged them not to hurt Doctor-saheb, but they forced me to leave. They said if I looked back they would kill me, too."

I wanted to run from his words; but I knew they were true. The kidnapping had happened and could not be reversed; all I could do was think of how to help. "The telephone might work in one of the neighbor's flats. I'll try to get through to the police, and you can explain which way they took the doctor."

"No. Doctor-saheb is dead. I tried to follow where they'd gone and found they ran a knife through him," Ishan cried.

And now my tears flowed, too, for Dr. Haq, the dedicated and gentle doctor who chose to work for the Red Cross instead of having a private practice. I had admired and liked him so much. He knew the danger of Direct Action Day but had gone out because he felt an obligation to save lives.

Jatin helped me guide the shaken driver upstairs and into the kitchen for tea. Wiping away my tears, I went into the library and tried the telephone. Still not working. I could not remember if the operators' strike was over or this was a new disturbance. The rioters could have cut telephone lines; they could do anything. How would I reach the Sens, to find out their situation? They could not stay where they were. Somehow, they needed to reach the White Town.

Inside the kitchen, Ishan was clutching a tumbler of tea and re-telling the story of Dr. Haq's murder to Manik, Jatin, and Shombhu.

"Hindus did that?" Jatin's voice was horrified.

Not knowing I'd come up behind him, Manik spoke with venom. "But the Muslims are killing ten times more than Hindus are doing. I would have let the doctor go, but I will fight the goondas attacking their neighborhoods. My knives are already sharpened."

The cook's crude boast made me want to shake him. Taking a deep breath, I said to all of them, "Anyone leaving this house to join the riots will never be allowed back. Ahmed has already lost his job."

"Didi, what is happening in the city is criminal. We must be prepared to defend." Shombhu was trying to sound authoritative, but his damp, flickering eyes told me he was afraid.

"Of course it is criminal. But remember that true Hindus respect all forms of life, and if they fight Muslims or anyone else, they will not have a good rebirth." I looked at Ishan. "If you are feeling better, we can go out in the van together. Let's start at the Control Room, where we can hear the safest streets to travel. I would like to get to College Street and give first aid to those who need it."

Ishan shuddered like a leaf being tossed about in a monsoon wind. "I'm sorry, Kamala-didi, but I am not going out again into the madness. This area where you live is safe. After the tea, I would like to stay for a while, if you will permit it."

Ishan was utterly distraught. I'd been insensitive to ask anything of him. Feeling guilty, I said, "Of course, you may stay here as long as you like, even overnight—Shombhu, is there space in the garden house for Ishan to take a rest?"

"Yes, but . . ." Shombhu paused. "Didi, is it possible for my brother to bring his family here?"

"Of course—but how will he know it's all right to come?"

"I'm sure he's already trying to reach the White Town," Shombhu said. "Everyone who knows of a safe place is trying to reach it. And don't worry for us, madam. We will not go outside to fight. We will help Ishan and everyone who comes."

"Thank you, Dada." The word for older brother slipped from my mouth. He looked as surprised as I was, but I covered his hands with mine before leaving the kitchen. I was not saying good-bye, just making a silent promise I'd see him again.

In the hallway, I saw the driver's cap that Ishan had set down on the little rosewood table where we kept the day's newspapers and post. Next to his cap was the Red Cross van's key. I picked it up. The van wasn't much longer coming than the ambulance.

Did I dare? If I reached College Street, I could bring back the Sens to stay until it was all over. I remembered what Simon had said about Christians not being at risk. The danger wouldn't exist if nobody thought I was Hindu or Muslim. I had changed my identity so many times. This would be simple.

Squeezing the key in my palm, I went into my room and put on a freshly starched white sari bearing the Red Cross patch. In the bathroom, I washed my face, making sure the kumkum mark typical of Hindus was gone from my forehead. Around my neck I hung the silver crucifix necklace that was a gift from the orphanage staff.

In the hallway, I left a short note for Simon about going to the Sens to bring them here safely, just in case he reached home before I returned. And then, before any of the servants might catch sight of me, I slipped downstairs and out to the driveway.

The Red Cross van started easily, and I slipped into first gear.

CHAPTER
46

I now fear nothing—neither myself, nor anybody else.
I have passed through fire. What was inflammable
has been burnt to ashes; what is left is deathless.

—Rabindranath Tagore, *The Home and the World*, 1919

I drove north on Chowringhee: the usual route, only with no traffic this morning. At the Park Street intersection, flames shot from the windows of a Muslim kebab restaurant where I'd had many good dinners with Simon. A nearby Hindu-owned auction shop had already been burned to black. Christian households and businesses had painted their doors with crosses proclaiming their faith; these doors stood untouched. I thought of Kabita, still angry with me but safe inside Saint Joseph's Convent. She would never know it, but being locked up with the nuns in Chandernagore might have saved her life.

Going through Wellesley Street, I saw a tank with soldiers and raised my hand to them as I passed. Then I was in Bentinck Street, with more looted and burned buildings. Here, I saw the first corpses lying in the gutters and hanging from lampposts. The most gruesome sight was a man who'd been tied up to a tram system's electric control panel. Electricity must have jolted him repeatedly toward his painful death. Once this place had been called the City of Palaces; now it was Hades. It was as if Calcutta was besieged with the demons Thakurma often talked about in her historical stories. But this was real. I remembered Simon's plea for me to stay in, but not to go to College Street could mean leaving the Sens to die. A mournful voice inside me whispered, *If they aren't already slaughtered.* I told the voice to shut up.

In the side streets, men ran in packs from one house to another with cleavers and swords and lathis in hand. Most wore the ragged clothes of the poor, but others were in clean white kurtas and wore the white caps of the Congress Party, the erstwhile followers of nonviolence. Some had red tika marks on the forehead, meaning they were Hindus who had recently worshipped.

As I continued north, I found a fire burning in the road's center, just as Ishan had described. I veered left into a side street knowing it would just take a few turns to get back onto Chowringhee. But the street I turned into was filled with Hindus and Muslims battling each other with knives and tire irons and sticks. At the sight of my van, shouting erupted among them. A Red Cross van. They wanted it.

If I stopped the van, I would be lost. In terror, I stepped hard on the gas and shot forward so fast that I was thrown back in my seat. There was nowhere clear to pass, so I drove straight toward the mob, rather than let them surround me as Ishan had described happening earlier. The strategy worked; the men scattered except for a vicious-looking fellow who ran straight toward the driver's side door. I turned sharply, and the impact of the car pushing into him made him fly in the air and across the bonnet. Then he fell to the side as I roared down the next street, burned out already and now empty.

Another left turn, and I was back to the relative calm of shattered, looted Chowringhee. I was shaking, for I could not forget the man's shocked eyes as he faced me through the windshield. And I'd felt a bumping under the tires that I knew was his body and maybe someone else's too. Everywhere I looked I saw deceased: some of them women, judging from the ruined lengths of saris. And I'd seen a woman running among the rioters with a lathi in hand; she was as bloodthirsty as the rest.

Finally I entered College Street. Burned trams leaned drunkenly off the College Street track and the bookstalls were in flames or smoldering. All the stories and histories and poems inside their wooden walls were gone; the words so carefully set down for posterity meant nothing against mass violence. It was better that Tagore had passed away in peace five years earlier; these events would have been more than he could bear.

I maneuvered into the Sens' small street and parked in front of the business next door, Khan Typewriters, which was neither looted nor burned. Dutta Publishers, on the other side of the Sens, had its door kicked in. The windows were smashed at Chowdhury Teas, and I imagined the shop's valuables had been taken. On this street, it appeared that only Hindus had been attacked.

The metal grille was locked across the Sens' front door and window. This must have protected them from the fate suffered by their Hindu neighbors who hadn't had one. I thought it did not seem as if anybody had gained entrance. I walked around to the small window where I'd once called for admittance and saw a wooden board was nailed over it. Not much safety at all, I thought, as I called for someone to open the door to me. Either they weren't answering, or they'd already gone. They weren't dead; *no,* I said to myself, *they couldn't be.*

I had traveled through so much, and now I could not reach them! The impossibility of the situation made me want to scream, but I knew not to call attention to myself. As a few thick raindrops began falling, I looked up and recognized the Sens' flat roofline. And this gave me an idea.

If I could reach their roof, I might gain entrance through the roof's trapdoor and down the little staircase that went into their house. But

THE SLEEPING DICTIONARY 455

to reach the bookbindery's roof, I would need passage through another nearby house onto its roof. I did not know of any neighbors except the Nazims, who had come for tea once while I was there.

I ran down the street and knocked at the Nazims' door. A curtain shifted as someone from inside peered out.

"I am a friend trying to help the Sens. Will you let me in to explain?" I faced the window as I spoke, but the curtain dropped back in place. I waited a while longer, but nobody opened the door.

Belatedly, I realized that I should not remain so visible. I walked off, thinking of another way I could reach the Sens' roof and finally got it: Dutta Publishing. The door was gone, so I could walk straight in and presumably get to the top, if the upstairs was not locked.

Wary that looters might still be inside, I tiptoed into the building. To my relief, it was quiet and empty. I took the stairway but stopped short at the first floor. Two men were sprawled across the floor; they had been eviscerated. So much blood had flowed that it stained the floor and books that had fallen around them. The sight was frightening; I put a hand on the wall to steady myself because I felt faint. When I'd collected myself, I stepped over their bodies and continued up.

The trapdoor in the low ceiling at the end of the stairs was simple to unlatch. Then I was up on the flat roof, and it was a short walk along the row of houses to the roof I recognized from Mrs. Sen's red-bordered saris still hanging on the washing line. Red like the blood that smeared the edge of my sari as I'd walked over the corpses in Dutta Publishing.

The trapdoor into the Sen house was locked. Using the notched edge of the van key, I struck at the hinge until it broke. The trapdoor fell open, but in the next instant I faced the long, slim barrel of a rifle. I almost fell backward, I was so terrified.

"Don't move!" Supriya shouted and clicked the trigger into position.

"It's only me. Kamala!"

Abruptly the gun lowered. I saw that Supriya was dressed in her INA khaki uniform, jacket to jodhpurs. Her eyes were red and her face was drawn.

"Did the British let you keep the gun?" I asked. She could have shot me so easily; this knowledge made me shake.

"Of course not!" Supriya snapped. "It was borrowed from the Strength Brigade years ago. Come inside. Everyone's safe."

On the second floor, Mrs. Sen was peering around the corner of a doorway, holding a squirming Nishan against her wide body.

"Why did you come?" Mrs. Sen's hair was half down, and her face was wet with tears. "The goondas will certainly come back and finish us."

"Mashima, don't worry," I said, putting my arms around her. "I brought the Red Cross van. We will drive like the wind back to Middleton Street. I know the safe way."

"Your driver—what faith is he?" Mrs. Sen whispered. "Some of the rickshaw and taxi drivers are driving people straight to those who will kill them!"

"I am driving you myself. Have you organized your valuables?"

"We each have a suitcase, but—" Mrs. Sen broke off. "You are driving? You?"

"Women drive in the army, Ma," Supriya chided while showing me into her room where a small line of suitcases stood. She shot me a grin and said, "I'm so glad you have a way out of this place for us."

Sounding injured, Mrs. Sen told me, "We asked the Nazims to hide us, but they said they could not. After all these years of knowing each other—sharing food, and our daughters helping their children with studies."

"Everyone is trying to save his own skin," I said sadly. "Where is Masho?"

"He is gathering the most important books," Supriya said. "I asked him to keep watch but he said after the books are together. Oh, what now?" Supriya had turned away from me and was staring through a slat in the shutter covering her bedroom window. A group of about ten young men had surrounded the Red Cross van.

"Oh, no." My heart began to thud as I watched them try to get in through the driver's door. Finding it locked, they smashed the side window to pull out all the medicines. Walking around the van's outside, one man methodically removed the mirrors while another worked on the tires. How stupid I felt for parking the van where it could be seen. I had let down the Sens, and we would die together: not for the freedom of India, but as victims of our countrymen.

As quickly as the van had been emptied, the men backed away from it. A teenage boy was tilting a can over it. Petrol. He threw a match.

"No," I cried into Supriya's shoulder as the van burst into flames. And to my horror, I saw men using it like a kind of fire pit, taking broken pieces of furniture, setting them alight, and then running back to throw this lit tinder into certain houses.

"Oh, we must help the Duttas!" Supriya cried.

"They're already dead," I told her. "I came up through their building, and I saw them."

"Ramesh-uncle and Chetan. Oh, God!" Now Supriya pressed an arm across her face.

"Dutta Publishing is where we should go," I said, pulling her arm down so she could see the emotion on my face. "Their killing and looting is completed, so nobody will think to go back inside or to burn them out. And I left their roof door unlatched."

Supriya pressed her lips together, looking uncertain. "If we leave our place, it will surely be looted. Baba and I decided I should defend us with the rifle. I only have a few bullets, but I am a good shot."

But there were so many men on the street, she could not possibly defend against every one of them. I made my case and got her to agree to let me bring the valuables up to the roof.

Nishan was glad to get out of his mother's grasp to help with this project. I left him working and went to find Mr. Sen, who was inside the office.

He shook a finger at me and said, "You should not have come, Kamala. If you saw the way those goondas just exploded a Red Cross van, you would understand the risk."

I could not admit that I'd been the one who'd been thoughtless enough to leave the van in front. Instead, I said that we were bringing valuables to the roof, and asked if there was anything I could carry from his office.

"Yes!" His expression relaxed slightly. "I was working on some very important folios for the Asiatic Library."

"I mean things of your family's: money, bank books, important documents. The library will understand that its books should not come before your family's life."

"But they are hand-painted poems from the time of Emperor Akbar! This is an irreplaceable part of India's history. We must protect it with our lives because without it—" As Masho spoke, thick tears coursed down his wrinkled cheeks.

I knew what he was thinking. Without India's history, we would not remember what we once had been; we would become shells of beings like the savages outside. I understood that Mr. Sen loved books the way that I did; for him, these ancient books were a form of human life.

"Masho, I will be very careful with the folios. Please come."

Nishan came bounding down the steps. "The men are coming back down the street, and they have torches. Guess who is with them? Our darwan, Ali! He must have told them that we are hiding inside."

"Give me the folio," I said to Mr. Sen, who appeared to have gone numb. His fingers shook as he handed me a cracked red cover with a bundle of papers inside. I spied a burlap bag in the corner, wrapped it around the book, and followed him and Nishan upstairs just as the men bashed through the front door's grille.

CHAPTER
47

*Calcutta has earned a bad repute of late. It has seen too many
wild demonstrations during the past few months. If that evil
reputation is sustained for sometime longer it will cease to be
a city of palaces; it will become a city of the dead.*

—Mahatma Gandhi, *Harijan*, August 24, 1946

As we reached the roof, Supriya shifted into commander mode,
ordering us to creep low along with the suitcases toward the
Dutta Publishing building. I should have been relieved that we were
finally on our way, but a nauseous feeling settled in the pit of my stomach. So many men were massed below us, working on the grille; any
one of them could look up and notice us. I told Supriya that instead
of moving, we might be safer lying flat in the roof's center behind the
washing line still draped with saris until they'd gone.

"If we linger, I could shoot one of them," Supriya mused. "That
could scatter the crowd—"

"Or show them exactly where we are!" I retorted. "Tell everyone
to lie down."

"No, you must listen to me," Supriya whispered emphatically. "There can only be one commander."

"Daughters, do not argue," Mrs. Sen interjected; she was lying awkwardly on her belly. "Let's do as Kamala says and hide behind the washing. Then we can follow Supriya's guidance to the next place."

The way she'd included me as a daughter reminded me of Sonali. I'd heard her in-laws' fine house was in the predominantly Muslim area near Nakhoda Mosque. I whispered to Supriya, "Have you heard from your sister?"

"Fortunately, they all went to a wedding in Sindh," Supriya answered. "She will be worrying, when she hears about this."

"Ruksana lives near Park Circus," I said. "They have many Muslim neighbors. I suppose it's unlikely they will be targeted."

"But there are Hindus nearby. I worry for them." Supriya fiddled with her rifle and muttered, "There's something you should know; in case I die today and you survive."

"Don't talk such nonsense!" I began.

"Pankaj is in Delhi for the INA trials. Before leaving he asked me to marry him, but I didn't know how to answer. Now I have made my decision. Will you please tell him that I would have done it?"

A shiver ran through me at her words. How ironic that the man who'd almost married Bidushi had decided on Supriya. But I could understand why. The two had always had a comfortable, teasing relationship; and he was very proud of her for serving with the INA. And I was sure that his mother also approved of Calcutta's political darling.

"Didi? What do you think?" Supriya's eyes were focused on me.

"Pankaj will be yours, if you want him," I said. At least I'd never confessed my long-ago crush or the anger I'd held against him for his cavalier treatment of my emotions. If I had told all to her, her loyalty to me might have kept her from the man she'd always secretly wanted.

"His mother already spoke to my parents. Ma and Baba are a little worried that he wants me for the wrong reason—the political advantage. You see, he plans to run for Parliament after Independence," Supriya said. "But I don't care about his ambition. There is not another man in Calcutta like him."

"Yes, you're right about that," I agreed. Marrying an INA heroine would be like gold for Pankaj. But he admired her, too. I hoped the marriage would be a happy one. While I honestly wished her happiness, I was very glad not to be in her position.

"You are talking of romance, when death is stalking! Daughters, don't be foolish," Mrs. Sen hissed from the other side, letting us know she hadn't missed a word.

"All right, Ma. Watch this." And then Supriya was sliding forward like a lizard toward the roof's edge. She sighted along the rifle and pulled the trigger. The resulting blast was strong enough that I clapped my hands over my ears while her mother and Nishan screamed.

"They're running!" Supriya rose into a crouch and shot again at the retreating group. I joined her at the edge to see one man wailing and holding his arm; the other lay motionless. But there was no time to feel victory, because thick flames were licking their way up the Sens' storefront.

"We must go over to the Dutta building," I shouted at the Sen parents, who were still lying behind the washing line. "Get up."

Supriya, Nishan, and I led with the suitcases and folios. Mrs. Sen was too weakened by fear to carry anything, so her husband was consumed by supporting her, step by step toward the side of the roof. There was about a three-foot gap between the roofs. The jump had not bothered me, but this time, as I approached the edge and looked down, the three-story drop was dizzying. I tossed the suitcase hard to the other side; then I tucked my sari higher at the waist, ran a few steps toward the edge and leaped. I fell forward as I landed on the Duttas' roof, with the Akbar-period folio clutched securely against my chest. Supriya coached Nishan to follow, and he leaped with a squeal of excitement and was caught safely by me. Then Supriya threw the remaining suitcases and leaped herself.

I looked back to the other roof and saw the Sen parents standing at the edge. Mrs. Sen was crying as she looked past the rain gutters at the faraway street. With a wave of her hand, she indicated for him to go forward; she would remain. And now it was raining in earnest, though I doubted that it was enough to kill the fire.

"Ma, come on! There is no time to waste!" Supriya called. She was busy hauling suitcases toward the Duttas' trapdoor.

"I won't make it," her mother called back. "Go on yourself."

"Take Nishan down," I advised Supriya. "Don't look at them on the first floor. I'll help your mother."

"Not yet. I'll help her first," Supriya said.

For some reason, my knees had become weak; I had to steady myself before I jumped back to the Sens' building. I landed shakily but righted myself and smiled encouragingly at Supriya's mother as Supriya bounded over to join me. "See, Mashima, it's not hard," I said. "Your husband can pull you across with him! And Supriya can catch you on the other roof."

Mrs. Sen vehemently shook her head. "I have not jumped since I was a schoolgirl. I'll make him fall if he holds my hand—"

Her words were drowned out by the roar of motors below. I looked down and saw an army lorry had arrived. If only the army had arrived earlier, there would never have been a fire. But then I saw, pulling up behind, a massive fire engine. I felt faint, as if I were dreaming. Father McRae's angels had come together and saved us.

"Don't go anywhere," I said to the Sens, who were still teetering at the divide between the buildings. "Come look!"

The firemen jumped out, aiming the hose at the Sens' doorway, while others doused the burning Red Cross van with buckets of water. At the same time, soldiers ran down from the lorry bed and rushed into the Duttas' building, calling for them to come out.

Just one worker remained outside: a European in civilian clothes who kept circling the van as the firemen lashed it with water. When the flames had faded, the man looked inside the van; he came out coughing and sat down on the curb, putting his head in hands. I did not know any Europeans at the Red Cross who looked like this fellow; but I recognized the slump of his shoulders. It was Simon.

"We're here!" I called down to him, my heart swelling with the realization that he'd loved me enough to find me. But the noise of the fire hoses drowned out my voice. Simon hadn't heard; he was dejectedly standing up and turning away from the van. He wiped his hand across his eyes, and I guessed he thought that I'd been killed.

"Look up! We're here!" I shouted in English and then in Bengali; finally a soldier looked and gave a loud cry. What a sight we must have been: one woman in a bedraggled white sari and another dressed in an INA uniform. Behind us, Mr. and Mrs. Sen clapped and cheered.

"Captain Supriya!" one fireman called in excitement and another echoed his cry.

With all the commotion, Simon finally looked our way. I was too far to see his face, but I knew he recognized me because he held up his arms outstretched toward me. The embrace I had longed for earlier in the morning was finally almost mine.

As the group quieted, I called out that Supriya would bring down her brother through the Duttas' building, and the Sen parents would like to proceed through their own building, if the fire was out. After a fireman gave approval, we descended rapidly. I felt such a spring in my step that it was like flying.

But the strength was temporary. When we emerged on the street, my knees buckled and Simon caught me up in his arms.

"How did you know I was here?" I asked as he pressed his wet face against mine. He held me as if the past had never happened; as if he loved me like a newly wedded husband.

"Kamala, I am so thankful you left the note. Shombhu read it and came straight to the Control Room to tell me." Simon put his warm, dry jacket around my shoulders.

"You brought the army and a fire engine. How did you manage that?"

"Actually, it's the best way to get around," he said cheerfully. "And I had a feeling we'd save more than your skin. Now, let's go. We're quite safe in the army lorry, but they want us back in the European Quarter."

I could not go to safety without my friends. I began, "About the Sens—"

"I hope they'll come to stay with us! Shombhu and Jatin can prepare every room they might need."

He had thought of this already, without being asked by me. Tears of gratitude and love welled up in my eyes.

"But you're crying," Simon said, touching my cheek. "Don't you want them to come?"

CHAPTER
48

ILLUMINATION: . . . . *2. Spiritual enlightenment;*
divine inspiration; baptism.

—*Oxford English Dictionary*, Vol. 5, 1933

The slaughter did not end that day, nor for some time thereafter. As the Week of Long Knives continued with sporadic killings and burnings, we remained safely nestled in Middleton Mansions. Mrs. Sen moved into the kitchen, spending hours attempting to teach an annoyed Manik proper Bengali cooking. Schools were closed, so Nishan spent hours on the carpet, lost in a chess game with Simon. Mr. Sen bided his time in the library, reading through the collection. Supriya held court in the drawing room, where she gave interviews to journalists wanting a firsthand account of how the female INA veteran had cleared a riot with two shots.

"The *Times of India* reporter told me the government says only seven hundred and fifty died in Calcutta. It can't be," Supriya said when she and Simon and I were sitting in the garden having tea one evening.

"It's obviously false," Simon agreed. "I can tell you that more than five thousand corpses have been collected, and who knows how many others had been burned to nothing or swept from the gutters into the Hooghly River?"

And then there were the bodies not counted because they were cremated or buried as fast as their families could do it. We heard about Chhatri Sangha girls who had lost family members; Ruksana had survived along with her parents because they'd been hidden by Hindu friends. For every story of murder, it seemed there was a story somewhere else about good people who had hidden friends and neighbors within their homes. And there were some very canny individuals, like Pankaj's mother, who'd dressed herself like an old Muslim sweeper lady and sent away the rioters with a few glittering pieces she told them were the Bandopadhyay family's greatest treasures. After this tale, I was certain that Supriya would get on with Pankaj's mother; she had the same cleverness, and she would be a far better daughter-in-law than Bidushi or I could ever have been.

I knew all of this because Pankaj, who was still in Delhi, had been writing to Supriya. He wanted her to join him, and she was deliberating whether she should go, staying with family friends as he'd suggested. I told her it was a good idea, because in the capital, Supriya could very well begin a journey toward her own political success. And she'd see Pankaj enough to help decide if he really was the right man to become her life partner.

So many people were in our flat that when it came to my reunion with Simon, the experience was very muted. Only when we were sure everyone was asleep in the various bedrooms did we dare speak intimately. We made swift, quiet love with more tenderness than ever before. Three nights passed this way; then four.

"When this is all over," Simon said one night, "where will we be?"

"I don't know about myself, but you're taking a ship home to England." I had not forgotten the ticket order I'd seen on his desk. Nor had I forgotten the little girl who lived and breathed just an hour's train ride away and might someday relent and allow me to be part of her life.

"Yes, my berth number's come up for January," Simon said. "But I won't go anywhere until I know where I stand with you."

"I am here for you," I said, although it was not quite true, because of the secrets I still held. I could have told him about Kabita then, but I was scared of his pulling away.

"I never stopped loving you," Simon said. "You understood that, didn't you?"

"Of course I didn't! You said nothing to me for months, took your own room, treated me like an Untouchable—"

"But, incredibly, you stayed."

"I stayed because you are my husband," I said. "And because I am tired of running."

"Running from where? Please, won't you tell me?" Simon murmured. "What is it that has been driving you all this time?"

I would not risk the tenuous bond that was growing between us. So I answered the best way I could, by covering his mouth with my own.

*   *   *

BY AUGUST 24, the killings had stopped. Trams and buses were running, and shops and markets had reopened for business. The Sens' contractor was making repairs to the ground-floor entrance, which was the only part that had burned. The question was whether the Sens would stay or sell the place; for as Mrs. Sen said, "Not one of the neighbors we knew for more than thirty years helped us when we needed it. With friends like that, who would stay?"

The Sens had decided to move to a section just outside Calcutta called Salt Lake. It was still mostly swamp, but the Israni family thought it would become a popular place to live. Supriya planned to stay with them until her December wedding.

I busied myself with the Sens' departure to their new home, and then they were suddenly leaving Howrah Station with twenty suitcases and a flurry of embraces. The weekend stretched ahead. I was looking forward to having time alone with Simon, to see a film or eat dinner at a good restaurant as we'd once done. I wanted to replace the ugly memories of the Direct Action riots with what I remembered of the good life.

On the first night all of our friends were gone and we were finally alone, I sat in the garden with a glass of sweet lime, watching butterflies circle the jasmine bush. Mr. Chun's teak chair felt firm under my back, as strong as Simon's arms around me at night.

"Something for you!" Simon walked down from the veranda; he was home a little later every evening, but happier. He had been this way since his transfer from Lord Sinha Lane to Government House, where he had become the Bengal governor's confidential assistant for the transfer of power. Simon's role in securing the army's return on a night when Calcutta's government was paralyzed had been appreciated, and he was no longer anywhere near Mr. Weatherington.

"A letter for you!" Simon said, holding it out. "But I will only give it for baksheesh."

As I looked up to give him a kiss, which was surely the kind of tip that he was teasing me for, I wondered who had written to me. The cream-colored envelope seemed familiar, and when I saw the watermark, I recognized the stationery set I'd bought for Kabita. She had not written me any letters before. I held the envelope, studying Kabita's neat, rounded handwriting, trying to control the excitement I felt inside. A letter from Kabita. She had made the effort to communicate.

"Is it something you don't want?" he asked quietly.

"No," I said, realizing how grave I must have looked. "This is a letter I've eagerly awaited for so many years."

I slit open the envelope and drew out two sheets of paper written in the same neat English that had been on the envelope.

Dear Auntie,

I am not sure what you would like me to call you now. You never said. I am writing because I heard what happened in Calcutta, and I hope you are all right. Mother Superior let me ring Calcutta but there was no answer.

I am sorry for what I said the last time. I have been thinking of you every day. Some months ago you sent me some smashing stories. You stopped at the place where you and your friend are beginning to study together. I want to read what happens next. But if you don't write again because you're mad, I understand why. And I haven't forgot you!

Your loving daughter,
Kabita Zeenat Hazel Smith

She used her names—all of them. My daughter understood who she was and did not hide it. And this was more of a gift than anything I had ever received.

"Are you all right, my love? I see you're crying." Simon had settled in the chair next to mine without my noticing. Now he took up my hand.

"Yes, I'm fine. It's the best letter I ever had." I sat motionless, filling up to overflowing with emotion. I was so proud of Kabita, so wracked with love for her, that I could no longer hide her away. It was time to stop holding all my secrets. "Here, you look at it."

He read it slowly all the way through and then a second time. At last he said, "I don't understand. The writer of this letter calls you Auntie but also says she is your daughter. Is that an Indian custom?"

I took a deep breath and looked straight at him. "No. She's my little girl. Not so little, really. She turned eight over the summer."

"Damn it," Simon said, and blood slowly filled his face. "Damn."

"You're upset," I said, but still felt relief that the truth was out.

The bricks in the walls of lies were coming loose, freeing me from the prison I'd lived in since girlhood.

Simon put his drink down. "If she's eight now, you were young when she was born."

"Eighteen. And prior to that were terrible years that I did things no girl should ever have to."

Simon shook his head. "I'm sorry."

"Yes, I imagine you won't want someone like me in your flat anymore—"

"No. It's just that—" He broke off, and sighed. "We've wanted a child, and it seems we've had one all along."

We've had one all along. The sentence spoken so naturally made my pulse race. Did this mean Simon would have accepted Kabita in the past—or that he still might?

"You must be horrified by this information," I said, watching his face. "Any husband would be."

Simon shrugged. "What happened in this city over the last few weeks is what I'd call horrifying. Discovering that I am not your first lover is not. You already know that you weren't my one and only."

"Yes. Though I expect that I am, now!" My pulse was hammering, not out of fear but happiness.

"Yes. We must talk honestly—and obviously, Kabita's needs must come first. What is the situation with her father? Would he allow her to visit us on holidays?" Simon's eyes were on me, full of hope.

"Don't have to worry about her father, because he never accepted her as his. He was an Englishman." The words slipped free before my internal censor could stop them.

"Well, then. I'm relieved that he's not a part of your life, or hers." Simon was still looking steadily at me. "Please understand that whatever happened with him, or with the spying, or with your daughter, will not cause me to leave you. But I'd like to know more. If you're ready to tell."

Tears had come to my eyes again; I wiped them and said, "I've feared telling you because the story is filled with so many sad parts, and is quite long. It begins in a tiny village by the sea."

Simon took my hands in his. "Oh, but long stories are my favorites. Especially when I know the ending will come out happily."

CHAPTER
49

DARLING: 1. A person who is very dear to another; the object of a person's love; one dearly loved.

—*Oxford English Dictionary*, Vol. 3, 1933

Time, sweet time! For most of my life, time had passed with excruciating slowness, but now, the days rushed forward. The next morning, Kabita answered the telephone call I made to Saint Joseph's. Her soft hello sounded shy but not angry.

I told her that I'd spoken about her to my husband, and we both wanted her in our life. She could stay in the flat as often as she wanted; and if she were willing, he would formally adopt her as his legal daughter. Simon knew many of the judges in the Calcutta High Court, and he'd been advised to quickly bring a petition to them before independence.

"I've thrown so many long words and ideas at you," I apologized. "But what it really means is that you'll never be alone again. You will be with your father and mother, in a comfortable house, and you may attend school wherever you'd like."

Kabita was silent for a half minute, then asked if we could come on Friday to take her to stay with us for a weekend in Calcutta. I agreed and gave her details about our arrival time. Simon, who'd been sitting on the other side of the partners desk listening intently, gave me a thumbs-up. But I wondered if we could truly convince her, after she'd suffered so many disappointments.

※   ※   ※

"I'M MORE NERVOUS today than at our wedding," I said, holding on to Simon's hand as we walked together up the convent's drive.

"You are?" Simon gave my damp fingers a squeeze. "At least she knows you. She probably thinks I look like a blue-eyed devil!"

"A very handsome devil. Oh, there she is! The tallest one, with the brown hair." I had spotted her in a cluster of energetic young Indian and European girls. They had field hockey sticks and were battling for the puck on the grass near the school's entrance. Kabita did not see us, but her merry laugh carried.

"She's good at sport. Maybe the doll I've bought for her was the wrong gift." Simon sounded anxious.

"Well, there's plenty we can do with games in the garden." I was feeling optimistic. We would not be a typical family, but my happiness since telling Simon was not typical, either. He had listened to my life story over the course of three nights. At the end of it, he'd said that while many parts of my story broke his heart, all he felt was gratitude that I'd come into his life and stayed.

"Kabs! Your parents are here," shouted an English girl, looking over her shoulder at us.

How did she know we were her parents? I wondered, before realizing that everyone at school knew Kabita as Anglo-Indian. Simon was white, and I was Indian; the three of us looked as if we belonged together.

As Kabita loped toward us, her eyes moved from me to Simon. And then she put her arms out to me, and I inhaled her delicious schoolgirl scent of ink, coconut oil, and sugar. As I stooped to hug her, I smelled Bidushi and our shared past; but the aroma was all the sweeter, because this time there could be a happy ending.

"Kabita, thank you," I said, my voice finally catching up to my breath. "Thank you for coming with us this weekend. I can hardly wait to bring you home."

"Ma, what should I call him?" she whispered into my ear.

She had chosen to call me Mother; with my heart filled to bursting, I considered the question of Simon. "I don't know, darling. Maybe Simon-uncle, or—"

"Father." Simon had squatted so he was at our level, and his blue eyes looked deep into hers. "Or Daddy or Papa or Baba! You choose my name. I can never replace Hafeeza and Abbas, but I will treat you like my own."

"Really?" She pulled away from me a few inches and looked at us with her beautiful, wary eyes.

In her gaze, I saw all the people who'd died or vanished from her world. Why should she believe that this home we wanted to give her could be a permanent one where she'd be happy?

"Yes," I said softly, holding back the tears. "Your bedroom is right next to ours. It's just been painted pink. There's a teddy on your bed and a dollhouse set up on the carpet. Outside, the garden is full of flowers and a very large mango tree. Everything is waiting. You are the only part missing."

Kabita shifted from one foot to another, as if deciding. Then she said, "I like pink."

I looked at Simon, and he grinned. I'd been the one to insist on the rushed painting and decorating.

"Pink is a beautiful color," Simon said, picking up her hockey stick "Well, then. Let's all go home."

CHAPTER
50

Hindus and Moslems, freely mixing with each other,
are in Calcutta tonight wildly celebrating the approach of
independence. The former scenes of communal battles are now
happy meeting places for crowds of both communities who are
shouting and dancing in the streets. No incident has been
reported until a late hour tonight. Mr. Gandhi, Mr.
Suhrawardhy, who ceases to be the Premier of Bengal at
midnight, and a former mayor of Calcutta are beginning
a 24-hour fast to celebrate independence.

—*The Manchester Guardian*, August 14, 1947

I'd planned to serve our independence dinner by candlelight in the dining room laid on a silk tablecloth laden with all the favorite family dishes. But Simon was playing field hockey in the garden with Kabita and Pallavi, her new friend from Loreto House, the school just down the block. All afternoon and into twilight, the girls had run back and forth in the garden, chasing the balls he lobbed. In the end, they were altogether too sweaty to sit inside on velvet chairs, so I shifted the meal to the veranda.

We began dinner at nine thirty, timed so that while we ate pudding—a trifle made with fresh cream, mangoes, and pistachios, the colors of the new Indian flag—we could listen on the wireless to Mr. Nehru addressing the Indian Constituent Assembly. I was happy to see the girls dig in, but inside I felt some private guilt at the feast because of the fasting by Gandhiji and Suhrawardy in North Calcutta. They were staying together as an appeal to Bengalis not to fight like they had eleven months earlier. To let the new borders of India and Pakistan stay, even though Bengal itself would be split apart like sisters separated by a flood, never to live together again.

"At the stroke of the midnight hour, when the world speaks, India will awake to life and freedom." Nehru's voice cut into my bittersweet imaginings. "A moment comes, which comes but rarely in history, when we step out from the old to the new, when an age ends, and when the soul of a nation, long suppressed, finds utterance."

"Ma knows him," Kabita said casually to Pallavi, whose mouth made a little O as she gaped at me.

"Not quite, Kabby. We've only just said hello!" It was true that I'd met him at Supriya and Pankaj's wedding. When Pankaj had made introductions, he had praised my years of intelligence gathering, especially regarding the government's attempts to catch Netaji. Nehru had nodded in approval, while I said what I always did: I had never heard from the Bose family that the information had mattered, but it felt right to help in anyway possible.

As Mr. Nehru's address continued, I was filled with the realization that everything was linked, like the efforts Supriya and I had both made, as far apart as we had been. And while the political outcome I'd always longed for had come, it also meant the end of Simon's livelihood, because the new Indian Civil Service would be staffed by only Indians.

Simon had packed up his office two weeks earlier. Reams of

documents and photographs were nailed up in crates headed for the East India Office archives in London. Simon was allowed to keep duplicates that were not classified material. I wondered how we would fit all these new books and pamphlets and folios into the library; but not as much as I wondered what he would do for his next job.

We had talked about his taking an administrative job with the British Civil Service in London, like so many of his colleagues, including Mr. Weatherington, were doing. Another choice was moving to West Sussex, where his family had a variety of business interests. But Simon didn't particularly want to return to England. He'd considered taking his books to fill a shop in Bombay that he'd heard was being vacated.

I'd lobbied for staying put in Calcutta, selling books out of the library as needed to stay afloat.

Months earlier, I'd created a sales brochure about the most valuable books that Simon might be willing to let go. Mr. Sen spread the word to his collector customers throughout India, but their reaction was muted. The few inquiries that had come for the most valuable books were less than what Simon had paid to buy them ten years earlier. So he held on.

Prime Minister Nehru's address finished at midnight. Over the wireless came thunderous roars of joy that were soon drowned out by honking horns and fireworks on our street. India was free.

"It's come! Independence!" Simon said. I leaned over and kissed him, feeling a surge of elation that I was celebrating this day with him and my daughter. We were different from any other family in Calcutta, but no less happier. I turned to give hugs to Kabita and Pallavi and found them already standing by my chair.

"Ma, please! Listen to me; may we be excused?" Kabita shifted from foot to foot in an impatient dance.

"But why would you go off? It's Independence!"

"Yes! Jatin wants to set up fireworks in the road and give away all the leftover cake!" Kabita said, pointing to the vast expanse of mango-cream confection that was left.

"Giving it away is a good idea." I hesitated for a moment, considering whether her going into the street was a good idea. I escorted Kabita everywhere, even down the block to school, because deep inside—even though Simon had brought me immigration information proving Rose Barker had left India and settled in Brighton—I still feared that my daughter would vanish.

"Kamala-di, all of us will be with them. Just in front of the house, with the Mitra family," Jatin said, mentioning a Parsi family I'd grown to know and like. "They are serving refreshments also."

"Yes," said Simon to Kabita. "But remember, darling, you may only hold sparklers. And stay right with Jatin and the others. Ma and I will be along shortly."

After they'd skipped out of the garden, I asked Simon, "Will it feel strange to you to be celebrating on the street, an Englishman amongst Indians?"

"Why should I?" Simon poured a little more Darjeeling in my cup. "I worked for the transition, just as you did."

"I never dreamed that I'd live to see independence," I said, taking the cup with a smile. "When I was a girl at Lockwood School and then in Kharagpur, it seemed the British could put down any attempts at freedom."

"So when you found out about my work, you hated it," Simon said. "It took me some time to understand that I wasn't being helpful to anyone. But I know that I love India. Just as I love you."

I studied the man I'd come to love improbably but so deeply. "For a while, I thought I hated you. But the feeling inside me was—too strong. All along, it must have been love—mixed with disappointment at what I learned."

Simon pressed his lips together. "I fear I'm going to disappoint you again. I don't think any bookselling business could bring enough to support us. And then there's the question about you—how you'd like to spend your life."

I had been thinking about this, too. I wanted to do more than keep house, volunteer, and take care of Kabita, because in less than a decade, she'd be off to college. Slowly, I said, "I don't want to be a memsaheb. I wish I could afford to enroll somewhere and get the Cambridge certificate I always wanted. But a twenty-seven-year-old lady can't sit down at the desk with her daughter at school. It's too odd. You know how sensitive Kabita is; she'd be humiliated."

"I often forget you don't have that certificate, and it means so much to you." Simon paused. "I don't suppose you'd—no, you'd find it too cold."

"What's too cold?" I looked at him, thinking, Darjeeling?

"Someone invited me to apply for a position in Canada," Simon said. "The University of Toronto is seeking a lecturer on India's politics and modern history. If I did get the position, I would teach there—in that country."

I caught my breath, because I could tell he felt differently about this than the proposed government job in London. "I gather you'd qualify to teach the politics and history based on your Cambridge degree and your career experiences here?"

"Yes. And do you remember the essays I sometimes wrote about the books in my collection? Well, a few of them were published. People are interested in understanding how England treated India over the years. And how, in turn, India responded to the British." A flash of pleasure crossed Simon's face, an excited happiness that I'd never seen when he spoke about his ICS career. "If I became a lecturer, it would allow me—allow us—to return to India occasionally. And to further your personal interest in education, the University of Toronto might be just the place. A private tutor can help you with prerequisites. The academic system is different in North America, not as rigid as India or England."

But Canada was a dominion of the United Kingdom, just as India would remain for a few years before becoming a republic. I asked, "How English is Canada, really?"

He smiled wryly. "Well, most of the people there are supposed to sound like Americans, but there are quite a few Brits who've emigrated. Supposedly it's easy to find crumpets and marmalade."

"Many Anglo-Indians are leaving for Canada," I said, recalling a conversation at some recent Loreto House mothers' gatherings. "We might know people in Canada."

"There is a large Asian community in Toronto," Simon said. "Indians have been there for many years. They say that one can buy spices there. And real Indian rice."

I considered the myriad customs and words that the British had brought to India. Could Indians scattering throughout the world spread their own culture, too? And if I worked there, and had a profession of real value . . .

"Sailing by ship is relatively inexpensive, but it takes so long," Simon continued, not knowing the questions racing scattershot through my mind. "This is the way the government will send us out. But if we are careful with money, we might be able to return for our first visit by airplane."

"If *we* earn enough," I added. "After some of my experiences over the years, I feel called toward—becoming a doctor. Maybe if college goes well, I might qualify for medical school, although I always thought I would teach. I can't say which I'd prefer right now."

"Whatever you choose, I will support—and just think how proud Kabita will be." Simon's voice dropped; there was a catch in it. "But that doesn't take away the question of leaving India now. Would it break your heart?"

Once again, a wave had come and swept away the life I knew. This time, the wave was freedom. Children born into the new India would grow up in a nation where no foreign power could seize their rice or keep them out of hospitals and train compartments. Women would vote freely, and the caste system would be officially abolished. I would have preferred to linger in the new free India. But I could still witness India's growth from wherever I moved and feel proud.

"My heart is healed," I said, running my hand along the edge of

Simon's jaw and bringing it to his lips. "And you know that India will always be inside it, along with you and Kabita."

Simon kissed my hand. We looked at each other for a long moment, full of everything that had happened—and what would come. Then gradually, I became aware of car horns bleating in exultation. I heard the cheering, and singing voices, and even Kabita's high-pitched, merry laugh. Without saying anything more, Simon and I linked hands and walked out of the garden, toward the celebration.

A TASTE OF OLD
CALCUTTA

PERFECT RICE (BHATT)

Serves 6 with leftovers

2 cups basmati rice, white or brown, soaked at least 20 minutes (for white rice) or 2 hours (for brown)

3 cups water or low-sodium chicken stock (for white rice; use 4 cups for brown)

1 cinnamon stick

2 cloves

2 green cardamom pods

¼ cup chopped onion

1 tablespoon canola or vegetable oil

Rinse the soaked rice (once for white rice, 4 times for brown) to remove extra starch.

In a medium-size pot, add 1 tablespoon of oil and bring to medium heat. Add spices and, after a minute, the onion and drained rice. Sauté about 2 minutes and then add the stock.

Raise heat slightly to bring to a boil. When it boils, lower heat to a simmer and put the lid on the rice.

Cook rice until the water is almost gone (15–20 minutes for white basmati rice, about 45 minutes for brown).

Turn off range and let rice sit covered for 10–20 minutes to continue steam cooking. Then fluff with a fork and serve. Bengalis consider rice well cooked if the grains appear to be standing upright.

MUSTARD SHRIMP (CHINGRI BHAPEY)

Serves 6 as part of a larger meal

1.5 pounds raw shrimp,
shelled and deveined
3 tablespoons brown
mustard seeds
1 tablespoon poppy seeds

2 green chilies, seeded
1 teaspoon turmeric
powder
¼ cup coarse salt

Marinate shrimp in coarse salt for 10 minutes, then rinse.

Grind the mustard and poppy seeds and chilies in a spice or clean coffee grinder.

Mix the shrimp into this paste and put in a stainless-steel bowl. Cover tightly with foil.

Choose a stockpot large enough to contain the bowl. Add enough boiling water to the stockpot so that it will come a third of the way up the foil-covered bowl. Cover the stockpot and put on medium heat for a low boil. Cook the shrimp about 10–15 minutes total, then carefully (to avoid burning yourself!) lift the foil midway (turning off the stove temporarily) so you can stir the shrimp once.

Shrimp are ready when they are tender and the flesh is white. Serve with rice, dal, and a vegetable curry.

INDEPENDENCE TRIFLE

Serves 10

Approximately 18 double ladyfinger cakes, fresh or dried

1 pint of custard, made with Bird's Custard Powder or from scratch (store-bought vanilla pudding may be used as well)

Two 30-oz (850 g) cans of Alphonso Mangoes, drained (or 4 cups of fresh, ripe sweet mango slices)

1 pint heavy cream, whipped with 2 tablespoons of sugar

Apricot jam or orange marmalade

1 cup unsalted pistachios, shelled and roughly chopped

Reserve 1 cup of the whipped cream to use for topping. Mix the remainder of cream with the custard.

Cover the bottom of a glass bowl with ladyfinger halves, curved side down. Spread a little mixed apricot jam/orange marmalade on top of the ladyfingers. Lay enough mango slices to cover.

Top with half the custard-cream mixture and sprinkle with ⅓ cup of pistachios.

Repeat another ladyfinger, jam/marmalade, mango, and custard layer, sprinkle with ⅓ cup of pistachios.

Add remaining fruit and top with whipped cream and sprinkle with remaining pistachios.

ACKNOWLEDGMENTS

First, I must thank my parents, Subir Kumar Banerjee and Karin Banerjee Parekh, for temporarily removing me from elementary school in order to join my father's three-month sabbatical to India. I still treasure my illustrated diary recounting the unforgettable experience with my sisters, Rekha and Claire Banerjee: from giant lizards in the garden to mosquito net beds, Amul cheese, and kumkum. Since that happy period in 1973–74, I've traveled to India four more times, but I doubt I'd feel as strongly called to India if I hadn't had that marvelous childhood introduction. I am grateful to the many relatives in our Banerjee clan, based in Kolkata and Jamshedpur, especially my aunt Sumitra Sengupta and my cousin Gautam Sengupta, who smoothed the way for me into India's National Library. More relatives—the Chatterjees of Midnapur—kindly welcomed me to their historic hometown, Kharagpur, and Digha. Dr. Bharat Parekh, my mother's husband, shared some great freedom-fighting stories from elder relatives that inspired my account of Kamala's and the Sens' activities.

I also received very special assistance from my father's wife, Dr. Manju Parikh, whose family has been established in Kolkata since the 1970s. Manju's mother, Padmaben Parikh, and her sister,

Hemantika Puri, both recently died and are very much missed. I was so lucky to know them and will always be grateful for their introductions that led to my connecting with wonderful experts on the city, among them Sunita Kumar, who brought me into Middleton Mansions; Moina Jhala, the Browsers, Tiku and Rekha Ashar, who know College Street so well. Dr. Dilip K. Roy, a retired surgeon and my father's best friend from childhood, gave stories and reading suggestions, as did his son, Kaushik, and daughter-in-law, Dina. Damayanti Lahiri and her mother, the artist Shanu Lahiri, gave me a delicious taste of the city's intellectual-social energy. Thanks also to Rajashri Daspupta and Sushil Khanna for their hospitality and suggestions of historic walking tours, and Professor Madhu Mitra for helping with Tagore titles.

Several scholars of Indian history steered me to places I would never have found on my own. Geraldine Forbes, distinguished teaching professor at SUNY Oswego, inspired me with her memoirs of Bengal's women freedom fighters and gave me a kind introduction to the Oxford historian and former Gandhian activist, Tapan Raychaudhuri, who was generous enough to meet with me during his winter visit to Kolkata. Dr. Forbes also referred me to Professor Krishna Bose, the director of the Netaji Bhawan (and a former Member of Parliament and daughter-in-law of the late Sarat Bose), who graciously spoke at length with me about Bose family history at the Netaji Bhawan. Also during my Kolkata visit, I was blessed to have met Dr. Durba Ghosh of Cornell University, who shared information about the lives of jailed freedom fighters. Dr. Parna Sengupta of Stanford University offered insights into missionary schools in India. Dr. Hari Vasudevan, director of Maulana Abul Kalam Azad Institute of Asian Studies, gave a good picture of the social and international ferment during wartime. More details of old city culture came from Dr. Sweta Gosh of Saint Xavier's sociology department. Dr. Usha Thakkar, honorable secretary of the Mani Bhavan Gandhi Museum in Mumbai, gave me a wonderful house tour in Mumbai and an explanation of Gandhiji's role in the freedom movement. At Loreto College, I was happy to learn about the history of girls' education in India from Dr. Anuradha Chatterji, and I am appreciative to the faculty of La Martiniere Girls school to allow my visit to their beautiful, historic building. Mrs. Flower Silliman, a longtime teacher in Kolkata, used her fantastic memory to help me write accurately about the cultural life of the 1940s, from diamond rings to nightclubs. To the librarians at India's National Library's reading room near the Esplanade, many thanks for hauling down all those old *Amrita Bazar Patrika* copies—and the cups of tea!

The Sleeping Dictionary also took me to London. Before I'd reached the India Office archives held by the British Library, librarian Hedley Sutton alerted me to recently declassified files from a secret intelligence unit operating within the ICS's Bengal division. Thanks to him, Mr. Lewes found a profession!

Unbelievably, there really was a gentleman like Mr. Lewes—that is, a passionate collector of books and printed material related to the British rule of India. The real collector came from Saint Paul, Minnesota, and his name was Charles Lesley Ames. At the turn of the century, Mr. Ames began reading about India, and this led to his collecting books and government records of British India. In 1961, he donated more than twenty-five hundred books to the University of Minnesota, which established the Ames Library of South Asia, which has become one of the foremost Indian libraries outside of India. At the Ames Library, I received tireless and frequent guidance from its librarian David Faust. I also appreciated the efforts of my inspiring University of Minnesota Hindi teacher, Nadim Asrar, now a journalist working with the *Times of India* in New Delhi.

Research is the fun part of writing a historical novel. Sitting through dozens of rewrites is the hard part. I couldn't have pulled it together without my Minneapolis writers group: Gary Bush, Heidi Skarie, Maureen Fischer, and Stanley Trollip and Judy Borger. Also: the writers Neroli Lacey for her expertise on Britain, and Joyce Lebra for her insights on women in the INA. Subin Banerjee shared childhood stories of wartime Calcutta, and Karin Banerjee Parilch did a thorough copy-edit.

Online research put me in touch with so many knowledgeable people. Members of the India-British Raj LISTSERV that is organized by Harshawardhan Bosham Nimkhedkar within rootsweb.com, were able to answer detailed questions about wartime raids, school life, cars, and restaurants in 1930s and 40s Calcutta. My generous online helpers on the Anglo-Indian colonial experience include Nick Balmer, Sunny Kalara, Kabita Chhibber, Sylvia Staub, Doreen Grezoux, John Feltham, Warren O'Rourke, Dr. Stanley Brush, Blair Williams, and Roy Wildemuth, the assistant curator of the Antique Wireless Association's military collection. Anyone else I missed: my apologies, and I owe you a gin-lime!

I am so grateful for the steadfast support of Vicky Bijur, who has been encouraging me to write about India for more than a decade, and to editor extraordinaire Kathy Sagan for believing in this book, and her assistant, Natasha Simons. Most of all to my beloved husband, Tony, and our children, who understand my mental and physical absences. To every one of you: *Shukria*. Thank you so very much.

Sujata Banerjee Massey

BIBLIOGRAPHY

I read many books about India's history (in English) in preparation for writing this novel. I've listed most of them below along with the chapters where they appear. Rabindranath Tagore's poetry has appeared in many collections and anthologies and on many websites. I've used the most widely known titles, English and Bengali (if available to me) and the year of original Bengali publication and the name of that publication if I could locate it. Other important books that I used in research, but did not directly quote from, are listed as well.

Book I: Tagore, Rabindranath. "Golden Boat," 1894.

Chapter 1: Tagore, Rabindranath. "The Flower Says," *Chandalika*, 1938.

Chapter 2: Tagore, Rabindranath. "Sea Waves," 1887.

Chapters 3 and 10, and Book III: Denning, Margaret Beahm. *Mosaics from India: Talks About India, Its Peoples, Religions and Customs.* Fleming H. Revell Company, 1902.

Book II: Tagore, Rabindranath. "Two Birds," 1894. *One Hundred and One: Poems.* Bombay: Asia Publishing House, 1966.

Chapter 4: Yule, Henry and A. C. Burnell. *Hobson-Jobson: A Glossary of Colloquial Anglo-Indian Words and Phrases and of Kindred Terms, Etymological, Historical, Geographical and Discursive.* London: 1886.

Chapter 7: Carey, William. *A Dictionary of the Bengalee Language,* 1825.

Chapter 8: Tagore, Rabindranath. "Number 18," 1937. *One Hundred and One: Poems.* Bombay: Asia Publishing House, 1966.

Chapter 9: Tagore, Rabindranath. "The Night Express," 1940. *One Hundred and One: Poems.* Bombay: Asia Publishing House, 1966.

Chapter 11: Tagore, Rabindranath. "Urvashi," 1895. *One Hundred and One: Poems.* Bombay: Asia Publishing House, 1966.

Chapters 12, 39, 42, and 46: Tagore, Rabindranath. *The Home and the World.* Macmillan, 1919. Originally published in Bengali as *Ghare Baire* in 1915.

Chapter 18: *Travel in India, or City, Shrine and Sea-Beach: Antiquities, Health Resorts and Places of Interest on the Bengal-Nagpur Railway.* Times Press, 1916.

Chapter 31: Godden, Rumer. *Bengal Journey: A Story of the Part Played by the Women in the Province, 1939–1945.* Longmans, Green Ltd., 1945.

Chapter 37: Porter, Cole, and Robert Fletcher. "Don't Fence Me In," originally written for the unproduced film *Adiós, Argentina* in 1934.

Chapter 44: Tagore, Rabindranath. "Rahu's Love," 1884. *One Hundred and One: Poems.* Bombay: Asia Publishing House, 1966.

Additional Bibliography

Banerjee, Bibhutibhusan. *Pather Panchali* (Song of the Road), originally published by Ranjan Prakashalay in Bengali in 1929, translated by Indiana University Press, 1968.

Bose, Subhas Chandra. *Netaji's Life and Writing: The Indian Struggle, 1920–34, Vol. 11.* Calcutta: Netaji Publishing Society, Thacker Spinks and Company, 1948. Originally published by Romain Rolland, London, 1936.

Bose, Subhas Chandra. *Netaji Speaks: A Collection of Speeches and Writings, Vol. 1.* Calcutta: Jayashree Prakashan, 1973.

Bose, Subhas Chandra. *Selected Speeches of Subhas Chandra Bose.* New Delhi: Ministry of Information and Broadcasting, Government of India, 1962.

Brush, Stanley Elwood. *Farewell the Winterline: Memories of a Boyhood in India.* Santa Rosa, CA: Chipkali Creations, 2002.

The Calcutta Key. India-Burma: Information and Education Branch, United States Army, 1945.

Chaudhuri, Nirad C. *The Autobiography of an Unknown Indian.* London: MacMillan Publishers Ltd., 1951.

Cohn, David L. *This Is the Story.* Boston: Houghton Mifflin Company, 1947.

Craig, Hazel Innes. *Under the Old School Topee.* London: British Association for Cemeteries in South Asia, 1996. Reprinted by author, 1996.

Das, Hari Sadhan. *This Is Midnapur.* Midnapur: Smt. Reba Das, 1999.

Day, Rev. Lal Behari. *Folk-tales of Bengal.* London: MacMillan and Company, 1883.

Dipti's Calcutta & Howrah Guide with Map. Calcutta: Dipti Printing and Binding Works, 1963.

Fay, Peter Ward. *The Forgotten Army: India's Armed Struggle for Independence 1942–1945*. Ann Arbor, MI: The University of Michigan Press, 1993.

Forbes, Geraldine Hancock. *Indian Women and the Freedom Movement: A Historian's Perspective*. Mumbai: Research Centre for Women's Studies, SNDT Women's University, 1997.

Lebra, Joyce C. *Women Against the Raj: The Rani of Jhansi Regiment*. Singapore: Institute of Southeast Asian Studies, Singapore.

Martyn, Margaret. *Married to the Raj*. London: British Association for Cemeteries in South Asia, 1992.

Prasad, Bisheshwar, ed. *India and the War: Official History of the Indian Armed Forces in the Second World War 1939–1945*. Delhi: Manager of Publications, Government of India, 1966.

Ray, Bharati. *From the Seams of History: Essays on Indian Women*. New York: Oxford University Press, 1995.

Roychowdhury, Laura. *The Jadu House: Intimate Histories of Anglo-India*. London: Doubleday, 2000.

Sahgal, Lakshmi (Geraldine Forbes, ed.). *A Revolutionary Life: Memoirs of a Political Activist*. New Delhi: Kali for Women, 1997.

Sahgal, Manmohini Zutshi (Geraldine Forbes, ed.). *An Indian Freedom Fighter Recalls Her Life*. New York and London: M. E. Sharpe, 1994.

Sena, Manikuntala. *In Search of Freedom: An Unfinished Journey*. Stree, Calcutta, 2001, originally published in Bengali as *Shediner Katha* and published by Pabapatra Prakashan in 1982.

Thapar's Calcutta Pocket Guide, Including Industry Directory. Calcutta: Thapar Publishing, 1958.

GALLERY READERS GROUP GUIDE

THE SLEEPING DICTIONARY

Sujata Massey

Introduction

When a tidal wave wipes out a tiny village on Bengal's southwest coast, a young girl known as Pom is set adrift in the world. Found near death by a charitable British headmistress and her chauffeur, Abbas, Pom is christened Sarah and becomes a servant at the Lockwood School for British and upper-caste Indian girls. When Bidushi Mukherjee, whose family owned Sarah's home village, arrives at the school, Sarah believes she's found a true friend. Bidushi is engaged to a handsome young lawyer, Pankaj Bandophadhyay, and the two girls dream that Sarah will become Bidushi's personal ayah after Bidushi marries. Sadly, Bidushi succumbs to malaria, and Sarah is accused of theft and runs away. With the help of Abbas, she makes it to the larger town of Kharagpur, where she hopes to work as a children's teacher, but her lack of qualifications make this impossible. A glamorous Anglo-Indian woman, Bonnie, invites her to luxurious Rose Villa, where she is re-named Pamela and inadvertently falls into a life of prostitution. Rose Villa caters to British railway men and military officers, and Pamela's unhappy experiences there spark her interest in the burgeoning freedom movement. Secretly, she plots to save enough to leave Rose Villa for Calcutta, where she hopes to study for a teaching certificate.

Her hopes are dashed yet again, this time by an unwanted pregnancy. Believing it's the best thing she can do for herself and her newborn daughter, Kabita, she leaves the baby in the care of Abbas and his wife and sets off for Calcutta, hoping to find respectable work. By a stroke of luck, she becomes the librarian and house manager for Simon Lewes, a young British Indian Civil Service officer who has a massive collection of books on India. She tells him her name is Kamala Mukherjee and allows him to believe she is well-born and well-educated. With her new freedom-fighting friends, Kamala reconnects with Pankaj Bandopadhyay, although he does not remember her as the servant girl from

Lockwood. At his urging, she spies on Mr. Lewes's work and finds that he's tracking Indian revolutionaries. As they work together, she wonders if he could ever look past the unknowns about her and become her husband. However, as time goes on, Simon becomes more sympathetic to Indian independence, falls in love with Kamala, and convinces her to marry him. And, while their relationship is tested by the stresses of World War II, the reappearance of Kamala's daughter, Kabita, and the truth of Kamala's difficult past, their love for each other and for India carries them through.

Discussion Questions

1. After losing her family, Kamala goes through several identities—from Pom to Sarah, Pamela, and finally Kamala. Can any of them be said to be more "real" or "true" than the others?

2. Kamala's life is strongly shaped by loss: her family, Bidushi, even Abbas, the Lockwood School's chauffeur. How do these deaths shape the course of her life? How effectively does she deal with these losses?

3. Discuss the race relationships in the book as exemplified by the administration at Lockwood School, the clients at Rose Villa, and Kamala's relationship with Simon. Are there generational forces at work, as well as class and caste, in terms of how the British and Indians interact?

4. Instead of treating her sympathetically, the Indian housekeeper at Lockwood goes out of her way to bully and abuse Kamala. What inspires Rachael's antipathy toward her? What does it illuminate about relationships within Indian and British society?

5. There is a large gap between the paths of the Rose Villa girls and the activist Chhatri Sangha girls. How is Kamala able to move

from one world to another? What real differences (if any) are there between these young women that lead to their respective circumstances?

6. Kamala decides to give up her daughter, believing she is making the right choice both for herself, the child, and Abbas and his wife. Do you believe it was the right decision, considering what we know about Kabita's life at the end of the novel? What would you have done in Kamala's shoes?

7. Kamala has three real friendships throughout the novel: Bidushi, Lakshmi, and Supriya. How do these friendships shape her and her ambitions? How do they impact her life, for worse or for better?

8. When Pankaj discovers who Kamala works for, he asks her to spy on her employer. How does this subterfuge affect Kamala's feelings about Simon Lewes?

9. Is Kamala wrong to hide her past of poverty and unwed motherhood from the people she meets in Calcutta? Does she become a less likable character because of her dishonesty, or do you think she's doing what she must in order to survive?

10. Would Pankaj ultimately have been a better match for Kamala than Simon? Were you surprised at the way their relationships turned out?

11. Simon is surprisingly accepting of Kamala's daughter and past. What does this show about his character's development?

12. How much of Kamala's success does she attribute to luck, how much to her own hard work, and how much to destiny?

13. What did you already know about India and its struggle for independence? Were you particularly struck by any of the historical details in the novel? How does it compare to other fiction set in the same time period?

14. How does the inclusion of real historical figures (Gandhi, Jawaharlal Nehru, Subhas Chandra Bose) affect the reading experience? Do they add additional dimensions or pull you out of the narrative?

Enhance Your Book Group

1. While novels like *The Sleeping Dictionary* are set in real historical situations, they are ultimately fiction. Discuss the group's attitude towards historical novels: How much do you expect to be accurate and how much fictionalized?

2. PBS's *Story of India* offers a full history of India, and includes background on Nehru, Gandhi, and the Indian National Congress. Learn more at www.pbs.org/thestoryofindia.

3. Sujata Massey offers information about the inspiration for the book on her website, sujatamassey.com. She is also willing to join book clubs by phone, if time permits. Email sujatamassey@mac.com for details.

4. The novel mentions many delicious Indian dishes. Have each member pick one to make for the group's meeting! A few recipes are included here.

5. Explore the role of Indian women in the colonization and independence of India. Consider figures like Commander Lakshmi Swaminathan, who commanded women's forces in the Indian National Army during World War II, and the Rani of Jhansi, Lakshmi Bai, who was killed fighting against the British in 1858, and Indira Gandhi, the world's longest serving woman prime minister.

A Conversation with Sujata Massey

In your website's introduction to The Sleeping Dictionary, *you mention the difficulty of switching from writing about one culture to another. Tell us more about that; did you have to employ different writing techniques, along with doing new research?*

Up until the present, I've been writing a long-running mystery series set in Japan. I had the ease of continuing characters in every book and a very familiar setting where I'd once lived. Writing those mysteries was like slipping into a warm old jacket. I'd say *The Sleeping Dictionary* was more like a slippery, shimmering sari—quite tricky the first time you wear it, and for a long time thereafter, too.

Although one side of my family is from Bengal, and I've enjoyed visits there and to other parts of India, I faced the challenge of not having really lived in India nor been able to speak Indian languages. For this reason, I hesitated to write about India, but as Kamala's story formed in my mind, I longed to share it. I was writing the book while living in Minnesota, where I could not find a Bengali language course. I was able to study Hindi for a year to get the sentence structure, idioms, and feeling for dialogue. I did most of the historical research at the Ames Library of South Asia, within the University of Minnesota, which turned out to be a treasure trove of rare books and documents relating to colonialism. Some choice snippets from these books are shared in the epigraphs. Midway through writing the first draft, I took a research trip to Kolkata, Midnapur, Kharagpur, and Digha, to walk through all the locations of the book. I also did research at the British Library in London where all the old records of the India Office are stored.

You also mention on your website that you interviewed many Bengalis for the book. What was the most interesting or surprising thing you learned during those interviews?

I was very interested in meeting *anyone*—Bengali or not—who could recall daily details of life and politics in 1930 Calcutta. In India, I met a former Gandhian freedom fighter, Tapan Raychaudhuri, who endured a prison experience, and also Krishna Bose, the widow of Sisir Kumar Bose, the nephew who aided Netaji in his daring escape. But my favorite interviews were at home with my father, Subir Banerjee, who grew up in Bengal and Bihar. From a child's perspective, he recalled incidents like the Japanese bombings of Calcutta, and his father angrily railing against English soldiers who wanted to throw their family out of a train compartment. He also revealed that a relative on his father's side, Womesh Chandra Bonnerjee, was the founding president of the Congress Party—and that going back a bit further on his mother's side, those ancestors, the Sabarna Roy Choudhury family, leased to the British the three villages that became Calcutta. So the beginning of colonialism, and the struggle to end it both are a part of me.

There were so many possible paths for Kamala to take as her life develops. How did you decide on her trajectory?
I originally wrote an even longer story, giving Kamala a few more work experiences—as a children's ayah, and also as a nurse during the war—but I realized that I might lose my reader with an 800-page book. Streamlining the novel into four discrete books that are narrated by Pom from childhood through womanhood hopefully make the mother-daughter story, as well as the love story, have more of an impact. I was tempted to follow Kamala to the West after her marriage . . . but that story could be picked up in another book.

Kamala's time at Rose Villa is complicated from moral, ethical, and racial standpoints. Was it hard to find a balance in portraying the different characters and their interactions?
There were many times I wished I didn't have to send Kamala to Rose Villa, but I felt that with her vulnerable status, this would really have

happened to her, as it continues to happen to young homeless women worldwide. The basis for Rose Villa was a prewar high-class brothel one of my elderly sources described as located in Chandernagore and staffed by beautiful French women. Each patron, upon leaving, was given a bottle of French perfume for his wife. The existence of places like Rose Villa points out the hypocrisy of the British saying they were uplifting the moral development of Indians. Natty, Doris, Bonnie, and Rose Barker also illustrate how families were broken and left in poverty when many English soldiers repatriated to England. At the same time, it's important to know that only a minority of Anglo-Indians became prostitutes; most lived comfortable, respectable lives.

What issues did you consider when writing Kamala and Simon's relationship?
I knew it would be controversial to have a relationship between a British man and an Indian woman that could turn out to be nonexploitative. Some might have preferred a fairytale ending with Pankaj. But I felt that Simon had grown so much through the years of knowing Kamala that he really was the right person for her. I believe that our hearts dare to go where our heads won't, and that we always need to listen to the heart.

Which sections of The Sleeping Dictionary *were the most fun to write? Which were the hardest?*
I found the Rose Villa section the hardest to write, because of my concern for all the girls' well-being. It was also wrenching to leave the baby Kabita behind when Kamala pursued her new life. Bringing the old Calcutta alive, with all its intellectual hangouts, pastry shops, and residences, was the best part for me, because I love the city so much.

How do you feel about the way the struggle for Indian independence is portrayed in novels? Do you have any favorites written by other authors?

I very much enjoy the writing of Amitav Ghosh, who touches on the history of colonialism in many of his novels, as well as Rabindranath Tagore, whose novel *The Home and the World* was significant for Kamala. British writers like E. M. Forster, M. M. Kaye, and Rumer Godden have written novels and memoirs that share the British perspective beautifully. My complaint with most novels about the British colonial era is that there are few Indian female characters playing any type of role, although we know from historic accounts that this was not the case. Young women walked away from their families to serve with the INA. Mahatma Gandhi's wife, Kasturba, died while a political prisoner. I hope this novel, in some small way, celebrates these strong women.

How do you balance historical accuracy with the demands of plot? Were there any liberties you were afraid to take with the historical details, or is all fair in fiction?
I did the best I could to make sure every real event that happened is reported at the right time and place, such as the Christmas Eve bombing of Calcutta and all the details of Bose's escape. There are of course some events that are fictional—like the particular Subhas Chandra Bose speech in Town Hall and a train sabotage—but they are based on real happenings during the period. The newspaper quotations I've included are all real, as are the various political leaders and Chhatri Sangha, the female students' group.

Do you plan to write another book set in India, or to continue writing about any of the characters from The Sleeping Dictionary?
Yes, indeed! While I am continuing my Japanese mystery series about Rei Shimura, I'm planning another historical novel, possibly featuring Kamala's daughter, Kabita, as its narrator. There is so much exciting South Asian history over the last seventy years—and fortunately, people who are still alive to tell me their stories.

There are many fascinating historical figures woven into Kamala's story, including some, like Subhas Chandra Bose, who may be less well-known to Western readers. Were there any figures you wished you could have written more about, or featured differently in the story?

Yes. I wish I could have done more with Subhas Chandra Bose, but there is so much concern about what is true and untrue about his life and death that I didn't feel it would be appropriate to create any fictional dialogue for him or place him in fictitious situations. I also dreamed of Miss Richmond inviting Rabindranath Tagore to visit Lockwood School, so Kamala could be truly inspired, but it turned out he was staying in Japan during those years. I originally wrote a young Mother Teresa into the famine section, but when I went to do research at Mission of Hope, I learned her activism with the poor didn't start until after the war years.

Aside from the enjoyment of a good book, what do you hope your readers will take from The Sleeping Dictionary?

I hope readers get an inkling of why religious communities are so divided; and that while the caste system in India is tough, it is not insurmountable; and to understand how strong Indian women are, from peasants like Pom's mother to political activists like the Sen women. I will be thrilled if this book leads readers to explore more about India and travel there. Kolkata is a tremendously artistic, un-touristy, and friendly city where English speakers abound. For more about visiting sites from the book, or to have me join your book club by phone or Skype, please visit my website, www.sujatamassey.com.